Solarium-3

Book One of the
Solarium-3 Trilogy

JOHN R. SPENCER

Overhead Diagram of the Solarium-3 Pods

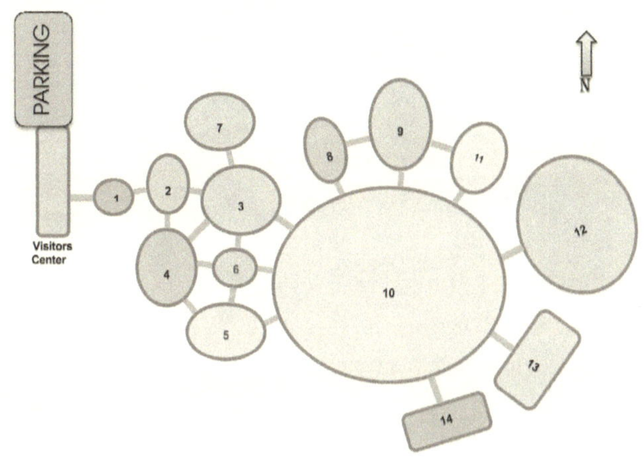

Legend

Pod 1   Entrance Pod
Pod 2   Communications Center (Comm.)
Pod 3   Research Center
Pod 4   Residence (House)
Pod 5   Recreation & Pool
Pod 6   Aviary
Pod 7   Infirmary
Pod 8   Maintenance Shed
Pod 9   Large Animals Housing & Research
Pod 10 Main Agriculture Area, Crop Fields
Pod 11 Small Animals Housing & Research
Pod 12 Ocean, Aquatic Plants & Marine Animals
          Research
Pod 13 Equipment Storage & Main Supply
Pod 14 Fuels & Fertilizers

1

Tuesday, May 13th

Insistent evening winds created whimsical havoc through the trees as two little nuthatch eggs crashed together in their rickety nest atop a high unsteady branch. The chill Wisconsin air bathed the flimsy nest, ready to initiate them into the cold reality of life.

The comforting warmth of their mother's belly would never again shelter them. Twenty minutes ago she left in search of food and, as things go, was herself swallowed up and moving through the bowels of a prowling Siamese-mix cat.

High above the nuthatch nest the winds whisked burgeoning clouds through a sky that continued to darken. Low clouds crested over higher ones like vaporous waves, plumes of thick wetness splashing against some heavenly shore. The nuthatch nest bucked in the wind but clung tightly to its host, wedged between two twig-like branches not much bigger than pencils. The destiny of two unborn nuthatches teetered in the weak grasp of an ancient great-grandmother Oak who, not knowing why, stubbornly clutched the shreds of straw and grass and bark chip and mud. Great-grandmother, her stiff aching back creaking in the wind, nearly thrust both eggs from her unprotected womb.

An odd place to entrust the lives of your young.

The tiny eggs smacked each other again. *Critch . . . nyaack . . . snick.* One shell cracked and wiggled. A cramped, sticky nuthatch pushed weakly, seeking escape. A last, sudden smack against her brother's shell worked. She stretched harder, forcing her way out as the nest bucked in the wind. Her infant talon instinctively grasped a sprig of straw. She hung on for dear life, such as it might be.

A violent burst of wind whipped the other egg from great-grandmother's hand as from a slingshot. It plummeted to earth with an inaudible crackle, a tiny shipwreck dampening the soil. His scrawny carcass lay stillborn, his neck broken. One sticky wing—animated by the wind—fluttered momentarily as if to protest, then dropped lifelessly onto pieces of shell.

The winds diminished. Menacing flashes lit the sky. Strange electrical discharges that looked like heat lightning rippled far to the east. Like unearthly convulsions of light the flashes progressed from east to west relentlessly, a hot, shimmering terror blistering the sky above the serene countryside.

WALKING IN from his dairy barn near Amherst Junction, a farmer jerked his head up quickly as he saw the strange flashes approaching. He winced, then crouched as if the eerie lights might somehow club him, or carry him away. He caught his breath but held it. Nothing happened—except a six-year-old light bulb on the back porch brightened, then blew out.

His skin tingled for an instant and his mouth went dry. The air smelled of rancid steam. As he drew breath he could taste bitterness in the air. The flashes of light ricocheted silently overhead like some demonic upside-down pinball game, shards of light contending like warriors in some invisible battle. He spit. *Never tasted lightning before*, he thought. He backed toward the porch, watching the show. The volcanic sky seemed to signal some unspoken warning. He had no inkling of what. The strange lightning moved off to the west. He shrugged, spit again, and went in for dessert.

BARELY A mile west of his farm, the damp body of the surviving nuthatch had dried quickly. Her fragile eyes were assaulted by these unnatural bursts of light racing along overhead. She clung tenaciously to her nest, watching the eerie light show, a carillon of silent, luminous bells of menacing light. To the little nuthatch they were just one more incomprehensible feature of the inexplicable world into which she had awakened.

The hoard of angry flashes overhead painted large swaths across the sky, galloping west. As they neared Stevens Point, all the city lights flickered—and went black.

SIX HUNDRED miles further west, John Haskins sat in his quiet office suite, fourteen floors above the nightly hubbub of Omaha. He'd just gotten back from a late supper at the Gibson Girls Grill. The smell of grilled steak and beer lingered in his suit jacket. He picked unconsciously at a small piece of meaty leftover with a soggy, splintering toothpick. Moonlight powdered the carpet near the floor-length windows and shimmered faintly on the polished cherry desk. A brilliant lamp over his shoulder crowned his balding head with the sheen of a faint but undeserved halo.

He'd spent the hour just before supper arranging files on his desk for a final review. He wiped his glasses with a perfectly clean handkerchief and readjusted them on his face. He picked up a large heavy folder labeled SOLARIUM-3 — PROJECT MASTER FILE.

He flipped past three inches of specifications, blueprints and photos, to the section tabbed PERSONNEL that would occupy the rest of his evening.

The real meat and potatoes, he reminded himself. The people, the ones who would ultimately make this project a success—or a failure. Unfortunately, it was the thinnest section of the whole file. Because of the four-year length of the project, only 246 people had applied.

He thumbed through the potential team members, remembering one name in particular, until he unburied the pages he wanted.

Clayton Block, 44; born Denver, CO; Def# 564981784480; White/Male; Height: 6'03", Weight: 225; Brown Hair, Blue Eyes.
Probability Of Program Success: High
Stress Compatibility: Excellent
General Intelligence: High
Focus Area: Life Science, Group/Team Leadership
General Information: Lieutenant (Retired), U.S. Army (Rangers). Military background suitable to disciplinary needs of the project. Married, Michele Anne Peavy. Stationed mostly in Germany. Three tours in the Middle East. Granted an emergency discharge due to problem pregnancy of his wife back in the states. Widowed (wife died from complications of delivery of a stillborn son); no other children. Parents deceased: Father (alcoholic) due to liver disease, Mother, due to cancer. One younger sibling, Barbara, died in a car accident (driving drunk). No long-term relationships or ties. Versatile. Outgoing. Friendly, but unlikely to form intimate relationships with other project members.
Recent Update: See Addendum A.

Haskins flipped to Addendum A.

Update: Block has just completed Methodologies and Analysis of Advanced Life Support Systems at UW-Stevens Point / Life Sciences Department, Stevens Point, Wisconsin. Older, but highly capable student. GPA: 3.861.

The lamp behind Haskins caused a bead of sweat to slither down the crest of his forehead. The sleeve of his free hand wiped it away while his other continued digging at a particularly stubborn piece of steak. He flipped back to the previous section.

Overall Assessment: Not the best, but the best that's available.
Recommendation: Team Leader.

Haskins had studied all 246 applicants carefully. None were anywhere near Clayton Block in the race to capture the key position of Team Leader. This was the man they wanted. Haskins felt a calm assurance that Block would be the key to success for the Solarium-3 project.

As he dictated the letter of hire into a small recorder, the office lights flickered momentarily—and went out. Haskins waited in silence. Moonlight took over the room making ghosts of the furniture, and Haskins, too.

He paused the recorder, set his toothpick in an ashtray, and walked over to the windows. Every building he could see had gone dark. As he flipped open his phone to call Security, the power came back on. Recessed fluorescent lights flickered back to life. He sat again and finished the letter to Block, then walked back to the windows that formed the entire outer wall of the office. The city's lights glowed steadily again, sending a reassuring glow up against the broken clouds where the moon, skating between them, began its slow decline toward the western horizon.

ON THE high plains of southeastern Colorado, seven hundred miles west of Haskins, forty construction workers labored into the evening, pushing hard to put the finishing touches on the Solarium-3 complex. Inside the huge plastic domes and connecting walkways the smell of new concrete filled the air, competing with the odor of freshly laid sod. All was nearly ready for the INSIDE team's arrival in just four weeks.

Twenty feet up in the top of an arched ceiling in one of the podwalks, two men on stepladders were installing a cumbersome eight-foot light fixture. One of them, a man about 60, held his end as he tried to secure the bolt that would anchor it to a crossbeam. A sudden wave of vertigo overtook him—something he had never felt before. Instantly dizzy, he fell backwards. As his shoulder hit the floor, his head smacked the concrete walk with the sound of a home run leaving the bat. Blood spattered from his lacerated scalp.

His son on the other ladder dodged the light as it swung toward him. Narrowly missed by the heavy fixture, he leaped to the floor in panic trying somehow—impossibly—to break his father's fall. The adrenaline shock to his heart competed with his tears. He rushed to his dad who was motionless on the concrete. He shook him. Nothing. His father lay unconscious, a small puddle of blood growing beneath his head.

His son yelled for help to workers in the adjacent pods. Someone called an ambulance from La Junta, several miles away. Within moments, every man and woman in the giant complex was hovering near their fallen co-worker.

The son knelt by him, trying to comfort him. But his father remained unconscious, unaware of everyone else's fears. Blood mixed with sweat from his balding head stained the pristine concrete.

Suddenly every light in the huge complex flickered spasmodically, then died. Outside, high above the domed pod roofs, a spectacular but weird light show erupted across the sky, sprinting east to west.

Time seemed to hang in suspension. A workman ran to the parking lot outside the complex and watched a distant point on the highway, hoping to see the flashing ambulance lights that would signal help. But everyone else's eyes followed the strange lights across the sky as they were swallowed into the haze of a dying sunset. Amber light penetrated the pods of Solarium-3 as the last ugly spears of unearthly light peppered an otherwise clear evening sky.

Time shuddered. Everyone in the complex seemed to hold their breath. In what seemed like an hour—but was only 11 minutes—an ambulance arrived. As they worked with flashlights checking the fallen man, the lights in the complex sputtered back to life. His shallow breathing mimicked the unsteady lights. He was sinking into a coma, loitering somewhere between life and death.

No time to lose. They loaded him on the stretcher and rushed him into the ambulance, which sped back toward town.

BACK IN the dark Wisconsin woods, the tiny newborn nuthatch clung tenaciously to her bouncing nest, a flimsy ship in a wild ocean of air. If she'd had a rational soul, she might have glanced down with tender sorrow and wept over her dead brother. As things were, she just braced herself against the hellish cruelty of the night air.

Her rubbery beak let out a pathetic squeak that couldn't pierce the bragging wind. Her eyes closed tightly. She forced them opened again, trying to take it all in. A curious place, indeed, to entrust your young.

The wind subsided. The moon, with a longing nod, had set. The nuthatch's tiny heart fluttered to near agony as she stared out into the darkness that enshrouded the damp forest around her.

2

Thursday, May 22nd

A trickle of dew sought its way down the glass of Clayton Block's balcony doors. The early morning sun was at just the right angle to break the droplet into its secret prismatic colors.

The second-floor balcony overlooked a thick pine forest across the road in Plover, Wisconsin. Block lay catty-corner across his sofa, one leg over the arm at the far end, intently watching the drop of dew make its way down. To the left. Down. Now angling right, like a slow-motion running-back intent on breaking through the line. His eyes fixed on this insignificant event as if it were of some great importance. Maybe he had too much time on his hands.

Rays of sunlight pranced like young mustangs through broken clouds outside his balcony. The thick aroma of coffee rose from a cup perched precariously on the worn arm of the sofa. Without looking, he reached for the cup and sipped. His eyes tried to focus on the colors of the droplet through the steam rising from his coffee. But what took his glance was the turquoise sky beyond.

It was one of those moments, unique and impossible to reproduce. Hidden within that moment was a sense of contentment, a bit of perfection in his very imperfect world.

His bulky, muscular body pressed into the mushy couch cushions. Today was a day of relaxation after the end of his—hopefully—last semester of college. After the usual struggles of a "late" student, he managed to complete a degree in Advanced Life Support Systems. He had worked very hard for what seemed like a ridiculously small diploma hanging cockeyed in its $4.98 Taiwanese frame over the TV.

He sipped again, stretched his broad shoulders, and stared out the door. A rabbit hopped across the road between his building and the woods and nibbled nervously at some leafy morsel. After only a few bites it dashed off as two storm-trooping chipmunks invaded the area.

The morning news dribbled aimlessly from the TV. Transient images flipped across the dusty screen. Block reread the letter from Haskins that had arrived last week. His mind ignored the newscaster, preoccupied with thoughts about his impending move to Colorado. One news item caught half of his attention.

"The sudden widespread power outages that struck most of us about ten days ago still have utility experts puzzled. The massive May 13th power failures reported from coast to coast were accompanied by strange lightning. While the outages caused general disruption of communications and electronic media, experts say they caused no permanent damage.

"What has the experts baffled are the similar power failures earlier the same day in Australia, Asia, Africa and Europe. Researchers at the Washington-based National Association For Public Utility Development say they'll continue to investigate the cause of the domino-like failures.

"Some sources think the outages were triggered by faulty computer switching between several wide-area power grids. Others say that what we saw was an unusual display of the Aurora Borealis that could easily disrupt electric transmissions around the globe. Research continues."

Block chuckled. "'Research continues.' Means they don't know squat." The newscaster droned on in her artificially musical voice.

"In other news, officials at the Omaha-based Lifeline/New World Exploration Corporation formally announced today the launching of their next project, Solarium-3."

Block's ears perked up.

"The new project gets underway in a remote area of southeast Colorado next month. Like the last two projects, Solarium-3 could result in significant advances in life-preservation techniques and food and energy conservation, a spokesman said. Once construction of the complex of fourteen huge, plastic domes is complete, the facility will operate primarily on solar energy in a self-contained environment with its own atmosphere. Lifeline/New World researchers predict Solarium-3 will pave the way toward the eventual development of human colonies on other planets."

Canned file footage of the large greenhouse-like Solarium-2 complex in northeastern Utah flashed on the screen behind the announcer's back, partially obscured by her flamboyant auburn hairdo. Block watched the footage carefully, imagining the newer, much larger Solarium-3 that would soon be his new home. When his letter from John Haskins had come, he let out a whoop and danced a little hop-step right there in front of the apartment building. The neighbors probably thought he was drunk, even though it was only 9:00 in the morning.

He was still excited—though it didn't show much—because he knew how tight the competition had been. More than two hundred applicants had competed for the seven "INSIDE" positions, a team that would spend the next four years sealed INSIDE Solarium-3.

The news-less news ran on. Block's eyes drifted from the TV back to the faint trail of moisture left by the drop of dew that now hung suspended near the bottom of the patio door, fighting gravity, and running out of energy. Survival. Which way to go? This way? Or that? He stared again pointlessly at the stuck water droplet.

The sun ditched behind a cloud. A dimly lit corner of Block's newly trained mind calculated. It was cool outside, in the mid-50s. How many seconds of radiant heat through the thermal-pane glass would it take for the little droplet to live again, to reach its destination? *Like the world itself,* Block thought, *suspended in a chilling universe.* He sipped his coffee. Ghostly arms of steam continued to rise from the cup, but not as fast now.

The news wound down. The last segment drained into his memory almost without notice.

"And finally, this," the Auburn Hairdo said. "The latest news from the world of astronomy has some scientists puzzled. Astronomers at an observatory atop Mauna Kea, Hawaii, released preliminary reports yesterday on a mysterious 'dark shadow' they've observed in outer space, a galactic cloud of some nearly invisible substance. Asked by our on-the-scene reporter what he thought this mysterious space cloud might be, Ariel Winthrop, chief of the observatory, had this to say."

A close-up of Winthrop's head appeared. As he spoke he pulled at the side of his beard, which hid the large blotches of acne scars that marred his face. He spoke with authority and confidence.

"It's something— Something, certainly. We're not quite sure what. Yet. But certainly nothing to worry about."

The on-the-scene reporter, visible only as an outstretched hand holding a microphone, dug deeper.

"Doctor Winthrop, could it be we've finally seen living proof of 'anti-matter'?"

Winthrop sighed almost imperceptibly.

"Whatever this substance—or whatever one calls it—whatever it was, our best equipment did not detect its approach to earth. When we finally spotted it, it registered on most of our instruments as nothing more than a filmy membrane."

"A membrane?" the Hand asked.

"Well, yes, something like—like indistinct ripples floating through space. But nothing to worry about."

The Auburn Hair at the news desk reappeared.

"And so, we won't. That's all for now. Join us today at five. This is Harriet Hampton. Have a *gerr-rate* morning!" Her perfect, thoroughly fraudulent smile blessed the television viewers once again as she departed into electronic oblivion.

Block missed her disappearance as he scrutinized the shrunken droplet suspended on his balcony door, waiting for—hoping for—some last movement. Out of nowhere, a small gray-and-white bird landed on the rough wooden balcony railing. The fledgling tried to see through the glass, only a mirror from its side of things. The eleven-day-old nuthatch was lost, unable to find her way back to a nest that, dislodged from its branches, was suddenly gone.

She leaned forward and walked down the corner post—head first. Block's eyes abandoned the water droplet and watched the bird walking upside down.

"Darndest thing I ever saw," he mumbled.

The white-breasted grayish-blue bird pecked an invisible insect egg out of a deck plank. A scarf of black feathers wrapped the back of her neck. A breeze rippled the feathers like a musician's fingers stroking upward across the strings of a harp. Block squinted, his mind barely capturing the motion. His chirping phone ringer detonated the silence and the frightened nuthatch flew away.

He lurched across the far end of the couch and grabbed the phone.

"H'lo?"

"I'm calling for Clayton Block."

"Yeah? Telemarketer?"

"John Haskins here."

"Oh, I'm sorry—"

"That's all right. Get your letter?"

"Yeah—" He caught himself. "Yes sir. Got it. Last week." Block sat upright as if Haskins could somehow see him. His heart started jogging. "I faxed the acceptance form back. Didn't you get it?"

"Not yet. Probably down in my box. Just wanted to let you know we've finalized your teammates. I've got their files here in Omaha. Wondered if you'd pick them up on your way to Colorado. Give us a chance to meet, since I wasn't in on your interview."

"I didn't plan on coming through Omaha."

"Change plans."

"I don't like changing plans."

"I know. That's one reason we hired you. Look, things are pretty much ready at the site, so we've moved the start date up a couple of weeks. We want you to report June twelfth."

Block's lips mimed the date as he jotted it on a scratch pad.

"Got it. I'll be there." He scratched the back of his ear with the receiver as he glanced at the calendar over his desk. "I could stop at your office on Tuesday, the tenth. In the morning?"

"Good. See you on the tenth. We're very excited about this project, Clayton. And we're glad to have you on board."

"Thank you, sir. I'm glad, too. See you on the tenth."

His lazy morning preoccupations suddenly gone, he went back to digging through piles of old books and papers in the spare room, sorting what to take and what to store. He stared at sixteen different piles on the floor.

Why in the world am I still dragging all of this junk around? he wondered.

Four years INSIDE Solarium-3, he thought. He searched for the few things he really wanted to reread. He flipped open the torn cover of an old college notebook labeled "Modern Civilization."

"Just think," he said aloud, "and it all fits in one little notebook." He tossed it into a storage box.

Call the movers, change the date.

He went over to the desk and flipped through shards of paper tossed near the phone book for the number.

"Hi. Yeah, this is Clayton Block. You did a bid for me a last week? Clayton. I never use Clay. Yeah. Oakwood Lane. Can you load up on the 9th instead?" There was a pause. "Yeah? Good. Yeah, change of plans. Seven a.m. on the ninth. Thanks."

He went back to not packing, and spent the better part of an hour thumbing through papers and wandering the apartment plucking books from shelves that peppered its walls. He recovered a lost can of Friedrich Brau perched precariously atop two uneven books. Two-day-old beer. He swigged it down.

"Waste not, want not."

He found a browning banana that was no longer able to hide in the back of the gradually emptying refrigerator. He peeled it and chomped off half. The phone chirped again.

"Yeah?" Block mumbled as his teeth mauled the banana.

"Well, still eating—after all these years?"

"Who's this?"

"It's me, Clayton. William."

"William who?"

A familiar voice, Block thought, but not registering.

"William who? William the 2nd!"

Block swallowed the whole mouthful and tossed the rest of the banana at the waste basket, which he missed.

"Willy? William Atchison the 2nd?"

"Memory like a steel trap."

"Sorry, Will. Are you kidding? William the 2nd? Sure! R&R on the Riviera. All those beautiful women. What a killer time! Sorry, buddy. You took me by surprise. How long's it been?"

"Too darn long, Clayton," Atchison said enthusiastically. "Anyway, we're about to fix that."

"Whad'a'ya mean?"

"Would you believe me if I told you that a guy named John Haskins just called me?"

"You're kidding!"

"No. He tells me you've been picked to lead the Solarium-3 team."

"Yeah." Block was puzzled. "Why'd he call you? Background check?"

"No, Clayton. I'm telling you, you won't believe it. I'm picked, too."

"No way!" Block said, astonished.

Atchison reacted with his Midwestern drawl.

"Come on, Clayton. You know I never could tell a joke worth a dang. No, buddy, I'm serious as sweet potatoes. I've been doing agricultural research for Lamont Corporation the last two years. They're in on it, you know. Bunch of their money, anyway. So I got picked. Hand-picked. Like an overripe ear of corn. I'm *their* man INSIDE."

Block repressed a grin.

"Four more years of R. and R., huh?" he said. The grin spread across his face.

"Can you imagine the great time we're gonna have in that place? They've even got a beach in there!" Atchison said.

"Absolutely, you old fart! We'll have some more brain-bashin' good times. You bring the whiskey again, OK?"

"Think I can sneak it in?"

"Probably won't need to. I bet they've hand-picked that, too!"

"Extended furlough, old buddy," Atchison said, "inside those big plastic bubbles. Humidity, hogs, homemade soup! It'll smell like heaven, I'll bet."

The imaginary sensations passed through Block's nostrils.

"You gotta be the only guy in the world who actually likes the smell of hogs, Willy!"

"Yeah, well, I always did have a nose for manure."

"So what've you been researching for Lamont? The chemical complexes of the cow pie?"

"Somethin' like that." Atchison crackled out his bellicose laugh, almost bursting Block's eardrum.

"June 12th, huh?" Atchison asked.

"The 12th. Come prepared, buddy. I'm now a college grad-u-ate—and a nightmare to work for!"

"I'm scared, big-time scared! Look, I'll be going through New Mexico. Gotta stop and see my folks. They retired down there, you know. But I'll be on time. Don't worry. See you on the 12th, boss man."

"See ya."

Block hung up, smiling at the thought of a reunion with his long forgotten military buddy. Atchison was just three years older and they had become great friends. In between stints in Germany, they spent eight months detached to a small NATO office in the Balkans. After a lot of begging and three bottles of imported American whiskey, Atchison managed to bribe their Belgian C.O. into giving them a two-week furlough to the French Riviera—just three weeks after they arrived. Willy used to joke that their bodies aged ten years in those two weeks of "rest and relaxation."

It was one of the best times Block could remember, and "William the 2nd" Atchison had made it happen. Block could still see Atchison strolling—stumbling actually—along the moonlit beach with his hairy pot-like belly hanging over the edge of low-slung swim trunks and his burly brown mustache stained with various foods and lipsticks. Every 10th step, counted exactly, Atchison would let out a loud, long, triumphant belly belch. Block laughed almost uncontrollably just thinking about it.

What are the odds? he asked himself. *William the 2nd!*

Still chuckling, he went out to the dumpster behind the building for more cardboard boxes. *Atchison*, he thought. After Block's emergency discharge, Willy weaseled his way into army intelligence. Block read somewhere that Atchison stirred up a hornet's nest for reporting a couple of French colonels in the Balkans. Caught them for extortion, scamming the locals. It must have been after that mess that Atchison decided to go into agricultural research. What better place to hide?

Block scraped some sticky hamburger wrappers off a heavy cardboard box from the bottom of the dumpster and carried it up to his apartment.

JOHN HASKINS' phone stayed busy for another three hours as he located his five remaining Solarium-3 team members to confirm they had received their letters and to give them the new arrival date. He tracked down Mai Ker Moua on a vacation trip in the mountains near Flagstaff, Arizona, where she was camping with her brothers and sisters. A ranger at the state park managed to coax her to a telephone at the park gate.

"Mai Ker Moua?"

"Yes. Who's calling? I'm on vacation."

"Not for long."

"Who is this please?"

"This is John Haskins. I'm project leader for—"

"Oh! You're—" Her heart rate spiked. "—the Solarium project! I got the job? Did I get the job?"

"Yes, Miss Moua. Didn't you get your letter?"

"No. I mean, I've been gone." She grabbed the surprised park ranger and gave him a bear hug.

"Well it's probably waiting in your mail box. But we've moved the start date up. You need to report June 12th."

"Yes—thank you, Mister . . . ?" Her mind went blank.

"Haskins. John Haskins. And we're very pleased you're coming on board, Miss Moua."

Then it hit her.

"Oh no! June twelfth! That's too quick. I'm in Arizona. How can I—?" She composed herself, and reverted to her professional voice. "Thank you. Of course I'll get there. Can you email me directions, please? You have my email? Yes. Yes. I'm pulling my tent down in five minutes! Yes, I'll be there sir. Thank you very much. You're a very kind man. Thank you."

She stood another moment holding the receiver, after the dial tone returned. Then she gave the surprised ranger another hug. Her large brown eyes sparkled. Her heart raced as she tried to take it in. She had applied on an impulse, and never seriously thought she'd get the job. She sprinted back toward her campsite to pack.

In Omaha, Haskins was still smiling at Moua's excitement as he dialed again. He loved it when people were so enthusiastic to come to work on one of his projects. He felt like Santa at Christmas.

Bridget Listner's reaction was also a bit of confusion mixed with enthusiasm. Haskins reached her by pager at a hair appointment in downtown Sacramento. She was in the middle of a perm.

"Mr. Who?" she was saying into a cordless phone.

"John Haskins. The Solarium-3 project."

"Oh, Mr. Haskins. Could you just get this out of my face for a— Not you, Mr. Haskins, I'm sorry, I was just—the stylist—no, just wait a second, this stuff smells raunchy—"

Bridget masked the phone with her palm. Muffled grumbles were all Haskins could hear. He shook his head, suppressing a smirk.

"I'm back. Sorry," Bridget said. "Start again, can you?"

Haskins finished his brief spiel about the new start date. Bridget was now sitting straight up in the salon chair pulling everything out of her hair, trying to get the huge bib off, and juggling the phone.

"Of course, I'll be there. And thank you for this great opportunity! Thank you for calling me personally," she said, pushing the hair stylist away. She shoved a $20 bill into the woman's hand for the half-started perm and fled toward home.

Pamela Hansen, Jimmy Algood and Sarajane Haug all got similar calls over the next hour. All had their letters, and all bubbled with delight at their selection.

Pamela Hansen assured Haskins they wouldn't be sorry for picking her and that she would do everything she could to make the project "a wonderful success."

When Jimmy Algood got his call, he listened in stunned silence to Haskins' voice, like Moses hearing words from the burning bush. Jimmy knew the Solarium projects had become temples of modern science. And he had been called INSIDE. It was the chance of a lifetime.

Sarajane Haug took the phone call in stride, another piece of life's puzzle falling casually into its place. She thanked Haskins, jotted down the new report date, and also asked for a map.

Haskins hung up the phone and sat back. Sometimes, all the work and anxiety and preparation for these projects actually felt worth it.

"That was fun."

He smiled. A creature of habit, he walked over to his floor-length windows, looking out. He took a long, slow breath, gazing out over the city. At times, the world seemed a beautiful place indeed. But slowly a frown spread over his face, as he remembered the real reason for moving up the start date. The frown darkened, like the face of a man who has just secretly mortgaged his grandmother's house.

3

Monday, June 9th

By 10:00 a.m., the mover had the van loaded and pulled away. Block went back to his apartment for the last time, grabbed his shaving kit and suitcase, and a few remaining odds and ends of clothes. He gave the empty apartment a quick once-over for any left-behinds, then pulled the door shut on the latest chapter of his life.

He tossed the shaving kit and clothes carelessly into the back seat of the cramped two-door. Its odometer had spun past 100,000 miles a year and a half ago. He squeezed in and patted the steering wheel gently.

"Hope you can make Colorado, old paint," he said, firing up the clattering engine.

The sadness of leaving his comfortable surroundings gnawed at his stomach but began to subside the minute he pulled out of the parking lot.

"Dang it!"

He lurched to a stop, roared backwards into the lot toward his empty garage, and crawled out.

"Stupid cord." He flung the garage door up and peered into the darkness. There it was, hanging on the back wall, the orange extension cord that had been his engine heater's life-line through three bitter Wisconsin winters. He snagged it and it flew into the back seat. He wedged back into the car and took off. He would make Omaha late tonight if the road construction wasn't too bad, pick up the files from Haskins early tomorrow, and be in southeast Colorado by late Tuesday night.

He punched the car down the street. The bright

morning sun flashing through the rows of tall pines created a strobe effect across his hood, and dazzled his eyes as it ricocheted off building windows along the street. Fleeting nausea again gripped his stomach. This had been a beautiful place to live, but there were only a handful of friends he would leave behind. He wasn't two blocks down the street when his eyes caught a dark flutter coming at his windshield. It thumped the glass and was gone.

"Dang it!" he yelled to the deaf car. He slammed down the brake pedal and skidded to a stop in the middle of the street. He walked a few paces back to find a stunned bird quivering near the edge of the pavement.

"Way to go, Block," he said aloud. "Always killing some dang thing."

He cradled the almost weightless creature in his hands. It looked familiar. Then he realized. It was just like the little bird on his balcony a couple of weeks ago. They all looked alike, of course—at least to Block. Was it the same one? He entertained the thought, then dismissed it as the most improbable fancy. But while he didn't believe it, as practical as he was, it *was* the same little nuthatch that had teased him on the balcony that day, the unfortunate creature that had lost her mother and brother the night of her birth.

Feeling like a worm, Block laid the bird on the warm hood of his car.

"What the heck do I do now?" he asked as if she might understand and help. "Can't leave you here. And I can't take you home." It dawned on him in a new way. "No home."

He looked the little creature over, trying to figure out if it was dead, or just stunned. Its neck seemed OK. He could detect a slight muscle tension. That was good. One wing was either broken, or severely bent. The stunned bird moved slightly. It gave a hesitant shiver, but obviously wasn't going anywhere under its own power anytime soon.

Block let out a sigh. He went back to the open the door and rooted around in the back seat for some kind of container. He opened the box holding his new mountain boots and flung them on the floor. A couple of smelly pairs of socks were in a small plastic bag, laundry that didn't quite get done. He arranged them in the box and doctored up a nest.

"Here you go, little guy."

He babied the injured bird into the make-shift nest, parked the box on the passenger seat, and crawled into the car again—completely oblivious to the two cars which had pulled up and stopped behind him. The other two drivers patiently marveled at his care of the injured bird.

"Gotta feed you now, too, I suppose," he told the bird. "You're just gonna have to go along. If you gotta die, at least you'll be with me."

He started off for the third time. At a stop sign, he fumbled for a nearly empty bottle of soda on the floor, poured some warm pop into the bottle cap, and nestled it into the nest. He chugged down the rest of the soda, which was two weeks old.

As if in a rush now, he headed for the highway and was off to Nebraska. He drove hard all afternoon with only one pit stop. The sun slowly descended into the afternoon sky. He kept glancing over at his fragile little passenger.

"Wonder where we're going, huh?" He tried to whistle a bird-like tune. "Me, too."

He stroked the bird's tiny neck with a fingertip. "Looks like you're going to Bubble Heaven. Maybe I can sneak you in. One more bird can't hurt anything. Better get your wings back. There'll be plenty of room to fly."

He wasn't all that optimistic about the bird's

recovery, but felt better having tried to cheer it up. At one point along Interstate 80 early in the evening, feeling a little drowsy, he got to staring at his little passenger, and almost ran off the road.

Block pushed himself on. A spectacular red sun grew into a giant orb kissing the horizon. Its stretched arms radiated across the sky, clinging to the day's end. He drove on, coffee in hand, hoping to make Des Moines by 9:00 p.m. That would put him into Omaha around midnight.

The little nuthatch lay in her makeshift nest, slowly recovering, safe once more from the loneliness of the coming night.

4

Block's room in the Bent Motel was stifling. The air conditioner was broken, like everything else. But it was the last operating motel in Las Animas, Colorado, a small town on the high, arid plains of southeastern Colorado along the Arkansas River.

The badly-worn carpet showed years of deterioration from mountain-bound tourists who failed to realize so much of eastern Colorado lay between them and the glory of the Rockies. The motel, built just after World War II, was now a seedy mixture of twisting boards, shabby plaster that looked like a grade school chalk board that had been erased too many times, and shabbier drapes. The one picture on the wall had cost 79 cents when it was new.

The tourist trade in this part of Colorado withered long ago like the summer weeds that had reclaimed the little motel's front yard and gravel parking lot.

Block arrived just after 1:00 a.m. Wednesday morning after the long haul through Nebraska, down into western Kansas, then across the seemingly endless desert-like prairie of eastern Colorado.

EARLY TUESDAY morning he had stopped as promised at John Haskins' office in the Lifeline/New World Exploration headquarters in downtown Omaha. The secretary escorted Block down a marbled hallway and into Haskins' office, sheltered away on an upper floor of the plush high-rise. Haskins stood to greet him.

"Good morning, Clay. Thanks for stopping."

Haskins looked nothing like what Block had imagined from his voice on the phone. He was considerably shorter than Block, a little overweight, with a bushy shock of gray hair hovering over each ear. The rest of his head was bare. Dark green smiling eyes studied Block through a pair of thick glasses.

"Thanks," Block said. "By the way, if it's OK, I always go by Clayton."

"No problem. You excited?"

"Yeah, pretty much," Block said with a casual nod. He was trying to look professional and mask the true excitement bubbling inside. He was conscious of sweat seeping from every pore in his body although the air conditioning was working fine.

Haskins smiled again.

"I have the personnel files on the others." He sat and pulled open a drawer of the credenza behind his desk.

"Believe it or not, I know one of them already," Block told him.

"You do? Who?" Haskins asked, his eyebrows flattening with curiosity.

"Will Atchison. We were in the service together— for a while. Just before my wife had problems with the baby."

"That's amazing." Haskins smile broadened. "Did that include the infamous trip to the Riviera?"

Block was caught off guard. He swallowed hard.

"You knew about that?"

"Of course, Clayton. We do our homework. Don't know how we missed the fact that Atchison was *that* Atchison."

Block quietly cleared his throat. He was beginning to wonder how he ever landed the job. But Haskins kept smiling. Two dimples appeared in his chubby cheeks.

"It's not a problem, Clayton. I have to admit we missed the connection."

"Nobody's perfect," Block said politely.

A grudging look of admission crossed Haskin's face.

Block was curious just how much of that Riviera debacle they actually knew—especially the two days in that French military garrison. He grinned, remembering Atchison's escapades with a certain belly-dancer. He could still see her belly-button winking at Atchison, and William the 2nd roaring like a spastic grizzly bear.

Haskins interrupted Block's wandering.

"Don't worry about it, Clayton. I hear it was a pretty wild trip. But nothing to disqualify either of you from this project." His face went dead-pan. "But there won't be any expensive French wine in Solarium-3."

"That's good to know, sir." Block relaxed.

"Actually, Atchison was quite a find. Highly recommended by our search team. Been at Lamont. He's done some amazing stuff with agri-genetics."

Block relaxed even more.

"I'm really looking forward to this project," he said. "And I really appreciate the great opportunity you're giving me. This is once-in-a-lifetime stuff."

"Yeah," Haskins said, "it could well be. You're efficient, organized, clear as a leader. Your military background, your discipline—all pluses. That's what I need for my leader INSIDE." He shoved a large stack of folders across the desk. "Look these over. We found you a great team."

From the height of the stack, Block knew Haskins had indeed done his homework. The secretary brought a box to carry the files out.

"How far you going tonight?" Haskins asked.

"I got a line on a little motel out in Las Animas, near the project. I'll drive straight through. Anxious to get there, see the place. That'll give me a full day to study over these."

"I'll fly out the morning of the 12th. We'll have a

short presentation and tour for the shareholders, then team orientation will start."

"Thanks again," Block said, offering a handshake. "See you then." He hiked back through the marble hallways, laden with the box of files. He searched out his car in the maze-like parking ramp and shoved the box into the little remaining space in his back seat, trying not to disturb his little feathered friend napping in the front seat. He pulled his bulky frame into the car and headed west.

THE ANCIENT motor-court on Bent Avenue wasn't much but it was convenient as his last stop, eleven miles east of the Solarium-3 site. Block was stretched out in the flimsy chair, his feet propped on the edge of the bed in the oven-like motel room. It was a little after 11:00 p.m. Wednesday night. The television droned vacantly in the background. With no cable, the screen was mostly ghosts and shadows.

He had the personnel files stacked on his lap and working through them, trying to absorb the few details they provided about his teammates. He looked at Willy's first.

File:
   William Atchison, II: 47; born Kansas City, MO; Def# 391468973201; White/Male, Height: 5'08", Weight: 195; Brown hair, Hazel eyes; Agricultural Specialist; M.S., Biology.
   Probability of program success: Good
   Stress compatibility: Good
   General Intelligence: High
   Focus area: Genetic engineering
   General information: Atchison is a versatile individual with a varied background. He began graduate studies in theology but abandoned the seminary after several disputes with his

denominational heads. Pursued a military career, eventually working into army intelligence in London for a number of years. Served tours in the Middle East and the Balkans. Honorable discharge. Went back to college for a graduate degree in biology. Taught plant genetics and food research at Mills College in North Carolina. Also did some preliminary research in the cross-breeding of marine and land-mammals toward the futuring of species. Currently a researcher at the Lamont Corporation (develops crop hybrids and fast-growth fertilizers). No current attachments. Married a female researcher at Mills College; marriage ended after 18 months. Never remarried. No children. Apart from his brief unsatisfactory marriage, Atchison has demonstrated a high degree of stability, reliability, and intellectual proficiency.

Overall Assessment: Intelligent, creative, somewhat of a Maverick, but a good scientist.

Recommendation: Primary Geneticist, Technician, General Maintenance.

This oughta be fun, Willy and me together again, Block thought, tossing the file aside. He scanned through the next two.

File:

Pamela Hansen: 36; born Louisville, KY; White/Female; Height: 5'09", Weight: 138; Brown hair, Blue eyes; B.S.N, minor in Psychology, second minor in Archeology; Registered Nurse; M.S. in Nutritional Science and Home Economics; second M.S. in Psychiatric Nursing; specialist in human and animal nutrition, wellness, and preventative mental health care.

Probability of program success: Good

Stress compatibility: High

General intelligence: Good
Focus area: Physical health/animal health
General Information: Although born in Kentucky, Hansen was raised in Wichita, Kansas, where she has spent most of her life, most recently working the psychiatric care unit at The Thornton Institute. Started out teaching at a junior college in nutrition and home economics, but gave this up in favor of the hospital setting. Well-versed in all aspects of nursing (a generalist is hard to find these days) but also has a special interest in veterinary care. Describes herself as "a people person."
Overall Assessment: Team player, pleasant, good with others.
Recommendation: Project Nutritionist, Relationship Maintenance Coordinator.

File:

Sarajane Haug: 34; born Rochester, MN; Black/Female; Height: 6'02", Weight: 165; Brown hair, Brown eyes; B.S., M.D., Specialist in bacteriology; did internship at University of Colorado Medical Center, Denver.
Probability of program success: High
Stress compatibility: Good
General intelligence: High
Focus area: Medical programming / research
General Information: Born in Minnesota, her parents moved to Santa Fe, New Mexico when she was 4. Haug did her undergraduate work (dual major in biology and physics) at the Sandia Institute, a small private college outside Albuquerque. Accepted to C.U. Medical School, Denver, where she was cited as the outstanding intern of her class; special success in diagnosing and working with the victims of a highly volatile, degenerative tissue disease that claimed many lives

in the Denver area. Highly organized, not outgoing, but a good team player. Single, no children, no significant ties.

Overall Assessment: Brilliant mind, somewhat withdrawn, but not to a fault. Should do fine in team environment.

Recommendation: Team Physician; Systems Monitoring, Animal Care Specialist.

Block's eyelids were drooping and his head jerked suddenly as he almost dozed off. His heart wasn't in this tonight. It was late. He would read the rest some other time. He closed Haug's file and tossed them all back into the file box.

He leaned his head back into the pillow that was propped on the upper edge of the mushy, deteriorating chair and stretched his arms and legs like a turtle coming out of its shell. His little nuthatch was resting on another pillow on the lumpy bed. Block stood and started for the bathroom. The movement startled the nuthatch and she abruptly took to the air. She circled the ceiling madly, bumping it several times, then perched on top of a horrendously ugly orange swag lamp that hung in the corner near the window.

Block watched in amazement. It was the first time she'd flown since smacking his windshield. He smiled.

"Tough little booger, huh?"

He tried in vain to capture her and realized how easily he could reinjure her fragile wings. So he ignored her. When he came back from the bathroom, he scrounged through his jacket pocket for a bag of leftover sunflower seeds he had bought somewhere in northwestern Kansas. He dumped some seed into the lid of his deodorant container and put the makeshift feeder into the socks that lined the cardboard nest. He quietly pulled a T-shirt out of his suitcase and settled back onto his chair. He sat very still, looking innocent.

Within 30 seconds the nuthatch took the hint and flew several narrowing circles over its box on the bed, then floated down into the smelly nest. Dirty socks, and foul deodorant. It was a wonder she would even consider food from such a source. But she rapidly plucked at the sunflower seeds.

Block swiftly flipped the T-shirt over the box, trapping her inside. She didn't protest. He could hear the *click-click* of her beak cracking open sunflower seeds. He found masking tape in his bag and fixed the T-shirt around the box, then slid it to the foot of the bed. He slid himself in under the covers.

He hoped he wouldn't dream again about the INSIDE of Solarium-3. So far it was only pictures, real and mental. But he knew he would. He tried to calm his mind. The anxiety of the *new*. He'd be there soon enough. Right now he badly needed sleep.

Click-click . . ..

The nuthatch finished her snack. Block faded off.

5

Thursday, June 12th

Block was up early, butterflies in his empty stomach. He shaved and dressed faster than usual, then loaded the files and his bags into the car. The last thing out was the nuthatch's box, in the co-pilot's seat.

"Hope they don't complain about me bringing you in," he told her.

He walked to the shabby office to settle with the manager, who looked as worn-out as the parking lot. Stubby gray whiskers protruded from the man's old, bony face. Stubby hair covered his reddish scalp. His grungy T-shirt proclaimed *LIVE FAST, LIVE HARD* in huge red letters. Under the logo was an utterly pathetic drawing of a sailor dancing with a blond bombshell whose dress was falling off her shoulders.

Block did everything he could to conceal his smirk. He handed over $48.58 cash, most of what he had left. The old man's arthritic fingers scratched "paid" on the faded blue room card.

Block meandered through the gravel streets of the town hoping to find some breakfast. *Where are all the people?* he wondered. Many houses were crudely boarded up. Every third or fourth one had a FOR SALE sign out front. *Strange,* Block thought, *my last morning of freedom spent in what feels like a ghost town.*

He passed two long-abandoned cafes. Finally he spotted The Faded Sombrero. It was clinging to life. He could make out the movement of a waitress's white apron through the dirty front window.

He snuck in and sat near the window, which was

cracked from top to bottom. The waitress, who was apparently also the cook, appeared from the kitchen. Her grimy apron was as dirty as the front window.

"Breakfast?" she asked.

"Huevos Rancheros with biscuits. And an orange juice, please. And coffee."

She gave him a genuine but tired smile.

He chased the greasy breakfast down with the orange juice and two hurried cups of coffee. The waitress hovered on her stool by the counter. She was reasonably pretty, early 30s, with jet black hair. Maybe this would be her Knight in Shining Armor. She looked out at his beat-up car. *Guess not,* she thought. She ventured a few words.

"Gonna be staying in town long, honey?"

"About three more minutes," Block said, trying not to sound rude. But he knew that kind of smile. "I'm working out at the new Solarium project." This didn't register with her at all.

He paid, gave her a decent tip, and scooped a few biscuit crumbs from his plate on the way out the door. He had left the car windows down a little but it was already hot in the car. As he aired it out, he fed the crumbs under the edge of the T-shirt to his little passenger.

"Not much longer, little one, and maybe I can let you loose again."

He took out the computer-generated map Haskins had sent with his letter. After two wrong turns he found his way back to the north end of town and barreled his little car west on Colorado 194 toward Solarium-3.

The newest Solarium was just east of the Bent's Old Fort National Historic Site on the north side of the Arkansas River. The fort was one of the first European settlements in Colorado in the early 1800s and housed a busy trading post frequented by the Cheyenne and Arapahoe tribes, European explorers, fur traders, and military men. It was abandoned, then mysteriously destroyed about 1850, whether by drunken mountain men, or maybe the owners themselves, no one ever knew.

The long-abandoned ruins were rebuilt by the National Park Service in the 1970s using authentic adobe materials so it would look just like the original. But, just like the original, the adobe walls quickly fell to pieces. No drunken mountain men were needed. Just erosion, and U.S. government planning. It was rehabilitated, but with declining visitors and government revenue, Mother Nature had her way.

With the fort in ruins—again—the government put some of the land up for sale. No one wanted it. So when the Park Service heard about Solarium-3 and offered to donate the land, project planners snapped it up like Block's nuthatch going after sunflower seed.

Twenty-one months later, the enormous, gleaming domes of Solarium-3 sprawled across sandy fields just above the river. Even before the mammoth complex was in sight, Block ran its design through his mind again. He had memorized the blueprints in fine detail.

The walls of Solarium-3 would last a lot longer than the new Bent's Old Fort. The giant geodesic "pods" of the Solarium were supported by special structural beams made of aluminum and titanium alloy. The domes were fabricated out of clear, space-age plastic that had originally been designed for the now defunct U.S.-Russian mission to Mars. The Solarium planners discovered that ten years' worth of materials fabricated for the Mars trip were piled up in a storage yard in central Oklahoma. They snapped these up like birdseed, too, at one-twentieth their value. Fine pickings. Thank you, Uncle Sam.

The nuthatch was trying to fly inside the box, making bumps in the T-shirt. The winding, little-used highway followed the bends of the Arkansas River as they drove west. For the first time since his letter from Haskins arrived, Block began to feel real nervousness. He was confident—probably overly confident—that he could run the INSIDE team perfectly. On the other hand, four years locked up in a set of big plastic bubbles with the same six people would be a long haul anyway you looked at it. Block had lived alone since the death of his wife, Michele. He preferred it that way, preferred his privacy, his freedom to come and go. As excited as he was, he had some misgivings about the "social" environment he was getting into, except for Will Atchison, of course. There would be a general lack of privacy, and no freedom to come or go anywhere at all. But then there was the pay, $504,000 for the four years. Very hard to say no to that.

But four years. Forty-eight complete months sealed in the Solarium. One thousand, four hundred and sixty-one entire days INSIDE.

That queasy stomach he felt pulling away from his apartment in Wisconsin was back. Which was worse? Leaving the old, or entering the new?

THE OLD '76 Chevy equipped with four completely shot shock absorbers, one fully-rusted fender, and Mai Ker Moua at the wheel lumbered along Highway 194, coming east from La Junta toward Solarium-3. She quietly hummed the song on the new satellite radio that had been crudely cobbled into the dash.

Her heart was beating faster than usual. She knew she was close to the project site and was getting excited. Just a few more miles. The highway bent hard left, then hard right around several sharp corners.

Without warning, a brown mule deer bounded out of the trees—not twenty feet away. Mai Ker's short legs both hit the brake pedal at once. The car screamed violently sideways. It skidded off the shoulder into a shallow irrigation ditch and slammed to a stop, narrowly missing a huge elm. Her chin and chest slammed the steering wheel. Blood burst from her lower lip. The deer never saw her, never broke stride, never looked back, never cared.

She caught her breath, shaking. She wanted to cry but didn't. She was too stunned. Her heart pounded. The veins in her neck throbbed. Her mouth went dry and she thought she would throw up. She stared through the windshield at the rough bark of the imposing elm tree twelve inches from her front bumper.

"I could've died." She whispered it to herself. Then her whole body began to tremble. Several minutes past. No other cars were in sight.

The shaking subsided. She hung out the window and looked. The front wheels were in the water, but didn't look stuck. She reached down and took the neglected seat belt and buckled it, then put the transmission into reverse. She managed to back up the gradual slope and stopped diagonally along the north edge of the highway.

Finally an old pickup showed up, coming toward her from the east. The scruffy looking driver laid on the horn, swerved past her without slowing, and yelled some obscenity out the passenger window. She shook again.

"Great timing, Mai Ker . . ." she told herself.

A GLISTENING flash of light off to his left caught Clayton Block's eye, like a signal mirror flashing a warning. He squinted. The flash of sunlight was a reflection off the highest dome of the Solarium-3 complex, just visible over the tree tops two miles ahead.

Block slowed down. Why was he going so fast? It was still early. Suddenly there was no hurry. He slowed even more. He was—as usual—two hours early. He swallowed some stale milk from a small carton that had sat on the dashboard since Tuesday afternoon. This made the queasy feeling worse. He took a long, deep breath and stretched his shoulders back. A faint expression of anxiety shown on his face. He peeked under the edge of the T-shirt at the nuthatch, which was trying to nap.

"I hope you know what you're gettin' me into here."

He rubbed the back of his neck as the car had rolled almost to a stop. His companion made no reply. She wasn't much for words—or peeps. The entrance to Solarium-3 came into sight. He slowly turned into it, his tires making a sticky squeaking sound on the shiny new asphalt.

Block stopped in the drive and looked up, taking it all in. The complex was much larger in real life than it had been in his head. The place was monstrous, in fact, a behemoth sprawled out across 162 acres of fallow Colorado soil.

It lay about 200 yards north of the trees that lined the Arkansas River. Fourteen geodesic pods of thick plastic, each supported by an internal metal framework, rose to various heights between 40 and 130 feet. The sheer magnitude of the place almost overwhelmed him. For a fleeting moment it looked to Block like a steel and plastic dragon that some futuristic knight had slain and left to rot here on the high plains.

A deep-pitched horn blew behind him. He flinched in his seat, realizing he was still stopped dead in the drive like a tourist. A glance in his left mirror—the only one left—revealed a pretty oriental woman in a huge Chevy stopped behind him. Large pieces of mud hung from the car's front bumper. Her reflection smiled at him in his mirror.

Block pulled ahead to the guard booth. After a quick examination of his ID, the guard sent him through. He drove the final quarter mile to the parking area in front of the Visitors Center and parked perfectly square between two lines of new yellow paint.

"This is it, partner," he told the nuthatch. "We're home." He looked toward the highest dome again. "Too late to turn back now." His stomach began to settle.

As he reached for one of his bags in the back seat, a voice by his window startled him again. He flinched and turned. The same young woman who had pulled in behind him was standing there, the same broad smile on her face.

Block pushed his door open and greeted her.

"Hi."

"Who are you?" she asked. "Are you INSIDE, or OUTSIDE?"

"INSIDE. I'm Clayton Block. The team leader."

"Oh, this is wonderful, isn't it?" She gestured toward the domes. "I'm Mai Ker Moua. I will be with you."

He studied her quickly. She was a small woman, petite, not a ravishing beauty but very pretty in a unique way. The most predominant features of her face—and personality—were large brown eyes and the most engaging smile he'd ever seen.

Block pointed to the large clump of fresh mud and grass hanging from her bumper.

"Have some trouble?"

"Oh. Just a small accident," she said with an embarrassed grin that actually improved her smile.

They cleared through security at the Visitors Center and were greeted by John Haskins in the hall.

"Good morning," Block said as if he'd known Haskins for months.

"Glad you're here," Haskins replied, also with great friendliness. "The Board of Directors insisted I be here for the orientation tour. But I wouldn't miss it. Been working this thing up for the last six years—even before Solarium-2 was over."

Haskins looked at Mai Ker whom he recognized from her picture.

"Miss Moua . . .?"

"Yes, I'm Mai Ker. Thank you for hiring me. I can't tell you how exciting this is."

Mai Ker, Haskins thought, followed by, *My my, lovely . . .*

"Well, let's hurry on, shall we?" Haskins said. "We moved up the welcome ceremony to 11:00 o'clock. Some of the big people are here—want to see it—see you all go in for the first time."

"Big people?" Block asked.

"Investors. You know. Want to see some of what they're getting for all that money. And a couple of military consultants who'll be working with us."

"Really?"

"You are not moving up the Seal-In date, are you?" Mai Ker asked.

"No, you'll still have two full weeks of orientation INSIDE before Seal-In. But let's hurry. You're the last two. Your teammates beat you."

This impressed Block—but upset him a little—to realize the others had reported for duty even earlier than him. *Quite a team they've picked,* he told himself. He smiled, anxious to see his old buddy, Will Atchison.

Haskins led them down a glass corridor at the far end of the Visitors Center to a small oval meeting room where several impressively dressed men and women were seated around a cherry wood conference table. Without taking time to introduce the last two arrivals, Haskins hurried to the plastic podium.

"Let's begin. I'm happy to welcome you all. I know some of you are on tight schedules, so we'll start with a brief tour. Shall we?"

The group rose and followed in a lazy herd after Haskins. For the big day Haskins had replaced his thick glasses with contact lenses that he thought made him look younger. They didn't help. His stocky frame filled a rather expensive suit, with an expensive pen clipped neatly into his coat pocket.

Block went right to Atchison's side and grabbed him around the shoulders, smiling broadly. He looked around and recognized Pam Hansen and Sarajane Haug from their file pictures. He had not yet studied the other files, but Bridget Listner and Jimmy Algood were not hard to pick out.

Each of the team acknowledged his look with a brief smile. Bridget Listner seemed a little shy. When Block looked her way her shoes suddenly needed inspection. Although the team had not seen Block before, they sensed from his demeanor who he was. When he wasn't looking, Bridget studied him from a distance. He was a tall, heavy built man with short, dark, curly hair and was clean-shaven. His clear blue eyes seemed to penetrate everything they saw, including Bridget's glance. Except for a lack of fur, he looked remarkably like a friendly gorilla, at home in his new zoo. His walk betrayed no sense of the inner anxiety he was still feeling.

Haskins led them through several short corridors in the museum-like Visitors Center. From here they made their way through the first podwalk that led to Pod 1. Here they were greeted by a sturdy metal door with a large window in it. Haskins pulled at the handle several times, not grasping why it wouldn't open. Then it dawned on him.

"Locked," he smiled, as if this was news. "Security of course is critical. This is the only point of access—or exit—from the rest of the pods."

He fumbled in his coat pocket and produced a hand-held radio, and pushed a small ear piece into his ear.

"Control?" The response obviously came quickly. "Haskins. We're at the main door. Can't get in."

He listened.

"Of course it's supposed to be locked. But we're on the tour."

OUTSIDE Control in the basement of the Visitors Center apparently talked back. The others could hear the faint electronic gurgle in Haskins' earpiece. Block and Atchison glanced at each other. Haskins became impatient.

"Just let us in will you? It's just a tour!" He gave an apologetic look to the others. The gurgling in his earpiece was heard again. "No such thing as 'just a tour' they say. We have to be patient."

"Looks like we're getting what we've paid for," said one pudgy young investor. His squinty eyes scanned the others, several of whom nodded.

"You can bet your life on it," Haskins said with confidence.

The remotely controlled lock finally made a *clack* and they hurried cautiously through the door, as if it might bite them at any instant. They gathered in a small knot in the little Entrance Pod.

"This first pod is primarily an airlock," Haskins explained. "If it should ever be necessary for someone to leave in an emergency, this prevents the complex's air seal from being broken, since that would damage the integrity of the whole project."

The outer door locked behind them, and another *clack* came from the inner door leading toward Pod 2. Haskins pulled it open.

They all felt a subtle change in air pressure as the control system sealed out the outer world and their ears adjusted to the INSIDE air.

Haskins led them down the podwalk to Pod 2. At once, they were barraged with a torrent of the rich, humid aromas of the Solarium. Air pumping through the massive circulation system bathed them with the smells of hundreds of plants, animals and fertilizers.

"See, I *knew* it," Atchison told Block. "Already

feels like home."

It was like walking into a rain forest in a giant barn. They could literally taste life in the air.

The door out of the Entrance Pod had re-locked. Haskins took them proudly into Pod 2 which held the Communication Center, the brain of the whole complex. He gave a quick speech, an overview of the many obviously expensive communications and computer consoles, then moved them along quickly through to the Research Center building housed in Pod 3. Tables, counters, cabinets, computers and lab equipment—most of which Haskins could not explain—filled the building.

"Our team knows what to do with all this stuff," he assured the investors, pointing to Block and his teammates.

They crossed another podwalk into Pod 10, the main agricultural pod and the largest of the domes, 550 feet across and just over 130 high. Everyone finally felt the magnitude and sheer size of Solarium-3. The complex seemed twenty times larger INSIDE than it looked from OUTSIDE. Even Block, tall as he was, suddenly felt small and insignificant, as if he were in a colossal medieval cathedral.

"It's beautiful," Bridget Listner said quietly, venturing out of her shyness for a moment.

Haskins beamed at her, then the others.

"Yes," he said with obvious but dignified pride. "I designed it for functionality—but for aesthetics, too. We wanted to be sure you're all as happy and comfortable as you can be—as far as plastic and metal allow," he chuckled.

Several investors smiled.

"As you can see, the skeleton of each pod is very elaborate," Haskins went on, "and extremely strong. The entire framework is a special aluminum-titanium alloy that was developed for space craft. The domes themselves are Stellar plastic, also developed for space. It's a full inch thick. Each section is between 28 to 40 feet long, and 18 to 24 feet wide. They're perfectly clear so the team will feel at one with the surrounding environment."

"And you're sure it'll be completely airtight?" one of the visitors asked.

"Absolutely. If you look closely, you'll see that over every seam between the Stellar panels, on the outside, we've laminated a foot wide piece of more Stellar. Acts like a shingle. The edges are beveled toward the roof so water won't pool there. These pieces are secured with a special epoxy glue, made just for Stellar. It's impervious to water, and to air."

The team and visitors gazed skyward as Haskins explained all this, studying the complex structural system that supported the immense plastic dome. The unique space-alloy beams didn't look large enough to support themselves, let alone the obviously massive weight of the plastic pods. It seemed like an optical illusion, but was entirely real. The interlaced beams running at various angles looked like a child's creation, a rigging of giant metal toothpicks held together with invisible glue. Yet somehow they supported the gargantuan shell.

Will Atchison had stopped and bent down, running his fingers through a patch of broken soil, checking it, smelling it. Jimmy Algood was still staring straight up.

"Funny. The sky looks—bigger somehow—in here," Jimmy said.

"Really," Haskins commented, looking up as if he doubted him.

"Yeah," Jimmy said. "It seems more . . . present, I guess. Like looking up through the ocean when you're diving."

Block recalled his last scuba dive to a depth of 125 feet in the Caribbean. He remembered the pressure on his body and the overwhelming sense of all that water over his head. He looked up with Algood. Jimmy had put it well.

"Swimming in an ocean of air," Sarajane Haug observed casually.

Block turned and looked at her, and back at Jimmy. *Very perceptive people*, he told himself.

"Well, shall we get on?" Haskins asked, oblivious to the moment of silent insight several of the team had just shared.

Everyone dutifully followed Haskins through several more pods. The tour didn't cover all the areas. They visited the critical "life-centers" including the animal research pods and the artificial ocean in Pod 12, eventually circling back toward the Residence Pod by way of the aviary in Pod 6.

Pam Hansen suddenly stopped so abruptly that one of the women in suits bumped into her.

"What are—?" the woman got out before Hansen cut her off.

"What's that?" Pam asked, pointing to a dark, rust like stain on the podwalk. As soon as she asked, she realized what it was.

"Oh, um, sorry," Haskins said with great embarrassment. "There was a little mishap toward the end of construction. Someone fell. But he's all right, I hear. At the hospital in Pueblo."

"A worker?" one of the investors asked, visions of insurance lawyers dancing in his head.

"Yes," Haskins said. "Fell from a ladder. But things happen. Just careless, I suppose."

But Pam Hansen frowned. Already, a blotch on their pristine new home.

"We'll certainly get it cleaned up before Seal-In of course," Haskins assured everyone. "Shall we see the house?"

Haskins lead them into Pod 4 that held the team

residence. The team members had seen it indistinctly from a distance driving in. Now, directly in front of them, stood a beautiful, hand crafted two-story Victorian. It was pale yellow with evergreen trim and greeted them with warmth. The smell of fresh deck stain from the porch, the final touch, filled the pod. Haskins escorted everyone into the house. Having seen the blueprints, Block was the only one not surprised by what they found.

"Most of you will have a roommate," Haskins explained, telling them, for the benefit of the investors present.

"You'll have to be the odd man out," Block told Jimmy Algood. "Nothing personal. Atchison and I are old friends, so we'll bunk up together."

"Fine with me," Algood said. "I don't mind a little privacy."

Atchison looked around and leaned toward Block.

"This sure ain't the Riviera, Clayton."

". . . and then four main bedrooms upstairs," Haskins was saying. Gesturing down the hall, he added, "Plus an extra bedroom down here to the right. All your clothing needs have been seen to, besides whatever you brought along. And, of course, we've supplied all your necessary personal articles."

One of the women on the tour, a well-dressed public relations specialist for one of the sponsoring corporations, smirked at Haskins.

"And why do you need an extra bedroom?" she asked with a bit of a leer.

"Well . . ." He hesitated, and was careful to look at none of the team. "Seven people cramped up for four years. You know, there may just be times someone needs a little extra privacy."

The woman started to chuckle but a man next to her gave her a slight elbow jab as if to say, "Shut up, Helen."

"Let's move on," Haskins said.

After an hour and a half, the special guests—many who had poured millions of personal and corporate capital into Solarium-3—were duly impressed but tired. Haskins guided them back to Pod 1. Without thinking, he grabbed the handle of the inner door and pulled at it hard—with the same result as before.

After another call to OUTSIDE Control and a brief wait, the door unlocked and the temporary prisoners shuffled into the air lock. The inner door locked, the outer unlocked, and they reentered the Visitors Center.

They returned to the conference room where those in the most expensive suits took the few comfortable chairs. Block stood alone to one end. The rest of the team sat nearby.

"I hope this has been helpful," Haskins said to the guests. "We've put a lot more time into this plant than Solarium-1 and -2. Learned a lot from those trial runs. This will be more like the real thing. Six years of intensive planning. Now four years of research work. I think I can guarantee you this will be the most successful Solarium project ever. We have great hopes of gaining lots of new knowledge. This will be the first entirely sealed, self-sustaining complex we've tried. Nothing comes in, nothing goes out, during the project. Absolutely free-standing, no interaction with the physical environment OUTSIDE. Except necessary communications, that is."

One of the military consultants raised a hand.

"Yes, Colonel Mahham?"

"I don't want to criticize. But that's not totally accurate, is it?"

"How do you mean?"

"Well, this close to the river, isn't there going to be seepage, and some natural interaction with the ground water under the complex? Won't that affect a number of variables, and skew results?"

"A very good question," Haskins answered. "But actually, we thought of that. Not only is the complex totally airtight, it's completely watertight, too. Before the pods went up, we excavated the whole site 60 feet down—a pretty good trick, by the way, this near a river. We poured a two-foot thick concrete tank and lined it with lead, then filled it all in with rock and soil. So in the pods where you see ground, you're actually seeing a completely isolated piece of planet Earth. The pods are absolutely sealed from all environmental interference—above, and below."

"I'm reassured," Mahham said.

"We wanted this to be a real test of complete environmental independence, as it would be on another planet. We'll see how it works out."

There was a minor round of applause.

"And each of you will have the satisfaction of knowing you've helped make it possible," Haskins concluded.

More applause rippled around the conference table. Block even found himself involuntarily offering his congratulations. For what, he wasn't sure.

"I suppose," Haskins admitted, "I really should have made introductions earlier. Jeanine and Edward, I know you've got to leave. I'll finish briefing you later. Thanks for coming." He nodded toward them as they left. "I'm sure some of you introduced yourselves during the tour. Let me formally introduce the INSIDE team leader. Clayton Block. Clayton? Would you come forward?"

Block walked over to Haskins, hoping this was "forward" in the oval room. He looked like a school boy who has just won the spelling bee.

"Clayton has the experience and credentials of a first-rate team leader. You've seen his file. We were very lucky to capture him for this project. And I want to thank him in advance for the fine work that I know he'll be doing INSIDE. Thank you, Clayton," he said, offering his hand. Block took his hand with a grip that could have lifted the smaller man off the floor.

Rubbing the hand behind his back for the next few moments, Haskins did perfunctory introductions of the rest of the team, telling the tour group a little about each person, with fewer and fewer words as he went. He came to Will Atchison last. Atchison looked fresh out of a hardware store in a bright yellow shirt, baggy khakis, and a sincere but cockeyed grin. The white plastic pocket saver in his shirt held its mandatory ballpoint pen, two mechanical pencils, and a black felt-tipped marker. Haskins could not contain a smile.

"And this is William Atchison, who's been working for the Lamont Corporation."

"An excellent choice," said a fragile-looking man to Haskins' left, obviously the representative from Lamont.

Block quipped under his breath, "You can take the boy out of Kansas, but you can't take Kansas outta the boy." Fortunately, only Jimmy Algood was close enough to understand it.

The same pudgy man Block noticed earlier went around and pinned a small enamel "Solarium-3" pin on each team member. He was followed by a woman who handed them each a small gift-wrapped shoe box.

"Care packages," she smiled warmly. "My daughters helped me." Each team member forced a little smile as they accepted the package. Smiles were everywhere, infecting the room like a happiness virus.

Atchison whispered to Block, "Clayton, feels like we're goin' to scout camp or something."

Block shushed him with a little shove. Atchison held his little shoe box up to his ear and shook it gently. He leaned closer to Block and spoke in muffled, confidential tones.

"I'll bet you a quarter there's at least two flashlight

batteries and a pair of shoe laces in here.

Block broke out laughing. Everyone stared at him. He bit his lip, and scowled at William the 2nd.

"Well," Haskins announced quickly, "it's nearly noon and the team's afternoon schedule is pretty full. So we'll call our tour to a close. Clayton, we wish you and your teammates the best of luck."

The remaining visitors worked their way down the line of team members as if they were greeting the bridal party at a wedding, then excused themselves, hurrying off for a business lunch at Pueblo Airport before their flights home.

THE FEW furniture items that Block and others had shipped ahead were already installed in the house. The project planners had allowed each to bring along several small pieces of their own furniture so they'd feel more at home. Most of Block's was in storage.

The team members had lunch in the Visitors Center cafeteria, then collected their remaining personal belongings from their cars. But before lunch, Block retrieved the little nuthatch from his front seat. The bird had given up every attempt at escape. She had grown used to the comfort of her make-shift home in the boot box and was nesting quietly. Just before Haskins escaped to Pueblo, Block got permission to take the extra bird inside.

"Not sure we have any nuthatches," Haskins said.

"Thanks," Block said, "Darn near killed it on the way here. I want to nurse it back to health."

The words touched Haskins in a way he had not expected. He looked at Block for a moment, unsure what to say, and not wanting to say too much. When he spoke, there was an uncharacteristic fervor in his voice.

"God bless you, Clayton. You're a big man, with a big heart."

The unexpected compliment struck Block as

somehow out of place. It was like a father counseling his son who was going off to war. He didn't think of himself as soft-hearted. But Haskins' words, and the look in his eyes, touched a chord.

"Keep it safe," Haskins said as he walked away.

The bird, Block wondered, *or my heart?*

THE AFTERNOON was spent in on-site orientation led by several of the OUTSIDE Control team, beginning with a more thorough inspection of each pod and the equipment they would be operating day-to-day INSIDE. Work would be home, and home would be work, for four years. The next twelve days—with no days off—would be intense as the Solarians began settling into their new habitat, preparing for Seal-In. Days off, Block realized, were a thing of the past.

As the day wore into the evening and wore down, so did Block. He settled into a chair in the bedroom he would share with Willy. Willy was somewhere else, doubtless out on the porch with some—or all—of the women.

Block found the box with the personnel files he had brought from Omaha. He pulled out the three he had not yet read. He began with Moua's.

File:

Mai Ker Moua: 26; place of birth uncertain, possibly California, but probably Laos (Laotian Hmong family immigrated from Laos); Oriental/Female; Height: 5'02", Weight: 103; Black hair, Brown eyes; Daughter of immigrants, now a naturalized US citizen; B.S., dual major in Chemistry & Biology; Ph.D., Genetics; specialist in organic agriculture and plant genetics.

Probability of program success: Excellent

Stress compatibility: High

General Intelligence: High

Focus Area: Bio. and Ag. Research

General Information: Moua earned her undergraduate degree from UCLA by the age of 20; just received her Ph.D. in genetics from Stanford. Special field of interest is applying the organic farming methods of her parents' native Laos to the modern agricultural systems. Applied for team membership after utilizing some Solarium-2 data in her doctoral dissertation. Search team leader recommended her as "a brilliant mind and buoyant, joyful personality." Single, no children.

Overall Assessment: Excellent scientist, perhaps a little pushy, but should be all right after an adjustment period around teammates.

Recommendation: Agricultural Specialist; Research Technician, General Maintenance.

File:

Jimmy Algood: 29; born Eden, Louisiana; Black/Male, Height: 6'01", Weight: 205, Black hair, Brown eyes. Research technician, scientific & atmospheric research. Ph.D. / Physics.

Probability of program success: Good

Stress compatibility: High

General Intelligence: High

Focus area: Biological and agricultural Research.

General Information: Algood is a bright, well-recommended research assistant at the Altercaster Foundation, a private research group working on the development of future environmental systems. He was raised in a small town near Alexandria, LA; very bright in high school; did his undergraduate work at L.S.U.-Shreveport on a full academic scholarship. Ph.D. (with honors) from M.I.T. No military experience, but a well-disciplined individual who works well under pressure and

deadlines. Single, no children.
Overall Assessment: Hard worker, intelligent.
Recommendation: Plant/Animal Research Manager, Air Quality Controller, Facility Manager.

File:

Bridget Listner: 31; born Winnipeg, Manitoba, CAN; White/Female; Height: 5'06", Weight: 120; Brown hair, Brown eyes; B.A. / Biology, minor in Communications; M.S., Computer Research Technology.
Probability of program success: Good
Stress compatibility: Good
General Intelligence: Good
Focus area: Communication/information systems
General Information: Listner is one of the most technically adept information systems experts available and brings a background in biological science as well. Wrote analytical programs for biological research at Barstow College, Winnipeg; did independent study in veterinary medicine as well. Extremely adept at analyzing preferential data; created a new specialization she has dubbed "Conscireology," the predicting of future consciousness in animals using computer modeling. Single, never married; bore one child (baby girl) when she was fifteen; child given up for adoption.
Overall Assessment: Computer whiz, quick mind, strong but pleasant personality that should blend well with others selected.
Recommendation: Information Systems Programmer and Manager; Research Assistant, General Maintenance.

Block put the files carefully back into the box, this time alphabetizing them. He put the box into a locker in the back of his closet where the files would be locked and under his care. Not that there were any big secrets. He was sure that before long he and the other six would come to know far more about each other than the spotty details which the project management team had decided to include in these short summaries.

He looked over at the nuthatch in her cardboard home.

"Got to come up with something better than that," he said to her quietly. "Maybe tomorrow we'll make you a real home."

He got her some fresh water from the bathroom sink and put it in her makeshift cage. She was already a blessing of sorts, an easy distraction from the mountain of work, anxiety, and uncertainty that his new life here would involve. He thought about going down to join Willy and the others. Instead, he changed and got into bed. There would be many days, many evenings, they could spend together.

6

Wednesday, June 25th

The two weeks of orientation and training raced by. The Solarians covered every inch of the complex with three project instructors who had been part of the design team. The INSIDE team had to learn the engineering details and mechanical equipment of each pod to make everything run smoothly, according to the master project plan.

They studied the electrical schematics and systems drawings. They mastered operating of the multiple well and drainage systems that would recirculate water through the natural rock and soil filter that was part of the giant concrete "tank" that underlay the whole complex.

The intriguing wave machine for the artificial ocean in Pod 12 was a series of giant, angled air pistons that created underwater surges forceful enough to generate surface waves. When he first saw the bustling waves, Will Atchison was anxious to try them out.

"Wish I hadn't forgotten my surfboard."

"Didn't know they made one that heavy-duty," Block quipped.

The air circulation system was especially complicated. There had to be a constant inter-flow of air throughout the complex, including the podwalks, so that normal oxygen and carbon dioxide interactions would take place, nourished by the pods that were richest in plant life.

Due to OUTSIDE temperature fluctuations and the intense greenhouse effect of the pods, the massive solar-driven heating and cooling system was maintained by a separate computer, with a redundant backup. The system would always do more cooling than heating, even in winter months. This was intentional, to mimic what would occur on the surface of a low-to-no-atmosphere planet where solar heating would be intense. The planners had to find out if the cooling units could handle the constant load.

The project planners also didn't want any wasted productivity time if someone got sick so every team member had to learn how to operate every piece of equipment. This was no small challenge but the new Solarians managed it. Each of them had to become proficient in operating the high-tech communication systems that tied the pods together and tied them all to the OUTSIDE Control facility under the Visitors Center. The basic system was wireless, but a hard-wired system backed it up. The mysteries of the elaborate computer network were explained in great detail to insure the team would not only maintain proper communications with OUTSIDE, but also archive daily research data on the internal systems. OUTSIDE would then feed all research data to project headquarters in Omaha each day.

By yesterday afternoon, the 24th, their training was complete and they woke up this morning to prepare for the Seal-In. They gathered with their main instructors one last time in the Visitors Center cafeteria for lunch. A few jokes, most not very good, were exchanged about how long four years really was. Mai Ker gave each of the instructors a long hug as the team left for the Entrance Pod.

Bill Becker, the grandfatherly lead instructor, reassured her.

"Don't worry," he said, "we're gonna be right here on the other side of the glass."

"Plastic," Mai Ker corrected. She nodded and

followed the other Solarians into Pod 1, where the outer door clacked shut behind them.

Atchison brought along his "last can of OUTSIDE soda" as a souvenir. The nervous tension between them was percolating as they stood close together waiting for the airlock to transition. Their ears felt the air pressure change. The warm moisture and smells of the Solarium began to greet them, comforting them with familiar sensations that had become routine during the two weeks of training. The pressure change itself had become routine as they moved between the OUTSIDE and INSIDE world. That routine stopped today. Each realized they wouldn't make this passage again for many months.

The silence became pervasive. It all began to sink in.

The lock of the inner door clacked open. Bridget flinched. Will Atchison broke the silence.

"OK, kids, let's go have some fun," he said as he strode forward.

The emotional relief from his humor was palpable. They poured into the Solarium with the new-found energy of school children clamoring off the bus on a field trip.

Will led them down the podwalk to the Comm. Center in Pod 2. Here they held a final briefing with Omaha. Nothing new. More routine stuff. Sarajane, the last one into the room, leaned against a counter at the back wall. *Research on a whole new level,* she told herself. She was amazed, and very pleased, that she was here.

One of the technicians in OUTSIDE Control sat down at his computer and keyed in the final sequence for the Seal-In. Graphics and preprogrammed orders began to cycle down his three large screens. Every graphic and command was paralleled on screens of the Comm. Center INSIDE. At the same instant, replicas of the information poured across screens at the project Monitoring Center in Omaha. A master computer in OUTSIDE Control raced through a labyrinth of technical commands and codes.

INSIDE, the Solarians felt the refreshingly cool air circulating through the pods as several fans and vents readjusted. Air purifiers kicked in at the right moment, fine-tuning the air quality throughout the fourteen pods.

After twenty minutes of computer programs and graphics dancing across the screens, the dance partners OUTSIDE, INSIDE and in Omaha all came to a prearranged rest at the same instant, like the end of a graceful ballet. A small green dot appeared in the upper left corner of each screen showing that the entire INSIDE system was running smoothly. The computers were all happy and shook hands. Harmony and stability had come to the Solarium complex. The Seal-In was complete. Solarium-3 was up and running perfectly.

LATER THAT evening Block stood alone on the porch of the house in Pod 4. He felt as he often did scuba diving. Things were quiet, too quiet in a way. He felt he was now floating, weightlessly, through life. For a few seconds he felt an inner peace and calm he sometimes felt during a dive—that paradoxical sense of feeling completely free, yet somehow unusually contained.

He walked along the wraparound porch that encircled two sides of the house. He looked out through the surrounding pod walls, and the near blackness beyond them OUTSIDE. He stared for the longest time up through the pod roof into the almost cloudless sky. The skin along his back and neck tingled. He felt now a different sense, one he couldn't shake for several hours afterward. He knew he would be here for four years, yet for some inexplicable reason he felt like a man just sentenced to life in prison.

He was not alone. Most of the team wouldn't sleep

very well tonight. Their minds and conversations had buzzed all evening, trying to adjust to the reality of finally being *sealed* into the complex. The small talk got smaller, and they began to act more naturally with each other. Atchison was the glaring exception. He tried out his "batteries and shoe laces" joke again, shaking his unopened care package in front of Sarajane who was trying to read. She said nothing, just looked over the top of her glasses, and took her book to another room.

An hour later when Block went up to the bedroom he would share with Atchison, he found Will out cold, and snoring loudly. *Forgot that part,* Block mused. He realized he hadn't had a really good night's sleep since leaving Wisconsin. Will's snore certainly wasn't going to help.

He laid down and tried to unwind. He watched his little nuthatch flit about in the large, baggy cage of netting that he'd rigged up over the foot of his bed. But he couldn't sleep. He couldn't even relax. Will sputtered like a pregnant machine gun. Block watched the little bird fly circles INSIDE her own little habitat.

"You know, little critter, you need a name."

Block dropped a pillow over Will's head as he left the room, but Atchison never stirred. He was dead to the world. Too much excitement.

Block walked down the faintly lit stairs, out onto the porch, and wandered over to the Research Center in Pod 3. Under the dim night-lights he scanned several books in Center's impressive scientific library, but—rather curiously—found nothing about bird species.

"I guess it's all in the box these days."

He sat down at one of the four computer stations and flipped on the desk lamp. He brought up an inquiry screen and typed in "wildlife, non-domestic fowl." He scrolled through page after page of digital photos until one popped onto the screen that seemed to match his pet. He clicked the little square icon by the photo, a little three-dimensional box with the word "Detail" popping in and out of it. As he clicked, a lengthy article sprang up alongside the picture.

"Electronic books," Block said wearily. The picture auto-shrunk into a corner of the screen. He scrolled through the article:

White-Breasted Nuthatch. Scientific name: *Sitta Carolinensis*. This small, stocky creature is usually about 5 inches tall with a short, squared-off tail. A very strong bill helps it in searching out insects in tree bark and cracking open seeds and nuts, especially hickory nuts and acorns, on which it thrives during the winter. May visit suet and other feeders.

"And large Solariums," Block said half-aloud. He read on:

The male and female are similar, with a grayish-blue upper body offsetting a white face, breast and underbelly. The male sports a black cap and neckband. The female has the black neckband only and a blue-gray cap. Found across northern hemisphere, Canada into Mexico.

Its song is a steady *"whi, whi, whi,"* or *"who, who."*

A curiosity: like other nuthatches, *Sitta Carolinensis* is known to routinely climb down trees head-first.

"That's my girl," Block said.

He clicked the photo again and studied the female version. Without intending it, the whole article was sucked electronically back into its little box.

"Yep. You're the one."

"Talk to yourself a lot?"

The voice, though soft, startled him. He lurched around to find Bridget Listner standing across the room.

"Sorry. Didn't hear you come in."

"I was here when you came in," she told him. "Over there." She gestured to a work cubicle at the far end of the room.

"Sitting in the dark?"

"Yeah." She rocked her head a bit. "Just trying to get used to it. The whole idea. You know?"

"Being 'stuck' you mean?"

"Yeah. Like that. It was OK. Until tonight. After sundown." Then she hedged, remembering she was talking to her new boss. "It's not that I'm claustrophobic or anything. It's just the time. You know? Four years didn't sound like much. Well, on paper. In here, tonight—seems a lot longer."

"I know. That's why I'm not sleeping I guess."

"What were you reading?"

"Birds. You saw her, didn't you? In my room."

"Why would I be in your room?"

"I brought her in that first afternoon."

"In that big mysterious shoe box?"

"Yeah."

"Why would you bring a bird along? And no cage?"

"Well, I almost killed the darn thing leaving home. Couldn't leave it there in the road. So I just brought it along. Trying to get her well. Seems to be OK now. She's flying a lot more."

"Very noble. How can you tell it's a she?"

"Noble, huh? Wouldn't say that." His expression changed to a very self-conscious smile. "She's a she because of this little black scarf thing. Here." He pointed to the picture of the female.

"Good at spotting females, huh?"

Block gave her a look, but ignored the remark.

"I was trying to think of a name."

"You having a baby?"

Block gave her another look. But he enjoyed her friendly teasing.

"For the bird?" he said.

"Let's look," Bridget said.

She leaned over Block's shoulder and looked closely at the picture. She clicked the little icon again and the article erupted again from its hiding place, flooding the screen.

"Well, that's simple," she said.

"It is?" Block looked up into her face hovering alongside his. Her long, sandy brown hair smelled like coconut oil. His hands were a little sweaty.

"Caroline," she said.

"Who?"

"Her name. It should be Caroline."

"After who?"

"Nobody, Clay. It's right here."

Block pulled his gaze away from her and looked back at the screen. "*Sitta Carolinensis*" jumped out at him.

"Of course. You're pretty smart."

"Thanks. Well, I'm going to bed. You?"

He foundered a little, but realized she didn't mean what he thought.

"Yeah, I think I can get to sleep now."

Bridget smiled down at him. "Pleasant dreams, Clay."

"Clayton," he said. "I always go by Clayton."

"Pleasant dreams, Clayton. Get some rest. Shut the lights off when you're done."

She had disappeared into the house by the time Block reached the porch. He went upstairs and laid back down. Will was snoring even louder.

He thought about Bridget's teasing, and the smell of her hair. *Don't let that start,* he lectured himself. *Remember, you're the boss.*

"*Tick tick tick tick.*" The nuthatch pecked at the bark of the small branch that Block had arranged in her netted home. "*Who, who who.*"

"Good night, Caroline."

She ignored him. "*Tick tick, tick tick.*"

In a few moments Block drifted off into a light sleep.

7

Saturday, September 20th

Jimmy Algood sat with his lanky legs propped up on the Comm. console in Pod 2. He brushed a few beads of sweat off his dark, glistening forehead and ran his fingers through his hair. It felt warmer than usual.

He was eating one of the crunchy snack bars Pam Hansen had been experimenting with for a week. She called them "Christmas cookies" although Christmas was months away. They were long rectangular bars cooked in a flat pan that looked nothing like what the folks back home in Louisiana called a cookie.

The term "Christmas cookies" had already caused a minor controversy among the teammates. Clayton, Pam, Will and Sarajane had nominal Christian roots but none of them showed any inclination to talk openly about their faith, if they still had any. Mai Ker seemed to hold some traditional Eastern views but she too kept these to herself, and admitted her family had never actually practiced any religious ceremonies. Early on, the team made an informal pact that during the next four years there wouldn't be any religious displays—in particular Christmas festivities—INSIDE. So Pam's decision to make "Christmas" cookies provoked a short debate one day at lunch. It was hard to have strong feelings about a cookie. But they finally agreed cookies could be an exception. The less religious teammates, in fact, couldn't understand why a cookie could have special religious significance anyway. What really drove the decision was simple: they all loved Pam's cookies. The name, after all, had nothing to do with the taste.

Although it was fall OUTSIDE, it still felt like summer INSIDE. The greenhouse-like effect of the pods would keep the Solarium fairly hot even come winter. The solar-powered cooling system ran almost continuously, until well after sundown each day.

The summer months just past had put a heavy strain on the cooling units. The OUTSIDE temperatures some days soared to 110 degrees or higher. INSIDE the Solarium, without constant cooling, the pods would have jumped to 130-140 degrees. The high-efficiency cooling units in the top of each pod were designed to keep the INSIDE at a moderate 70-90 degrees year around. Over the summer, they worked overtime. But due to brilliant design, even under the magnified solar radiation INSIDE the units shot out a continuous blast of arctic air, unless the computer system told them to slow down.

The planned benefit, as with any greenhouse, was that the solar heating created a near-tropical climate with a constant growing season. This would enable Atchison, Algood, Moua and Haug to continue agricultural research uninterrupted throughout the various OUTSIDE seasons over the four years.

The designers had also put an elaborate sprinkler system high overhead that recycled filtered water from the underground basin and acted as the rain source for the fields, lawns and plant life. Maintaining the right balance of flora INSIDE was critical to the air quality. The "rain" sprinklers were also triggered by a computer, whenever humidity or ground moisture dipped too low. But the system allowed the Solarians to produce "rain" manually if they thought it was needed. Human sensitivity to dryness or moisture had to be considered, as it would in any long-term project on another planet.

The team was judicious with the rain, though. Too

high a humidity would over-saturate the air and intensify the heating effects of the sun. And when the pod walls cooled at night, the condensation would trigger *real* rain INSIDE as the moisture dripped down.

All in all, it was a tricky system to maintain, especially in the first few weeks. It had become mostly routine now. The whole INSIDE ecosystem had to operate in a precise balance. Each system affected and interacted with all the others. And the team took great care to follow the master project plan and timing of certain experiments—timing that had been worked out months in advance by intricate computer modeling. So far, both agricultural and animal research was on schedule.

One of Jimmy's responsibilities, and the reason he spent far too much time at the computer console, was managing the atmospheric recycling units that continually circulated air through the pods. The air quality was, of course, affected by the animal life in the complex. Just as oxygen production by the plant life was essential, so was the absorption of carbon dioxide and other gases that the team and the animals added daily to the mix.

The air system included filters that could "scrub" the air in an emergency by reducing the carbon dioxide level. But one of the project's goals was to use these only in a true emergency, and to work to maintain a "natural" balance in the Solarium. Over time, the "scrubbers" would become fouled. In a long-term environment on another planet, this could be a problem.

Bridget Listner stayed busy either in the Comm. Center or in the Research Center in Pod 3 updating logs and generating progress reports that were uploaded daily to OUTSIDE Control and to Omaha. When she wasn't tied to a computer she spent a lot of time with Block helping with general operations and maintenance of the physical plant.

The Solarians held regular team meetings three times a week to refine schedules and smooth out bumps in the operational routines. By late August, those routines had finally become truly routine. They all stayed busy, often working alone or in pairs in various pods, and seeing the group only at lunch or supper around the large oak table in their Victorian home.

THE MOST unsettling thing—and something none of them even thought about when accepting the job—was that the complex quickly became a popular tourist attraction. Cars and vans rolled into the parking lot every hour of the day. All sizes and shapes of people filtered through the Visitors Center or prowled around the OUTSIDE sidewalks that encircled the perimeter of the fourteen pods.

So they found themselves living in a fish bowl. It was worse at night, when others could see in, but they couldn't see out very well. At first, it was impossible to ignore the overly curious visitors, so the team would acknowledge them with a wave or high-sign. This got old quickly. Visitors, especially the kids, often stood and stared with very peculiar expressions on their faces—when they weren't snapping pictures.

"Didn't know I'd be an animal in a zoo," Will Atchison said one day. Then he did a frantic pantomime of a gorilla, which for Will was actually quite easy.

"Behave," Jimmy said. "Pretend you're running for office."

"Ain't that what I just did?" Atchison laughed.

But by early September, even the presence of these daily visitors had become routine. It was rare now if any of the Solarians looked up or acknowledged a visitor. It was as if those INSIDE felt they had become invisible to those OUTSIDE.

AN EXCEPTION happened on September 6th. OUTSIDE sent an email to Block announcing a "special visitor." Block called the team together in Pod 2, expecting to see some politician or dignitary on the podwalk OUTSIDE.

As they waited for the last two to reach the pod, a second email arrived from John Haskins himself, characteristically late:

TO: CLAYTON BLOCK
FROM: J. HASKINS
:: BLOCK: YOU'LL HAVE A SPECIAL GUEST AT THE VISITORS CENTER THIS MORNING, CALVIN JOHNSTON. HE'S THE WORKER WHO WAS INJURED FINISHING THE COMPLEX. PLEASE GREET HIM WARMLY. HE SUFFERED A SEVERE SKULL FRACTURE AND HAS NOT RECOVERED VERY WELL. HIS DAUGHTER WILL BE WITH HIM. HE HASN'T BEEN ABLE TO SPEAK SINCE THE ACCIDENT, BUT THE DAUGHTER (REBECCA) SAYS HE WROTE A NOTE LAST WEEK THAT HE WANTED TO VISIT THE COMPLEX TO "SEE IT IN ACTION." HE APPARENTLY FEELS PRETTY PROUD TO HAVE BEEN A SMALL PART OF OUR PROJECT.
THANKS. HASKINS. ::

With all the team assembled Block walked them outside the Comm. Center building to the edge of the pod. Coming along the sidewalk OUTSIDE was a woman pushing her father in a wheelchair. The man's hair was very short on one side, still growing back after the third surgery.

This was the first personal visitor the Solarians had seen. They were all at a loss. Finally, Bridget stepped close to the pod wall and gave Calvin a little wave and a smile. She turned slightly and beckoned the others with her eyes, seeking support.

Block walked to Bridget, waved to Johnston, then used a sweeping arm gesture to indicate the rest of the pods behind him. He gave Calvin a thumbs-up. Johnston managed half a smile, making several slow nods of his head. He raised a nearly limp right arm part way and repeated Block's thumbs-up.

Sarajane applauded him, applause Johnston could see but not hear through the inch-thick Stellar plastic. Johnston's daughter waved a *thank you*, then pushed her father along, taking him around the entire perimeter of the complex.

"Wasn't that fun," Bridget said sourly, as they all walked into the Comm. Center, trying to hide.

"Well, Haskins wanted us to say 'Hi,'" Block said. "He's not just a visitor. He's the guy that got hurt when they were finishing construction."

"The blood on the podwalk," Sarajane commented.

"Yeah. Guess he's not doing too well."

"Yeah, well let's get back to work, OK?" Atchison said.

Everyone nodded silent agreement. It didn't take much.

THREE HOURS later Atchison came back to the Comm. Center where Jimmy was alone, working at a console, and nibbling Pam's Christmas cookies.

"What's cooking, Jimmy?"

"Cookies," he said, holding one aloft.

"You are *such* a funny guy. I mean what's new from the OUTSIDE? Any more special visitors planning to stop by?"

"Nah. Just waiting for a feedback report on the air quality data I sent out yesterday—and confirmation on my lab analysis of those new green bean hybrids you've been working on."

"From the big brains in Omaha, huh?"

"Big computer brains," Jimmy said. "I tell you, Will, the main computers they've got there are pretty smart. And fast? I can't believe it. They're scary. The guys back there tell me a couple of the systems are so advanced they've almost reached the point of 'artificial intelligence.'"

"Well, it ain't nothing new, Jimmy," Will chuckled, picking up a cookie. "That's what the human race's been operating on for a long time."

Jimmy laughed. "*You're* the funny guy, Will. Hey, I've been meaning to ask you. How come Block calls you 'William the 2nd'? What's with that?"

"Oh, just a little private humor from Lieutenant Block. See, when we were in the service, we had a couple of long R&Rs. One time I kinda overdid it—you know, a little too much rocket fuel. Block was outside this restaurant on the Riviera, winin' and dinin' some French lady. He came back in and found me dancin' with a much *prettier* French lady. Except I was wearing a badly beat-up toilet seat for a hat. A crown. Now I don't remember this myself, mind you. But Clayton swears it's true. And he's pretty honest. Anyway. He said I looked good in my crown and started callin' me 'King William the 2nd'. Smart aleck."

"I hate to say it, Will," Jimmy smiled, "but I have no trouble believing Block on this one." He laughed louder.

"Well, let's just keep it to yourself, OK? We have genuine ladies here, and they don't need to hear about it."

"Not a word, buddy. Not one word. I never cause trouble." But the image of a dancing Atchison crowned with a toilet seat made Jimmy's whole day go better.

"Yeah, we had some wow times together in the service. But I gotta admit, I had a real problem with the booze back then. Toilet seat probably got stuck while I was ralphing up my guts in the men's room. Took me a lot of years to straighten out."

"You obviously did, huh?"

"Yeah, had to. That, or croak."

"Good for you," Jimmy said.

Atchison pulled a chair up to the console and swiped another cookie from Jimmy's pile.

"So, how's it going for you? I mean, how you like it here so far?"

"Good," Jimmy said. "Hey, I love this. This *place*. It's a dream come true for me."

"How's that?" Atchison asked, brushing cookie crumbs from his bushy mustache.

"Reminds me of when I was a kid. Me and my brother and my two sisters used to play 'spaceship' under a big table down in the basement."

"Spaceship?"

"Yeah. We got the idea one night when we were all hiding under the table during a tornado warning. The table was right in the southwest corner of our basement—my dad always claimed that was the safest place to be when the big tornado hit that was always gonna hit us. Course, it never did—so we never got to test his theory. But one night I said to my brother, 'This would make a cool spaceship.' The next day we covered up the table with blankets hanging down to the floor, and we set up a whole bunch of old junk switches and rheostats that my dad had lying around with his model railroad stuff. It was the cabin of our space shuttle. We stored in a bunch of peanut butter sandwiches and chips and warm soda. One time that summer we camped out in there for four and a half days, 'cause we were flying in space. Mom said, 'You children, you've all lost your marbles.' 'No, ma'am,' I said, 'we got them under here too!'"

Atchison laughed at Jimmy's little joke.

"My dad didn't really know much about it cause he was hardly ever home anyway. Always running around selling this thing or that. I knew my friend's dad better than I knew my own. But we had a fantastic time under that table. I bet we would've stayed under there for a month if we hadn't run out of peanut butter sandwiches.

"My mom would come down every few hours to check on us—but we wouldn't look out or anything. She'd talk, then we'd say 'You have to send us a message over the space radio, we can't hear you.' And she'd wander back upstairs muttering to herself."

Atchison laughed again.

"I made my mom mutter a lot, too," he said. "So Solarium-3 is like hiding under a table, huh?"

"Oh, way better! We get to stay. And we don't have to eat peanut butter three times a day!"

Atchison was laughing again when one of the terminals beeped and Jimmy's report popped up on the monitor. He punched a key and a nearby printer disgorged nearly a ream of lined green paper at high speed.

But in the middle of the printout the computer barked out a loud interrupt signal. The printer froze, and "*MESSAGE WAITING — PRIORITY: URGENT*" flooded the screen in large red letters. Jimmy hit the RECEIVE key as Atchison watched the screen with curiosity.

The screen scrolled on in red, "*REPEAT— PRIORITY: URGENT. NEED CLAYTON BLOCK IMMEDIATELY.*"

"That's par," Jimmy said. "Guess I'm not good enough for these big boys to talk to." He said it only half-jokingly.

"I'll go find him," Atchison said.

He headed for the recreation area in Pod 5. He'd seen Block and Bridget a half hour earlier working together—as was becoming more and more common—cleaning the swimming pool filter.

8

Saturday Evening, September 20th

Atchison found Block and Listner, as he expected, getting the pool ready for a late afternoon swim party. Both were sitting on deck chairs wiping away sweat. Parts of the pool filter assembly lay on the ground. The sun OUTSIDE in a cloudless sky was causing the air conditioners more overtime.

"Clayton, sorry to bug you. Jimmy's got an urgent bulletin or something for you in the Comm. Center."

"Well, it can wait till after we swim."

"I dunno. Looked pretty darned important. For your eyes only."

"Bridget—you can finish this, can't ya?" Block asked.

"Yes, thank you, numbskull. Remember who showed you how to take it apart in the first place?"

Block gave her a blank look. "You?"

She frowned at him. Block looked embarrassed—something easy for him to do.

"That's right, you did. I forgot." He gave her a fake, toothy grin. "Thanks. I'll be back in time for that swim. Got a new pair of cutoffs to break in."

Bridget rolled her eyes. Block was not into high fashion, especially at pool parties.

Block followed Atchison back to Pod 2, but when Block saw the large red "SECURE" icon in the corner of the screen he asked Will and Jimmy to leave for a few minutes.

"Sorry, guys. Looks like one of those security-type things. I'll let you know what's up in a few."

"It's close to swim time anyway, isn't it William the 2nd?" Jimmy asked.

"Hey now, you promised—" Atchison started.

"No, I only said, Not in front of the ladies."

"You told him?" Block asked.

"Slipped out," Atchison said, with a sheepish grin.

He and Jimmy went to the house to change. They knew certain management communications were routinely shared only with Block as the team leader— but they still resented these little exclusions when they happened. As the Comm. Center door shut itself behind Jimmy and Will, Block keyed in his security password to unlock the message.

BLOCK ONLY!: PRIORITY.
FROM: J. HASKINS
ENTER   SECONDARY   DE-SCRAMBLE
KEYWORD.

Block entered his second pass code which allowed the message onto the screen.

:: MESSAGE: NEED YOU TO JUMP AHEAD TO ATMOSPHERIC STUDIES GC-401 THROUGH GC-442, ORIGINALLY PLANNED FOR NEXT MARCH. FOLLOW SAME PROCEDURES, WITH MODIFICATIONS WHICH WILL FOLLOW THIS MESSAGE. **NOTE: THIS IS PRIORITY.** CONTINUE ALL OTHER PROJECT ACTIVITIES AND INTERMEDIATE ASSIGNMENTS AS POSSIBLE, BUT THEY ARE NOW SECONDARY. THANKS.
PS: THIS IS CONFIDENTIAL, NOT FOR DISCLOSURE. ALGOOD WILL HAVE TO BE TOLD TO HANDLE RELATED COMMUNICATION, BUT KEEP IT LOW PROFILE.

DETAILS OF THIS CHANGE ARE NOT, REPEAT NOT, TO BE SHARED WITH OTHER TEAM MEMBERS. JUST HAVE THEM FOLLOW THE PROCEDURES WE'RE SENDING IN. THANKS. HASKINS ::

Block's normally high level of curiosity went through the roof. What could be this important? He initiated an on-line "chat" with Haskins. There was a half-minute pause, then this.

:: J. HASKINS IS NOT AVAILABLE. NO FURTHER INFORMATION IS AVAILABLE. ::

Block shook his head. He keyed in another secure "receive" code. The remainder of the message spilled across the screen like flood waters rushing over a dam. The printer kicked to life again and spewed out several more reams of scientific data and new procedures onto the last page of Jimmy's printout that was interrupted a few minutes earlier.

Block ripped the whole thing off the printer and scanned it quickly, with the pages of Jimmy's report leading his. He read quickly over the revised testing procedures Haskins had sent.

"This is stupid," he said half-aloud. "How do they expect us to pull this off?"

He scanned a few more pages, and gave up in frustration. He tore the pages apart and threw the air quality and green bean reports into Jimmy's mail tray, not realizing the first lines of Haskin's message were on the last page of Jimmy's printout. Block took the message from Haskins to the house and locked them in a small safe in his room.

"Later . . ." he said, changing into his cut-offs. The jeans had shrunk from too many washings in hot water—which was why he decided to cut them off. His legs bulging out at the bottom, along with his growing belly, created a rather comical look, as if he'd been poured into them then blown up like a balloon.

"Wonderful," he frowned in the mirror. "Oh well, it ain't a beauty contest, Block." He headed off to Pod 5.

"Well, slow poke, finally," Sarajane laughed as Block hurried onto the pool deck, barefoot and bulging out of his trunks. "Nice shorts, Clayton!" she snickered.

"Sorry—got tied up at Comm."

"So what was so darn important that we're not in on it?" Atchison asked, scratching at his hairy, barrel-like chest.

"Probably a new recipe for Pam," Jimmy teased Block.

"Well—actually, Jimmy—you're kind of warm. It's some . . . well, just a few revisions Omaha wants us to implement. Some tests. A little different than what was planned—but I guess they always know what they're doing."

"Awfully important message for just some stupid test," Atchison said skeptically.

Block mixed a cold drink at the pool-side bar.

"Tonight?" Mai Ker protested with a whine in her voice. "We have to work tonight?"

"Don't worry, not tonight," Block said. "It doesn't affect you, Mai Ker. Jimmy and I can get on it in the morning. I need some time to read over the new specs."

He wasn't really anxious to read the new test specifications or start what looked like rather bizarre testing for that matter. He hated changes to the routine.

Block sat back on a deck chair and watched his teammates in the pool. He didn't often study people like this, but being thrust together for many weeks now had piqued his interest. Absorbing their behavior and personalities was becoming a hobby since, besides Caroline, he didn't have any hobbies. Each day he noticed something new about them.

His eyes went to Bridget first, of course. She was clad in a brightly colored bikini that showed off her beautiful curves. *More curves than a mountain highway,* he thought. Her sandy brown hair, sprinkled with droplets from the pool, flowed over her shoulders and flipped in all directions when she laughed, which she did a lot. Her eyes sparkled when she glanced at him—which she also did a lot—but they sparkled for everyone else, too. Intriguingly, her eyelids always seemed not quite open. It was like she was looking out at the world sleepily, as if in a curious dream. The bright yellow swimsuit matched her personality well. She was a lively woman, not over-confident, but not a wallflower, either.

Pam Hansen, on the other hand, was dressed conservatively in a dull, dark blue, one-piece swimsuit. She was slightly taller and heavier than Bridget but was also very attractive. It wasn't that her figure couldn't have withstood the exposure of a two-piece but the conservative look reflected her interior landscape. There was always something going on in there, but it didn't always show. She was somewhat of a puzzle to her teammates. Reared in Kentucky and southern Kansas, Pam retained a Southern drawl that was a confusing mix of quick jabber-talk and slow, stretched-out words.

Jimmy was splashing around in a camouflage swimsuit and sleeveless T-shirt. He was a powerfully built man who could have commanded any crowd, yet his manner was always one of politeness and attempts-to-please. To Block he seemed to be the kind of person who could stand in front of a tornado without flinching but would give you the shirt off his back in a pinch.

William the 2nd presented a stark contrast to Jimmy. Willy, as Block called him, showed up in baggy, beige Bermuda trunks. The draw string and some belly hair bulged out at the waist. His first

"torpedo" dive sent shock waves through the pool—
and the air. When he surfaced, the thick matted hair on
his back looked like the soggy spikes on a drenched
dinosaur.

"Willy," Block shouted, "you look like a drowning
snapping turtle!"

This was all the excuse Atchison needed to try to
imitate that very reptile. From alongside the pool,
Sarajane watched him in complete bewilderment with a
look that could have equally been amazement and
disgust.

"What is *that* supposed to be?" she called.

"That would be the American Red-bellied Basking
Turtle," Atchison hollered, just before he swallowed a
mouthful of water.

"P. rubriventris," Mai Ker called from her deck
chair.

"Beg your pardon?" Atchison retorted, gasping for
air.

"P. rubriventris," Mai Ker repeated.

"What'd she say?" asked Jimmy.

Mai Ker laughed.

"That's its scientific name," she said. "The
American Red-belly."

"Ah-hah-hah!" Atchison laughed, and started
splashing away again—arms flailing, head pumping up,
down, searching from side to side. He was quickly
exhausted by this little display and reverted to a
pathetic breast stroke down the remaining length of the
60 foot pool.

Block roared with laughter and melted into the
evergreen cushion of his deck chair. Sipping his iced
gin and tonic he tried to relax, which was, in this
environment, a huge challenge. Sweat continued to
trickle down his forehead from the heat in the pod,
though the brilliant sun was finally setting. It struck
Block how the refracted amber light shining behind the

pod's framework cast strangely twisted shadows across the team.

Mai Ker next caught—and held—his attention. She sat near him on a lounge chair in a rather plain bikini that amply covered her. The white suit made a striking contrast to her warm brown skin. *She is really a pretty woman,* Block thought. He still remembered his first glimpse of her in his rear-view mirror that first morning. Her large brown eyes still fascinated him. There was a kind of secret joy about her all the time, as if she alone knew the meaning of life and was floating through it on a pair of gossamer wings. Her constant, pleasant smile seemed to exude not just from her lips but from her whole body like a halo. Her rounded face and lovely eyes were highlighted by thick, dark eyebrows. She was considerably smaller than the other women, and more fragile looking.

Block went to the poolside bar for more ice. This was partly to chill his drink but also to water it down. The first one was too potent. As he turned he noticed Sarajane sitting on a bare plastic chaise lounge on the far side of the pool. She was usually the first one into the pool but also the first one out. As she slowly air-dried, her dark brown skin still glistened from the short dip she had taken a few minutes earlier. She noticed Block's glance and gave him a little wave, which caught him by surprise. But that was all the attention she granted. She went back to reading her paperback, the pages of which were damp with drops falling from her hair. Sarajane was a big woman, just an inch shorter than Block. She had on old brown khaki shorts held up by a leather belt—even while in the pool—and an Army-green T-shirt. Her long, twisting brown hair was tied up in some kind of womanly knot on her head. She, too, was a bit of a mystery. She obviously enjoyed everyone's company, but she rarely took much of an active part in anything they did, other than to be present.

Block realized he was no longer sweating like a mule climbing out of the Grand Canyon. The sun was finally below the horizon and the pod was a little cooler. He laid back on his deck chair, perching the cold glass on his bare stomach. The scientist in him took over, studying the sky OUTSIDE. It seemed bluer than normal. The air had a faint bluish tinge, like that momentary coloring that permeates the air after an electrical discharge.

Off in the distance to the southeast, rapid lightning flashes began to punctuate the darkening sky as a thunderstorm brewed. The storm moved toward them along an uncharacteristic path, driven by a strong southeast wind, heading northwest. The thunder that surely accompanied the lightning was completely inaudible INSIDE the Stellar plastic of the Solarium. Before long, heavy rain pelted the pod but INSIDE the pool party rolled on into the evening.

After several drinks, Atchison jumped out of the pool and yelled, "OK, everybody, ready for a little skinny-dippin'?" He turned his back as if ready to yank down his trunks. Bridget turned her face away and leapt from the pool, intending to make a run for the house.

She was stopped by everyone's laughter. Sure enough, William the 2nd had yanked down his Bermuda trunks. But he had a set of racing trunks underneath. He tossed the Bermudas as hard as he could toward the pod wall, where they stuck with a *splap!* He shook his hips a few times, and did another torpedo.

"April fool!" he bellowed just before he went under.

Sarajane said, "It's September, bone head," but he didn't hear.

As Atchison surfaced with a broad shark-like grin, Bridget wagged a finger at him.

"Very funny, Will," she said, only half angry.

"Gotcha!" Atchison retorted, with a bellicose laugh that jiggled the water around him.

Bridget slipped back in the pool as if entering an actual shark tank. Jimmy was now out of the water and toweling off.

"Boy, we dodged the big bullet that time," he said to Block in a pretended whisper that everyone but Willy heard.

"You're not a-kidding. I spent time in the service with him. I promise you, you've never known abject terror until you've seen William the 2nd buck-naked."

Jimmy did all he could to contain a nearly uncontainable laugh.

As the sky darkened and lights came on in the pod, Block's nuthatch, Caroline, joined the party briefly. After just a month INSIDE, Block abandoned the idea of keeping her caged up in his room. Even though no other nuthatches had been provided for the Solarium, he decided to let her take her chances with the other birds flying around INSIDE. The planners in their wisdom had provided Pod 6, a beautiful aviary with a large, open cage. This pod was a hub centered between the Research Pod, the Residence Pod, the Recreation Pod—known by the team as "the three Rs"—and the huge Agricultural Pod. Most of the birds in the complex made #6 home but they were free to fly wherever they wished. The arched Stellar tunnels that covered the podwalks had 16-foot ceilings so the birds were able to navigate them with little trouble without getting stuck.

Caroline visited the aviary almost daily but Block found she still knew where her real home was, as long as he kept a little seed lying about in dishes around their bedroom. A bedroom window left open a bit gave her easy access. Atchison objected for a couple of weeks about having to wipe up bird splatter off the carpet every day but he finally gave in and accepted

Caroline as a legitimate resident of the room.

As she flew into #5 to investigate the party, she circled twice around the top of the pod, dodging beams, then touched down on the stanchion of one of the pool area lights. Block waved to her with one finger, something like a child saying goodbye to an old friend. Then, obviously showing off for Caroline, he left his lounge chair and dove in right behind Bridget, who was standing midway across the pool with her back to him. He dove under her legs and hoisted her, unsuspecting, onto his shoulders. Bridget shrieked. Then she slapped Block across the side of his head in protest and laughed.

"Clayton—you rat! Put me down!" She shrieked again, about to lose her balance but obviously not too unhappy. "Put me down!"

"On your feet or your head this time?"

"Just let me down—you're embarrassing me again."

"It's the only thing I'm good at."

Jimmy dove back in, landing belly first in front of Block. He got his footing, grabbed both of Bridget's hands, and pulled her over Block's head, somersaulting her over his own head. She landed flat on her back with a loud *slawaapp* and began to sink to the bottom.

Pool parties never change.

Jimmy dove after Bridget, afraid he had drowned her. Despite the hard landing she came up laughing, and wriggling around with Jimmy like two spawning salmon. Atchison, in his very unattractive racing trunks, sat on the edge of the pool grinning, slowly shaking his head. Caroline, obviously finding nothing of interest in such human nonsense, flew off to the aviary. The Solarians, including Block, continued to laugh and play happily like kids, except for Sarajane who was now deeply engrossed in her novel.

ABOUT 8:30 that evening, Pam found Sarajane in their

bedroom, curled up on her bed, still glued to her book.

"What'ya reading?"

"A fantasy," Sarajane answered. "Really strange story about this whaling ship."

"Ah. *Moby Dick*."

"No, actually. It's called *Sailing Through The Night*."

"Sounds scary," Pam said as she sat down at her little vanity table and began to brush out her hair. "An old-time fantasy?"

"No, a modern whaling ship, diesel powered. But there's this whale, this mysterious whale. It keeps showing up on sonar, but never surfaces. It just seems to follow the ship around, or maybe lead them. It comes and goes every few days—but they never actually see it."

"A mystery whale." Pam contemplated the image.

"Kind of like Atchison in the pool today," Sarajane said in a monotone.

Pam laughed loudly.

"I like Will," she said. "I think he's nice. And kind of cute in his way."

"For a whale."

"More to love," Pam said with a knowing look to her roommate.

Sarajane was reading again, ignoring her.

"You sure like to read," Pam observed.

"Yeah."

"You kind of keep to yourself a lot, too."

"Yeah."

"Are you comfortable having me as a roommate?"

"Sure." Sarajane looked up, as if confused by the question. "Why?"

"Just don't want to be bothering you. I guess I could take that extra room downstairs. I mean, if you'd be happier by yourself."

"No, Pam. I'm fine. I like you fine. I just like

reading."

"More than people?"

"Books have people."

"Yeah," Pam said. "So?"

"The difference is, in a book, you can set them aside whenever they start bugging you."

Pam looked at her long hair in the mirror and kept brushing.

"True." She thought about this. "Except people in books don't breathe. You know?"

"They breathe on paper."

"But they don't live real lives."

"Sometimes I think their lives are more real than most of ours," Sarajane answered.

Pam, reflecting, was quiet for nearly two minutes.

"You think Will's a pretty decent man?" she finally asked with a certain cautious distance in her voice.

"As decent as they probably come." Sarajane thought. "Except his jokes are lousy."

"Lousy?"

"Stupid. 'Batteries and shoe laces'?"

"OK, I can agree with 'stupid.' You're right. His sense of humor leaves a lot to be desired." Pam smiled. "But he tries."

"But what male was ever truly funny?" Sarajane asked.

CLAYTON BLOCK and Will Atchison ended up in half-dried swimsuits reclining against two bales of hay in the horse stable in Pod 9. They both stared up at the aluminum trusses that held up the metal roof of the stable. Their bloodstreams were polluted with various mixtures of alcohol and soda but each managed to balance a warm, nearly empty beer bottle on one knee.

The topic this time was not the Riviera but another R&R near a secret NATO installation in Greece. Atchison's recollection of this "vacation" included an overly friendly woman he had run across in a dingy restaurant. He knew not one word of Greek. She spoke perfect, if slightly broken, English. Only now, after many years, was he ready to reveal to Block the details of his three-day romance with this lady who had three children at home, but no husband.

"Her shtinking husband just up and disappeared one day. No note, no explanation. Just gone."

"So—you can be honest, Willy," Block said slowly, trying to carefully enunciate every word.

"About what?"

"About—you know."

"Never."

Block almost lost the bottle off his knee.

"Never," Block repeated, trying to verify that his hearing was still functioning. "Willy, she was an absolute stunner. You're telling me—"

"Zero. Zero sex."

"Zero?"

"Zilch."

Block's head flopped sideways toward Atchison. He could only stare.

"This is not the Willy Atchison I once knew. You-sirrr, are an impostor. You are not William the 2nd! Will the real Will Atchison please stand up? 'Will the real Will,'" he repeated musically, his tongue stumbling. He was entertaining himself tremendously.

"Couldn't stand up if he wanted to," Atchison said.

"Let me check your fingerprints," he said, grasping Atchison's hand and shaking four floppy fingers. "You are a definite impostor—a charlatan, a fake, a quack, a duck—a pretender to the crown of Atchison!"

Atchison pulled his hand back.

"Honest to the Almighty, Clayton. I did not sleep with the woman. We sort of . . . well, yeah, we were in love—yeah, I admit it. Here amongst these delicious smells of hay and road apples, I confess. I did love her.

But we didn't do the crocodile rock."

"I'm shocked, Will," Block said, now with a terrible seriousness in his voice, and trying to right his body into a more vertical position. "Very surprised. Tell me, old friend. Is anything—wrong?"

"What?"

"You know, *wrong*? Any of the moving parts not moving anymore?"

Atchison, without looking, gave Block a shot to the upper arm, knocking Block's beer into the haystack.

"Moving parts are jush . . ." he muttered, ". . . *just* all fine, m'friend."

Block, for some unknown reason, was trying to wipe up the spilled beer as it trickled down into the hay. Atchison spoke quietly, seeming momentarily sober.

"For some reason, Pam kind of reminds me of her."

Block peered at him.

"You really *are* drunk, Will."

"No. Really." Atchison was very serious now.

"Will. I remember the woman. I can see her as well as you. I mean, as well as I can see you. Her hair was luscious—dark brown, right? Her eyes were on fire. She was a walking bonfire. Now, Pam . . ."

"Some people's bonfire is on the inside, old buddy."

"Some people have lost their matches, old Willy."

"I wonder." Will swallowed back some warm beer that was trying to escape his gullet.

"You ssshouldn't have got me started on this stuff today, Clayton. I gave it up, you know. Had to."

"Yeah. I knew that. But I forgot. Sorry. I'm old enough to know better."

"Me, too." Atchison belched loudly. "No more after tonight. Ginger ale, that's it." He swallowed again. "I will be a sick dog in the morning."

"You have an excuse. You've never been in prison before."

"Just one night in southern France."

"Doesn't count. Wasn't four years."

"You're really startin' to get bugged by this place, aren't you," Atchison said as if suddenly sobering up.

Then it was Block who sounded sober.

"Four years is a very long time, Willy. Very, *very* long. So, about Pam. Don't fumble yourself into anything stupid."

Atchison belched slowly, but politely this time.

"You'll look after me if I do, Clayton. You always did."

"Yeah. I did, didn't I?" Block smiled. "Huh, I sure can't see many stars tonight," he said, sounding curious.

"Nope," Atchison confirmed. "That's cause we're inside the stable, dummy."

They both smiled a stupid smile at the aluminum rafters.

9

Early the next morning, Block called Jimmy Algood into a small room in the Research Pod to tell him about the change of plans from Haskins. Jimmy beat him to the punch.

"Something funny about those new green beans, Clayton," Jimmy said, dropping several sheets of paper on the table.

"Whad'a'ya mean?"

"Take a look at this report."

Jimmy fanned the pages apart, exposing the last page of his printout from the day before. At the bottom was the beginning of Haskin's emergency message:

BLOCK ONLY!: PRIORITY.
ENTER   SECONDARY   DE-SCRAMBLE
KEYWORD.

:: MESSAGE: NEED YOU TO JUMP AHEAD TO ATMOSPHERIC STUDIES GC-401 THROUGH GC-442, ORIGINALLY PLANNED FOR NEXT MARCH. FOLLOW SAME . . .

"How'd you—?" Block looked at the heading on Jimmy's report: "Analysis: Green Beans, plot 412.07; 19 SEPT." He looked at Jimmy, who was unruffled.

"I guess your top secret stuff yesterday interrupted my bean report."

"And I thought I was so careful."

"What's up with this, Clayton? Why all the

secrecy?" He was frowning. "What's in the rest of that message from Haskins?"

"The secrecy? I don't know, Jimmy. Just got these change orders from Haskins—with no other explanation." Block laid the rest of the message from Haskins on the table. "He wants us to move some of the atmospheric experiments ahead. And change them."

"Why?"

"Doesn't say. Just that it's urgent—priority one."

Jimmy looked at the revised instructions. He frowned even more.

"But what difference does it make when we do this stuff? I mean these are just atmospheric composite tests—with some changes. Slightly different air mixtures." He read further. "Up the nitrogen levels for a few days, up the oxygen during the night-time. What's the point?" He looked closely at Block. "And what's the big darn rush?"

Block was getting irritated with all the questions.

"I don't know, Jimmy. I told you."

"Come on, Clayton. Don't play me dumb. You've gotta know. You're the boss."

Block's irritation turned to a tightly controlled anger.

"Look, Jimmy! I'm telling you—as the boss—I don't know! And at this point, if I did, I wouldn't tell you anyway."

"OK, OK," Jimmy said, his palms toward Block, "calm down."

"Well, just keep asking pointless questions if you want to get under my skin." Block calmed himself. He wasn't feeling very professional at the moment. "I tried to get Haskins on the chat, couldn't find him. You know as much as I do."

"This stuff's pretty strange," Jimmy said suspiciously.

"Maybe so," Block replied, "but it's priority one.

They hired us to follow orders, not nitpick." But looking over the instructions again, Block knew Jimmy wasn't nitpicking. "You think these tests will have any long-term effect on anything? Habitat, agriculture products, things like that?"

"I don't know. I don't think so. Might produce some excess carbon dioxide for a while. I just want to know what's the big deal. Why the hurry?"

"Got me, Jimmy. I just work here."

Jimmy studied the procedures in more detail. He pulled a large operations manual down off a shelf and flipped to a section in the middle. After a few minutes, he paused and looked at Block, who was sipping coffee as usual.

"There're some significant changes here," he told Block. "Some of these air mixtures they want are completely different from what I have in the original manual. And check this out. They want us to do some high-voltage electrical arcing. INSIDE!"

"I saw that. Like artificial lightning."

"But why? I mean, we've got the equipment. We can make it happen. But it's gonna be risky, especially for some of our sensors and electronic equipment."

Block now was the one with the curious look.

"Something to do with the growth cycles maybe? You know. Make the tomatoes grow faster or something?"

"Yeah. Next thing you know they'll have us singing to the peaches and petting the potatoes."

Jimmy examined the revised instructions for a few more minutes as Block slurped a sip of coffee. Jimmy stopped, shaking his head.

"Nope. Clayton, this isn't right. Doing the stuff they've laid out here—it won't speed anything up. If anything, it'll beat up on the produce we already have in the ground. Look," he said, pointing to a bracketed section, "some of this procedure could actually be harmful—not just the plants, it could hurt the smaller animals. And look here." He pointed to another section. "Look at these voltages."

"Dangerous?"

"Dangerous? I dunno. Exciting maybe. My point is, it's just unnecessary. It doesn't mimic any normal weather patterns or predictable atmospheric trends. It's like trying to calculate agricultural trends on Pluto or something." He paused, rubbing hard at his forehead. "And it sure doesn't fit the plan."

"Headache again?" Block asked him.

"Yeah. Darn aspirin doesn't work anymore either. I must be allergic to something in here. Wish to heck I could figure out what."

"Well, look, this artificial thunderstorm—and all this other stuff—if it's not dangerous and we have the equipment to do it, let's just get on with it. It'll make March a lot easier schedule-wise."

"I guess—if we can keep up with everything else between now and then. There were no slackers on that planning team, lemme tell ya."

"You can work on this stuff this morning?" Block asked. It was his indirect way of giving an order, something Block was fond of.

"What the heck? All pays the same, right?" Jimmy shrugged.

The meeting room they were in had warmed up rapidly from the morning sun. The Research Center had movable aluminum louvers overhead that acted as a ceiling when closed, and a sunroof when open. At the moment they were open and the heat was aggravating Jimmy's headache. He gathered up the data sheets and started out of the room.

"The rest of your green bean report is in your basket. Jimmy—one other thing. Haskins, he . . ." Block hesitated. "He doesn't want to upset anybody's routine or anything. So let's not talk about these test changes until we have to. OK?"

"Understood." Jimmy grabbed the bean report out of his box and started for the door. He paused and turned back. "Doesn't care if he disrupts *my* routine, does he?" He held another palm up toward Block. "Yeah, OK. Mum's the word. My lips are hermetically sealed. I'll get to work on the tests."

"Buy you a beer after work, Jimmy."

"Yeah, maybe it'd help this headache," Jimmy snorted as he grumbled down the podwalk toward the central agricultural area in Pod 10.

Block laughed as Jimmy groused away.

JIMMY, AS usual, was fast and efficient. With Sarajane's help throughout the day, he re-rigged several of the portable electrical modules and set up several large, open electrodes at various angles in Pod 10, the largest open space they had. He wrote a revised computer program to manage the tests, working from the sheets Haskins had sent. He then fed the program into the main INSIDE computer.

That evening, the thunderstorms broke loose in Solarium-3. Jimmy's new test program first brought the temperature in the pods up to 90 degrees to simulate a humid summer evening. Then the show began.

With computer-controlled timing, high voltage was fed to the eight open electrodes. Artificial lightning arced between them. Unlike the night before, when silent flashes of lightning punctuated the sky OUTSIDE, the lightning INSIDE could be heard—and felt—throughout the complex. The resulting thunder was colossal and shook the plastic pods to their footings. The Solarians shook, too. Not only did Jimmy create a perfect thunderstorm INSIDE, he rattled the brains of his teammates.

Then, at the precise moment given in Haskins' instructions, the sprinkler system in Pod 10 was triggered, washing the electrified air with thousands of gallons of artificial rain. Throughout the tests that ran for two and half hours, Jimmy injected—in precise quantities prescribed in Haskins' instructions—certain chemicals into the air: nitrous oxide, methylene, and several thiazine compounds.

One result was a lot of involuntary giggling among the Solarians.

These odd chemical combinations, as Jimmy and Block knew, were not part of the original tests. And they seemed to serve no purpose in the research plans for Solarium-3. All day, as Jimmy prepared the series of tests, he kept rubbing his head, massaging it, trying to figure out why Omaha wanted these chemicals injected into their atmosphere. He could not come up with an answer. By late afternoon, his best guesses proved wrong, and his head ached worse than ever.

Now, as the artificial lightning thundered throughout the pods and rattled the interior buildings, his head throbbed like a jackhammer in 80-year-old concrete. He wondered what in the world he was doing. The lightning bursts from the electrodes were so violent he worried that he might damage the pods, strong as they were.

Amidst the flashes and crashes, the noise was giving him a stomach ache on top of his headache. Sarajane stood close beside him under a heavy rain tarp manning a portable computer that coordinated the labyrinth of electrodes generating the electrical storm. She shuddered with each new crack. Her intense brown eyes darted about, wincing with each flash of make-believe lightning. They both wore special goggles to protect their eyes from the intense streaks of energy snapping around them.

Jimmy was keeping his eyes on the aluminum-alloy beams that knit Pod 10's superstructure together. The beams quivered with each crash of thunder.

"Man, I hope they knew what they were doing!" he shouted to Sarajane.

"Great show, Jimmy!" she said in a loud growl. "But I still don't understand why we're doing it. Isn't this dangerous? Some of the new plants are just germinating. We might flood them."

"If we don't electrocute them!" Jimmy shouted over the noise. He remembered Block's warning. He couldn't let any details slip with Sarajane. He was about to cook up some fraudulent answer to her perfectly reasonable questions when he was rescued by the sight of Block himself walking toward them under a ridiculously huge, multi-striped umbrella, under which he carried a steaming mug of coffee and a moronic looking grin. Rain poured off the umbrella by the bucket-full.

"Crème de cacao and coffee . . ." Block conjured up his most boisterous and melodramatic voice. ". . . the only way to fly on a dark and stormy night." He sipped a few drops from his "BECAUSE I'M THE BOSS" mug. "That last one scared the crapola out of me, Jimmy! Can you turn your stereo down?" He laughed and slurped down more liquored coffee.

"Huh, that's a hoot!" Sarajane shouted. "Come on, Clayton," she said satirically, "you jump like a nervous monkey every time the intercom buzzes."

He swigged more of his home brew to unfasten his mood.

"No need to be snide, madam," he said, swallowing a huge slurp. "Some of us don't have your total control over all the universe." A belch slipped out that no one heard but Block.

Sarajane gave him a murderous look. Block cackled, wiping a bit of saliva from his lower lip.

"Go on, Jimmy," Sarajane said. "Turn it up. All the way!"

"You asked for it," Jimmy told her. In the playful

mood of the moment—and reacting, no doubt, to one of his all-time most unscientific twinges—Jimmy did exactly what she asked. He carefully rotated a large rheostat.

Block had started walking slowly away, apparently trying to make sure of his footing with every step. As the rheostat in Jimmy's hand hit maximum power, a screamingly high-pitched whistle split the air over their heads for a millisecond, just before two jagged bright flames of omnipotent light ricocheted off opposing beams near the top of the pod and raced to beat each other to the ground. They struck the soil violently, leaving a blackened parchment of earth where they hit.

Everything rattled, including Block's knees and teeth. All his high-test coffee splashed down his chest, staining the front of his shirt and a large area near the crotch of his baggy white shorts. Sarajane recoiled from the light and the noise as if she'd been shot. Jimmy jerked his hand off the rheostat feeling he'd been electrocuted—though he only imagined it.

There stood Block, his pants soaked, scowling at them both. Sarajane stared at him. Then she burst out laughing, pulling blindly at the back of Jimmy's T-shirt, trying to hide her face in it. She couldn't get a single word out between bursts of laughter, but none were necessary. Jimmy looked at Block. His diaphragm snapped out one unpreventable laugh. At the look of wrath in Block's eye, Jimmy caught himself and quickly looked down at his instruments, biting his lips. He could still feel Block's burning scowl piercing his chest.

Sarajane backed away from Jimmy and continued to roar with laughter, as Block took out a large orange handkerchief and began wiping the front of his pants. He then took what seemed—at the moment—the only course left open to him. He walked straight to Sarajane, thrust an arm around her shoulders and pulled her close to his soggy front. The pungent smell of spilled and exhaled alcohol drifted up between them.

"You really pushed my buzzer tonight, baby," he said with all the sarcasm he could muster in his present state. He puckered up in a mock kiss.

She slapped him once across his puckering jowls and pulled away. Not quite sure how he might react, she backed up a few steps and surveyed him up and down. Then she started laughing hilariously once more.

"Jimmy," Block said with a giggle, trying to regain a little bit of dignity, "the nitrous oxide was especially great tonight." He sucked in a deep breath and patted his stomach at the same time. "Let's do this again sometime, kids," he smirked. He inhaled expansively, made a woozy bow to them and started toward Pod 6. Sarajane went after him.

"Did I hurt you?" she asked with a hint of genuine concern, but standing her ground.

Block stopped and, not sure of the answer, investigated quizzically by rubbing his jaw and cheek. He morphed into the formal, English manservant, accent and all.

"Don't worry, madam. They picked me for this job because I have a very goll-danged hard head, what?"

Sarajane, standing there with the sprinkler system still pouring out artificial rain, was getting soaked. As if in sympathy, he shoved the empty mug into a bulky back pocket and folded his umbrella. In moments he too was drenched.

"Turn off the lights before you go to bed, will you dear?" Block chuckled. He tried to wink at Sarajane but his eyelid just sort of flickered. The coffee had done its job. He turned and used the umbrella as a cane, escorting himself in a properly distinguished fashion back toward the podwalk into #6.

Jimmy, wiping a mixture of sweat and dense humidity from his face, and realizing he'd gotten a little out of hand, looked over his test notes. He gave Sarajane a thumbs-up sign and said, "We're done."

She went to her computer and helped power down the equipment. Unexpectedly, a last pent-up burst of static shattered the air with a final, tumultuous clap of thunder. Block, who had just reached the podwalk, lurched and did a brief, involuntary dance step. His nerves were shot and it took all he could muster to stumble on toward the house.

Sarajane was embarrassed, and still giddy. She wrapped an arm around Jimmy's waist and gave him a little squeeze.

"Served him right," she said with great satisfaction.

Jimmy smiled. "I concur, Dr. Haug."

10

Friday, January 16th

The Solarians were now over eight months into their stay. Life INSIDE had become more and more routine, even for little Caroline the nuthatch.

As the mid-morning sun bathed the outside of the house through the pod roof, Caroline was snipping up bits of bird seed that Block had put in a saucer on top of his bathroom light fixture. She seemed to like this as a feeding spot. Maybe it was the warmth of the light that drew her.

If anyone had been around to watch, they would have seen a slight shudder in her body. As she finished her snack and launched into flight, her wings seemed to fold and she fell toward the floor. But like a glider pilot recovering at the last second she pulled up and landed on the edge of the tub. She sat dazed for several seconds. She hopped to the floor, since walking headfirst down porcelain was beyond even a nuthatch's skill.

She sat very still, her tiny breast heaving rapidly. Both wings stretched out as if being tested. A shudder ran again along her back feathers and rippled off her tail. Then, in a renewed burst of strength, she flew out of the house through the aviary in Pod 6 and on into Pod 10 searching for insects, and her friend, Clayton Block.

BLOCK AND Bridget Listner were in the Research Center, seated at the two largest computer consoles. Block keyed in his daily activity summaries using his labored but reliable four-fingered typing method.

Bridget was reading an agricultural manual and tracking the other Solarians on the INSIDE locator screen as they went about their routines. Each Solarian showed as a flashing purple dot on a computerized graphic of the Solarium complex. Jimmy and Will were working in the large agriculture Pod, Sarajane and Mai Ker were doing a monthly supplies inventory in the maintenance shed in Pod 8, and Pam Hansen was in the test lab over in Pod 11 working on a blood analysis of several caged squirrels that had been looking sickly over the last week. Bridget watched the dots and tried to read, but her mind was elsewhere.

Block's mind was buried in masses of numbers and data that weren't all clear to him but that he knew would make sense to the lab techs back in Omaha, two floors below John Haskins' office. Block's responsibility was to be certain all the daily project data was keyed in correctly so that the technicians receiving the information at project headquarters could make sense of it all.

Feeling more and more trapped, Block was becoming frustrated by having to communicate with OUTSIDE solely over the data terminals. But one of the intentional handicaps of the project was that there was to be no direct verbal or video communication between the INSIDE and OUTSIDE teams, either the on-site Control in the basement of the Visitors Center or the team of researchers in Omaha. All data for OUTSIDE had to be sent electronically as if the Solarium were on some distant planet. The project planners wanted the Solarians as focused as possible on their daily tasks so that the rigorous research schedule would be kept. Verbal or video communications would distract them.

So there were no phones, radios or televisions INSIDE other than the hand-held radios used for communication between the pods. They had been allowed the luxury of CD players and music pods with their favorite music. But to protect the integrity of the project, all OUTSIDE radio and TV signals were jammed by a perimeter system around the Solarium. Their only link to the OUTSIDE world was the email and chat link with OUTSIDE Control and Omaha. The planners wanted the Solarium to be their entire world for the whole four years.

And it was working. For the Solarians, it was indeed like living on another planet, cut off from the rest of humanity. The one exception was visual contact with the daily visitors who wandered the walks OUTSIDE the Solarium. But the physical barrier of the pod walls, preventing transmission of any sound from OUTSIDE, created an eerie, other-worldly sense INSIDE. It was as if those OUTSIDE were all silent, and therefore not quite real. As they toured the walks around the complex, the visitors seemed to be lip-syncing through life.

So, not just Block but all the Solarians were all beginning to feel increasingly isolated. One result was a greater intensity developing in their relationships INSIDE. While this was welcome in some ways, it was disconcerting in others. They were unavoidably stuck with each other. There was no way to get any real distance from each other, and sometimes this drove them a bit crazy.

As Bridget continued to vaguely monitor purple dots and study her manual, she was also running analytical programs that compared and correlated research figures that Block had keyed the day before. She was also daydreaming about an old boyfriend she had dated for two years in college. And she was unconsciously reacting to the warmth and humidity of the complex, a sense of being back in the womb. So she paid little attention when Jimmy's voice keyed over the monitor from his voice-activated radio.

"You guys awake in there?"

"We're here," a startled Bridget said.

"Listen, I'm finding some anomalies in a few of the new veggie plots. These carrot tops in plot 3107 are wilting. Look puny, too. Actually, they look awful. But they looked fine yesterday."

Will's voice keyed his radio, gargling in over Jimmy's voice.

"My new 8410 corn plants don't look very spiffy either, folks. Frankly, they look like garbage. They germinated OK, but they look pretty darn pathetic now. It's not like we're not getting 'em enough water."

Block switched his voice-actuated mic on.

"You sure?" he asked.

"Heck, Clayton, the water and fertilizer mixture's been perfect all week, but—" Will hesitated. "—they're not thriving like they oughta."

"Check the fertilizer mix again guys. You know how touchy the stuff is the way Omaha's got us blending it."

" 'Touchy' doesn't even come close, buddy," Will said under his breath, but his comment whispered through the intercom. "Never saw any real farmer this picky!"

Bridget laughed.

"I know, Willy," Block responded. "But the boys and girls in Omaha want it just right."

"Clayton," Will protested, his voice booming, "darn it, I've been doing this stuff more years than most of those kids in Omaha have been changin' their own diapers. I don't know how to be any more careful!" Atchison, who had been bending over the plants, straightened his stiff back and wiped beads of sweat from his arms and bare belly. "And those kids in their fancy fashion ties in Omaha don't have to work out here in the zoo!"

He looked out at a clump of visitors OUTSIDE along the east side of Pod 10, pursed his lips together and let out an elephant-like trumpet roar, spraying a circle of saliva across the surrounding crops. He made an imaginary trunk out of his arms and started swinging them around, blowing another elephant blast.

Jimmy watched this latest display with a grin.

"Good one, Willy, good one! Know how you feel."

A woman OUTSIDE in a purple sleeveless top, orange shorts and green tennis shoes smiled and waved enthusiastically at Atchison as if she thought this was perfectly normal behavior.

"Un-be-lieve-ab-le," Will said. "Don't know what the heck those folks out there expect to see." This accidentally broadcast over his radio before he realized it.

Block and Bridget frowned toward each other.

"OK, Will," Block said. "Look, if plants are dying, you guys are the experts. Figure it out."

Jimmy had gotten Will into a loose bear hug, trying to stop his antics toward their dumb-founded visitors.

"Clayton," Jimmy called over the mic, still trying to stifle laughter, "how come the only time you ever call us experts is when you're stumped yourself?"

"What're experts for, Jimmy?"

Bridget finally paid half attention to the research summaries pouring across her computer screen.

"Guys. I'm getting some bad numbers on yesterday's statistical analysis, too. Will, Jimmy, why don't you guys run over here when you're ready for a break. We'll look them over together."

"Rodger-dodger, Sky King," Jimmy said. A click over the monitor signaled his mic switching off.

Block leaned over Bridget's shoulder.

"There's a problem with my numbers?" he asked skeptically. "I enter something wrong?"

"I don't think so, Clayton. But the average growth

numbers for yesterday show almost all our products are down from two weeks ago. They should be up."

"Maybe the instruments aren't giving the right readings."

"I doubt it. Those things are near-perfect. I've never seen any equipment that can measure growth and chemical reactions as accurately as they do. No, it's not the equipment. It's—something else."

"Well, I need a break, too. I'm going to take a walk, then go over to the house. You and Jimmy and Will can look this stuff over. Let me know what you find."

"Sure."

Block left the Research Center and took a roundabout walk out through Pod 10. Jimmy and Will were cleaning up at a wash station at the far side of the pod. It felt warmer than usual in #10. It was clear and sunny OUTSIDE and the sun beat down on them relentlessly through the protective Stellar plastic.

He circled into the podwalk leading to the aviary in Pod 6, and stopped abruptly. His eyes caught something on the ground by a small sage brush bush. The something turned out to be two birds, both obviously dead. His heart jumped a beat until he recognized that neither was Caroline.

He stooped and picked one up. Still warm, not stiff. Definitely dead though. He looked it over, and then the other. Neither had any sign of injury, so none of the animals had killed them. There were more than a dozen cats around the place but they were so well-fed and domesticated that they rarely gave a bird or mouse a second glance. Too busy sleeping, mostly.

Block picked up the two small carcasses and cut back through an adjacent Podwalk to the Research Center, arriving on the heels of Willy and Jimmy. Without thinking, he laid the birds on the counter near Bridget, who almost jumped out of her chair.

"What the—?" she yelped.

"Calm down. What do you make of this?" he asked them all.

"Where'd you find these?" Jimmy asked, picking one up.

"In Pod six."

"What happened?" Jimmy quizzed again.

"Don't know," Block said tersely. "Kind of shook me. Thought one was Caroline. Gotten kind of fond of her, you know."

Will carefully picked up the other bird and examined it.

"Nothin' obvious," he remarked. "Pretty odd."

"Heat maybe?" Block asked.

"Don't think so," Atchison replied. "It's a little warm today—but not that bad." He looked at one of the computer screens. "Eighty-eight. Not enough to bother these little guys."

"Maybe they got into something," Jimmy speculated. "Some fertilizer concentrate or something."

"Could be," Will said. "Sarajane can check 'em out. Do some toxicology tests."

"Well—I'd like to know," Block said with a certain commanding tone in his voice. The oddities of the day were multiplying too rapidly. "Maybe they're just a couple of birds, but everything in this ecosystem is important to everything else. If one thing's affected, could affect other things, too."

"You think there's a connection between the birds and your plant problems, you guys?" Bridget asked.

Jimmy and Will looked at each other.

"Hadn't dawned on me," Will said, "but—yeah, it's sure possible."

Block kicked into his habitual commander mode again.

"OK, look, Jimmy, take these little guys over to Sarajane and tell her I want a certified death certificate in two hours. Willy, take some of the plant specimens you're concerned about and have Mai Ker do chemical workups. ASAP."

"Where's she at?" Atchison asked.

Bridget checked the purple dots.

"Pod eight. Sarajane, too. They're doing inventory this morning."

Jimmy and Will left quickly to carry out their assignments. Several unusual events had meshed—for no apparent reason—and everybody's curiosity was up.

SARAJANE'S POSTMORTEMS and toxicology tests on the birds took more than four hours, as did Mai Ker's analysis of the sickly looking corn and carrot plants. But just after 7:00 p.m. both women, having skipped supper, came back to the house. They found the rest of the team in the dining room, engaged in their normal after supper banter.

Mai Ker carried a file folder and Sarajane a ring-bound notebook.

"What's the word, ladies?" Will asked first.

Both women looked at each other. Sarajane gestured toward Mai Ker.

"Well," Mai Ker began, "your plants are sick because they're chemically imbalanced. High concentration of CO_2, carbon dioxide. And the nitrogen balance is wrong—an unusually high concentration of nitrites. It's affecting the photosynthesis."

"Why?" Block asked.

"I can't tell you why yet—not from these preliminary tests."

"Whad'a'ya think's causing it?" Jimmy asked. He obviously hadn't paid very close attention.

"I just said, Jimmy, I don't know," she said brusquely. "The other thing, there's also an unusually high nitrogen concentration in the leaf systems. The root systems seem about normal, but the stems and leaves are too rich in nitrogen compounds."

"I've never seen that before," Will said skeptically. "You sure?"

"Yes. I am sure."

"The whole plant system's usually balanced pretty much cell by cell," Will said. "Doesn't matter what part of the plant."

"I know that," Mai Ker said, her voice implying that she didn't need his mini-lecture. "I do not know the reason. But I know what I'm seeing. I don't understand this either."

There were several moments of thoughtful silence. Block looked around the table at the others. Bridget shrugged her shoulders with a *Don't look at me* expression. Will looked genuinely puzzled. Jimmy frowned.

Pam Hansen broke the moment with her usual nurturing sweetness. A delicious smell was coming from the kitchen.

"Well, while you're pondering, anybody want some desert? I have fresh cheesecake. With cherries."

"Wait, Pam," Block said. "Let's hear from Sarajane."

Pam looked momentarily crushed, as if nothing should take precedence over warm cheesecake.

"Well," Sarajane began, "call this coincidence if you want. I mean, I haven't talked to Mai Ker all afternoon. But your birds died of an overdose of nitrogen."

"What?" Pam exclaimed, forgetting the cheesecake.

"Nitrogen poisoning. The lung tissues were over-saturated with nitrogen. Their little lungs are very sensitive to this sort of thing. Resulted in oxygen starvation."

"From what?" Block asked her.

"Gosh," she said with a tinge of sarcasm, as if Block the scientist should be able to answer his own question. "Where can a poor bird get nitrogen these days?"

They all went quiet again. Then Jimmy stated the obvious.

"Where we all get it," he answered, voicing what they already knew. "Air."

"Right," Sarajane said. "But why? The concentration in their cells was way too high, Jimmy. Air is normally about eighty percent nitrogen, about twenty percent oxygen. But these birds had concentrations of nitrogen that were way above normal. It's like they've been sucking on pure nitrogen gas.

Block's own frown suddenly darkened.

"Jimmy," Block interrupted, "what about back in September?"

"What about September?"

"You don't remember? Those special tests that Haskins had us run. Didn't you shoot some nitrous oxide into the air?"

"Yeah, Clayton, but that was months ago."

"Jimmy's right," Sarajane said. "Something that long ago—if that was the problem—it would've killed these little guys long before now."

"What is it, then?" Bridget asked, getting a little agitated.

"It has to be a high concentration of nitrogen somewhere. Gradually absorbed into their body cells— their tissues became saturated with it. It's like a scuba diver with a case of the bends. A high nitrogen pressure builds up in the body tissues. You get weak, sick, headache, disoriented. Pain in the joints. Pretty quick, it kills you."

"Like Sarajane said, birds have very sensitive systems," Mai Ker added. "That's why miners used to carry them—to detect methane, or a lack of oxygen."

"Somehow," Sarajane said, "they've been exposed to a higher than normal concentration of nitrogen—and it killed them."

The same question kept bouncing off Sarajane like

an echo.

"But how?" Pam asked.

Sarajane was getting as frustrated as Mai Ker.

"Like we said, we don't know yet. It wouldn't take much because they're so sensitive. Their respiratory systems are very fragile. A slight change could affect them dramatically."

"Like my corn plants," Will said.

Block looked at him. Then he moved quickly from the table to the computer terminal built into the dining room wall and brought up an inventory listing of materials and supplies in storage around the complex.

"We don't have any concentrated nitrogen gas stored, do we?" Block asked, typing away. "Something they might have put in for agricultural use? A small leak maybe?"

"Nope," Will said. "Closest thing is those nitrous oxide tanks—the ones Jimmy used—" He broke off.

"—back in September," Block finished.

"None of this makes sense," Jimmy protested. "And I don't think birds know how to turn on tank valves."

Sarajane interrupted again.

"Clayton, I told you. It's too long ago. All the birds would've croaked months ago. It's got to be something else."

Complete silence fell again, like a monastery at prayer time.

"Listen, Clayton," Jimmy finally said, "if the plants are suffering from too much nitrogen, too, I doubt it's those storage tanks."

"Wait," Mai Ker said, looking troubled. She had been sitting quietly, listening, head down, eyes closed, thinking. She now looked intently at each of them as if a flood light had just popped on in her head. "Jimmy's right. It's not the tanks. Will, there is more I did not say yet. Your plants—they also had a high concentration of carbon dioxide. Something is wrong."

Pam's face reacted before the words even sank in with the others. A chronic worrier, her expression went completely blank, as if all emotion in her had instantly been wiped clean.

"What do you mean 'wrong'?" she asked, deadpan.

Mai Ker looked at her. She read her expression, and went on cautiously.

"The air. Our atmosphere here in the complex. If it became imbalanced—which might account for the nitrogen concentration in the birds, this would mean the plants were exposed, too. Too much nitrogen in the air—it would affect the water, the soil. Maybe the plants are compensating somehow, retaining carbon dioxide. It would slow the photosynthesis process."

"You make it sound like these plants have brains," Pam protested weakly, some semblance of emotion once again overtaking her features. The emotion was controlled, but clear. It was fear.

"No," Mai Ker said. "But they have very sophisticated genetic coding. You would be surprised how they can compensate, adapt to their environment. Just like us. If photosynthesis is slowed, less oxygen is released. And you compound the problem. Too much nitrogen concentration in the air, not enough oxygen."

Block was frowning, a deep crease across his forehead.

"If they're getting too much nitrogen, the higher nitrogen concentration in the stem and leaf systems might correlate—another compensation."

"I don't know," Mai Ker said. "I've never seen this process occurring before."

Block looked up, visibly disturbed. He bolted from his chair and ran up to his bedroom, looking for Caroline. She wasn't there. He checked under the bed, where she had been known to hide on hot days. Nothing. He ran back down to the dining room, arriving winded, and noticeably agitated.

"Anybody seen Caroline?"

"How would we know?" Pam asked.

"'Cause she's the only one I put a pink leg band on," he said, somewhat embarrassed.

All the heads said no. Block started to swear, but stopped.

"I wish—" The words hovered on his lips, then he swallowed them. He was about to bolt out the front door in search of Caroline but hesitated, looking at each of them. With great effort he calmed himself and spoke.

"All right. Let's get back to the problem. Jimmy, how long for you to manually check the air quality in each pod?"

"Well, if we shut the interlock doors and measure the pods individually, maybe 48 hours. For a good clean printout. I mean, if you want it completely accurate."

"I do. Do it. Sarajane, anything more you can do with those birds? To give us a better direction?"

"I don't think so, Clayton. I did all the standards. Everything else looked perfectly normal. Just too much nitrogen in their systems."

"Well, if anything dawns on you, try it anyway, before they rot."

"Sure. I'll keep them in a fridge in the lab."

"No dessert?" Pam asked, searching in vain for something else to talk about, and realizing her fresh cheesecake was probably going to sit on the counter all night spoiling. Everyone's mind had quickly flown elsewhere.

"Not tonight, Pam. Thanks," Atchison said absently. "Clayton, I'm gonna go rerun some numbers from the last few days and take a closer look. Maybe we've missed something."

"Thanks, Willy. What was it, Pam?"

"What?" she reacted, distracted.

"What was dessert?"

"My St. Louis Cheesecake."

"Maybe I'll have some with breakfast," he said as he hurried out of the house, searching for Caroline.

Pam grimaced. *Cheesecake for breakfast?* She grimaced again, thoroughly disgusted, and talking to herself aloud. "And probably on top of his usual drink of raw eggs. Sounds like a perfectly Clayton Block breakfast." Her nose scrunched up.

Block hurried through most of the pods but didn't find Caroline. As he finished searching the ocean area in Pod 12, Jimmy came along behind him setting out special sensors to monitor the air overnight.

They sealed #12 up. It was the furthest pod from the house and the Comm. Center, and the least used at this phase of the project. Jimmy promised Block he would do two or three more Pods tonight, then seal the rest tomorrow.

Despite the much bigger problems, Block was preoccupied the rest of the evening looking for Caroline. He felt driven, as if trying to protect her from some unseen peril.

He finally gave up in frustration after nearly two hours of searching. *Don't worry, lots of places the little gal can hide,* he told himself. His attempt at reassurance was dashed immediately. Coming into Pod 9, where most of the large animals were housed, he found another dead bird on a sidewalk by the horse corral. This one was a sparrow. It was bigger than the first two he had found, but just as dead. He picked it up. It was already cold.

A sudden, overwhelming sense of despair began to oppress him, but he pushed it back. He sat dejectedly on a bench by the corral, resting the limp bird in his palm. He looked around, peering through the nearly invisible walls of the dimly lit Pods, surveying the small world over which he held sway as the team leader of Solarium-3. He was searching for Caroline, but for something else, too—something his mind couldn't get a clear hold on. He shook his head silently, still agitated. He knew Caroline might already be gone. He resigned himself to it.

Bigger problems here, he told himself, looking around through the pod walls. *She's just a bird anyway—like this one.*

He stroked the neck of the dead creature gently with one finger, wanting to restore life to the dead. The image of Caroline hitting his windshield flickered in his mind, then a memory of her limp body on top of his ramshackle car.

Guess she's lucky she's made it this long.

He just didn't know how right he was.

11

Sunday, January 18th

A day and a half had passed since the anomalies first appeared. Jimmy worked fast. For nearly 40 hours since their discussion Friday night, Jimmy had confined the others to the house in Pod 4, while he worked feverishly in the Research Center in #3, catching cat naps on a cot as often as he could. His mind raced as fast as the data flowing across the many computer screens. Searching and analyzing facts, data, life. A microcosm of the human condition.

Block did find Caroline. Saturday morning, just after Jimmy sealed them up in Pod 4, Block found her sitting on top of the bathroom light fixture again nibbling quietly at her birdseed. She had snuck in during the night wobbling like a drunken teenager when no one was awake to notice. Block had propped both screen doors open just in case. When he found her she looked healthy enough, but wouldn't fly—even with prodding from his finger.

"Must have walked home, huh?" he said to her. "Probably too drunk to drive."

After the brief, one-sided conversation he set her in her netting nest over his bed and fixed up a dish of water, and more seed.

"Don't have much of an appetite either, do ya, kid?" he asked her.

Though of course she couldn't answer, she did let out a faint *whi, whi,* which was good enough for Block. He chose to believe she actually had answered him.

He was still frustrated with waiting for answers

from Jimmy. They had not yet alerted OUTSIDE to the possible aberration in their air quality or to the plant problems—or the dead birds. It was likely the OUTSIDE teams already knew, since their monitors picked up all the information flowing from the INSIDE sensors. If they knew, they hadn't said anything either. But Block wasn't going to highlight the problem until he thought he could explain it. And at this point he didn't have enough information to give Omaha a clear picture of what the problem might be, let alone how to fix it.

Apart from six dead birds, none of the other animals seemed affected. And—so far—all the human animals in the Solarium were doing fine, except for Jimmy's chronic headaches.

About noon, Jimmy's voice came over the intercom telling the rest of the Solarians they could open the doors between the pods and move about normally. His voice was ragged and tired.

He came dragging into the house looking like last week's dog food and ate several sandwiches Pam had waiting. He then went with Block, Will, Sarajane and Mai Ker to the Research Center to look at his test results.

Jimmy kept rubbing his aching eyes as if this might make the answers clearer to everyone. His whole body felt like he'd been beat up. The lack of real sleep left him punchy, his words tripping over each other.

"I wish I could be more peci—specific, Clayton," Jimmy started, "but I'm kinda confused. I closed everything up—sealed each pod separately—so I'd get a good measurement for each one." An uncontainable yawn escaped. "Did that in case the animals or the crops in each pod might have a"—he carefully focused his tongue to the front of his mouth—"specific effect in that one pod. So anyway, here it is. I'm getting *slightly* different readings in the different pods—but overall

I'm getting an over-rich nitrogen pressure in every area of the complex."

"How rich?" Mai Ker asked.

"Nitrogen pressure is running eighty-four to eighty-five percent of the total, so it's displacing the oxygen pressure accordingly. Right now we're surviving on about a fifteen to sixteen percent mix of oxygen in the air. No wonder I'm gettin' these darn headaches." He rubbed at his eyes and forehead again.

Block's hands tilled the air, prodding Jimmy for more.

"Normal oxygen is about nineteen to twenty-one percent, right?" Block said.

"Right. About three PSI, out of a total air pressure of about fourteen PSI."

"But I don't get it," Atchison chimed in. "Why is there *any* variation between the pods? I mean, air's air. It washes, blends. If the balance of nitrogen and oxygen is off in one pod, it oughta be off the same amount through the whole darn place."

"Maybe not," Mai Ker said with careful and precise words. "The doors and passages between the pods are small compared to the total air volume in each pod. That might account for some of the variation. The air will transition between the pods through the circulation system. But since no OUTSIDE air mixes in, the blending of air between the pods might take place slowly. Leaving slight variations."

"Which pods are the lowest in oxygen?" Sarajane asked Jimmy.

"Pods nine and eleven."

"Which of course makes sense," she said, aiming at some lurking thought. "That's where we have the highest concentration of animals. The cattle and horses in number nine, and the small animals in number eleven. Just their normal air consumption would draw down the oxygen levels in those pods. Their systems are going to absorb as much oxygen as possible with each breath—especially if the oxygen pressure is low to begin with."

Block broke in. "So, you're all telling me—what? Our air is all screwed up?"

"Essentially," Jimmy said. "Put simply, yes."

"How? Why?"

"That's what I don't know yet," Jimmy said.

"That will take more time," Mai Ker added. "There could be many complex factors, interacting. But I think you need to let OUTSIDE know." She hesitated, and looked down at the shiny tiled floor. "I mean, this could become more of a problem."

"What could be 'more of a problem'?" Block asked, although he knew as well as she did. He was hoping against hope she would suggest something other than what he already suspected.

"Well, a problem for us," she said. "The birds are more sensitive. It affected them first."

"But we're all breathing the same air," Sarajane said, helping her express what no one really wanted to hear.

"Yes," Mai Ker continued. "The animals. And us. It's likely to have an effect on us. Eventually."

"Like Jimmy's headaches?" Block asked.

"Probably," she said. Then, always cautious when it came to her science, she added, "And it *could* get progressively worse."

Block was beyond frustration and getting angry. He'd been waiting almost two days and was hoping for something more solid than this to give to Omaha.

"And this is what I'm supposed to tell Haskins?"

The tension in Jimmy's voice was thick, too.

"I've done the best I can, Clayton. This stuff takes time, OK? If you can do it better—or faster—well, go get it!" Jimmy was equally angry and headed for the door.

Block was not immune to sarcasm. His face showed a momentary cloud of shame.

"All right," he said, stopping Jimmy. "Sorry. I'll get on the wire to OUTSIDE. But I need more answers. You've got to get me more specifics. They're gonna want to know 'why?' Details. Spell it out."

"Can't spell the words out when you don't know what the words are," Jimmy said, completely exhausted.

"Then find out!" Block ordered, his face brightening with color. "That's why we're all here, isn't it? To figure things out? Learn? Discover? We're the experts, right? The science freaks? Well let's earn our keep and get on with the figuring out part!" His big chest rocketed a frustrated sigh across the room.

Moments after this eruption of Mt. Block, when the others had cleared the office with more than their normal haste, he drew several deep breaths and sat down at a terminal to send an email to OUTSIDE.

FROM CLAYTON BLOCK: SPECIAL ATTENTION, NATHAN DANIELS, CHIEF, CENTRAL RESEARCH; CC: JOHN HASKINS:

:: ANOMALY NOTED IN OUR ATMOSPHERIC CONDITIONS. INITIAL TESTS INDICATE AN IMBALANCE IN NITROGEN / OXYGEN MIX THROUGHOUT PODS. DON'T HAVE CLEAR ASSESSMENT YET ON CAUSE. WORKING ON THIS.

NO MAJOR DISRUPTIONS HAVE RESULTED. HAVE SOME CONSEQUENTIAL PLANT SPECIES RETARDATION, AND SEVERAL BIRDS HAVE GONE TO THE GREAT PODS IN THE SKY. TRANSMITTING SOME PRELIMINARY TEST DATA ATTACHED TO

THIS MESSAGE. REQUEST NATHAN LOOK THIS OVER AND MAKE SUGGESTIONS FOR RESTORING CORRECT BALANCE. WE'RE WORKING ON THIS TOO. MORE INFO WHEN AVAILABLE. EVERYTHING ELSE ON SCHEDULE. C.B. ::

He felt more than a little foolish asking for OUTSIDE help when clearly the real experts were supposed to be locked up in here with him. But what bothered him most was the seemingly sudden onset of this problem—and the fact that their instruments had not automatically picked it up and alerted the INSIDE control consoles. The whole project site had been so tightly laced with highest grade sensory instruments available that nothing should have escaped notice. Those sensors, Block knew, should have triggered an alert long before those first birds keeled over.

YESTERDAY AFTERNOON and evening, from her remote terminal in the house, Bridget had spent twelve grueling hours looking back through the data files for clues, looking for any unretrieved sensor alerts that might have miscued into data storage instead of coming up directly onto a monitor. While she had found a few threads of data that probably should have triggered an alert, she ran into numerous dead ends. Their INSIDE monitoring system in each case, for some reason, had channeled the suspect data immediately off into an analysis program rather than into the alert cue file. If this data had gone—as it should have—into the alert cue, it would have triggered audible and visual signals throughout the complex, warning the team of the developing problem.

This apparent mistracking of data disturbed Bridget the most. What had gone wrong? She kept this discovery close to the cuff. She told only Block and

Jimmy what she'd found.

BLOCK SAT thumping his fingers on the Comm. console like a bored third-grader, wanting a reply from OUTSIDE. He was struggling with emotions, trying not to think about the worst-case scenario that could emerge from the air problems. The truth was, contrary to the purposely controlled tone of his last message, all the Solarians were now completely off task, preoccupied with questions that lacked answers, dealing with ungraspable fears, distracted from their normal responsibilities.

Even Pam Hansen, in charge of meals and nutrition, was off center—and the stomachs of the others were beginning to suffer. When the chief nutritionist doesn't pay attention to business, various and sundry gastric problems start appearing. The Serbian goulash she had whipped together for supper last night had tasted like burned diesel fuel and the grainy white sauce on the green beans had the consistency of grade school paste. Pam was obviously as uneasy as everyone else.

Human beings being who they are, it wasn't surprising that this break in routine had thrown the teammates into a tailspin. Block was the least affected so far—once he found Caroline—but both Jimmy and Mai Ker seemed unusually distracted as they went about their non-routines. Pam, doubling as the "Relationship Maintenance Coordinator," had to take time out of her schedule to take Jimmy and Mai Ker aside one at a time to counsel them about the importance of focusing, and paying attention to detail.

"Distractions can lead to fatal errors," she told each of them, in words reminiscent of some advice once given to her by an ICU nursing instructor.

Of course, this was like the pot calling the kettle black, but it had the intended effect on Jimmy and Mai Ker. They were now more on track, paying more attention to the critical details of their work.

This, Pam knew, would make Block happy.

BLOCK'S MESSAGE to OUTSIDE Control was answered in only two and a half hours, a near record, which surprised even Block.

> TO: CLAYTON BLOCK:
> :: LOOKED OVER WHAT YOU'VE SENT SO FAR. NOT VERY CLEAR. NEED MORE DATA. DO YOU HAVE PRELIMINARY THEORIES ON CAUSE / EFFECT? WE'D LIKE TO KNOW WHAT YOU THINK. WE'LL BE HERE WHEN YOU NEED US. ::
> N. DANIELS. Ph.D.
> CHIEF OF RESEARCH

Block shook his head, reading, unfortunately, the exact words he expected.

Bridget was also in the Comm. Center when the message came back but she couldn't see the screen Block was on. Muttering, Block printed the message, then erased the stinging blue letters from the screen, sending them off into cyber storage. Bridget caught the clear tone of disgust in his voice.

"If we knew the stupid cause and effect, we wouldn't be begging for help, would we, Nathan!"

"What'd he say?"

"Typical round-the-bush B.S.," Block said, handing the printout to her. "Dog-A chasing its own tail-B. Numbskulls."

She reacted just as he had.

"Well for crying out loud, Nathan!" she said. "Of course it's 'not very clear.' If it was clear, we'd've fixed the problem! Bonehead." The frustration had leapt from Block's throat to hers. "What're you people in Omaha being paid for, anyway?" she barked at the screen as if Nathan Daniels could hear.

"Guess we just keep working on it," Block said, eager to get beyond his sense of helplessness. "We give them crappy information, they give it back. What's new?"

"Don't worry, Clayton. Jimmy, Mai Ker—the whole team—they're good. They'll find you answers."

He looked at her and his eyes narrowed. He felt a fleeting sense of sadness for her habitual optimism.

"I'm not sure we know the questions yet, Bridget."

"You seem really bothered by this." Her voice became softer, inquisitive. "You OK?"

"Yeah. I guess. It's just—" He hesitated, not sure if he wanted to expose these particular feelings at this particular moment. He felt she was prying. He didn't like it. But he went on anyway.

"I'm feeling cooped up. Again. Like the first night here. Stuck. And now I'm stuck wrestling a monster I can't get my hands around. When you're on a battlefield, you have a known enemy. You get your hands around his throat—and you wring it. But this stuff—feels like—" He was shaking his head. "I don't know. It's like wringing out a soggy ball of invisible cotton. Nothing there. Don't know who the enemy is!"

"We don't have to look at this problem as an enemy, Clayton."

"Why not?" he said almost scowling at her. "Sure looks like one to me. It wants to kill us." He saw the confused expression on her face. He realized he was just making things worse. "I'm sorry," he said. "But that's how I get when I get frustrated. Every frustration becomes an enemy."

"You get frustrated about a lot of things, don't you Clayton?"

It seemed, he thought, she was always calling him Clayton now.

"What's that supposed to mean?" he asked. His eyes

had been focused on his desk top, as if he were Superman trying to burn a hole in it. Now his head snapped to attention and his eyes went to Bridget again. She shrugged.

"It means what it means. You get edgy sometimes. Really easy. 'LFT' they call it."

"Low frustration tolerance, huh?"

"Yeah," she said. "It just kind of surprises me. For a man with your background. You know. Your experience. I'd've thought you could handle any old frustration that came down the pike, armed or not."

"Yeah. Well, I used to think so, too. Maybe it's just this place. I like being free. Roaming. Kicking loose. Here—I just haven't felt right. Ever since we got here."

Bridget's thoughtful eyes studied him. She saw him with new depth. Block was beginning to come out of his hardened shell. He was slipping, allowing himself to become almost a real human being to her. A surprise, but it was a pleasant surprise.

Their eyes locked. Block looked away first.

"What you looking at?" Block asked her.

"Was I staring?" she asked.

"Yeah."

Inexplicably, after so many months of keeping her at a distance, Block felt a powerful attraction. It was coming from her deep brown eyes.

"You . . ." She stopped abruptly. *How to put it?* she wondered silently. "You intrigue me, Clayton Block."

"Ooh—I *love* intrigue!" Playful sarcasm was his only remaining defense, an attempt to ignore the magnetism of her smile.

"Don't joke all the time," she chastised him. "I mean it. You're a very forceful personality, you know. But there's something more. Behind all that power. I'm curious. That's all."

"Well, if you figure it out, clue me in, will ya?" he said in the same joking manner. It was Block's standard tactic with women, particularly those he found especially attractive. Keep 'em laughing, so they won't get serious.

She laughed lightly, joining the ploy.

"Oh, I will." She smiled at him. "You can bet I will."

BY LATE afternoon, Jimmy and Will had come up with a plan that might correct atmospheric imbalance throughout the pods. They discussed it with Block. By manipulating the circulation system between the pods, they hoped to reach a more neutral blend that might restore normal air quality.

"I'm still not certain what's happening, Clayton," Jimmy told him. "Could be a combination of some of the fertilizer fumes and the plant and animal waste in the pods. Might have triggered the whole episode. We're a completely closed ecosystem. Nothing gets in, nothing gets out."

"This isn't news, Jimmy," Block said impatiently.

"I know. But it's new. A complex of this size, I mean. They've tried similar stuff on the space station, and the simulation capsules down at NASA. But nothing of this magnitude. We don't really know how all the various systems are going to act—and interact. I mean, that's why we're here."

"I know that, too, Jimmy," Block said. "So why didn't Solarium-1 and -2 have this kind of problem?"

"Well, they were nearly airtight, but not totally. They weren't totally closed. Didn't have the catchment pond under the complex like we do, so there was some interaction with ground water, too. I browsed through some of their air records on the main computer today. See, on both those projects OUTSIDE monitored air quality and when they had to, they'd do some venting—purging bad air out and pumping fresh air in—to balance things out."

"Cheating," Block said.

"Yeah."

"But our place here," Atchison said, "was designed to be the next step—a totally closed, *totally* self-contained system. The way it would have to be on another planet. Totally self-sustaining—with no OUTSIDE help or intervention."

"Yeah." Block sounded completely discouraged. "So my call for help to Omaha was probably a waste of time, wasn't it," he said sourly.

"Not at all," Jimmy said. "Just 'cause they can't vent us up doesn't mean they can't help. They've got some good minds back there, Clayton. They may strike on something we're missing."

THE GOOD news of the day was that by early evening the air recirculation seemed to be having an effect. Nitrogen pressure in the air was down slightly and everything seemed to be holding steady on Jimmy's instruments. And no more birds had been discovered dead.

The team began to breathe easier, assuming normalcy would return in a day or two. This shared belief brought a great sense of relief. Even Pam's Beef Stroganoff that night brought a sense of reassurance, a delicious break from nearly two days of worry, queasy anxiety, minor confusion—and admittedly lousy meals.

Will Atchison pushed slowly back from the table after gulping down the last of his huge mountain of Stroganoff, steamed peas, and greenish "frog-eye" salad.

"We never did get into that cheesecake, did we Pam?" he asked, a twinkle in his eye.

"No, that's right," she said. "But I think it will still be fresh."

They all knew this was a white lie, the kind of thing Pam was rarely guilty of. She looked around at them.

"Well, pretty fresh," she conceded. "I knew sooner or later it'd tempt someone. Who's interested?"

Seven arms went into the air like synchronized swimmers, because Atchison held up two. Pam went back to the kitchen to retrieve the large pie dish of cheesecake with a secret look of triumph in her eyes.

There's nothing in this world, she silently smiled, *that a little good dessert can't fix.*

12

Monday, March 2nd

"What the—!" Jimmy yelped. "I can't believe this!"

Startled, Mai Ker almost jumped off the couch. The book she was reading after lunch dropped to her lap.

"Jimmy, what's wrong?"

Jimmy, sitting next to her reading daily reports, flapped the pages in the air.

"This can't be right. It's back!" He shook his head, dismayed, and flipped back through several printouts.

"What's back?" Mai Ker demanded, shaken by the panic on his face.

"The air problem. This is bizarre! Everything's been fine for over a month. Then—wham—it's back! It's like a darn virus or something."

"Are you sure?" she asked.

"I was sure the air was fixed! But here it is—out of the blue!" He scowled, his anxiety sky-rocketing. It felt as if he had just finished building an 80 story high-rise and then found a crack in the foundation. He was on his feet now.

"I've gotta find Block. This can't be happening."

"Wait," Mai Ker said, pulling him back down on the couch. "Let me see."

She scanned the printouts, her lips pinched tightly together. Jimmy sat impatiently, wanting her to hurry up so he could find Block. He pointed to the latest air quality readout that triggered his outburst. Her eyes narrowed, then widened. Her fingernail scratched unconsciously at the paper, as if this might somehow eradicate the data she saw.

"Why is this happening again?" she said, mostly to herself. There was no doubt the problem was back, detailed in black and green. The sensor data showed the same kind of atmospheric imbalance in Pods ten, twelve and thirteen. The nitrogen pressure was high, the oxygen pressure too low. It appeared gradually over a period of three days. And this time Pods nine and eleven—for some reason—weren't involved.

"What's happening to us, Jimmy?" Mai Ker said plaintively. "We've been so careful. I don't see why this would happen again."

"I still don't know why it happened the *first* time!" Jimmy said with a tone of defeat. "And this looks worse. Why haven't we had an alert? I'm gonna have Clayton call the team together. We've gotta get on this fast."

Mai Ker gave silent assent with a nod. They tried the hand-held radio with no response from Block. They left the house to find him. Finding someone in the Solarium was not an easy task, even though the pods were clear plastic. The task was complicated by the maze of buildings, trees and plants that peppered the pods. They made a cursory search of three adjacent pods, then found Bridget in the Comm. Center.

"Can you see Clayton on the monitor?" Jimmy asked.

"Right there," she said, pointing to a purple dot on the house graphic, "in his bedroom."

"We just left there," Mai Ker said. "I thought I saw him go out after lunch."

"You were reading," Jimmy said. "You probably imagined it."

Mai Ker frowned and failed to laugh. Normally she liked Jimmy's friendly jabs but was not in the mood.

"Bridget, we need everybody back at the house," Mai Ker said.

"What's wrong?"

"Problems again. Just get everybody home."

Now Bridget frowned. She put an "all-call" over the intercom for everyone to gather in the dining room. When the three of them got there, everyone else was there except Block. Atchison went up and found him in the bedroom, sitting on his bed and stroking Caroline's back as she lay on his pillow.

"Didn't you here the all-call?"

"Something's wrong with her again, Will. She's hurting."

"Something's up, Clayton. We need you downstairs. Everybody's waiting."

"What's going on?"

"Don't know."

"Can't it wait?"

"I don't think so. Come on."

Block trundled Caroline into his hand and carried her down to the dining room. She was in no mood to try to escape.

"Well?" Block asked as he and Atchison arrived. His voice was impatient. He obviously wanted to go back to nursing Caroline, who he set down on a pile of napkins in the middle of the table.

"Clayton, it's starting again." He held his hands apart in a gesture of helplessness.

Block looked blankly at Jimmy.

"Charades, huh? Give me a better hint. What's started?"

"The air problem. Oxygen pressure is dropping again. I found it in my printouts after lunch. Mai Ker agrees. It's back. I thought it was solved. It's not."

"Why?" Pam asked.

"Haven't got a clue. I don't know what's happening—let alone why."

Will scowled at the floor.

"You said this was all resolved," he said. "Last month."

"Well—it *was* resolved—at least, I thought so," Jimmy said. "I wasn't getting any more odd-ball readings. And we haven't gotten any alerts."

Mai Ker tried to help him.

"But see we never did figure it out—really—did we? We never were *sure* what happened in January. Or why. We got the oxygen and nitrogen balance back to normal—"

Jimmy cut her off.

"—and assumed everything was fine."

"It was fine," Sarajane said.

"Well, it's not fine now!" Jimmy fumed. "I'm tellin' you, it's got me stumped."

"I thought it was just a one-time anomaly," Block said.

"That's what I thought," Jimmy said. "After we rebalanced the air in the pods, I thought we had it fixed." He looked at them all. "Obviously we don't."

"Obviously," came Block's ominous echo. He, too, looked from face to face. No one spoke. "What now?" he asked.

"Well, we can try to rebalance again," Jimmy said. "But I don't understand why we're not getting alerts. The sensors must be picking up the problem, but the computer isn't generating the required alerts."

"Could be a programming bug," Bridget said.

"This is like a disease, a virus in the air or something," Jimmy frowned. "But it's not biologic, or bacterial. Nothing like that. It's atmospheric. The pressures have just changed, with no reason. But it *acts* like a virus. It recedes, it hides—and whammo—it's back!"

"You're sure it's not biological?" Pam asked.

"Ninety-eight percent sure," Mai Ker said in her always precise way. "We checked it all before. There was no explanation for the air imbalance. That we could find."

The room went silent again. They looked at each other, at the floor, out the window into the yard. Each face bore a unique expression: curiosity, mild fear, confusion. Pam's had a look of dread. *So much for cheesecake,* she told herself.

They remembered the dead birds. They all knew what this meant. Jimmy's reminders that they were in a totally closed ecosystem rang into memory like a bell tolling. This was their worst nightmare.

The silence became a suffocating vapor clogging the room.

"Let's get on this," Block said abruptly. "Does OUTSIDE know?"

"That's what really busts my chops," Jimmy snapped. "They're getting the same data we are. They must know. Even if the alert system was down on our end, why didn't they see this?"

Atchison spoke in a low, bass timbre.

"Maybe they did."

Everyone stared. No one spoke.

"I've been thinking," Atchison continued. "There is one thing. Only one thing that doesn't fit. Didn't fit, I mean." Muddled faces waited. "Those tests they had us do. Back in September."

"Willy," Block said, "we talked about this last month. We decided that wasn't the problem."

Atchison's response came in careful, plodding words.

"Well, maybe—just maybe—we were wrong." He feigned a sneer. "Not that humans have ever been wrong before." He waited for a smart comeback that didn't come. "Look, guys, it's possible—possible, I'm saying—that those tests did something to our air. Fouled it somehow." He scratched at several not-quite-shaven whiskers on his throat. "I don't know. Just wondering. What was that all about?"

"Willy," Bridget asked with disbelief, "why would

OUTSIDE have us do something that would mess up the project?"

Until this moment, such an idea had never crossed anyone's mind.

"She's right," Sarajane said. "No way. No way are they going to have us do something that would screw up the project. Are you kidding? With the kind of money they have tied up here?"

Again the silence took hold, but only briefly. Mai Ker momentarily closed her eyes tightly, thinking, then opened them.

"Maybe Will's right," she said. "There is nothing that we have done—nothing beyond the master plan—except those tests in September. Isn't this true, Jimmy?"

It was obvious to everyone that Jimmy didn't want to respond. He had done those special tests on orders from OUTSIDE. Why should he have to defend them? Finally, his tense face distorted into an angry frown.

"OK, Mai Ker. You're right. OK? But I can't see how those tests could cause this problem. This is more like—" He searched for a word. "—like pollution or something. Something is not right in here. But there could be a hundred reasons. A thousand!"

"Or even just one," Atchison said forcefully, but quietly.

Mai Ker tried to break the tension.

"Nobody is saying this is your fault, Jimmy." She walked to him and looked up into his eyes. "You were just doing what they told us." She took his upper arm and squeezed it gently. "What about the chemicals you used. Did they trigger something? Maybe?"

He looked away, thinking. His scowl turn to puzzlement.

"Well, there was the nitrous oxide. But I mean, the quantity was so small. Compared to the huge volume of air in this place." He flopped into a chair, exasperated.

"I don't know!" he almost shouted. He grabbed his head. He would have torn it open if it would have helped him find the answer.

"Let's just go back and look," Mai Ker said.

"I don't believe this," Sarajane said with disgust. She, too, dropped into a chair at the dining table.

The tension in the room was thicker than cheap peanut butter. Block finally slashed through it with as much authority as he could muster.

"Look guys. There's no reason to get at each other's throats. We've got a little problem on our hands, that's all. And we're gonna deal with it like we always do. We'll fix it. We're a team. Let's act like it."

"Clayton, nobody's accusing anybody—" Bridget began to say, but Block cut her off.

"And we're not going to start. We all know what we're thinking. Let's be honest. I'll email OUTSIDE right now and find out what they know. Jimmy, go over those September test specs again. With a fine-toothed comb. Mai Ker, you and Willy help. This is top priority until we straighten it out."

Jimmy's temper was stretched thinner than a piece of tissue paper but he knew Block just helped him down off a very large hook. He nodded, and headed for the Research Center. Even though he didn't want to think about what Atchison had said, something deep in his gut told him that Willy was on to something—as usual. Atchison looked like a plodding tree sloth at times but his mind was sharper than Perseus' sword.

Caroline was still cuddled up in the napkins on the table. She turned herself in little orbits, responding to all the voices and moods around her. She seemed agitated but was unable to pick herself up. Block carried her back up to her nest. Bridget followed him, watching how he gently handled the tiny creature. She stood in the doorway, watching in silence, suppressing her desire to compliment him on the care he showed for his little pet.

"At least now I know why you're having problems again," he said to Caroline with resignation. He stroked her back but she made no sound.

Block turned and saw Bridget.

"Come with me, would you?"

They went to the Comm. Center where Block typed out a quick message to Omaha:

TO: J. HASKINS
CC: N. DANIELS
URGENT, URGENT.
:: PROBLEMS AGAIN IN HERE. ALGOOD REPORTS FINDING SAME ANOMALIES IN AIR QUALITY READINGS. VERY SIMILAR TO JANUARY. WE'RE LOOKING FOR EXPLANATIONS. WHAT ARE YOU READING? ANYTHING MORE FROM JANUARY? PLEASE RESPOND ASAP ::
BLOCK

He hit the SEND key and the message was sucked off the screen and zipped OUTSIDE to Omaha. He sat back, preoccupied.

"Clayton?" Bridget asked.

He keyed the intercom mic.

"Sarajane, what's the smallest oxygen tank in the infirmary?"

Her purple dot on the nearby monitor flashed orange as she spoke.

"There's some 160-liter ones in the storage closet just left of the cleanup room."

"Thanks."

Without another word to Bridget, Block left and jogged through Pod 3 into Pod 7. He checked the storage closet Sarajane described, found the green cylinders, and grabbed one. He rummaged around for plastic oxygen tubing and some nipples and couplers.

His jog back to the house bordered on a dead run. He grabbed two large, clear garbage bags from the kitchen and bounded up the stairs. He threw all the gear onto his bed and dug through the bottom of his closet for the old boot box in which Caroline had arrived at Solarium-3. Some of the same socks were still in it. He threw these aside and arranged some clean ones and set it on the floor at the end of his bed. Carefully, he put Caroline in the new nest.

In minutes he had rigged up a floating oxygen tent by doubling one bag inside the other, then taping them tightly to the floor around the box. He cut a small slit near the top and taped an oxygen tube into the tent. He worked so fast he was winded. Done, he opened the cylinder valve just enough to inflate the doubled-up bags, then turned it until it was barely open, letting a weak stream of oxygen seep into the tent and out through a small flap cut near the floor.

The slow oxygen flow kept the tent inflated. He could no longer touch Caroline but at least he could see her and monitor her. She was safe from the corrupted air in the pods.

"Your own little Solarium," he nodded to her.

He watched her for a few more minutes, savagely intent on keeping her alive, though he didn't know why.

With scissors and tape he made a small food door and put in some water and seed. Through all this, Caroline lay perfectly limp on the rumpled socks. Though still, her eyes were open and moving. Once in a while her beak would quiver, as if she wanted to protest this oppressively unfair world.

Block knew exactly how she felt.

THERE WAS no response from Omaha that afternoon. Block sent a second request about 5:30, then spent the late afternoon and evening checking with the team, each engaged in various tests around the complex checking air and water quality, animal activity, plant metabolism.

Jimmy was glued to a terminal in the Research Center, going over and over Haskins' instructions from September. About 7:45 that evening he called Block over the intercom.

"Clayton. Come over to the Research Center. I want you to look at this."

"Be there in ten."

Block had been checking several animals with Sarajane in Pod 11. He went by way of the aviary in Pod 6, where he hadn't ventured all afternoon. As he feared, four birds lay dead in the bottom of the main cage. Many of the others looked lackadaisical. There was no chirping, or singing.

Jimmy was waiting impatiently when Block arrived, drumming his hands nervously on the console desk.

"Whad'a'ya got?" Block asked.

"I've gone over and over those test specs that Haskins gave us. I can't find anything conclusive. But the readouts from the last few days—they look just like January. The nitrogen pressure is pushing up again, and the oxygen pressure is falling off. I don't get it! This just doesn't happen."

"It doesn't, but it *is*," Block corrected.

"Well, it stinks like you know what. I mean, we're talking *huge* quantities of air. Mammoth numbers of oxygen and nitrogen molecules. The balance of pressures—the percentages—they just don't change like this."

"So, what are we saying?"

"'We' are saying it's impossible! You know the science, Clayton. There's rules. We're talking so many quadrillions—centillions—of oxygen and nitrogen molecules—even in our little piece of heaven here, that—well . . ." He broke off. "I don't know."

He sat, stumped. He shook his head like he was trying to shake off the after effects of a three-day drunk.

"Go on, Jimmy." Block's voice offered encouragement.

"It shouldn't be happening. Nature's balance in the atmosphere has gone virtually unaltered for eons. I can't understand how anything we've done could change it like this! It's not like we've got a volcano in here or something!"

Block had become a non-essential presence. Jimmy was arguing with himself.

"Then what caused it?" the non-essential asked.

"That's what frosts me! I can't tell. I've checked everything I can think of. I've run a hundred computer simulations. I can't make it happen."

"So something's happening that's not in our control."

"Yes," Jimmy sighed with futility in his voice. Just as suddenly his temper flared. "Look. I'm not paranoid or anything—but we're in seriously deep tapioca here. It's not just birds that're gonna be keelin' over. Do you read me? If we don't get a handle on this, we're gonna have to get out of here—and quick."

Block scanned down the batches of data on Jimmy's computer, his back stiffening.

"Look at this!" Jimmy said. He scrolled through several more screens showing Block more bad news, the effects on the plants, the animals, every living thing in the Solarium. The atmospheric gas mixtures—which normally displayed on one screen as green bars—were now partly red. The oxygen and nitrogen pressures were changing in inverse proportion. The oxygen pressure was decreasing. If the problem persisted, the nitrogen pressure would soon become toxic. The growing imbalance of these primary gases would quickly become fatal to the animals, including the human variety.

"Can we boost the plant population enough to compensate?" Block asked.

"No. Well, not fast enough anyway. The volume of plants we have are just right to keep the natural balance. We'd have to plant every square inch of soil in every pod. But there's no time. The oxygen is dropping too fast."

Block knew his question was pointless. The oxygen they needed to survive was gradually being squeezed out of the Solarium's air. If the air continued to tumble out of balance, the whole ecosystem would be affected.

"So where's the excess nitrogen coming from?" Block asked him.

"I only wish I knew." Jimmy had struggled with this question all day.

"All right. So what do we do to stop it?"

"I have *no idea*."

"Well, use the brain God gave you, Jimmy!" Block said.

"Don't get rude with me, Block. I'm trying, OK? This thing—" he said, waving his arms, "—it's a living monster!"

Block accepted the rebuke.

"Sorry," Block said, suitably reprimanded. "So?"

"So I'm stumped. OUTSIDE has to fix this. Or, we open up and leave."

"I'm working on them. No response yet. Slower than molasses in January. Any other ideas?"

"Well, we could kill off some of the large animals. They're consuming a lot of oxygen."

"Will the air react quick enough?"

"Well, probably not."

"OK," Block said, "what else?"

"We could try to boost the oxygen pressure with direct O_2 infusions. We've got some pretty large tanks of the stuff in the main storage shed. For welding, that kind of thing. But with our total volume of air, I don't know if that's gonna have any impact. I mean, you're talking 8.7 million cubic feet of air in this place! I don't know if the oxygen tanks are gonna have much effect."

"Any other barnstorm?" Block asked, his colloquialism for brainstorm.

"Not at the moment." He stared at Block. "I was kinda counting on you having one."

Jimmy took a huge bite of the candy bar that was his supper. Block sat down and chewed at the inside of his lip. The muscles in the back of his neck tightened more.

"What if we did both at once?" Block asked.

"You mean kill some animals and try the gas infusions—both?"

"Yeah."

"I dunno." Jimmy thought about it. "Might work. But we won't have much left to eat except vegetables and insects. And whatever meat we can freeze."

"And that might shorten our stay in here," Block mused with unrepentant glee.

"Yeah. And royally tick off the bigwigs in Omaha."

"Well, life's full of little trade-offs, right?"

"Look, Clayton, the simplest answer is we just call it quits. We leave. That's our only sure bet. Or, you convince those turkeys in Omaha to vent in some fresh air from OUTSIDE."

"Come on, Jimmy. That's not going to happen. They'd sooner we quit. If they vent in air, it bastardizes the whole project."

"I know. It'd completely contaminate the whole complex," Jimmy admitted. "We wouldn't get the long-haul results they want." He looked squarely at Block. "But you could ask."

Block tried to picture this. He saw himself as David standing across from Goliath, polishing up one little rock for his slingshot.

"I've never sold cars, but I could try."

"A shorter-term stay, fewer results. But some successes."

"They won't like it."

"Beats a shorter-term life."

Block nodded.

"I know it's only 8:30, but I'm done in," Jimmy said. "I'm hittin' the hay."

Jimmy left for the house and Block went to the Comm. Center in #2, hoping there might be some response from Haskins to his earlier messages. He was greeted by a blank screen.

He punched in a new message:

TO J. HASKINS:
CC: N. DANIELS
URGENT
:: JOHN: WE'RE IN REAL TROUBLE. NEED YOU TO OPEN UP AND VENT IN SOME FRESH AIR. SAME PROBLEM REFERRED TO EARLIER THIS DATE. WE HAVE NO FIXES IN HERE THAT DON'T HAVE LONG TERM DETRIMENTAL EFFECTS ON THE PROJECT. THIS SEEMS LIKE THE QUICKEST AND BEST SOLUTION. ONLY OTHER SOLUTION IS TO CALL IT QUITS. PLEASE RESPOND AS EARLY AS POSSIBLE. ::
BLOCK

He knew there was no point in sitting here waiting. Haskins had certainly gone home hours ago. Block was angry that he hadn't answered the earlier message. And Daniels was ignoring him, too. So much for good communications.

He walked to #4 and up onto the front porch of the house. The sky OUTSIDE was dark, the Solarium's interior lighting turned low. He went up to his bedroom to check on Caroline. She was standing very still, but was at least on her feet. This made him feel better.

He walked down the hall and tapped at Bridget's door. There was no response. He tapped again.

"Yes?" her voice said.

"You decent?"

"Always."

This was cute, but didn't tell him what he wanted to know.

"Can I come in?"

"Sure."

Bridget was on her bed, propped up with three pillows. She had been reading but the book had been carelessly tossed aside, hanging half off the bed. Block sat down on Mai Ker's perfectly made bed opposite Bridget's.

"Where's Mai Ker?"

She ignored the question.

"What's going on Clayton?"

"I was just talking with Jimmy. Same thing as before. The air's being poisoned. Too much nitrogen. There's no easy solution, as far as we can figure—unless Haskins agrees to vent in some air."

"Will he?"

"Don't know. He hasn't responded. He's pretty thick headed. Got a lot of pressure on him from investors. Lots of money riding on this deal."

"Nothing else we can do?"

"Yeah. Leave. They're gonna love that one, too."

"You going to ask him?"

"Already did."

Bridget pawed the spine of her lifeless book, looking pensively at the far wall. She took a slow breath, and looked at Block with a mixture of worry and sadness.

"How's Caroline?"

"I made her a tent. I think she's OK. For now." He

hesitated, a somber look in his eyes. "There were four more dead ones in the aviary."

"I figured. Just didn't want to go look."

Her bedroom was cool, but Block felt warmer than usual. He was conscious—too conscious—of the blood heating his face. Bridget saw it, too.

"What's wrong, Clayton?"

"What do you mean?"

"You get red like that on purpose?"

He became flustered. He struggled for an excuse, a rationalization.

"Caroline's really the only thing in here I care about, Bridget. She gives me a purpose. Whatever happens, I just want to keep her going—you see?"

"I see." The disappointment in her voice was subtle, but there. "Lot of investment in a bird."

"And . . ." He hesitated again. "Well, there's you, too. Last couple of weeks, I don't know, I feel kind of like that toward you . . ." He stopped himself. *Where do I go with this?* His mind froze up. He rolled his burly shoulders back, his usual manner of saying, *I'm stuck.*

"You see me like a bird," she said hesitantly, trying to make a joke.

"You know what I mean, dang it."

"I know. Just teasing."

"Well, you do that a lot." He looked at her. "I don't usually feel this way. I mean, about Caroline. In combat—well I always kind of felt like this for my men. Keep 'em alive, at all costs. But I have that feeling for you. Now. In here."

"I can't imagine."

Now he couldn't tell if she was still teasing or serious. In any case, she was doing her best not to help him out of his bewilderment.

"I guess I've grown to like you a little." He sounded just like a fifth-grader, which is how he normally felt when he was attracted to a woman.

"A little," she repeated. Her lips rumpled. "Thanks, Clayton. It's nice to know." She smiled.

He didn't know what to do next, so he stood up.

"Want to go down to the kitchen and get some dessert?" His grand idea of a date. It was the most romantic thing he could think of at the moment.

"A little," she said, laughing.

Block smiled at his own foolishness, a foolishness he knew he'd never get over if he lived ten thousand years.

They went down to the kitchen. Pam wasn't around so they were free to peek through everything she'd stashed away in the three refrigerators. Two strawberry shortcakes sat there at the back of the main refrigerator, helpless, forgotten. They snatched them out, took stools at the breakfast counter, and gobbled the delights down, giggling like two naughty school children sneaking around grandma's house after midnight.

ABOUT THE same time, Mai Ker had found Jimmy sitting forlornly on the living room couch. He had planned to go to bed, he couldn't. He was once again shuffling pages of reports. She knew he was blaming himself for not catching the problem sooner.

Of all the team, Mai Ker and Jimmy had become the closest over the last eight months. A natural attraction had been spawned between them after only three weeks in the Solarium and had grown into a close, though not yet intimate, friendship.

"Still at it, Jimmy?" she asked.

"Uh-hum."

"Sorry if I was critical earlier. When I talked about those tests you did. I know you were just following orders."

He looked at her, appreciative of her apology.

"Not your fault, Mai Ker. We're all tense. And after looking at these numbers all afternoon—we oughta be!"

"Have you found something?"

"Well, after the initial rebound last month, our atmosphere has slowly gotten worse. Very gradual. There was this short lull," he said, pointing to a printout, "right after we worked on the problem. But then the nitrogen level started back up—very slowly." He slapped the couch cushion in frustration. "I just don't understand why our sensors didn't trigger the alert system. If I hadn't caught it in the analytical report today, we still wouldn't know."

"Are the sensors malfunctioning? Maybe the system is off-program or something."

"I don't think so," he said. "Everything looks OK. But no alerts. The sensor program seems to be running normally—it should've sounded alerts every day. But no alerts!" He flipped his hands in the air. The papers fluttered to the floor.

Mai Ker sat down by him and rubbed his shoulders and neck.

"Relax, OK? We will figure it out. Don't be so worried."

"I was born to worry," he said. "That's probably why they hired me."

She nodded unconsciously, though he couldn't see. She knew Jimmy well enough to know this self-description was pretty accurate. His voice relaxed a little with her massage.

"Don't know what else to do." He said.

"Could we try some oxygen infusion?

"Clayton and I talked about that. I don't know if we have enough in storage to have a real effect. We even talked about slaughtering some of the bigger animals, to conserve."

"A lot of work down the gutter," Mai Ker said.

"Down the drain," he corrected her.

"I wish we could go home."

"I hate to break it to you. For now, we *are* home." Faint desperation trailed off with his voice.

Mai Ker gave two final squeezes to his shoulder muscles sending a warm sensation down the full length of his back.

"Maybe so," she agreed, though she wasn't sure why.

BRIDGET WENT back up to her room to change her blouse, the front of which was now richly colored with wide drips of strawberry syrup and whipped cream from her dessert-fest with Block. She hadn't seen Sarajane all evening, so she stopped and tapped on her door.

Sarajane, who had been reading all evening, said, "Come in."

"Hey, Clayton and I are raiding the ice box. Want to join us?" She scooped a splotch of whipped cream off her sleeve and licked her finger.

"Thanks. I'm kinda in the middle of a chapter. I'd rather finish."

"You sure? You been kind of hiding out from the rest of us lately," Bridget said.

"Not hiding. Just got a lot on my mind. And I haven't been feeling the greatest anyway."

"What's wrong?" Bridget asked her.

"Just feeling a little tired."

"I could whip us up some spiced coffee. Put a little lead in your pencil."

"Thanks, Bridget. But I think I'll just take it easy tonight. Had a hard day."

"Yeah. Guess we all did. What're you reading?"

"Oh, some medical update stuff. You know, trying to keep brushed up on things while we're locked away. I don't want to come out of here in three and a half years and be completely in the dark on medical advances. The chief project doctor in Omaha emails me stuff every two or three weeks."

"Sounds boring," Bridget said. "Do technical work all day, and read technical junk all night? Come on, give it a break. Come have some fun with us."

"You guys go ahead. I'm having fun."

Bridget's eyebrows went up a full inch at this one, but she just laughed and told Sarajane to "Enjoy, enjoy." She went and changed her shirt and rejoined a messier-than-ever Clayton Block in the kitchen.

BY TRUE coincidence, another pair of Solarians was at work in another part of the complex. Pam had gone to the fuel shed in Pod 14 to connect a new propane tank to the supply line that ran underground to the residence. Will Atchison had been walking an inspection detail around several of his corn plots in Pod 10 and saw Pam headed to #14. He was bored staring at plants, and feeling more than usually alone.

"What's cooking?" he said when he found her squeezed between several of the large propane tanks.

"Pressure to the stove was running low. Time for a new bottle."

"Like nursing a baby," Atchison observed.

"Today, this whole place seems like nursing a baby."

"Yeah." He reflected on this, but mostly watched Pam. "Want to go for walk? I mean, instead of back to the house?"

She didn't answer.

"Got time?" he pressed.

"I suppose." She finished tightening down the line coupler over the tank nipple and hung the large crescent wrench back on the wall. She reached a hand forward.

"Yeah?" Will asked, not sure what she wanted.

"Your arm, sir?"

"Oh. Yeah," was his embarrassed reply. "A little off

my form tonight."

"I'd say."

He offered his bulky arm and escorted her out of the fuel shed and back into Pod 10, through fields of crops, plants, flowers, with many varieties of small shrubs.

"You know," Pam said, "they built this place to prove we could support life out there, on some distant world." Her eyes strained through the pod roof toward the heavens. "We could be walking on another planet right now. Imagine." She looked at the darkened, star-lit sky OUTSIDE. "We could be on the moon."

"It's not a planet."

"What?"

"It's a moon."

"Wise ass."

"My daddy taught me that. Better to be a wise ass than a dumb ass."

"Dumb ass."

They walked silently for several minutes toward Pod 12, enjoying the quiet. As they entered the podwalk into #12, they heard the gentle waves splashing quietly along the artificial ocean's shore.

"Why'd you come here, Pam?"

"To walk with you."

"No," he said. "Why'd you come *here*? Why'd you take this job?"

"Let's see. You want the truth, or one of my prepared lies?"

"Truth."

"The money," she said. "I was broke, Will. I went to school a lot. My whole life, it seems. Never made enough money to even pay back my school loans from my bachelor's degree. I thought this would be my ticket out of debt."

"Really?"

"Well, here I am, earning a great salary every day, and I can't spend a penny. When we get out, there'll be

48 direct deposits sitting in my savings account. Plus what's left of the sign-on bonus that I didn't get spent before I got here. I'm going to pay off every one of those college loans, buy a small house in some little secluded town in the mountains in Wyoming."

"Sounds fun."

"I'll stock in a whole shed full of cashews and treats, another whole shed of stitching and craft projects. Maybe someday open up a little year-round Christmas craft shop." He saw her plans lining up, thread after thread, on the loom of her imagination. The tapestry was still very sparse, but Atchison could imagine the picture taking shape. He liked what he saw.

"Sounds real fun," he said. He took her hand off his arm and put it in his hand as they walked the shore. He waited for the obvious question.

"Why'd you come here, Will?"

"God only knows." His voice was quiet. "I guess I felt I'd done about all the damage I could out there— OUTSIDE. Yeah, the money's good. But I think it attracted me because it felt like settling down. At least for four years."

"That's settling down?"

"For me, yeah. I don't think I've ever lived in one place more than a year and a half my whole adult life. This felt like a steady job. And when I found out Clayton was going to be here, that cinched it. Can't think of a better man to work for."

"Haskins is really the boss."

"For you maybe. Not me. I work for one guy— Clayton Block. Won't find a steadier guy on the face of this earth. I've been places—I ought to know."

"Yes, I heard a story. Something about a jail on the French Riviera."

"Not just that. Well, yeah, that part's true, too. No, I'm talking about me and Block out there in the thick of it. Front lines. Hundreds of anonymous souls out there trying their very best to kill you. Block saved my butt from a whole lot more than French jails. Thing is, he never takes credit."

"Sit?" Pam stopped, pointing at a concrete bench near the water about a third of the way around their ocean.

"Sure."

Will gazed out over the water for several minutes. The quiet roll of the waves was soothing after their tense day. Pam let him wander in his memories. Finally, he spoke.

"This ocean would be a whole lot prettier if there wasn't that big plastic bubble sitting over it."

"Life doesn't always have to be pretty, does it?"

"No, but it sure helps when you're an old fart like me."

"You're not old," she gently scolded him.

"If I'm not, then you are—because your eyes must be going."

She put her arm around his thick shoulders and pulled his head to hers.

"Even the blind fall in love."

Atchison stared straight ahead, across the water, but sat up a little straighter.

"Is that what we're doin'?"

Pam had to stop and think.

"No. Not yet."

Atchison chuckled loudly. His laugh scared a small sea turtle that jumped off a nearby rock headlong into an incoming wave.

SARAJANE WAS still alone in her room. She sat on her bed, legs pulled up to her chest and the medical reports in her hands, sobbing quietly. She had lied to Bridget. These were not the usual medical updates from the project doctor in Omaha. These were different. She had specifically requested these, information on recent therapies for various respiratory diseases. On such illnesses, Sarajane had made herself an expert.

She brushed drying tears from her face and took a long breath. The inside of her chest burned. She got up and pulled a small lock box out from under her bed, a box she kept carefully out of sight when anyone was around. She opened it, took out two small inhalers, and slipped into the bathroom that she and Pam shared.

She took several long puffs from each inhaler—several more than usual. She sat on the edge of the tub and took long, deeper-than-normal breaths, trying to slow the spasms and get her lungs to fill. Peeking out the bathroom door to make sure Pam hadn't come back, she quickly replaced the inhalers in the box, locked it, and shoved it back under the bed. Her little secret. A secret kept from the team—and from the chief project doctor when she first applied. He now knew. She had revealed it in a confidential email three months after Seal-In. She had snuck a large supply of inhalers in with her personal belongings. She didn't think, frankly, it was anybody's business, as long as she did her job.

She curled up on the bed again. The medication began to help. Her chest burned less, her breathing slowed down. Her heart still raced a little, a reaction to one inhaler. But her breathing felt better.

She was tired, restless, feeling oppressed and confined. She wished now she had taken Bridget up on her offer. It was too late now. Surely by now, she thought, Bridget and Clayton would be off somewhere by themselves, enjoying each other. Why would they want her interfering?

The walls seemed closer together tonight. She had to do something, keep her mind busy. She got up and pulled open the bottom drawer of her built-in bureau. From under some slacks she pulled out a large photo album and sat on the edge of her bed. Her eyes scanned the walls, ordering them to stand back, then started through the album, from page one.

They were pictures of her family mostly. Herself and her brothers and her sisters as babies, then as little kids. With each page, her mother and father aged. Eventually, too, so did the kids, but it took them much longer. There were many more pictures of them as babies and toddlers than as youngsters and adolescents. Somehow parents manning cameras always seem to lose interest as the kids grew out of infancy and turned into little adults.

She turned more pages. Eventually it was the kids behind the camera, and mom and dad looked older than ever. Ancient, from a kid's eyes.

One more page turn, and her dad was no longer there. A heart attack, at age 52. Instantly, mom looked far older. Nieces and nephews appeared here and there in a corner of a page, smashing a birthday cake, pulling a dog's ear here, a little bare butt searching for a diaper there. Sarajane laughed. Little Justine. What a hilarious kid. Except for the brace on her leg, and the limp that would tag her forever.

Another page, mom again. Even older, but so healthy. Opposite was Sarajane herself, graduating from her Master's program, about to enter the University of Colorado Medical School in Denver. Then another photo, as she launched into her resident internship at CU-MED Outreach. Her sister held the camera that day, as Sarajane held her mom in a sideways hug.

She took another deep breath before she turned the page. There would be no more pictures of mom. For two frantic years during her internship in Denver, she worked tirelessly to find a cure. A cure for a terrible, infectious bacterial disease, a degenerative tissue disease that attacked human flesh and ate it away like a school of fish attacking the remains of a drowned sailor.

For two exhausting years, she worked frantically. Nights, weekends. Lots of cancelled dates with promising young men in the medical school. Frantic work. Hellish work. Eyes exhausted from staring into microscopes. And none of her colleagues had known why.

Finally, she did it, created the cure, a combination of chemotherapy and laser therapy that stopped the disease in its tracks, eradicating the grisly bacteria in mid-bite. The cure would be called miraculous by some of her physician instructors. They lauded her.

But it came three months too late for her mom. While Sarajane slaved madly in Denver, her mother had succumbed to the gruesome disease in Santa Fe. Although her colleagues didn't know it, her mother's diagnosis two years earlier was what drove Sarajane to pour such intensive research into the disease. The work had gone quickly. But not quickly enough.

She turned the page, searching for some purpose in her life after the horrible tragedy. One photo of her mom's grave. Then one of the plaque: her CU Outstanding Achievement Award for finding the cure—the same plaque hanging on her wall here INSIDE Solarium-3.

Another page. Another page. Brothers, sisters, their spouses. More nieces, more nephews, all cute, all cuddly. No boyfriends for Sarajane. No children. "No significant ties," as her file said. Just blank pages. Waiting for something. Waiting for some*one*.

A few fresh tears splashed down on the plastic photo page, and ran slowly sideways. Saltwater from the ocean inside of her. This would have been a picture worth preserving. But she brushed them away. She inhaled deeply, believing with all her hope that the empty pages would someday look like the rest.

13

Friday, March 6th

Within four days, the Solarians were in a complete nosedive. Anxiety and friction had erupted among the teammates. All routine work and research had crashed.

On Tuesday Sarajane became seriously ill and was taken to the infirmary where she worsened over the last two days. At first she experienced only mild breathing discomfort, but by Thursday night this worsened into severe chest pains and labored breathing.

Early this morning, as she had for almost 48 hours straight, Pam went to the infirmary to tend Sarajane who was still bedded down there and taking oxygen.

"How're you feeling?" Pam asked.

"Like a dog that's had the crap kicked out of her."

"Do you want to try the injections again?"

"I don't think it's going to help, Pam. I've had severe asthmatic reactions since I was little. If anybody was going to be affected by this air problem, it was bound to be me."

"The epinephrine seemed to help the spasms a little yesterday."

"Yeah, but we're just treating the symptoms—not dealing with the problem. Too much of that stuff is bad—it'll keep over-stimulating my heart till it stops."

"What else can we do?"

"My lungs just can't get enough air. I'm just slowly suffocating."

"You're going to be OK, Sarajane. The oxygen should be helping."

"A little bit."

"Look, you're going to be fine. You've just got to rest and take it as easy as you can—and stay on the oxygen. Until we get this air thing under control."

"They've been at it four days!"

"I know, but Jimmy says it's been brewing for weeks. Maybe months. Who knows? We can't fix it overnight."

"I know," Sarajane said, panting slightly. "But you know how I feel lying here, helpless. I hate it! I want to be up, helping."

"Well, you can't, and that's that."

"Maybe try a lower dosage of the epinephrine. Just enough not to mess with the heart. Maybe I'll try getting up a little later."

"I've worked up a special diet for you, too, for the next few days. That may take a little stress off your system. But you need to stay in bed."

"Thanks, Pam. You're like a mom."

"Excuse me? I am not anywhere old enough to be your mom!"

"But you're nice enough," Sarajane smiled.

Pam tried to smile, too, as she gave the injection, but inwardly she was scared. She could see Sarajane was suffering tremendously even though she tried to mask it. The oxygen therapy seemed to help but Sarajane had been flat on her back for the last day. The only solution was doing exactly what they were doing, keeping her as still as possible so her heart could rest a little as it tried to get oxygen to the rest of her body.

Atchison had been feeling generally cruddy for the last twelve hours, too, but being Will, didn't let on to anyone. When it came to hiding behind a smile, he was a master. Weakness and nausea crept over him every half hour or so. This, he was sure, was just from worry and lack of sleep. He'd had too much of the first and little of the second for four days. If it was a warning sign of some kind, he paid no attention. He had been a lot sicker before.

Just the stress, he told himself. *Just slow down, take it easy.* He repeated this mantra to himself several times. His personality was such that he generally couldn't recognize, let alone deal with, anxiety. He was always able to conveniently repress his feelings.

In the Comm. Center things were dead. Block had not received a single satisfactory response to any of his emails. Haskins sent back only a perfunctory answer to the first email, about what OUTSIDE found after the first air problems in January. As for Block's request to vent in some fresh air from OUTSIDE, Haskins had passed the buck over to Nathan Daniels, who responded by writing that a small committee was studying options but hadn't reached a decision. Late Thursday, in his typically obscure way, Daniels cluttered the screen with this gem:

BLOCK:
:: STUDYING THE INTRICACIES OF YOUR REQUEST. COMPLICATIONS ARE BEING ANALYZED FOR CONCURRENT POTENTIALITIES AND CONSEQUENTIAL EFFECTS. THE INHERENT DEFECTS OF YOUR PROPOSAL ARE APPARENT, AND OF GREAT CONCERN. CONSIDERING OTHER POSSIBILITIES. WILL ADVISE SHORTLY. ::
N. DANIELS

"Shortly" apparently meant something very different to Nathan Daniels than to Block. If Block hadn't already been feeling queasy this surely would have done it.

Jimmy and Mai Ker were the only two actually feeling fine, except for serious frustration and lack of a decent night's sleep. The oxygen levels in several of the pods had now dropped to 15 percent of total air volume. Pods 9 and 11 were being affected again due to the consumption of oxygen by the sizeable creatures housed there. The plants in #10 and the aquatic plants in #12 were also suffering obvious distress.

The increased nitrogen and decreased oxygen pressures also affected the carbon dioxide level in the pods. Plant life in the Solarium didn't know if it was coming or going. Less and less carbon dioxide to absorb slowed plant metabolism. This in turn meant less and less oxygen being expelled. Leaves and petals were wilting rapidly as if dried up by a hot desert wind. There was no wind, of course, except for the artificial variety produced by the large solar-powered fans adorning the tops of the larger pods. But no desert wind could have had a more devastating effect than the heightened nitrogen level that was searing the atmosphere INSIDE the Stellar plastic domes.

JUST BEFORE noon, Pam left Sarajane in the infirmary and caught up to Block as he came into the maintenance pod to wash up after doing soil inspections in Pod 11. What little grass was left in #11 to support the smaller animals was rapidly disappearing. And it didn't look like it would grow back.

"Where are we at, Clayton?" Pam asked.

"Nowhere new. Still waiting on Haskins." He flashed an angry look. "I can't believe they're taking this long!"

"Can't you prod them?"

"I've tried. I get no response," he said loudly. "Just stonewalling. If I could unlock this place from INSIDE, I'd've walked out by now."

"Look. I hate to be the worrywart. But Sarajane's not doing well. She's a lot worse today. She won't admit it of course, but she's in a lot of pain. I'm managing to keep her still but she wants to get up and help."

"I know. She's a trouper. But you can't let her. Tell her to be patient. We're doing our best. Either Jimmy's going to get a handle on this or OUTSIDE will. It's just a matter of time."

"Bridget was looking for you. She came by the infirmary."

"She can find me on the console anytime she wants."

"She wasn't at the Comm. Center. She came right from the house to see Sarajane and me. I said you were probably in number eleven or number twelve."

"Well, she managed to miss me. What'd she want?"

"Didn't say."

Block gave an exasperated sigh.

"All right. I'll find her."

He dried his hands and went scouting for Bridget, with no luck. He worked his way back through the Research Center in #3, which was vacant, then the Comm. Center. The purple dot marked "B.L." was blipping in Pod 6.

He found her sitting on a wrought-iron bench at the far side of the aviary. Nearly a dozen birds lay dead in the bottom of the main cage—recent deaths, since the cage had just been cleaned yesterday afternoon.

The look on her face was as wilted as the plant life Block had just inspected. He sat beside her.

"Got you pretty bugged, huh."

"That's not even *close* to the right word, Clayton."

"Gimme a break. I'm just trying to minimize things. As usual."

"Think that'll make it better?"

"No. I was doing it for your sake."

"Well, don't. It won't. I'm a big girl now."

His mouth tightened. He broke the news.

"Pam says Sarajane's pretty weak. A lot worse."

"Doing better than those poor birds," she said,

gesturing with her eyes.

Block stared at them, always thinking of Caroline.

"Yeah, thank goodness," he said.

"I feel totally worthless today," she complained, staring down at the dead birds. "Helpless. Don't know what to do next. I'd rather die quick like them—than worry to death."

"Let me worry."

"Think you can do that for all of us?"

"You could help Jimmy over in the main supply. He's doing an inventory of seed supplies to see if we can replant enough stuff—once we get this problem under control."

"Wow. Inventory. Sounds thrilling."

"It'll keep your mind off things."

"No, it won't."

"Go on, Bridget. It won't help sitting here looking at a bunch of dead birds."

She turned finally and looked deep into his eyes, searching for something. What, he couldn't tell.

"Caroline OK?" she asked.

"Yeah. Checked her a couple of hours ago. The air tent's working. I just have to keep an eye on the oxygen bottle. So it doesn't go dry. She keeps flying against the tent, trying to get loose. Doesn't understand why I won't let her out. Thinks I'm being mean, probably." Even he knew he was rambling. "She doesn't understand. In there is her only chance."

Bridget slowly shook her head, doubtful that Caroline had reasoned all this through in such depth. She smiled at Block, then pinched her lips together, choking down emotions she didn't understand. She still felt helpless, which she didn't like.

"All right. I'll go help Jimmy." She stood and looked down at Block. "Let me know if you want me back at control."

"Yeah, I will." He stood, put his arm around her

shoulders and squeezed. He didn't want to let go, but finally did.

Bridget crossed through the fields in Pod 10 and found Jimmy in #13, their main supply and equipment storage. Block went to the Comm. Center, hoping to finally find a *useful* message from Haskins or Daniels.

Still, not a word.

"Nobody talking, huh?" He chewed at the empty space between his teeth. "What in the name of God is wrong?" He kicked the chair in front of the console. It bounced off the desk and rolled back at him lifelessly. He yanked at it, sat down hard, and started hammering at the keyboard.

"All right. Enough is enough. Time to wake up, Mr. John Haskins."

The keys continued to click away.

DEAR JOHN:
:: GET OFF YOUR LAZY BUTT, YOU GOOD-FER-NOTHIN. WE NEED ANSWERS. LIFE'S GETTING ROUGH IN HERE. WHAT'S THE PROBLEM?? I NEED AN ANSWER. I NEED IT YESTERDAY! I'M BEING POLITE. IF YOU DON'T BELIEVE ME, KEEP STALLING. ::
BLOCK

This at least provoked a response—in less than two minutes.

DEAR MR. BLOCK:
:: I KNOW YOU THINK WE'RE IGNORING YOU. BELIEVE ME, WE'RE NOT. I'VE BEEN OFF MY BACKSIDE FOR DAYS NOW. YOU DON'T KNOW WHAT TOUGH IS. YOUR REQUEST IS NOT AS SIMPLE AS YOU THINK. WE ARE WORKING ON EVERY POSSIBLE OPTION. I'M SORRY, YOU HAVE TO BE

PATIENT. A WHILE LONGER. ::
HASKINS

Block stared at the screen in disbelief.

"Patient!" he hollered at the deaf computer screen. "I've been patient for weeks, you dimwit!"

In the weeks since January, when the Solarians first discovered the air problem, OUTSIDE had not given them the slightest concrete analysis of the data Jimmy sent them. It was now four days since Block's latest cry for help, and all he got was another "be patient."

"The pompous, illegitimate—!" Block hollered at the walls. "Thinks he runs the world!" The computer keys were trampled as if by a stampede under his next stinging message:

HASKINS:
:: I TAKE IT ALL BACK ABOUT YOUR BACKSIDE. YOU AREN'T ON ONE, YOU ARE ONE. YOURS PATIENTLY. ::
BLOCK

He stormed out of the Comm. Center and went to the house to find some lunch. Pam was back in the infirmary with Sarajane, so it was every man for himself in the kitchen. He slapped together a bologna and cheese sandwich with no mayonnaise but plenty of dill pickles. It fit his mood perfectly. He was busy wolfing this down with some corn chips when Atchison came in.

"Want some lunch, Willy?"

"Nah, not right now, thanks. I'm just gonna lay down for a while. Pretty tired today. Must've been your snoring last night."

"I haven't snored for years."

"Bull manure. You're just never awake to hear it, old buddy."

"You want me to make you a sandwich for later?"

"Nah. I'll make something when I get up. Listen, I've got another idea about this air problem. Maybe a new perspective. I'll talk to you about it. After my nap."

"You do look tired. If you want to nap through dinner, go ahead. We can talk in the morning."

"We'll see," Will said. "We don't have a lot of time to waste, do we." It was not a question.

"I know. Go on, catch a catnap."

Willy looked pale. Block even wondered if he hadn't lost a pound or two. *Understandable,* he thought, considering the worry and strain they were all under. He hoped it really wasn't his own snoring that was keeping Willy awake.

He finished his sandwich and soda and went to find Jimmy and Bridget. He was halfway across #10 when the fast triple beep tone sounded over the intercom, signaling an urgent new message coming into the Comm. Center. He silenced the tone from his intercom radio and hustled to Pod 2.

"PRIORITY" flashed at the top of the main screen. Block keyed in his password.

TO CLAYTON BLOCK:
:: CLAYTON. SORRY. I KNOW YOU DON'T WANT TO HEAR THIS. YOUR REQUEST TO VENT IN OUTSIDE AIR IS DENIED. CAN'T GO INTO THE REASONS RIGHT NOW. YOU HAVE TO TRUST ME ON THIS. I NEED YOU TO WORK UP OTHER OPTIONS. MORE DETAILS TOMORROW. ::
HASKINS

"More tomorrow? Sorry, guys, that don't cut it." He hammered the keys again, infuriated.

:: ATTENTION: HASKINS, OR SOMEONE ELSE LISTENING WHO MIGHT GIVE A RIP: TOMORROW IS NOT GOOD ENOUGH. SARAJANE IS VERY ILL. NEED TO EVACUATE HER NOW. IMMEDIATELY. IMMEDIATELY! REQUEST PERMISSION TO EGRESS HER AND COORDINATE AIR VENTING AT SAME TIME. I'M TRYING TO BE NICE ABOUT THIS. LET'S HAVE COFFEE AND TALK YOU BUTTHEADS. IF YOU DON'T UNLOCK THAT DOOR PRETTY QUICK I *WILL* FIND A WAY. ::
BLOCK

Thirty minutes went by. No response. Block stayed glued to the console, becoming even more impatient and angry. He wanted to throw something, but almost everything in the room was screwed down or bolted to something.

"What in creation are those people doing back there? Playing poker?" He kicked the metal back panel under the console. It responded with a loud *blang*. Finally, after forty-five minutes, the answer came.

TO BLOCK:
:: CLAYTON. CAN'T DO. WE CAN NOT OPEN UP OR ALLOW EGRESS AT THIS TIME. DO THE BEST YOU CAN. YOU'VE GOT TO HOLD IT TOGETHER IN THERE. A LOT IS RIDING ON THIS. I'LL EXPLAIN LATER. ::
HASKINS

"So when is later?! You idiot!" Block was almost shouting, his breathing labored. Another *blang* rang out. He felt like a box of malfunctioning Fourth of July fireworks. His gut was in knots. He didn't want to do what he now had to do. Go see Sarajane—and tell her she was stuck in this rat trap with bad air. And no way out.

At that moment, though Block didn't know it, Pam was wiping pinkish froth from Sarajane's mouth, violently expelled from her lungs by repeated coughs. Pam was near tears, but trying valiantly to hide it.

When Block got to the infirmary, Sarajane was alone, panting, but trying to breathe normally. Pam had left moments before for a quick break, a snack, and a chance to try to compose herself.

Block said nothing at first. He saw Sarajane's pain and the dregs of sticky moisture around her mouth. He walked up and laid a hand on her shoulder.

"How you holdin' up, little lady?"

"Little lady? The air's affecting your brain, Clayton." She coughed again. "You obviously can't see who you're talking to."

He grinned, trying to hold on to his own composure.

"I'm a tough old hen," she said. "You don't have to worry about me. Pam's doing a good job."

"I'm glad you're this spunky."

She coughed again, and swallowed what came up. Block was amazed at her ferocity.

"You just get this air thing straightened out and I'll be up and jumping in no time," she wheezed.

"We're going to fix this, Sarajane. I promise you, we're gonna beat it. I just don't want you to worry. Jimmy and Mai Ker and Willy have got some ideas. I think we can solve it pretty quickly. I know it's tough on you. Just hang in there for me, OK?"

"I'm not hanging in for you, Block. I'm hanging in for me."

"Whatever. Just do it. We'll need your help to get everything back on schedule once we fix this little problem."

"Little problem," she said sarcastically. "You make

it sound like a lousy mosquito bite—instead of a fatal air flaw."

"There's no problem that can't be solved. We just need time. A little time."

"Just another mosquito, huh?" She looked at him and tried to smile.

"Any word from OUTSIDE?" Pam asked as she came back through the door.

"Yeah," Block admitted. Here was the lead-in he needed. "We can't vent any fresh air in. They won't say why. Just that it's impossible. I tell you, I knew they planned this project tight. But I never thought it'd be *this* tight. This borders on crazy."

"Come on, Clayton, face it," Sarajane said, "if it wasn't a little crazy, none of us would have applied."

Pam laughed for the first time in two days. *Odd,* she thought. It was always the worst patient who could make her laugh the quickest. It was the same back when she worked in the hospital Intensive Care Unit. The dying ones, the critically injured—the most desperate—they always seemed to have the wildest sense of humor.

"I'm going back to the Comm.," Block said. "Check in with you girls later."

He walked away relieved. He had managed to slip the bad news in and make his exit. Now he didn't have to try to explain what he couldn't explain, the intransigence of OUTSIDE Control the last few days.

Jerks, he told himself. *Money, that's all it is.* "Has to be money," he mumbled. No right or wrong, just "the success of the project." He shook his head, outraged as he walked to the Comm. Center, hoping against hope for some different message he knew would not be there.

His feet ached. He had been up for nearly 36 hours straight. His body felt like he'd just left a boxing ring, the loser. The air smelled stale, and hostile. His stomach tightened again. He felt a bottomless regret over the day he saw the employment ad for Solarium-3.

14

Wednesday, March 11th

They made a very simple funeral of it. They had put if off now for four days, but it had to be done. Somehow, they needed to get past it.

The service was basically a memorial, since the body had been put into cold storage, for eventual burial OUTSIDE. A thorough autopsy would inevitably have to be done by experts.

Block read from the "Traditional" burial service format, one of several prayer services that had been unobtrusively supplied for them on the last pages of the last appendix to the Solarium-3 team manual. The remaining teammates gathered around in a small, aimless circle in the front yard in Pod 4. They stood, staring at the ground, as if it held something, only half listening. All but one. Sarajane sat propped up in a wheelchair, still too weak to stand.

"William Atchison died in his bed in the early morning hours of March 7 . . ." Block read, as if this was news to the others. He read without feeling, following the format numbly. ". . . of an apparent heart attack."

He stopped. It was too formal. He let the book drop to his side and looked down at the withered grass being mashed down under the toe of his shoe, which seemed a million miles away.

"His only close friends were those of us here. A place devoted to the study of life," he ad-libbed. Ironic, but the right thing to say. The sadness of this statement gnawed at Block's untreated ulcer. "He'll be missed by each of us. Me mostly." He stuffed back the tears. Always the brave leader. He lifted the prayer service back up. It all looked blank except this one phrase which he read out: "May God have mercy on his soul."

Block wasn't sure Willy needed mercy, or deserved it. He asked anyway.

Block realized, the morning of Willy's death, that he probably *was* one of the only real friends Atchison ever had, yet he had let so many years go by without so much as a phone call or letter after their time together in the military. Had it not been for the happenstance of them both applying for the Solarium-3 project, they probably would never have seen each other again.

Maybe that would have been better, Block felt.

What was most unbelievable about the present state of things was that when Block demanded OUTSIDE allow them to send Willy's body out for burial in his hometown of Kansas City, the request was denied. In the last few weeks, the only thing OUTSIDE had excelled in was denial of every reasonable request Block made.

Willy's death was utterly unexpected. He had just turned 48. Pam, under Sarajane's direction, had performed a basic autopsy, excluding the brain. The examination of the heart muscle was sufficiently conclusive, in Sarajane's opinion, to determine the cause of death. Toxicology tests would have to wait until Sarajane felt better. But there was no doubt Atchison's heart muscle had old damage from previous heart attacks, probably minor attacks that went undetected. There was also no doubt that their present situation, the depletion of breathable air, contributed to his death.

They were all feeling the air problem, to a greater or lesser extent. There were still no answers from Haskins, even after Atchison's death was reported. The team's frustration grew by the hour.

With Block's constant attention, Caroline had managed to survive in her little air tent. Most of the other birds, except the larger, heartier varieties, had died throughout the pods.

JIMMY AND Block sat on pool chairs in the Recreation Pod that afternoon after the funeral, in silence. They stared at the still water, smooth as a quiet evening lake. They retreated there from the Research Center, too depressed and disinterested to do any work.

The funeral for Willy had further spoiled what was bound to have been a rotten day anyway. By lunchtime Jimmy's atmospheric readings in the pods were fluctuating, but steadily deteriorating. Their air quality was going down the toilet and Block could not believe OUTSIDE was unwilling to intervene. Surely no scientific research was worth a man's life, not to mention the increasing risk to Sarajane and the rest of them.

Jimmy was ruminating on the same thing.

"I don't understand why they won't help," he said. "They should have done something—before this happened to Will."

Block nodded.

"But he might have gone anyway, Jimmy. The autopsy turned up old damage in his heart—probably been there for years. Don't even know if Willy knew. If he did, he wouldn't let on. William the 2nd—the invincible. His head was harder than a petrified tree."

"So what the heck, Clayton, let it be." Jimmy sighed. "At least he was doing what he wanted. And he was with friends. You especially."

It was a compliment, but all those years Block had ignored Willy after their military service made it sting.

"He died happy, Clayton, in a place he wanted to be. In his sleep, no less. What else could ya want?"

Block's mind grasped the truth of Jimmy's words,

but his heart couldn't accept it. Deeper down he was feeling sorry for himself, not Willy. He was hurting, all those taut feelings bottled up inside. And he felt stuck—more than ever—and not sure what to do next. He wanted to change the subject. He quizzed Jimmy on the status of their "little problem."

"Where do we go now, Jimmy?"

"I don't know. I've gone over it and over it. The nitrogen pressure keeps building and I can't figure out why. And I can't figure out how to combat it. Manipulating gases in small volume in the lab is a piece of cake. Trying to manipulate them in this kind of volume—with the complexity of the pod sizes, and the ventilation system—it's darn near impossible with the equipment I've got." His voice petered out in frustration.

"We talked about direct infusion—the oxygen tanks. We still haven't tried that," Block said.

"Yeah. But once we try it, we've shot our wad. If it doesn't work, we're really sunk."

"So the only real solution is convincing the birdbrains in Omaha to vent in some fresh air."

"It's the best. The quickest. I hate to see the project go down the tubes, too—but we're dangling at the end of the rope here!"

"Well, it's probably pointless," Block said, exasperated, "but I'll try them up again. Maybe if I—"

They both jumped in unison at a high pitched shriek rushing up from behind them. Mai Ker bolted into the pod with panic in her face. Her beautiful light brown skin had gone pale.

"Clayton—Jimmy, hurry! Pam needs you—the infirmary!"

Block launched from his deck chair like a ground-to-air missile and Jimmy flipped his chair backward trying to get his leg over it in pursuit. Mai Ker, on much shorter legs, tried her best to keep up but fell quickly behind.

The two men burst through the infirmary door in unison. Pam Hansen sat on the floor helpless, her legs fanned apart like a child playing marbles. Sarajane lay crumpled over Pam's leg, her face pressed down into a flat ugliness against the hard floor. Spasmodic tears erupted in spurts from Pam's eyes with each gasp of the ever more foul air.

"She's dead, Clayton. Jimmy—she's—" Pam gasped. She fell back into a slump against a chair that moved with her weight.

"What happened?" Jimmy asked, his eyes wide.

"She's gone."

"Oh my God," Block uttered in a despondent whimper, dropping to the floor to check Sarajane. She appeared lifeless.

Jimmy was too stunned to move. Mai Ker ran into him just inside the door and fell against Jimmy like a tree shattered by lightning.

The scene was repulsive, much more grotesque than when they had found Willy curled up on his bed, a hand clutched at his chest, his skin like cool wax, his pants soiled. Pam had been trying to help Sarajane out of bed when she fell. Sarajane struck her head against a counter on the way down, Pam doing her impossible best to break the fall. A trickle of blood streaked Sarajane's forehead and pooled on the white tile.

Block checked Sarajane's neck for a pulse. Nothing. She was absolutely limp.

"Good God . . ." he said quietly, desperately, uncertain whether he was swearing or praying.

From his post by the door, Jimmy supported Mai Ker.

"What happened?" he asked again.

"She just wanted to try to walk a little," Pam gulped. "She just—" She broke off in tears.

Block grasped Pam's shoulders and freed her leg

from beneath Sarajane's heavy, lifeless body. He held her as she sobbed convulsively. She desperately wanted to speak but hope for more words had fled.

Bridget appeared in the door. She had heard the commotion from the Comm. Center and watched three purple dots converge on the two in the infirmary.

In a ghostly echo, she said, "What happened?" The question glided through each mind like the hollow call of a sorrowful eagle reverberating off the walls of a deep canyon.

Pam still couldn't get another word out. Bridget and Mai Ker helped her up and took her to the house. Block and Jimmy put Sarajane's body up on the infirmary bed. The tension which seemed frozen into her body like early rigor mortis told them she had finally suffocated, deprived of sufficient oxygen one moment too long.

None of them were prepared to deal with another death. They were beaten into silence. What was there to say? Sadly they now knew just what to do. They put her onto a gurney—covered with plastic sheeting—and wheeled it to the cold storage in Pod 13. They placed her in a large cooler alongside Willy. A new routine, not found in the Solarium-3 manual. Odd, they felt, that they had been given a burial service, yet no hint of dealing with an actual death. But they were too crushed at the moment to wonder why.

IT WAS an hour later when they all gathered in the living room of the house. There was complete silence for several minutes. They all stared at, and through, each other. Pam finally recomposed herself enough to speak. Her eyelids were swollen and beet red, her nose still drippy. Every third or fourth word was helped out by the back of her hand brushing beneath her nostrils.

"She said she was feeling better. I gave her an injection about two hours earlier. Her orders.

Everything was fine. Her blood pressure was still pretty high. Then she pulled off her oxygen mask, said she wanted to walk a little. Maybe come over to the house for a book. I shouldn't have agreed, but I walked behind her. She's hardly been up out of bed for a week. She seemed OK, talking, joking about her pants sticking to her. Then she started wheezing—high pitched. It was horrid. I tried to hold her up. It was like some invisible thing grabbed her by the throat. Her back straightened like a post. And her knees buckled. We hit the floor and—I couldn't move her . . ." Her voice trailed off. Her eyes were looking for something that wasn't there.

No one spoke. The silence, they knew, would give Pam a chance to breathe. She did, in several forced breaths.

Finally Mai Ker spoke.

"What do you do when the only doctor dies?" Her eyes were empty, too.

Everyone looked at her, recognizing the heartbreaking irony.

"What do we do, Clayton?" Mai Ker pleaded. "It was not in the plan for our doctor to die. Was it? Was this part of their sick plan?" The vacant naïveté in her eyes changed into a look of horror. "Is that it? We're guinea pigs? They just cook us till we all die?!"

Bridget's temper broke. She jumped out of her chair, digging at the carpet like an angry bull looking for a toreador.

"This is garbage! It can't be happening. We're in a research center—not a B-horror movie! Clayton, you've got to end this thing—*now!*"

Now he blew up.

"Watch it, lady! Don't blame this on me! I've done everything I can. They're ignoring me!" he yelled. Bridget's insinuation was intolerable. "You think I haven't tried? Not done enough? You ready to take over?"

"I didn't mean—"

Block, exploding, cut her off.

"It should have ended before Willy died!" he growled. "It *sure* should've ended after he died! I've tried, Bridget! For Sarajane—for all of us. You know I can't open the door from INSIDE!" He fumed and paced, avoiding eye contact with Bridget. A weaker man would have taken a swing at her. In blind anger, he nearly ran into the wall.

Bridget was fuming, too. Jimmy felt helpless but had to break it up.

"Both of you! Stop! This isn't helping!" he almost shouted.

Bridget followed Block and grabbed his arm, turned him, and found his eyes. What he saw was love, not anger. His own anger deflated like a balloon torn open.

"I'm sorry, Bridget." He pulled away and dropped into a chair. "I can't get Omaha to listen. All of you, I'm sorry. I should have made them listen!"

"And maybe . . ." Pam's feeble voice hesitated. ". . . Sarajane and Willy—"

"It doesn't matter!" Block yelled, his temper snapping again. "They're dead!"

He instantly regretted it. The shock wave of his powerful voice whipped Pam's tear stained face and stripped it of all emotion. Block closed his eyes, searching for a way out. Even in combat he had never felt this kind of fear, or anger. He opened his eyes and saw Pam's frozen face. He went over and sat beside her, and took her hand.

"I'm sorry, Pam. It's my fault she's gone. Not yours. I just don't want to think about it right now." He wiped a very few uncontained tears from his face.

Pam's face became solemn, but resolute. She drew a long breath.

"Do whatever you can, Clayton," she told him

quietly. "We can't bring them back." She leaned her head against his shoulder. "I hate this."

Jimmy and Mai Ker, having absorbed all the anguish they could handle, looked at each other. They walked out onto the porch and around the corner of the house, clutching at each other. They both fought back an intolerable mix of emotions that neither could identify or name. They sat together on a porch bench and said nothing.

Bridget took Pam to her room and helped her lay down, offering to take care of dinner. Food was the farthest thing from Pam's mind. She felt physically and emotionally exhausted. The lonely image of Sarajane's final crisis—gasping and collapsing—consumed her until she finally drifted into a sleepy daze.

Bridget went back to the living room. Block was still sitting by Pam's now-empty spot, his eyes fixed on the floor. She walked over and offered a hand.

"I'm sorry, Clayton. I didn't mean to bark."

"I know," he said without looking up.

"But this is cruel. It's insane. They can't keep us locked up in here like this. Like a bunch of lab rats! Enough's enough for God's sake." Disgust permeated every word.

"I'm going to Comm. right now. Come on." He took her hand and kissed it as if he'd been programmed to do this. Bridget reacted with only mild surprise and stroked the back of his neck.

"Come on, toughie," she said.

He got up and they walked quickly to Pod 2.

"I'll write it, you proof it before I send it," he told her.

TO: JOHN HASKINS, *** URGENT PRIORITY ***

cc: TO ALL IN OUTSIDE CONTROL. OR ANYONE WHO GIVES A RIP:

:: SARAJANE IS DEAD. FATAL ASTHMA ATTACK. I AM TERMINATING THE PROJECT IMMEDIATELY. NOTIFY OUTSIDE SECURITY ON-SITE TO OPEN DOORS IMMEDIATELY AND ARRANGE TRANSPORTATION OF REMAINING TEAM MEMBERS FOR DEBRIEFING. REPLY IMMEDIATELY. ::
BLOCK

Bridget leaned over his shoulder and typed.

:: THIS IS NOT NEGOTIABLE. ::
BLOCK/LISTNER

Block squeezed her arm. "Right on the nail-head," he said, and hit the SEND key.

Almost instantly—to their complete astonishment—the terminal beeped three times and a response spit itself onto the screen:

FROM NATHAN DANIELS:
:: CLAYTON: UNDERSTOOD. I'M LOCATING HASKINS. HE'S NOT ON STATION AT THE MOMENT. SIT TIGHT. WE WILL RESPOND QUICKLY. I UNDERSTAND YOUR SITUATION. YOU WON'T LIKE THE RESPONSE. ::
N. DANIELS

"When I see that no-good—"
Bridget cut him off, wrapping her hand tightly over his mouth.
"Clayton. There's a lady present."
Less than ten minutes had passed when the terminal beeped three times again.

TO CLAYTON BLOCK, TEAM LEADER,

SOLARIUM-3
FROM JOHN HASKINS:
CLAYTON. I'M SADDENED BY THIS TRAGIC NEWS. BELIEVE ME I DID NOT WANT THIS. IT'S TIME WE TALK. I NEED TO GET SOME PEOPLE TOGETHER BACK HERE. HAVE YOUR WHOLE TEAM AT COMM. CENTER TOMORROW AT 0700. WE'LL BREAK THE RULES AND VIDEO CONFERENCE. YOU'RE RIGHT IT'S OVER. BUT NOT HOW YOU THINK. CALL ME ON-SCREEN WHEN YOU HAVE EVERYONE THERE IN A.M. THANKS :: HASKINS

"What in the world are they doing now?" Bridget said, maddened.

"Who the heck knows. All I know is tomorrow, I'm out of here! And you're going with me!"

"Is this a proposal?"

He looked stunned.

"I don't know."

"I accept."

He spun his chair around, catching Bridget behind the knees and dropping her gracefully into his lap. She smiled.

"So how do you want to spend your last night in this hell-hole?" she asked.

"With you." He kissed her, taking her completely by surprise.

"Well," she said. "I guess we've both been waiting a long time for this bus to arrive."

"So let's get on it."

"Later, cowboy. I promised Pam I'd make supper for everyone." The smile left her face. "Everyone who's left."

They walked to the house. Bridget checked on Pam. She was sound asleep, exhausted from the strain of caring for Sarajane for so many days. She rejoined Block in the kitchen and they worked on supper. There was no rush. Pam needed to sleep, and Jimmy and Mai Ker were nowhere in sight.

JIMMY AND Mai Ker were wandering aimlessly through the pods. It was late in the day and the Visitor Center had closed. There had only been two or three OUTSIDE Looky-Lous today, and they were long gone.

"It's funny," Jimmy was saying, "have you noticed how few visitors there are these days?"

"I guess we're just not news anymore."

"Would be if anybody knew what was really going on in here."

"I'm sure they're keeping everybody in the dark out there," Mai Ker said. "Why would they spill the beans that their big project is going down the sewer?"

They found themselves in Pod 11 where most of the small animals were housed. Mai Ker went to the rabbit cages and talked to several of them like they were best friends. Jimmy tagged along, lost in a myriad of feelings that he would just as soon have left behind in the house.

He looked at the bunny rabbits in their cages. Two of the largest ones looked tired, and not very animated.

"This is really horrifying," he said. "I mean, I came in here with all kinds of dreams and expectations. I was gonna make the world better—you know? Perfect some new technology, learn all kinds of new, important things. Maybe help feed all the starving people in the world. And whoosh—it all goes up in smoke."

"Not all of it, Jimmy," Mai Ker said, in her ever-optimistic manner. "You have done good here. We all have. Now it's just a matter of sharing it. Even with all this trouble, and quitting early, we've learned a lot about running a closed ecosystem. Someday it will pay off. Don't you think?"

"Yeah, like how to poison your friends with perfectly fouled-up air."

"You always look at the bad things, Jimmy. Look at the good things. There's always bad things to see, but there's good, too. You've got to look though. It's harder to see the good things."

"Like right now," he groaned.

She reached up and put her hands around his neck and hung there. He kissed her.

"Look," she said," just pretend you're one of these bunnies. They sit there, looking around. They don't know why they're here. But they're alive. And they take care of each other the best way they can."

"Great life. If you like living in a cage."

"Stop it!" she said. "This will be over. Clayton will do something. There's more life ahead, Jimmy. For you and me together—if that's what you really want."

"You know it is, Mai Ker," he said with a smile. "That's what keeps me going. We'll be outta here soon. Two big paychecks, and me and you. We'll go hide on an island somewhere. And raise bunnies."

"As long as the island isn't covered with plastic."

"Yeah. One that's open to that big, beautiful sky."

They looked out at the darkening evening sky. The usually reddish-orange sunset had turned to a deep bluish-purple.

"Looks funny, doesn't it?" he asked.

"What?"

"The sunset. See how purple it looks? I've never seen it that color before."

"You just haven't noticed," she said. "It's seemed more purple the last few weeks. Weather or something. Or maybe our Stellar plastic is tinting from too much sun."

"Well, I've had too much Stellar plastic. You're the only thing that's made these last few weeks bearable. I love you. I want us to stay together forever."

"Forever's a pretty long time."

"Then till we die," he allowed. "And if Clayton doesn't get something done, that won't be that much longer."

"Clayton will get it done. If anybody can," she said. "We should head back for supper. They're probably waiting."

He laughed. "Fat chance."

"Slim chance," she said, correcting him.

"Let's go."

THE AROMA of supper filled the air as they got close to the house. Bridget and Block had made a spiced hamburger casserole and canned carrots. There weren't a lot of fresh vegetables since the crops had all suffered so much. But for Jimmy the aroma of the casserole helped shelve the day's awful tragedy. They all desperately needed a little refreshment.

Bridget woke Pam up and helped her into the dining room in a semi-conscious state. Pam ate without speaking a word. Her eyes moved back and forth from her plate to a vacant spot on the table six inches in front of her plate. No one else spoke much either.

"Last supper here," Bridget said.

"That mean we're finally out of here tomorrow?" Jimmy asked.

"Yes," Block answered. "I told them no more stalling. Haskins called a big meeting for O-seven-hundred. All of us. He's gonna tell us why they've been such pig-headed jerks."

"I can hardly wait to hear that," Jimmy said.

15

Thursday, March 12th

An urgent morning sun pierced the pods through a blue-tinted sky. Just after 6:00 o'clock the team was up and hurriedly getting ready for the teleconference.

After the dishes were done last night, Bridget and Block had curled up on the couch and tried to read. Both failed, not for lack of interest in the books but because of their interest in each other. The belief this would be their last night locked up in the Solarium caused the magnetism that had developed between them to suddenly flower like petals unfolding under the lens of time-lapse camera.

Much the same happened with Jimmy and Mai Ker. They took another long walk through the pods after supper, a kind of farewell tour. Like Pam and Willy not many days before, Jimmy and Mai Ker ended up in Pod 12 by the ocean and laid down on a quiet, narrow beach, soft artificial waves splashing nearby and faint starlight hiding beyond the shielding Stellar plastic. The eyes of hundreds of thousand distant stars twinkled insistently at them, as if trying to get their attention. The dim night lights in the pod dome blocked the light of the lesser ones. The brightest stars winked playfully at the two humans there on the sand light-years away, winked as if they knew some important secret. But Mai Ker and Jimmy paid little attention to the stars after five minutes.

Pam, still in an emotional stupor, had half-slept through supper and gone straight back to bed.

Despite a giddy anticipation about good news from

Haskins, all had slept heavily, candles whose wax was nearly used up. Drifting overnight in other lands and times, transported on dreams that made little sense, they vanished into the warmth of their lovely Victorian home, resting and content as if they could be there forever.

But at breakfast, anxiety still creeping around like roaches, a brief spat erupted over who was really to blame for their predicament—OUTSIDE, or themselves. The argument went nowhere because no one really knew and they all kept changing sides.

"It doesn't really matter at this point—does it?" asked Pam, barely awake but trying as usual to mediate. "We'll know in a few minutes. Can't we just enjoy our breakfast in peace?"

Bridget, through a mouthful or cereal, agreed. The argument ended abruptly. They shoveled down their food which made Pam instantly happier.

They made it into their chairs in front of the video-conference camera in the Comm. Center just before 7:00 o'clock. Bridget keyed the camera into wide-angle mode so Haskins and his partners-in-crime in Omaha would be able to see all five remaining faces clearly.

OUTSIDE Control beneath the Visitors Center linked the teleconference with Omaha at 7:00 a.m. straight up. Haskins' benevolent face, like a late blooming dandelion, popped up simultaneously on four large monitors.

"So here we are, John, as ordered," Block said with a tone that could not be mistaken for anything other than bitterness.

"Good morning, team," Haskins said. He was trying to force a smile. It wasn't working.

The face of Nathan Daniels hovered a little to his left.

No one responded.

"We've held off having this talk because—until

now—I wasn't sure there was any real profit in having it." Haskins spoke like a father about to tell his kids about the birds and the bees. "Up till yesterday, we had every hope that you, in there, would be able to restore your normal atmospheric balance."

"Well, John," Jimmy butted in, "we fooled you then."

Block gave him a hushing look.

"We're concerned about your survival," Haskins said impassively.

"John," Block told him, "our survival at this moment depends on you unlocking that door and getting us out of here! It's becoming a mausoleum."

Haskins didn't respond to this, but went on.

"I know what you're all thinking. And you won't want to hear what I have to tell you." His voice cracked. "And you'll probably think I'm the biggest bastard on Earth for keeping this from you for so long."

"Not the biggest, John, just the best," Block said.

"Enough, Clayton" Bridget interrupted. "Can we just get on with this? What's the holdup, John? When are we getting out?"

"I know—" Haskins broke off again and let out a frustrated sigh with a look that no one in Solarium-3 took for meanness.

Suddenly all of their expressions changed. Haskins' eyes became wet.

"I know you just want me to let you out of there. So, here's the big news of the day. I can do that. If that's what you decide. But when we're done talking, you may feel differently."

"Drop the Greek, John. We don't speak it in here," Block said in a controlled voice.

Mai Ker, with her usual innocence, asked the obviously pregnant question, but a deep caution was in her voice.

"Why would we not want you to let us out?"

Haskins, shadowed by Daniels, frowned across the four monitors. His face changed to that of a slave who had just been tortured and whipped. His voice became grave. His lips and cheeks quivered.

"I'll make this as simple as I can. I know you've all gone through a lot of hell the last six weeks. Atchison's death, and now Sarajane. Believe me, we're as hurt by this as you. And we're just as stuck as you are. Maybe worse. It's been no picnic out here, either."

"John," Pam said with rusty agitation in her voice, "you obviously want to say something. Say it! What's so terrible you can't just say it?"

Haskins' steeled gaze went to the table in front of him as he rubbed damp palms together.

"Pam. You can't begin to guess what 'terrible' means."

"Is this a game show? Are we solving a riddle?" Jimmy demanded.

"Shut up, Jimmy," Haskins said bluntly, but with the look of a defeated general. A deep darkness hung about him and was somehow transmitted over the teleconference screen, infecting the room where the Solarians sat. They leaned toward the screens as if watching a horror film, gripped with fear, seeing the great dread that enslaved Haskins' face. Nathan Daniels' eyes were closed tightly, as if he could not watch.

"OK," Haskins finally said. "I'm sorry. I just don't know how to start." He pulled his tie loose as if it were strangling him and unbuttoned the top of his shirt. He looked sideways at Daniels again, whose eyes were still closed. No help there. He looked back into the camera.

"I hope nobody's standing up."

The five Solarians looked at each other, each face a large question mark.

"Let's go to the beginning. Do any of you remember last May? There were widespread power outages, almost simultaneous. Affected every continent."

"I remember it," Bridget said, "vaguely."

"About a month before you went INSIDE. The 13th of May, to be exact. Power failures affected every country in both hemispheres. In quick succession. If you remember, we were all at a loss. No apparent cause. Lots of speculation in the scientific communities. Maybe it was just a huge series of coincidences. Or a chain reaction failure—a domino effect across the major power grids. Of course, no one ever explained how such a failure could jump whole oceans."

"So?" Jimmy prodded.

"Stay with me, Jimmy. This gets a little complicated."

"Can't be as complicated as our life in here these days," he said snidely.

Haskins gave him a long-distance scowl but managed to control himself.

"No, Jimmy. Actually, it's a lot worse."

It was obvious to the Solarians that Haskins was dead serious, and not enjoying this conversation at all. "Here's the rest. About that time—well, now we know it was exactly the same time—Earth passed through a filmy cloud of some unknown matter in space. Some of the more sensitive telescopes detected it. Mainly radio telescopes. But even our best instruments couldn't accurately measure the stuff, and our best scientists couldn't describe it. And they still can't tell us what it was. Particles, space dust, radiation, some unknown gas—nobody knows. Something we've never encountered before. The honest to God truth is, we don't know *what* it was."

Haskins paused, wiping his forehead with what looked like an already damp handkerchief. He looked like the biggest loser of the biggest quiz show of all time. The Solarians sat in silence, afraid now to look at each other, afraid to ask another question. As if awakening, Haskins went on.

"Anyway, what seems to have happened—when we passed through this cosmic cloud last May—everything changed, upstairs. Whatever this stuff was, it altered every layer of the atmosphere. The various layers started changing. Degrading. Almost imperceptibly, from the highest levels on down. It was slow at first, but it's increasing. The different layers of the ionosphere are becoming unstable, erratic, breaking down. It's raining huge quantities of hydrogen and helium ions into the lower atmosphere. Lower down the nitrogen pressure has increased. We haven't figured that out yet. But that's part of what you've been experiencing. INSIDE."

He looked at Daniels, whose eyes were open again. Daniels spoke slowly, trying to help.

"It's like a flood of nitrogen sinking into the breathable level of the atmosphere. Like poison. And we can't stop it. It's causing all kinds of unpredictable chemical reactions, and normal oxygen molecules are deteriorating. That's the basics. As simple as we can put it. Our air is falling apart. Just like yours in there. Out here it's become almost unbreathable. Toxic."

Jimmy began to tremble as if a large hypodermic needle of gasoline had been shot through his veins. This sounded all too familiar. In an instant, the confused information that had been flooding his brain the last few weeks began to fall into place, and make sense. His mind still tried to reject it. He had demanded the truth. But he wasn't ready for this. He remembered how the number of their OUTSIDE visitors had been dwindling. He tried to form a mental picture of what must be going on out there. When he spoke, there was deep apology in his voice.

"You're not lying about this."

"No, Jimmy," Haskins said with a huge sense of

relief at finally finding the words. "I'm not lying about this. So far, over 850,000 have died. That's just North America. Mostly elderly people, children, asthmatics. People with weak respiratory systems."

Each of the team was trying to picture 850,000 caskets. Many of them small.

Jimmy sank against his chair, his jaw taut, his tongue pressed against his teeth. Bridget's eyes clamped shut, a futile attempt to hold in the swelling tears. They all sat frozen, stunned beyond belief.

Haskins continued like an undertaker carefully putting makeup on the corpse.

"We've tried everything. Nearly every lab and research facility in the world has been working on this since we realized what was happening. But we're no closer to any answers."

The lights all came on at once in Jimmy's brain, like someone who has just figured out a magic trick.

"Of course. That's what you had us do back in September. Those atmospheric tests. That was part of the research."

"Yes. One part of many, Jimmy. With the limited understanding we had of the problem at that point— about this cosmic cloud-matter stuff—we were trying to reproduce INSIDE what we thought had happened in the atmosphere OUTSIDE. Thought maybe we could speed up the process. Observe the whole thing in a controlled environment. We were trying to reproduce the same altered electrostatic and ionic and chemical changes we were seeing out here. See if we could get a handle on it, and find a fix."

"I don't believe this," Block said. He was going numb.

"Those special tests I sent you in September, Clayton, that was their purpose. We analyzed your test results closely. We were searching for clues. But they just weren't there. It's gotten much worse. It may be too late. With the chaotic changes in the ionosphere, Earth's magnetic fields have changed drastically, too. And of course that's affecting the atmosphere even more. It's like a chain reaction, but all unstable. Uncontrollable. The whole world's in a tailspin."

"So we were your guinea pigs," Bridget said with controlled fire in her voice.

A guilty nod of Haskins' head acknowledged her accusation.

"Yes. You could put it that way. But back in September, we hoped that in the Solarium, because you're a small, closed system, we hoped the atmospheric changes could be managed and a control protocol found. We could watch things happen. If there was any fix, we were more likely to discover it in there than out here."

Block's mind was racing now, but working. A sudden insight hit him with force.

"But you missed one important piece," he said. "Didn't you?"

"Yes, Clayton. We did. We weren't certain, but we were pretty sure the problem started in May. What we missed was the fact that by Seal-In last June your air was already tainted. So when we upped the ante with those tests in September—we aggravated your situation."

Pam was listening intently, not realizing she was holding her breath half the time. She gulped in several quarts of air.

"Your air was already in trouble." Haskins admitted. "We made it worse."

"You idiots!" Mt. Block erupted. "How could you possibly miss such a simple fact!" He threw the pencil he'd been using to take notes. It bounced off one of the monitors, leaving a faint gray mark over Haskins' right eye. "Why didn't you tell me before I put my people at risk!" he hollered.

Haskins was short and swift with his back swing.

"Don't you get it? *We're all at risk!*" Haskins shouted, on his feet now. His head was gone. Just shoulders and a torso paced close to the camera. "Everything. Every species, animal, plant. Everything! We're being roasted alive in a dying atmosphere. Wiped off the face of the earth. It *is* going to happen. Unless we find a solution!"

Bridget grabbed Block's arm.

"Let him talk, Clayton," she said. "I want to hear the rest." She looked bleakly back at the monitors. "All of it."

The predictable *blang* rang out from the kick panel near Block's feet. It took him several moments to rein his temper back in. There was silence on both ends of the electronic connection as the noisy vibrations of the kick panel subsided. At the same time, Nathan Daniels coaxed Haskins back into his chair.

"All right. I'm sorry, John," Block finally said like an overgrown kid trying not to pout.

"It's all right, Clayton. I expected this. We've kept all of you in the dark for a long time. I guess I thought we were doing you a favor." His expression showed he was sincere in this but still not certain it had been the right thing. "Look. You've probably noticed it's been hotter than expected INSIDE, even with the cooling systems. It's getting that way everywhere. As the atmosphere is changing, it's warming. Fast. We're not sure why yet. The higher nitrogen maybe? More solar radiation getting through? We're not sure. Maybe the gates of hell have cracked open." It was an attempt at a jest but was not remotely funny. "Whatever. Anyway, with the atmosphere heating up so is everything else. We're getting worried about coastal flooding. A lot of the ice is starting to melt. But—well, the fact is, nobody much cares. Our team here in Omaha doesn't think anyone will last long enough to see the coasts go under." A fatal dejection had crept into Haskins' otherwise professional voice.

Pam looked around. Her teammates were silent, engrossed. She couldn't stand the silence.

"You have no idea what caused this?" Pam asked.

"Nothing certain, Pam. One research group thinks that cloud in space could have been triggered by a supernova. Millions of light-years, and eons, away. One that went undetected. An explosion of that magnitude—nobody really knows what it could create, or throw out into space. It would have happened long before we had telescopes to watch it, and the debris trail only now reached us. It was essentially invisible. No one saw this coming."

He paused and collected himself.

"Other physicists think we just ran through something in space we can't identify yet. Let alone describe. It's off all the maps of science. Off everything we presently understand. And we don't know how to respond."

"So why did it affect the atmosphere?" Jimmy asked.

"We don't know. When we hit this space cloud last May—or it hit us—it triggered bizarre electromagnetic reactions. That's apparently what caused all the blackouts. Oh, the other thing. To make matters worse, the breakdown of oxygen molecules is adding ozone in the atmosphere. That should've slowed how much ultraviolet radiation is getting through. But for some reason it didn't." He paused. "At least I'll go out with a good tan." He tried to force a laugh.

Block shook his head.

"What *hasn't* gone wrong, John?" he asked. He was swallowing pride, ashamed of his earlier outburst.

"Well, Clayton, all in all, it's a rotten time to be alive." He tried to clear the dry phlegm out of his throat. He sipped some water to wash the cottony paste from his mouth. There was nearly a full half-minute of silence. Haskins was patient, knowing this all had to settle in. He turned and spoke quietly to Daniels, then looked back.

"How's your air in there today?" he asked.

"Stinks," Jimmy said. "Tell me something. I'm probably stupid to ask this. 'Cause I probably know the answer. But after we did those tests in September, how come our sensors didn't start triggering? To alert us to the bad air?"

"You're right. You probably know why," Haskins said without blinking.

"Tell us anyway," Block said, shaking his head slowly.

"We discussed it. For several days. We didn't want to mislead you. But we were afraid if we spilled the whole thing—you'd back out on us. Maybe refuse to do the tests. We couldn't risk that. We needed you. So we decided to keep you out of the loop. For a while."

"Doesn't exactly answer my question," Jimmy said.

"Well, don't get angry, Jimmy. But we reprogrammed the air alert sensors. We changed the sensitivity so they wouldn't go off. We had to, if we were going to keep you in the dark. We expected the air might worsen. We've watched it carefully. But none of us expected what happened to Will. And by the time we knew how sick Sarajane was, it didn't matter. The air out here was a lot worse than in there."

"And you managed to kill two of us," Bridget said. She had never in her life had the urge to strangle someone, until now. "If we'd known, we could've taken precautions. We all could've been on oxygen."

"Didn't save Sarajane, did it?" Haskins asked bluntly. "I know how unfair it seems. All I can say is we've been juggling the fate of the whole human race out here and—well, the reality is, you're just one small part of that."

It was cold, but it was true. And they all knew it.

"I saw the preliminary autopsy results you sent out on Atchison," he continued. "Looks like his time was just about up anyway. Just the normal work stress in there could have killed him. Let alone the bad air."

"Well, you can't excuse Sarajane's death with that line," Bridget retorted.

"No," he said quietly, "and I'm sorry. But she never disclosed her asthmatic condition to us until she was INSIDE. It was too late. And she would have died out here a lot sooner. A doctor, for heaven's sake. You would've thought she'd've been more honest about it." He gave a sympathetic shrug. "Look, we rescreened all of you. We made our best guesses. When we had you run the tests in September, we were confident all of you would be fine. We miscalculated."

"By a mile," Bridget spit out. She got up and started for the closest door.

Block yelled at her.

"Bridget! Where'd'ya think you're going?"

She stopped. She looked out the door at the grass, the pod roof, the overly-blue sky. She turned and looked around at her friends, her teammates, and Haskins on the monitors. Her eyes went to the floor. Drops of sweat and tears tarnished her face.

"I don't know." This hit her hard. She felt suddenly out of breath.

"I don't blame you for being angry, Bridget," Haskins said a little louder, hoping she would reappear on his monitor. "You won't believe me, but I'm pretty angry at myself. I was ultimately in charge of this thing. When the Pentagon came to me and asked for our help—well, I could hardly say no."

"And when was that?" Block asked him.

"Well, actually, it was just a couple of days before we hired all of you," Haskins admitted.

"And you didn't tell us," Block said slowly and

accusingly.

"Couldn't. Top secret. You know how it goes." Haskins wished he was anywhere else at this moment. "Look, everything's become a rotten mess-up. We were trying to understand cause and effect. And find the fix. We used you. Yes, we used you. But a lot was at stake. You understand that? We had to have you run those tests. And risk the outcome. Everything was on the line." He was breathing hard like he had just run a sprint. "Like I said, we miscalculated."

Bridget came back to her chair. Her face edged back into his picture, her eyes red.

"Remind me to write you a forgiveness card at the end of eternity." Her head started to go down on the console, but she held it up.

"How's everything else? Besides the air?" Haskins asked, trying to change the subject.

Jimmy again snapped at him.

"It all stinks, too."

There was a long pause on both sides of the cameras. Haskins finally popped the question.

"So. You can come out if you want. Today. And join us." Another pause. "Is that what you want?"

Block looked at the others. Nothing but blank faces, abandoned children looking for a mother. They now knew the final meaning of "tailspin."

"Well?" Block asked his team. Nothing. "I guess we'll have to talk about it, John."

"Yeah. If I were in there, I'd want to talk, too."

"How much time can we have?" Jimmy asked, not understanding the paradox of his question.

"Time," Haskins said, pathos in his eyes. "You don't have much time." His eyes narrowed. "On the other hand, if you can somehow fix your air in there—you may have all the time in the world. Compared with us."

It seemed like the completely wrong word but Block

said it anyway.

"Thanks," he said, still looking at the others. "We'll be talking about this real quick, John."

"I know it sounds hollow. But I really do wish you the best, my friends," Haskins assured them. "We're being crushed under the same avalanche." He paused. "Let me know what you decide."

"Yeah. We will," said Block.

Haskins disappeared from the monitors. Block keyed off their camera and microphone. His eyes scanned his teammates. No one made eye contact. It was too much for any of them to take in.

Block's mind felt numb, and like a stranger. He slid his fingertips back and forth along the edge of the console, as if testing to see if his senses still worked. An impossible weight had just fallen on his shoulders. Inexplicably, his mind raced into his distant past to, of all things, a Sunday school lesson: the first time he saw a picture of Jesus on the cross. The eyes of his mind focused not on the cross, but the face.

Must be like what you felt, Block supposed, *just before they drove the nails.*

16

Saturday, March 14th

Block sat by himself on a bench by their ocean. Caroline would have followed but was still cooped up in her oxygen tent.

It was early afternoon. A day and a half had gone by since they had heard the devastating truth. Much of the time he had stayed close to Bridget but this afternoon he needed to be alone. The whole human race was in crisis, but most pressing at the moment was that his own soul was in crisis.

His thoughts wandered and drifted and it was hard to focus on anything very long. Childhood memories continued to vault to the forefront of his mind. Considering the sizeable man he had grown into, his teammates would have been surprised that as a young teen he was the "class wimp." Sitting here now, aimlessly watching the artificial waves, he felt agonizingly like that little wimp again. The news from Haskins had triggered many bad memories, memories of feeling useless, helpless.

The ocean here in Pod 12 had become a refuge for several of the team. The soothing sound of the waves brought brief moments of respite from the terror of the decision that lay before them. How could they stay, knowing everyone OUTSIDE would die? How could they leave, when staying might offer the only glimmer of hope for survival of the human race? The questions were too large, the implications too immense. Some moments they tried not to think of it at all. But that was more daunting than facing the questions themselves.

Block's emotions were in disarray. As he looked out through the pod, the world seemed a blank, empty page. He sat, staring, like a writer with nothing more to say. His bare toes plowed grooves into the sand. He peered down at the grains of sand, particles that were nothing more than an impossibly large collection of the leftovers of life, the ground-down remains of millions of years of sea life, remnants of the shells of mindless creatures crushed into tiny specks over eons, washed against the land, buried and reburied in ancient fields, superheated into solid rock in the hills of time.

Block's soul cringed as his mind considered this. The immensity of time and the shortness of what lay before them. The scientist retreated, the bare-footed man stood forth to challenge life. What hand had wrought such wonders as the world they had known? What hand now brought such dread?

He thought of another inland beach, around Washington Park Lake in south central Denver where he grew up. Home was a small, unimposing house on Downing Street opposite the park. The park was beautiful most of the year and had been a haven for him as a youngster, as Pod 12 had now become. The lake was always crummy and dirty except when it froze in the winter and became a popular ice rink. In the summer, bored to tears, Block would sit along the small beach digging in the shallow sand—which was half Denver dirt—looking for souvenir bottle caps, stray pennies, or whatever other childhood treasures he might find.

He spent most of his days alone like that, after school, or on long, solitary summer days. He often scouted the park and knew every inch of it. He especially loved the treetops where he risked many dangerous climbs. There was a rickety, abandoned tree house that hovered precariously in thin air over the roof of the large winter warming house along the south side of the lake. The tree house was the crow's nest of his sailing frigate from which he plied imaginary seas.

His adventures in "Wash Park" insulated him from a noisy and contentious home life, where mom and dad rarely shut up at each other long enough to even notice the four kids, let alone play with them. He had made only one close friend, Robby. And Robby's first trip into the chaos of Block's home life was his last. After this, Block's goal was to spend as much time away from his house as possible, usually at Robby's house, where people talked rather than yelled and where parents regularly hugged their children.

Tears welled in his eyes. His mind drifted back yet further to when he was only three or four. It was late afternoon. He went to the kitchen looking for cookies just before Christmas one year and found his mother crying loudly. A neighbor woman tried to console her. He never knew the reason for those tears, but the image was stuck in his mind forever. Her sadness was so different from her anger, though she had trouble expressing either.

Why all this popped into his mind now he couldn't fathom. He bent by the shore and splashed warm water over his head as if to douse these thoughts. He sat in the sand. His mind wandered even further back to a deeply rooted memory. No sight, no vision, just a sensation of perfect comfort and security, cuddled on his mother's shoulder as she rocked gently in the old, white rocker that sat on their back porch. This was early on, when she still cherished his presence, before her depression swept all real feeling under some mental mat.

He found himself now rocking slowly back and forth, his knees drawn up into folded arms, water lapping around his feet.

Bridget came up behind quietly, and said his name very softly so as not to startle him. The sound flowed down his neck like his mother's breath. Bridget stopped several feet away and said again, "Clayton?"

When he didn't answer, she knelt alongside him and caressed his head and neck.

"What'ya thinking about?"

"Nothing," he replied. He felt frozen in time.

"Pretty solemn for 'nothing,'" she said.

Kneeling there, Bridget remembered herself running as a child on a beach along the northern Pacific coast, on one of the few vacations she and her parents had ever taken. There was the image of her father tossing sand in her hair, and her mother's melodic laugh nearby. She remembered tumbling into the cold water, and her father picking her up in a dance-like move. Pure delight, her memory told her, to have so much fun, to roll, to wrestle, with no one needing to win.

The memories and images soothed them both, distracting them from the problems at hand.

"It's time," she said. "The others will be waiting."

Clayton's somber baritone voice sounded stronger than it had for two days.

"I've decided. Before we do anything else, we're going to bury them. Over in number ten."

Bridgette was taken off guard.

"You're assuming we're going to stay," she said. "We haven't decided that yet."

"Let's go find out." He pulled something from his pocket. It was a small, rolled-up piece of notebook paper, twisted into a makeshift ring. "Here. I want you to have this. As a promise." He pushed it onto her left ring finger.

Bridget stared at it but Block immediately stood, took her hands and lifted her to her feet.

"Come on." He led her toward the podwalk, crossed through #10 and #6 and up onto the porch of the house. It was one of the most unusual engagements in history.

They found Pam sitting by herself in the Victorian

porch swing.

She, too, was somber, as if she'd lost a husband, the one she never married.

"Where's Mai Ker and Jimmy?" Bridget asked.

"Haven't seen them for a while," Pam said. "Is it time?"

"Yeah," Block said.

"They're probably walking again."

"I'll look," Bridget said. "Maybe you two could put a snack together in the dining room."

Block and Pam nodded in unison and went in.

JIMMY AND Mai Ker had their boots off, splashing feet in the swimming pool in Pod 5, blocked from the view of Pod 4 by the pool bar directly behind them. Mai Ker kicked away an inflatable pool mattress that had drifted by her feet.

"Why are we here, Jimmy?"

"At the pool?"

She gave him a wrinkled look, not sure if he was trying to be funny or was just that much out of touch with her thoughts.

"In this place," she said. Her lungs shuddered. "What brought us here?"

"Bad luck?"

"Was it? But maybe John Haskins is right. Maybe it is good luck. If we can survive. Not like everyone—out there."

"Yeah." His vocabulary shrunk at times of anxiety. "Look, Mai Ker. If we're gonna have a chance, we have to do something drastic. Fast. If we're going to stay."

"What's the point in leaving?" she asked. "We know what that means. Staying is the right thing."

He gave silent consent with a nod. He seemed far away for several moments.

"I've been thinking," he finally said. "Of a way.

I've got some ideas."

"Me, too." She looked at him. "We have to decide, Jimmy. We're just stalling. And it's not helping."

Bridget appeared at the podwalk entrance from Pod 6. Thinking the pair was somewhere in one of the animal pods she had headed toward Pod 10, but crossing through Pod 6 she caught sight of Jimmy and Mai Ker in #5 out of the corner of her eye.

"We're ready, you guys. Can you join us?"

"Right behind you," Jimmy said.

Pam and Block had chips, chocolate bars and soda on the table when the other three reached the dining room. The decision was pressing in on everyone's mind. Every minute they waited before confronting it was becoming unbearable. Besides, they had promised Haskins a quick decision, and that was two days ago.

Block, the steadfast but shaken team leader, began. Bridget knew his thoughts, the others did not. He began cautiously, not wanting his words to sway the others.

"All right. We've been talking this over. We have to let Haskins know."

Pam looked grim.

"I can't do this, Clayton," Pam said. "I just can't make a decision like this. We should just leave it in God's hands."

Block looked doubtful.

"Maybe his hands put us here."

"So, you mean he put this decision in our hands?" Bridget asked.

"Well, yeah. When you put it like that," Block said. "Unless we're going to blame him for everything we do from now on."

"I don't mean that, Clayton," Pam said. She began to tremble. "All I know is, I can't decide."

"Look, Pam," Bridget said, "if it makes it any easier, Clayton and I are leaning toward staying."

"Bridget—" Block interrupted.

"I know, Clayton," she said. "I just want to make it easier for her."

"No!" Pam said intensely. "It may be easy for you two. You've got a reason to stay. And Mai Ker and Jimmy. They've got a reason, too. But not me . . ." Her voice died out. She stood and walked out of the room.

Jimmy started to get up to go after her but Mai Ker pulled him back into his seat.

"Let her alone, Jimmy. Let her have some time."

Pam fled, bawling, to the infirmary, half hoping she might still find Sarajane lying there. From here she wandered to the animal sheds, seeking some kind of life, someone who wouldn't ask any questions or demand any decisions of her. Then, like a branch snapped from a tree by a violent wind, she bolted at a hard run into Pod 10 and ran through #3 and #2 toward the entry pod. She grabbed at the INSIDE door handle of #1. She pulled violently, shouting.

"Bastards! Let me out of here. I'm not gonna die in this hell!" She pulled at the handle wildly, but nothing budged. The door, held shut by triple locks, didn't even quiver. Pam smashed her forehead against the Stellar plastic window in the top of the door, tearing a tiny laceration over her left eye. She didn't feel it. She repeatedly punched the intercom switch by the door, but Control OUTSIDE offered no response.

"Bastards!" Her voice trailed off into a whimper. Tears cascaded down her cheeks. Sparkles of blood wet her forehead.

The others heard the noise from Pod 4 and ran to restrain her. Jimmy unluckily reached her first. He was met with a kick to his shins.

"Leave me alone!" Pam roared in a threadbare voice.

Jimmy pulled her into a bear hug, and held on. She tried to knee him in the groin but missed.

"Pam, there's no need for this," Jimmy said, trying

to console her. Block tried to help but Jimmy pushed him back.

"I wanna die! I just wanna die," Pam moaned. "I don't want to think about it anymore. Who cares whether it's in here or out there?"

"I care, Pam," Jimmy said softly

"We all care," Bridget said. "Come on back with us."

Pam let out such a long, painful sigh the others thought for a second she may actually have died there in Jimmy's arms.

"Let me go," she finally said in a pitiful voice.

"I'm not letting you go till you calm down," Jimmy said.

More than calm, she was virtually limp. Jimmy released his grip. Pam looked at them with terrible shame in her eyes.

"It's not you guys, it's not you," she whimpered.

"We know," Bridget said. "Come on Pam, it's going to be OK." She saw the bit of blood over Pam's eye. "Look, you cut your head. Let's go put something on it."

She started back toward the house and Pam followed as if tied by a tether. The others came behind.

Jimmy saw that Mai Ker was shaking slightly as she walked.

"You OK?" he asked.

She shook her head *No*.

"Come on, what is it?" he pressed.

She spoke quietly as they walked.

"I was trying to be brave about all this," her voice quivered. "I felt pretty good. Then when Pam went haywire. It shook me." She stopped and turned to him. "I'm scared, Jimmy."

"Mai, we'll figure this out. You know we can. We'll find a way around this thing."

She took his hand and squeezed it hard as they

walked back to the house.

"Let's sit in the living room," Block said, hoping to ease the tension. "Look, we're all shot. This thing's eating us up—like a boogeyman. We have to come to a decision. The sooner we do, the better we'll be."

Pam had regained control of herself but she again looked exhausted. Bridget cleaned her forehead and stuck a small bandage over the cut.

"Clayton," Pam said hesitantly, "is it all one way, or nothing? I mean, can some of us leave, and others stay?"

Block frowned. He hadn't even thought of this option.

"We can't do it," Jimmy said. "Too dangerous."

"Why?" Pam asked.

"Once we open that outer door—even one time, even for a short time—we'll further contaminate our air. It's worse out there. We'd be sucking in more problems."

"But Pod one is an airlock," she said.

"Yeah, in normal conditions," Jimmy said. "But if the inner seals aren't perfect, once that outer door opens, the risk of contamination is there. We'd be right in the same boat with everybody OUTSIDE. Either we all go, or we all stay."

Block frowned.

"I'm afraid Jimmy's right."

"Well," Bridget said. "So there it is."

Several moments of silence followed. Then Pam nodded, trapped, yet relieved.

"OK. I say we stay," she said.

"And I," Mai Ker added.

"Bridget already gave away our position," Block said. "Jimmy?"

"Mai Ker stays, Jimmy stays," he said with a smile.

They all let this soak in. The indescribable devil that had terrorized them for two days lay slain at their feet, foul, but gone.

"All right, then," Block said, trying to regain command of the jangled mass of emotions in the room. "I'll let Haskins know."

"I wonder what he'll think," Jimmy said.

"Does it matter, Jimmy?" Block asked.

"No. I just wonder."

"And we've got to make some fast decisions about the air in here," Block said. "What we tried back in January obviously didn't work. We need a better plan, everyone needs to work on it. There is nothing else, till we fix this. And we have to fix it." He looked around. "No time like the present."

"There is something," Bridget said cautiously. "I've been thinking. Just didn't know if I should bring it up."

"Well?" Block asked.

"Well, the animals. They're using up a lot of oxygen. I know they've been integral to the project. But we're at a crossroads."

"What are you saying?" Pam asked.

"I think we need to get rid of them," Bridget said. "Kill them."

Pam, only recently recovered, was hammered by this new shock.

"But why?"

"It'll conserve air."

"But they have a right to be here, too," Pam protested.

"Fine," Bridget said with fire flaring in her eyes. "So when we're all dead—they can have the whole lousy, rotten place!"

"Look," Jimmy said, "Clayton and I discussed this weeks ago. But that was before—" He broke off. "Well, before we knew. I think we have to consider it, Pam."

Pam chewed at her lip, then looked at Block.

"It will keep us alive?"

"It may help," Block said.

"You're talking about killing just some?" she asked.

"All." Bridget said it with regret but resignation.

"Pretty drastic," Block said quietly.

"The situation's pretty drastic, Clayton!" Bridget said.

"It's just not right," Pam protested again.

Mai Ker came to the rescue.

"The truth is, guys, we're just thinking short-term. But we need to think long-term. We're worried about staying alive. Today. We have to think about what happens if we do. We have to think about a future."

Everyone realized she was right and that their short-term panic could not blind them to longer-term needs.

"All right," Block said, "we cull them. We selectively slaughter most of the large animals, but preserve a breeding stock. Whatever we kill, we butcher. We've done that all along. We'll put as much meat as we can in the supply pod freezers. The small animals—well, that'll depend on how many we can catch. And what's edible. And what's not."

"I have a feeling everything's going to be edible pretty soon," Bridget said.

"We need to think about preserving species," Mai Ker said.

"Like the Ark," Jimmy said, taken back to his own Sunday school days.

"The what?" Mai Ker asked.

"Later," he said.

"What about the horses?" Pam asked with trepidation.

"I didn't think of them," Jimmy admitted. "What do you guys think?"

"They consume a lot of air," Bridget reminded them.

"Can we just keep a couple?" Pam asked. "For old times' sake?"

"I'm not sure there are any 'old times' anymore," Bridget said.

"Show of hands," Block said. "How many think we should keep a couple around—for old times?"

They all raised their hands, except Bridget. She gave up.

"I don't care," she said. "I guess we are in Colorado. What a bunch of sentimental toads you are."

"That's one piece. A little piece," Block said. "What else?"

"Well, we sure don't want any more electrical storms INSIDE," Jimmy said.

"What about your other idea?"

Jimmy looked blank.

"Which one?"

"Back in March. You talked about direct infusion of oxygen. From the storage tanks."

"It's an idea," Jimmy said. "But that's before we knew how bad it was. We have some large oxygen tanks over in the main supply. But I can't believe they'd be enough."

"I'm going out on the porch," Pam said, still pouting about the animals. "I need some air."

Three seconds ticked by and Pam was almost at the screen door.

"Wait," Mai Ker said, her eyes blossoming. "Pam—that's it."

"What's 'it'?" Jimmy asked.

"Air." Mai Ker repeated the word. "Don't you see. Not just oxygen. *Air!*"

"You've lost me," Jimmy said.

"Me, too," Block said.

"Me, three," Bridget added.

"Air," Mai Ker said again. "Maybe we are looking for a very complex answer when there is a very simple one right in front of us."

"Well?" Jimmy prodded.

"Air," she said. "Plain old air. Our air is out of balance. Too much nitrogen? So we add new air. We try to get the balance back with fresh air."

"Mai Ker—what planet are you *on?*" Jimmy said, exasperated. "There is no fresh air. Everything OUTSIDE is worse than in here."

"Not OUTSIDE air," Mai Ker said. "Fresh air, from INSIDE."

Jimmy just stared at her.

"Wait, Jimmy." The light came on in Block's head. He jumped at Mai Ker, hoisted her in the air and planted an obviously unexpected kiss on her lips.

"You're not only beautiful, you're brilliant! Am I thinking what you are?"

She dangled in his hands like a rag doll.

"I think so!" she said excitedly. "Put me down, please?"

The other three just watched, baffled.

Block set her down as if he might break her.

"What am I missing?" Jimmy demanded, half dumbfounded and half mad at Block for kissing her.

"We have more air in here," Mai Ker said. "Sealed up. Like that mattress in the pool."

Jimmy's arms flared out in front of him.

"Of course. Bottled air. Compressed air. We've got tons of it in the supply shed—and the working pods."

"And if we're lucky," Mai Ker speculated, "some of it was bottled up before last May—so it would not be contaminated."

"We free it. Let it all out," Block said, trying to explain what was now perfectly obvious to all. "We empty out every ounce of bottled air we have." In his mind, he was already typing the message to Haskins. "And because it's compressed hundreds of times, it'll expand to a much larger volume."

"How much do we actually have?" Bridget asked.

Block looked at Jimmy, the inventory expert.

"I don't know," Jimmy said. "Lots. I'll have to check. There's at least sixty huge tanks in number thirteen. That's besides the pure oxygen tanks Clayton and I talked about."

Block looked elated but was not yet satisfied.

"Look, we've got to think of every resource—every bit of 'fresh' air in this place. Where else can we find it? Think!" Block gave this order because at the moment he couldn't think clearly at all.

"The scuba tanks," Bridget said.

Block grabbed a pad and pencil and began scratching out a list.

"There's still quite a few oxygen cylinders in the infirmary," Pam offered. "The little green ones you've been using to take care of Caroline."

Block winced at the mention of Caroline.

"Yeah. OK. I just want to hang on to a couple of small ones. Until we fix this."

No one objected.

"What if we have a medical emergency?" Mai Ker asked. "Shouldn't we keep some back?"

"There's at least sixty in the infirmary supply," Pam said. "It would be smart to keep some back. Just in case, Clayton."

"Agreed," he said. He waited. "Well, come on. What else?"

Bridget leaned over to him. "Do I get a kiss, too? If I think of something?"

"Maybe," he said. "Just maybe."

"Tires," she said.

Jimmy grinned. "Bridget, you're brilliant, too," he said. "We've got, what? Six service trucks?"

"And two fuel trucks," Bridget added, "with dualies."

"Dualies?" Pam asked.

"Dual rear tires."

Jimmy ticked down the inventory in his head.

"Five four-wheelers. Two Jeeps. Four tractors."

Block jotted down "tires."

"The pool floats in the rec. pod," Mai Ker reminded them.

Block jotted them down. "Six floating mattresses. Four inflatable chairs."

"Wait," Mai Ker said, reconsidering. "We blew those up after Seal-In. So they're contaminated."

"Still might help," Jimmy said. "Our air is deteriorating by the day. Anything we blew up even a month ago might be better. Hey. And the inflatables. The rubber rafts, over in storage? Some use CO_2 to inflate, but I think some use plain compressed air. We'll have to check 'em."

"And we'll still have the two aluminum boats," Pam said.

Block wrote down "rafts" with a question mark.

"This isn't fair," Bridget protested. "You guys know what's in storage better than I do."

"Don't worry, Bridget," Jimmy said, "I'm not tryin' to score any kisses off old Clayton." He was just far enough away from Block to duck when the scratch pad flew past his head.

"Anything else?" Block asked, glaring at him.

Jimmy shook his head, and tossed the pad back, commenting, "You've got lousy handwriting, Block."

"You want to keep the list?"

"Nah. But I'll check the inventory database," Jimmy said. "Never know what might be holding air in here. I mean besides your head, Clayton."

The pad and the pencil just missed Jimmy's head this time. The pad hit the wall but he snagged the pencil in flight.

"Thank you, sir, I'll get right on it," Jimmy said, tucking the pencil in his pocket.

"Let's the rest of us do some scouting, too," Block said. "I want every inch of this elegant crypt turned upside down until we've found every last thing that has any air in it. When you find it, bring it to Pod ten. It's the biggest. And it's the only place we can get all the trucks and tractors into the same place at once. We'll work outward from there—"

Jimmy cut him off.

"And nobody opens any air containers until I say," Jimmy warned. "This can't be haphazard. We're only gonna get one shot at this. Our best chance is to crank out all the compressed air at once. Like a flood."

"And," Block cautioned, "eighty percent of what we let loose is still going to be nitrogen, so it's going to be tricky. We just have to pray enough oxygen gets out to help us get back close to normal."

All heads nodded. As they left to start their search, Block said a silent prayer of thanksgiving. Despite their agreement early on to keep religion and faith out of Solarium-3, he knew perfectly well a lot of praying had been going on the last 48 hours.

Jimmy went to the Comm. Center to check the computerized master inventory. He also cranked the lighting in all the pods so they would have enough light to search by once it started getting dark OUTSIDE.

The others scattered to various other pods, collecting the items Block had scribbled down. They came up with some extra finds: ten basketballs, twelve footballs, four soccer balls, and 26 cases of cleaning sprays whose labels showed only compressed air as the propellant. Most of the pressurized cans in the main supply—1,647 cans of hair spray, bug spray, air freshener, and miscellaneous supplies—were useless because they used chemical propellants.

Block soon came across two of the most obvious suspects in Pod 8, the maintenance area. He cocked his hands in the air, signing how stupid he had been to forget them. The maintenance garage housed two huge compressed air tanks the team routinely used to operate power tools, inflate tires, and so on. Both were on wheels, which enabled Block to move them by himself into Pod 10.

Jimmy's hunt through the computer inventory was successful but in smaller ways. He turned up two cases of spray paint which had been recently manufactured and used only compressed air as the propellant. The computer also located, on a high, remote supply shelf in Pod 13, ninety-six emergency tire inflators. They would contain highly compressed air. Jimmy patched together several printouts so he wouldn't forget a single thing.

THE TEAM locator showed Block's purple dot moving around in Pod 9 where the large animals were kept. Jimmy called over the intercom.

"We're doing good, Clayton. Stuff turning up right and left."

"Yeah, no lie. I forgot about the compressor tanks in maintenance. And I just came across three air sprayers here in number nine—the ones we use to dust the cattle for parasites. They have their own air cans."

"Air cans. Yeah," Jimmy said. "Thanks, Clayton." He clicked off the intercom. "Now how stupid is that?" he said aloud. "Why wouldn't they show up on my computer inventory?" He opened a storage cabinet at one end of the computer console. On the bottom shelf, at the back, was a large cardboard box marked "Computer Maintenance." From this he retrieved no less than thirty-three small air cans with tube-like nozzles used for dusting keyboards and computer cases.

"Sure—the one thing the genius planners forget to list on the computer inventory is the computer stuff."

The other Solarians continued to scour the pods for any hope of fresh air hidden away in a can, a bottle, a tube.

PAM HANSEN walked through the podwalk from #13 into #10, having finished her search. She headed back toward the house. As she passed a gate post by one field, some small black marks on the wooden post caught her eye.

The marks had been made with a broad tipped marker. A catch came into her throat. Surrounding a scribbled, child-like heart pierced by an arrow were the words, *Willy loves Pam.*

There was no telling exactly when he had put it there. Pam leaned against the post, and wept.

THE TEAM worked like maniacs late into the evening. Every air container they could find was assembled in Pod 10. By 9:00 p.m., the excitement had worn them all to near exhaustion and they collapsed again in the living room where the crazy project had begun several hours before. After a brief rest, they scraped together a light supper, and shortly after that Pam, Mai Ker and Jimmy headed to their bedrooms.

Block and Bridget cleaned up the mess, then settled on the sofa, trying to wind down. Finally, Bridget broke the ice.

"So, tell me about this paper ring," she said, producing it from a shirt pocket where it had been hidden away all afternoon.

Block's arms felt like used gelatin.

"Um," he hummed. "Well, that was my way of asking for a date." He paused and gathered his courage. "A very long date."

"Assuming a long date is still possible," she said.

"Right." He looked at her. "Look, Bridget. As soon as I knew I wanted to stay here, I knew I wanted to spend it with you—however long it might last."

"Yes?"

"Well, I'm pretty old-fashioned. If I'm going to be that close to you, I'm only going to do it the old-fashioned way."

"So this—thing," she held up the little ring, "this is a proposal?"

"It is."

"You never cease to amaze me, Block."

"Or myself."

She leaned into his chest and kissed him. "Thanks for asking."

"You're welcome."

She laughed. It was the first laugh INSIDE for two days.

"Go on to bed, Block," she said. "We can talk more tomorrow."

"See you in the morning, 'darling,'" he said sappily.

He found Caroline sitting placidly on a new hand-carved perch inside her oxygen tent in his bedroom. The tiny, steady stream of oxygen from her tank kept her free of the fate that awaited so many.

Without Willy occasionally knocking around the room, she was more isolated than ever. Her wings spread from time to time, longing for those times she had flown freely through the pods, swooping low through a doorway into a podwalk, emerging at the other end, then sweeping high toward a pod roof. Now here she was. Trapped.

Months had passed since the night of her birth, the night her brother fell into a silent abyss, the night the inhabitants of earth sailed unknowingly through that imperceptible cloud Haskins had tried to describe. Earth, like a great ship venturing uncharted waters, had sailed blindly through that cosmic void, puncturing space and time. Now, as billions of disrupted molecules rained down through the atmosphere, the great ship foundered on a reef of devastation.

Caroline, though, protected by a man and a love she had no way of understanding, was breathing normally. She jumped off her perch, made a short walk around the edge of her plastic tent, then stopped to peck at some half-eaten sunflower seeds that lay strewn on the floor of her little world.

Her protector was resting now, his bulky frame laid back against his pillows. Resting, but not sleeping. There would be little sleep tonight. Caroline hopped to her perch and stood guard. The morning would begin the strange battle to preserve Solarium-3, striving against what they could not see, boxing the air, hoping for hope.

17

Sunday, March 15th

Just as Block felt he had finally dozed off, the blazing Sunday morning sun flooded the Residence Pod, streaming light through every window and around every shade. He sat up with a lurch. His mind and eyes tried to focus.

In the excitement of their rescue plan and the search last evening, Block had completely forgotten to let Haskins know their decision. He dressed quickly and jogged to the Comm. Center. It was just past 6:30. He flipped on the teleconference camera and, unbelievably, saw John Haskins sitting at the console in Omaha.

"Had a feeling I might hear from you soon," Haskins said.

"You're up early."

"Haven't been to bed."

"John, we've made our decision. We're going to stay. We've cooked up a plan. Don't know if it'll work. But we're gonna try it."

"Let me guess. It involves oxygen tanks."

"Yes. But not just that. Mai Ker pointed out the obvious. We don't have much pure oxygen, but we've got tons of compressed air. That, with the oxygen tanks, might do it."

"Worth a try, Clayton."

"It's risky, though. I mean, it's a one-shot deal. We're going to trigger everything at once. But then we're done. I mean—done. We get just one chance at this."

"Well, there you go. You have a choice. One

chance. Or no chance."

"Hadn't thought of it like that."

"You would if you were out here," Haskins said.

"I'm going to have Jimmy transmit a list to you after breakfast with all the resources we've come up with. I need your team to double-check it, tell us if we've missed anything. Anything at all. No matter how small."

"We'll get it done. Get me the list."

"Thanks, John."

"Clayton. This has to work."

"I hope so."

BLOCK FOUND Bridget, Jimmy and Pam at the breakfast counter. He felt an urge to give Bridget a good-morning kiss, but didn't. It seemed out of place.

Mai Ker was still upstairs, singing quietly in her bedroom. The sound drifted down the staircase.

"What's for breakfast?" Block asked.

"Whatever you round up for yourself, Clayton," Pam said. "I'm not fixing any this morning. Maybe later."

He made a sour, sarcastic face at Jimmy, a face neither of the women could see, fortunately. He scrambled up four raw eggs in a glass, his favorite breakfast drink, and started to slurp it down.

Jimmy pushed two leftover pieces of toast toward Block, since he didn't have much of an appetite.

"Here, you can have these." The higher-than-normal pitch in his voice showed he was anxious to get going.

"Jimmy, I need you to go over and send Haskins a list of everything we've come up with. Air sources I mean. He'll have the project team double-check, see if we've missed anything."

"Good idea."

"But I want to get this show on the road ASAP. Have we got everything corralled into Pod ten?"

"Most of it," Bridget said.

"Clayton, I spent four hours last night going over all our previous air data," Jimmy said. "I can't find any sure way to exactly reverse the results of those tests Omaha gave us in September. So the oxygen and compressed air is all we've got going. We just have to pray it gets us back near to normal oxygen and nitrogen pressures." He swallowed the last of his coffee. "I also recalculated our total air volume in the pods, just to be sure. Our old numbers are right on."

"Good."

"And I projected the expansion of what I estimate we've got in all the air containers. Just a guesstimate, but if I'm figuring right, we may have a flying chance."

"Jimmy, you're amazing," Pam said.

"Oh, and I wrote a special ventilation program last night, too, to recirculate—"

"Couldn't sleep, huh?" Block said.

"Aahh, no. Anyway, to recirculate everything out of Pod ten and around the complex. The new program will reposition the circulation fans and shutters between the pods so everything flows outward from number ten and then back through the interconnect tubes."

"Will it work?" Block asked.

Jimmy looked at him gravely.

"It's gotta work."

Block swallowed the two pieces of toast nearly whole. He swallowed the rest of his glass of raw eggs in a gulp, followed with a chaser of milk, and wiped his mouth with a dish rag from the sink.

"And if this doesn't?"

Jimmy answered in his thickest, slowest Cajun drawl.

"Well then, Mr. Block, we are all comprehensively and permanently screwed."

THE TEAM assembled in Pod 10 two hours later,

dragging along the most recently scavenged sources of air they had found. All the vehicles and trucks had been brought in the night before and parked near the two tractors in the center of the pod. This destroyed a large area of very expensive hybrid wheat crop, but no one cared. When they were done, the assemblage looked like the staging area for an eastern Colorado Memorial Day parade and three-county flea market.

Jimmy had gotten the double-checked list back from Omaha. They had identified only two more items: two squat-looking air pistons that put the spring in the diving board at the swimming pool. These could only be opened by drilling them, so Jimmy had the needed equipment at hand.

Block had printed out a "hit" list of all the air containers and the exact sequence for opening them. Jimmy set up a laptop computer on the tailgate of a pickup with a wireless link to the Comm. Center so he could monitor the air quality panels and upload everything to OUTSIDE as they worked.

At 9:45, Block gave the signal. All five went to work, hustling like terrified little beavers trying to save their dam from an impending flood. Tires on all the vehicles were flattened quickly by removing the valve stem cores. The valves on the compressed air tanks were spun open in rapid-fire succession creating wild, blustering whistles and hisses, like the sound of a thousand steam locomotives and hissing snakes bearing down on top of them. Several of the largest tanks lay horizontal on the ground and the air blasting from them created whirling dust devils across the fields.

The pool floats were opened and rolled up tightly, squeezing every ounce of air from their innards. Next the scuba tanks were vented. Block hesitated slightly, knowing this meant no more scuba diving. He could live without it.

The spray cans came next, resulting in a temporary

but hideous stench throughout the pod, a mixture of perfumed hair sprays, bug repellent, deodorant, cleaning solvents, and paint. Footballs and basketballs were flattened quickly. Jimmy ran over them with a heavy metal roller to squeeze every ounce of life out of them.

The oxygen tanks were saved for last. Jimmy hoped that once all the compressed air was dumped, the sudden addition of the highly compressed oxygen would create a snowball effect, bursting the nitrogen "bubble" that had been devouring their atmosphere.

As the other four teammates spun open the oxygen valves, Jimmy ran to the laptop and keyed in the start sequence for the new air circulation program. Several of the large, reversible circulation fans housed in the overhead air shafts in the podwalks screamed in agony as the polarity of their motors was reversed. Their blades, howling like banshees, reversed direction. Motorized louvers on the ventilating shafts slapped open or shut throughout the complex. Smaller circulating fans high in the pod roofs spun faster and faster, impelling showering bursts of air down the walls of the pods. The team had also set up several large, mobile fans at the entrance to each podwalk around #10 to push even more air into adjacent pods.

The whole operation took nearly two hours. By the end of it, everyone's hands and fingers were aching from turning valves, turning wrenches, holding spray caps down. Their lungs and sinuses were aching from all the noxious substances they had vented along with their "fresh" air.

Jimmy monitored the air progress on several tiled panels on his computer screen. He flipped through other screens to watch changes in the ventilating system. He dropped into a desk chair that he had pulled up to the pickup's tailgate. The air sensors slowly marked a slight increase in overall oxygen pressure.

Jimmy spun his chair like a Tilt-a-Whirl, and let out a "hooo-whee!" He turned back, and held his breath. He flipped through several more screens. The colored nitrogen and oxygen bars on his monitor for Pod 10 both crept very slowly toward normal.

He spun his chair again.

"Hallelujah, dear Lord!" he almost cried.

He flipped to screens showing air quality in the other pods. The nine pods directly surrounding #10 also began to show very gradual but steadily increasing oxygen readings.

"Ride 'em cowboy!" Jimmy hollered with glee.

The other Solarians watched over his shoulders. Worried heads bobbing from side to side were giving way to little jumps and hops of excitement. Soon it was like the hoots of six crazed children whirling through a darkened fun house. Tears welled up in some of their eyes.

"Is it working?" Pam asked, breathing hard, her arms aching.

"Like a dream, like a dream," Jimmy said.

"We sure everything's opened?" Block demanded, turning to the three women. "We've gotta be sure."

"Let's check," Bridget said. "Double check everything!"

The four ran around again as Jimmy remained glued to the monitors.

"Come on baby." He coaxed the graphic oxygen bars upwards with his hands. He planted a kiss on the screen hoping this would somehow make the computer keep doing what he wanted.

Block and the women scurried from tank to tank, can to can. Mai Ker found one large compressed air tank whose valve had partially jammed. It was whistling like a frightened tourist in a dark alley. She tried to twist it. It didn't budge. She put all her force into it and twisted again. The valve wheel gave, and turned three more times. The faint whistle became the blow of a whale.

Bridget found a few spray cans that belched out little burps of air like babies that ate too fast. She squeezed down on each plastic jet until it gave up every ounce of air, or broke off.

Block and Pam started up each vehicle, driving them slowly backward and forward to force any tiny bit of remaining air out of each tire. But it was like squeezing blood out of a rubber rock.

Just before noon they were all exhausted again, more from a mixture of excitement and wild emotions than from actual physical work.

"It's not quite there. But it's holding," Jimmy told them. "We need to take a break, and see what happens."

They trudged to the house and made sandwiches, gulping them down with cans of soda. Pam found several pieces of cake in one refrigerator and put them on the counter. Jimmy ate quickly, then jogged to the Comm. Center to check with OUTSIDE and see what they were reading.

"Tonight," Pam announced, "I'm making a celebration supper. Steaks on the grill."

"I'll have two," Block told her. "Make them 'well done,'" he joked.

They forced a laugh at his little attempt at humor, the first time they had laughed together in several days.

AFTER LUNCH the women went back to #10 again to triple check everything, to be sure. Block went up to check on Caroline. The gauge on her oxygen bottle was near empty.

"Maybe I can let you out of there one of these days," he told her. She flitted about inside her little air tent. Four of the small oxygen bottles they had agreed not to vent were stored under his bed, the last remaining life support for Caroline.

He said goodbye to her and walked out to the Recreation Pod to see if they had missed any inflatable items by the pool. The place looked almost bare now. He thought of all their pool parties over the months. He thought of Willy, and Sarajane.

Going back to the house he went through the aviary in Pod 6. He realized that even if Caroline made it through this, she might have a pretty lonely existence. Most of the other birds were long gone. A few of the hardiest were still alive. Only two were in the aviary at the moment. He stopped, looking at the nearly empty cage, pondering the loss of so many of these beautiful, unique creatures.

When he got back to the house, the women were back, cutting up the nearly dried up cake. He stole a piece for Jimmy and hustled to the Comm. Center.

"Hey, Jimmy. I brought you some cake and another pop. How's it going?"

"Well, I think it's OK," he said, but there was caution in his voice. His exuberance from an hour earlier had disappeared.

Block's face fell.

"What's wrong?" he asked.

"It's not wrong. Exactly." He looked up at Block. "It's just not quite enough," he said. "Everything came up fast to start, toward the normal oxygen/nitrogen balance. Then it planed out. And there's been a drop— a very slight drop—in the oxygen level. In the last thirty minutes."

Block bent, tossing the piece of cake in his hand onto the counter. He studied the screen with Jimmy.

"Still dropping?"

"Seems to be steady right now. But I'm worried. I didn't expect to see it drop at all."

"We let loose everything we had, Jimmy. Everything. I don't know what else to do. Except wait."

"I checked with Omaha."

"And?"

"No ideas," Jimmy said.

"So, we just wait."

"No! We can't just wait. We're too close. So close. But not enough. There has to be something else! Something. Just a little more air—a little more—that's all we need."

"Jimmy, we've got nothing else. Nothing. Zip. Zero."

"Not exactly true, Clayton."

Block looked at him with a hardened face.

"Look, we talked about those spare oxygen bottles. We all agreed. Four for the infirmary—and the four under my bed. We're going to keep Caroline going as long as we can."

"I know what we agreed, Clayton. But we're so close. This close," he said, showing Block a fraction of an inch between his fingertips.

Block shook his head in frustration. He studied the computer monitors, then looked at Jimmy, who was staring at him with piercing eyes.

"All right," Block said angrily. "Come on. Let's tell the ladies."

They found the women still in the kitchen, munching cake crumbs. Jimmy explained what was happening.

"Oh no," said Mai Ker as she sank onto a breakfast stool.

"I can't believe this!" Bridget said angrily.

"There's nothing else we can do," Block told them somberly. "Except use the oxygen bottles we saved in the infirmary." He paused. "And the four under my bed." He looked like a man about to be shot.

They stared at him in silence. This wasn't the same man they'd lived with night and day for nine months. It wasn't like him to give up. He had kept his little friend alive through so much. Now he had given up. This change of character seemed somehow unacceptable. If he was rattled, it signaled something worse, for them all.

But even if he was giving up, Bridget wasn't.

"Are you really sure you want to do that, Clayton?" she asked.

"I don't see that I have any lousy choice."

Mai Ker swallowed a mouth full of pop too fast. Up came a burp.

"So you mean—" she began to say.

"Clayton . . ." Pam was saying.

"We have no choice!" Block snapped back.

"Maybe we—" Bridget began.

"Wait, you guys. Listen!" Mai Ker almost shouted. She forced up another burp, louder this time. She grinned.

Everyone stared at her.

"Soda pop," she said innocently. She belched again, this time quite loud.

"Unbelievable," Jimmy smiled. "You, woman, are completely beyond it all."

"What did I miss?" Block asked.

"Soda pop," Mai Ker repeated.

"They put carbon dioxide in it to carbonate it," Jimmy said. "And the carbonation creates pressure in the can—"

"—so there's some pressurized *air* in the top of the can," Mai Ker finished.

"So we shake the cans," Pam said, capping her soda can with her thumb and shaking it hard. She let loose and soda sprayed all over the counter, and Bridget's shirt. Pam laughed as if she would become hysterical.

Block stepped toward Mai Ker, beaming.

"You are definitely working on another kiss," he said.

"One from me, too," Jimmy said, beating Block to

the punch. Mai Ker squealed delightfully in Jimmy's arms.

"How much have we got left?" Bridget asked.

"Are you kidding?" Pam asked. "They loaded us up with enough of the stuff to last two decades. Must have been one of the corporate sponsors."

"I'll bet there's five hundred twelve-packs sitting over in Supply," Jimmy said, catching his breath.

The excitement erupted all over again, like kids let loose in a candy store.

"Will the trucks still roll on flat tires?" Bridget asked Block.

"They'll roll on the rims if we peel off the rubber— and keep them on the concrete."

"You might break up the walks," Jimmy warned.

"I'll tell you a big secret, Jimmy," Bridget said, "I don't give a rip!"

They headed for the big pod again. While Block and Jimmy cut and peeled tires off two pickups, the women began carrying packs of soda by hand from the supply shed in Pod 13. Once the trucks were running they relayed hundreds more out into #10, dumping them all onto the ground as hard as they could. Pam and Mai Ker tore open the cardboard and plastic wrappers and started pulling cans out, tossing them into huge piles.

Load after pickup load was brought in until the soda racks in the supply shed were empty. As Block and Jimmy loaded the last fifty 12-packs, they uncovered a colorful, professionally printed sign thumb-tacked to the warehouse wall. Emblazoned in bright red, white and blue letters they saw this:

GOOD LUCK FROM YOUR FRIENDS AT
YESTERYEAR COLA
HAVE A BLAST IN THERE!

There were now nearly 6,000 cans of soda thrown in

large piles near the center of Pod 10. They were all tired again but Block wouldn't let them rest. They started shaking cans, creating as much pressure as possible. Finally Block said, "Ready?"

Joined voices shouted "Ready!"

"Hit it!"

Five sets of hands went to work in a frenzy of pop-top-popping. Warm soda pop sprayed everywhere. In a few minutes, they were all drenched, along with everything else in range. The mania went on. They broke fingernails right and left prying the things open. Block grabbed some screwdrivers and pliers from a tool box and passed them around. Jimmy started puncturing cans with a claw hammer. Pam discovered that if she tossed them high enough and they landed on concrete, they would blow open on their own.

Jimmy and Mai Ker launched the official Soda Pop War, chasing each other in broad circles, firing pop cans at each other. It was madness, the kind of happy madness that only the truly insane usually get to enjoy.

After an hour they began to wear down but there were still several hundred cans left. Sopped in sticky pop, their hands and arms were harder and harder to manipulate. Pam stepped in with a large irrigating hose and saved them from drying up in the afternoon sun like human popsicles. Dirt and now mud from the fields made it all worse. But they kept at it, knowing they needed to free as much air as possible in as short a time as possible. It took most of another hour. Between hosings, they bore down on the few remaining cans.

The hundreds of gallons of pop they spilled out soaked into the soil or ran to the nearest irrigation ditch. This mess would take days to cleanup, but if the extra air from the cans worked it would be worth it. Grass, weeds and dirt clung to them, a tarring and feathering of their own making. When they finally finished, the team collapsed onto the ground. All except

Mai Ker, who stood over Jimmy still armed with one last can.

He held a hand up in surrender and struggled to his feet. Mai Ker shot the can at him but just glanced his side.

"Pam, one last time," he pleaded.

She got slowly to her feet and hit him with the hose for a full minute. He went over to his laptop shaking water from his hands—and found it dead. Pop spray had seeped into every crack and through the speaker covers, and fried the mother board.

He peeled off his drenched, matted shirt and limped on wobbly legs toward the Comm. Center to check the screens there.

Mai Ker, worn out but still on her feet, was now playing kick the can but no one joined in. Block was ready to vomit from the smell of all the sugar. Even if they had any pop left, which they didn't, he swore he'd never touch the stuff again. After a few minutes, Bridget got up and started checking to make sure they hadn't missed any cans. Mai Ker helped. Every can was open.

"I'm going for a swim," Pam announced.

"You're not going in the pool like this!" Bridget protested.

"The ocean."

No one needed a second hint. They dragged themselves toward the podwalk into #12 and were soon submerged in warm salt water, splashing around.

Jimmy had fallen into his chair at the Comm. Center console after wiping his hands dry. Several messages were blinking from OUTSIDE. He keyed up several monitors and started watching the numbers and bar graphs. He would have held his breath if he could.

AFTER FIFTEEN minutes of incredible refreshment the other four Solarians crawled out on the beach to dry.

"Anyone have a towel?" Mai Ker asked.

They all laughed.

"Clayton, would you mind going home and getting us towels? And some dry clothes," Pam asked, completely serious.

"Yes."

"You will?"

"Yes, I'd mind," he said, his face buried in his arms. He badly wanted a nap.

"Clayton, would you bring me that purple T-shirt and my brown slacks?" Bridget added, jumping back in the water. "And my underwear's in my top drawer." The water drowned her laughter.

Block sat up, not answering. *Where's Jimmy when I need help?* he thought. *Well, they all worked hard. They deserve the rest.*

Block refused to answer the women but started off toward Pod 4. He was half dry by the time he reached the house. He dressed quickly, then went through the two bedrooms, finding a T-shirt and shorts for each woman.

Let 'em get their own dang underwear.

He checked in on Caroline, then carried the clothes and three beach towels back to the ocean where the women were sitting together sunning on a large rock.

"Here y'are, ladies," he said. "Couldn't find much," he lied. "Must be close to laundry day." He dropped the clothes in the sand, turned and headed for the Comm. Center. "Thank you" followed him out of the pod.

He found Jimmy scanning six different monitors.

"Well?" Block asked. He was apprehensive but had to know.

"Looking better," Jimmy said. "A little better. I think this pop thing may have just done it. It'll take a while. To be sure."

"How long?"

"Hard to tell. Could be hours before we know if things are really stable. I don't want another false start, like earlier."

"What's OUTSIDE say?"

"They're watching, too. So far, so good."

"Let me take it for a while. Go get cleaned up," Block said.

Jimmy needed little encouragement since he was still sticky, and shirtless.

"A real shower sounds good," he admitted. "Just keep a close eye on Pod nine, the big animals. It's reacting positively, but not as quickly as the others. I've redone the circulation a little differently. Should help."

"So we'll have to implement the other part of our plan?"

"You mean the animals?"

"Yeah."

"I don't know," Jimmy said. "Let's wait. See what happens. I hate to kill more than we have to."

"All right. But not too long, Jimmy. We've shot our one bullet. We can't let this thing go backwards."

"I'll check back when I'm cleaned up. I gotta eat something. That sandwich and left-over cake didn't cut it. If anything starts looking funny—yell at me."

"Bring me back a snack."

"Sure."

PAM'S BARBECUE that evening smelled delicious. When it was almost ready Jimmy went to check in with Block. He found him dozing in front of the console.

"Asleep at the wheel again?"

Block jerked to a semi-erect position, yawning, unaware he had fallen asleep.

"Yeah. Sorry. Long night, long day."

"Long week. How's it look?"

They scanned the colored bars, graphs and readouts.

"Nothing's changed since you left. Holding steady," Block said.

"Fantastic."

"Number nine is starting to come up a little, too."

"Good job, boss."

"Thanks. I didn't do anything. Except sleep."

"Supper's on."

They found the three women already on the porch slopping down grilled chicken and mashed potatoes and cold baked beans. They all ate to overflow. The stress and work of the day had created huge appetites. Even the multi-flavored sugary smell wafting through the air system didn't spoil the supper.

"Pass the milk, would you Pam?" Block asked.

"More milk?" she said, looking at him with wide eyes. "So, maybe, we better keep a couple of cows around after all?" she joked.

They made small talk about the strangeness of all they had done today. It had been a bizarre kind of struggle. Yet they all knew it was, in fact, a battle against death. After a quick check at the Comm. Center, Jimmy reported that the nitrogen and oxygen monitors were near normal and holding. This news made dessert taste even better.

About 8:00 o'clock, Block and Bridget went back to the Comm. Center for one last check before bed. The readings were still steady. Block sent a confirmation out to Haskins.

Jimmy had headed straight up to bed after dessert but just a few minutes after Bridget and Block sat down at the console, he appeared in the door.

"Couldn't sleep," he told them. "Too tired. And wound up. Why don't you let me take it for tonight?"

"You sure?" Block asked.

"Yeah. I'm OK. I can flip out a cot in here and cat nap."

Block wasn't going to argue. His head had turned to

a bowl of cotton fuzz and his body felt like he'd just left a boxing ring.

"OK. See you in the a.m." Block and Bridget left him there and went to the house. Mai Ker seemed to be asleep on the couch, a book about wild flowers open beneath her limp arm.

Bridget checked her.

"Mai Ker? You OK?"

Mai Ker stirred, gave a sleepy nod, and rolled her face into the back cushions.

"Scared me a second," Bridget told Block as they went up the stairs. Block kissed her when they reached the door of her room.

"Want to stop in?" she asked.

"Not tonight. That time'll come. Soon. I promise."

She looked unsure but nodded, hugged him, and went in.

Block went on to his room. Will's bare mattress was a stark reminder of the nightmare that faced them.

What now? he wondered. *This certainly wasn't in the manual.*

He watched Caroline bumping around inside her tent. Though the air seemed nearly back to normal, he would not take any chance. He reached through the food flap to put in fresh seed.

"Hey, little kid. How's life in your pod tonight?" She landed on his finger. He bumped the finger up and down, giving her a ride. Then she hopped off. He stroked the clear plastic tent and she flew again toward his finger, but darted sideways just before she hit the wall. She flew circles, obviously feeling better. He taped the food flap shut and checked the gauge on her oxygen tank. It was near empty. He pulled one of the four remaining tanks from under the bed and switched them out.

He stared at the three remaining tanks under the bed. He looked at Caroline. "These may have to go tomorrow," he told her apologetically. "Last card in the deck."

He looked again at Willy's bed. "Why didn't we figure this out sooner?" he said to the empty bed. He had no answer. He was struck at that moment by the awesome—the overwhelming—human power to make choices. Real decisions, real consequences.

Can't be undone, he told himself. He thought about his four teammates. Four lives, now truly in his charge. His mind stalled.

"Oh, what the heck," he said aloud.

He pulled the three remaining tanks from under the bed and carried them quietly downstairs and out onto the porch. He sat in a rocker. Slowly, he cracked open the valve of each tank. They hissed with each other off-key. He closed his eyes and listened to the concert. *The end of a perfect day,* he thought.

When they reached the last measure he went back to his room. From under her tent Caroline sang, *whi, whi, whi.*

He smiled and laid down, still in his clothes. He felt heavy as he melded down into the mattress like a sunken ship settling onto the ocean bottom. In moments he was in a sound sleep.

18

Monday, April 7th

Two and a half weeks had passed since their valiant effort with the canned air and oxygen tanks. Near-normal air mixtures were holding constant. For three days after releasing "fresh" air INSIDE, the oxygen in their atmosphere actually jumped slightly above normal, then dropped into the normal range on day four.

Today, according to their air sensors, the oxygen pressure had slipped to 18 percent of the total air pressure, just a hair below normal. But Jimmy was confident they weren't facing a major drop again.

On March 16th, the day following The Grand Opening, as they now called it, Block transmitted this to Haskins:

TO JOHN HASKINS:
:: OUR TEMPORARY FIX SEEMS TO BE HOLDING. WE SCROUNGED EVERYTHING WE COULD FIND WITH AIR IN IT AND BLED THEM OFF YESTERDAY. JIMMY'S STILL WATCHING IT CLOSELY. WE HOPE THIS SOLVED THE PROBLEM. SORRY TO SAY IT CAN'T SOLVE YOURS. PLEASE CONFIRM OUR READINGS. AND LET US KNOW HOW YOU'RE DOING OUT THERE. ::

:: PS: JIMMY NEEDS TO KNOW IF YOU FIXED OUR AIR SENSOR PROGRAMS SO THEY WILL ALERT IN THE FUTURE. NEED TO

KNOW   EVERYTHING'S   WORKING
PROPERLY. PLEASE ADVISE. ::
BLOCK

The reply didn't come for over a day. Block was seated on a breakfast stool in the kitchen where Bridget was giving him a long-overdue haircut. Piles of brown, curly hair tumbled to the floor.

When no one answered Haskins' incoming voice message in the Comm. Center, it tripped over to the remote terminal in the wall of the kitchen. A loud "beep" went off. Bridget almost stabbed Block in the neck.

Cradling fragments of hair in the towel around his shoulders, he leaned to the wall and flipped on the audio monitor. Haskins' voice was sullen, and strained.

"Hey, team. John here. Guess you're not home. Sorry for the delay to your message yesterday, Clayton."

Block flipped on the mic.

"Yeah, John, we're here. Just over at the house. We're listening."

"Who said 'no news is good news'? I'm afraid this time it's more bad news. The air out here is deteriorating. Very rapidly. More deaths. Lots more. I can't even get an accurate count anymore."

"Sorry, John," Bridget said.

"I supposed you've noticed, not too many visitors there lately."

"Yeah," Block told him. "Haven't seen hardly a soul the last few weeks."

"I wasn't planning to tell you this. But—I guess we're beyond that now. One of your guards there in the OUTSIDE Control center died last night. We're sending a replacement, but I can't guarantee she'll make it—or how long they'll last. At some point, we need to turn over the outer lock controls to you

INSIDE. In case you change your minds. It just needs some circuits switched around in the basement of the Visitors Center, and some reprogramming at your INSIDE console."

"I guess that would be wise," Block said.

"Sorry there's not more promising news. I hope you're right about your fix in there, Clayton. Our systems people are watching it closely. They confirm your readings. Everything's holding. I hope it lasts."

"Yeah."

"If it's any consolation, you've got the purest air in the world right now. I wish we could bottle it somehow. For the rest us."

"Yeah," Bridget said, "but then somebody would try to sell it."

"No doubt," Haskins laughed. "There's been some talk about trying to launch a few teams out to the defunct orbital station. But too many glitches. Nobody's sure how many the station can support. Or how long. And the politics of choosing who goes from which country, it'll never happen. I suggested sending just the Gold medalists from the last Olympics. All I got was cold stares. Sounded fair to me."

"I bet 'fair' is hard to define these days," Block said.

"I think you're right. Too bad. Apart from you guys, it was our only hope." There was a lull with background static. "By the way, you weren't the only ones to come up with the compressed air idea. Every manufacturer in the world has been selling off their oxygen tanks. They're like pancakes at a Kiwanis breakfast! Ridiculously inflated prices of course. No pun intended. There's been a huge run on compressed air, too. People stockpiling. And lots of stealing going on. Nothing much changes, does it." This was a statement, not a question.

"Life goes on, as they say," Bridget ventured.

"As they used to say," Haskins replied.

"Sorry."

"Anyway, air merchants are making a killing. Wonder what they think they'll do with all that money? One tank a person. Maybe keep them alive six hours beyond the rest of us. Big deal. Anything for a buck I guess."

"Glad you still have a little humor left," Block commented.

"What else is there?" Another static pause. "By the way, tell Jimmy your air sensors are back online. Any problem, you should get an alert now. Sorry we played that little trick on you. It seemed like the right thing at the time."

"We're over it," Bridget assured him. "John. Just take care of yourself. And your family."

Haskin's "Sure" faded out with static.

EVEN THOUGH there was only one season in the Solarium, April made it feel like spring. Each new day brought a small shred of confidence to the team. But they had been stunned by the death of several animals over the last two weeks. Pam and Bridget said the animals probably had medical conditions that weakened their systems. Even though the air was now stabilizing they were too weak to recover from the effects of the oxygen starvation under which they had lived for so many weeks.

This raised again the remaining question in their survival plan, the plan to kill some, or all, of the animals in the complex. They were still jittery about the oxygen levels and the animals were consuming their share. Much of the plant life was still degraded, so oxygen replenishment was lagging behind what it should be. And they were still locked up together in a closed ecosystem. Each day they wondered: would the plant life recover in time to preserve the precarious air balance?

The team repeatedly analyzed the grand mix between soil composition, air, water, plant and animal life. All had to be kept in near-perfect balance. The gallons of sugary soda pop they had dumped in Pod 10 didn't help, even though it was what saved them.

The psychological stress of trying to maintain this thready balance was enormous. It weighed most heavily on Jimmy, Clayton and Bridget as they manned the Comm. Center controls 24 hours a day in shifts. By watering plants in a certain area one day—encouraging plant growth and photosynthesis—or changing ventilation patterns between pods another day, they were managing a delicate balancing act. They felt like a high-wire act hovering over an expectant crowd on the edge of their seats—expecting at any instant a terrifying fall.

FINALLY, THIS afternoon, Jimmy gave up the constant watch and asked Block to call everyone together around the dining table.

"I keep working the numbers. Things are steady," Jimmy said. "But not perfect. We're very gradually sliding into a hole. A tiny bit each day. But if we ignore it, it's gonna add up."

"So what do we do?" Pam asked.

"What we said. This is it. We're gonna have to kill some of the larger animals. Cattle, horses—I don't care.

"How many?" Mai Ker asked.

"As best I can estimate, about thirty. To start. Maybe six to ten more. It depends on what effect we get."

"We can eat beef," Pam said. "I don't care for horse meat."

"And most of us can't ride cows," Block added.

They reflected on this for several moments.

"How about thirty beef cattle and some of the hogs?" Bridget asked.

"Might do it," Jimmy said.

They all avoided Pam's eyes. But she had already come around.

"It's the only sensible thing, isn't it," she said with no hesitation.

"We'll start tomorrow," Block said. "Slaughter and butcher them as quick as we can, and into the freezers."

"Speaking of freezers and such," Pam said, "you all realize before long we could lose power from OUTSIDE."

"I know," Block said dryly. "I've been waiting for Haskins to clue us in on that. But he doesn't have a certain date. But you're right, could be anytime."

"Can the solar panels in the pod roofs keep us going?" Mai Ker asked.

"Not completely. I don't think," Block said. "So far they've supplied about forty percent of the electricity we use. So if power goes down OUTSIDE—"

"*When* it goes down," Jimmy corrected.

"When it does, we'll have to adjust. One of the big defects in the project design."

"We really need to start conserving now," Bridget said. "We don't want to wait till it's forced."

They all nodded. She went on.

"We need to look at all our electrical use and figure out what we can do without. That's the problem with the freezers. They suck a lot of juice. The lights and computers don't burn that much electricity, but the ventilating systems, the freezers, the big motors—they use a lot of wattage. The trouble is, we need them all."

"And the air conditioners," Jimmy said. "Without them, we're cooked."

"Literally," Mai Ker added.

"It was 106 degrees OUTSIDE today," Jimmy said. "Without the cooling system, it'd be 140 in here."

"We have a pretty good supply of tubing and sheets of plastic," Block said. "We can construct more solar panels, put them up wherever we can."

"What else?" Bridget asked him.

"Well, Willy was the real electrician. But I think I can reverse-wire some of the large motors, convert them to generators. We'll have to weld up some turbines for them."

"Can't weld anymore, Clayton," Jimmy reminded him. "No more oxygen tanks."

"Yeah."

"Wait," Bridget said, "I'm sure there's an arc welder over in number nine."

"I don't remember that on the inventory," Jimmy said.

"Jimmy, I saw it. It's inside a large cabinet in the back of the barn."

"Really?"

"You should spend more time around the horses."

"That'll work," Block said.

"What turns the turbines?" Bridget wanted to know.

Jimmy supplied the answer.

"We're talking the old style solar panels. Water-filled. We position the panels near the pod walls. With the greenhouse effect we should get 'em hot enough to produce steam. That drives the turbines."

"You know," Mai Ker said, "you could use a bicycle to drive a generator, too."

"How you gonna ride a bike in circles fast enough to turn a generator?" Jimmy asked, sure she didn't know what she was talking about.

"No. You weld a stand for the bike, to hold the back wheel off the ground. You pull a transmission out of one of the pickups and build a linkage from the bike axle to the transmission shaft. Couple the outgoing transmission shaft directly to the generator shaft. Or you can rig it with belts and pulleys. You start in low gear, as you get momentum on the generator, you upshift until you get it to high speed. That should put out a little juice."

Jimmy stared.

"What college did you go to?"

"My granddad showed me. They did it back in Laos all the time."

Everyone but Jimmy laughed.

"Well, we better get on this soon," Block said. "We don't want to be sitting here gabbing when the lights go off."

It was becoming obvious that everyone would need to learn new tricks and skills for their continued survival. Day-to-day routines would be very different from now on.

"Anyone for ice cream?" Pam asked. "Might not have it much longer."

Everyone agreed. She went to the kitchen and began spooning it out. *What was it,* she asked herself, *I used to say about desserts?*

19

Block, Jimmy and Bridget did most of the heavy work with the shovels this morning. Although the other two women joined in, their hearts were clearly not in this sorry chore. It was like slave labor, a necessary thing that had to be done.

There were no more eulogies. They had held another short memorial service right after Sarajane died. But now, knowing they were staying here, it only seemed right that she and Willy deserved decent burials and permanent grave markers.

Block had carved headstones for them on two pieces of sandstone he had robbed from an edge of their artificial ocean. Simple stones, names, dates. Jimmy suggested a Bible verse on each but they couldn't agree on which verse. Instead, both now read, "Your friends miss you."

So this morning, the graves opened along a wheat field near the perimeter of Pod 10, they brought the bodies in simple pine coffins that Jimmy had built from lumber stored in a shed in #13.

Block had gone through Willy's belongings and come across a gold wedding band. For his own reasons, Willy had kept it among odds and ends, despite the many years since his divorce. He put the ring back on Atchison's finger before the burial. He also found a birthday card he had given Atchison years ago on which he described Willy as "AFGHANISTAN'S WORST NIGHTMARE." He folded the card and put it into Willy's shirt pocket before the coffin was nailed shut.

Pam brought Sarajane's one major souvenir of life, her "Outstanding Achievement" plaque from her CU Medical School internship, from her bedroom and put it with Sarajane's remains, tucked under an arm.

The graves were side by side. Jimmy had stayed up late last night cutting wooden fence rails and slats and painting them white. After the burials, he erected a small fence around the double plot. He didn't want them forgotten. He made a silent pledge to keep the little graveyard looking nice. It was a part of his Christian upbringing that had stuck, this special respect for the bodies of those who had died. He had seen too many old family plots long-abandoned, overgrown with weeds and trees.

ON A Comm. Center screen, which sat unattended, a message grew line after line like a weed:

TO CLAYTON BLOCK AND SOLARIUM TEAM:
:: THINGS CONTINUE TO DETERIORATE OUT HERE.
EVERYONE'S BECOME DESPERATE. AIR BARELY BREATHABLE. MOST OF THE BOTTLED AIR AND OXYGEN IS GONE. YES— EVEN I GAVE IN. GAVE THEM ALL THE MONEY I HAD. FOR A LITTLE AIR. WANTED TO KEEP IN TOUCH WITH YOU. A LITTLE LONGER.
MANY MORE DEATHS. A LOT OF MASS GRAVES WITH HEAVY EQUIPMENT. THE ONLY WAY WE CAN KEEP UP. WHAT'S THE POINT? THE AIR COULDN'T SMELL WORSE. I GUESS IT HAS TO BE DONE.
LOTS OF RANDOM KILLINGS. EVERYONE LOSING THEIR MINDS. FIGHTS, SHOOTINGS

IN THE STREETS. EVERYONE'S GONE FULL-TIME TERRORIST. KNIFING OR GUNNING EACH OTHER DOWN FOR NO REASON. IT'S HIDEOUS, MY SHELTERED FRIENDS. AND ALL TOO HUMAN.

I DON'T THINK WE CAN KEEP THIS UP FOR LONG. THE AIR THE WAY IT IS, DON'T THINK ANYBODY HAS GOT ENOUGH ENERGY TO GO ON KILLING LONG.

SORRY TO SOUND SO FATALISTIC.

HOW ARE YOU ALL DOING? BETTER I HOPE? YOUR AIR MONITORS STILL SHOW GOOD. ENCOURAGING. WISH I COULD JOIN YOU. WISH WE COULD GET JUST A FEW MORE IN THERE. BUT IT'S IMPOSSIBLE. CAN'T RUN THE RISK OF OPENING THAT SEAL EVEN A CRACK. EVEN WITH THE AIR LOCK, I WOULDN'T TRUST IT. ONE TINY BIT OF CONTAMINATION AND YOU'RE SUNK. LIKE US.

Several empty lines scrolled down the screen. A pause.

GUESS NO ONE'S ON THE COMM. RIGHT NOW. SORRY I MISSED YOU. WE'VE TRIED TO KEEP YOUR PRESENCE QUIET, BUT THERE WAS A LOT OF PUBLICITY LAST YEAR. MOST EVERYONE'S FORGOTTEN YOU NOW. BUT A BAND OF REFUGEES STOPPED BY HERE A FEW DAYS AGO, INQUIRING. THEY KNEW ABOUT THE PROJECT, DIDN'T KNOW THE LOCATION. SAID THEY WERE JUST CURIOUS. I THINK THEY'RE MORE THAN CURIOUS. I LIED TO THEM, SAID THE PROJECT HAD CLOSED DOWN BECAUSE YOUR AIR WAS

CONTAMINATED, TOO. THEY WERE HEADED WEST WHEN THEY LEFT OMAHA. BE CAREFUL.

WE'RE THINKING ABOUT YOU. ENVIOUS. YOUR LITTLE PLACE LOOKS PRETTY GOOD RIGHT NOW. LUCKY. FOLKS ARE PRAYING FOR YOU, TOO. LOOKS LIKE YOU'RE THE LAST HOPE.

The message rambled on. Haskins needed someone to talk to.

POWER'S STARTING TO GO DOWN IN VARIOUS SECTORS AROUND THE COUNTRY. MOST OF OMAHA IS ALREADY OUT. WE'RE ON EMERGENCY GENERATORS HERE IN THE BUILDING. THAT WILL ONLY LAST AS LONG AS OUR FUEL SUPPLY.

MOST SMALLER POWER PLANTS HAVE SHUT DOWN. SEVERAL NUCLEAR STILL ON LINE. THOSE WILL BE POWERED DOWN SOON. SO THEY DON'T MELT DOWN AFTER WE'RE GONE. BUT WHY WOULD IT MATTER?

DON'T KNOW HOW MUCH LONGER WE'LL BE COMMUNICATING, GUYS AND GALS. RIGHT NOW I WISH I'D HIRED ON TO MY OWN PROJECT. YOU DON'T KNOW HOW MUCH. LIFE'S FULL OF STUPID DECISIONS.

WE'RE TURNING THE OUTER DOOR LOCK CONTROL OVER TO YOU TONIGHT AT 21:00. OUTSIDE CONTROL THERE ON SITE STILL HAS TWO GUARDS. FOR A WHILE. YOU UNDERSTAND.

FOLLOWING THIS MESSAGE IS A FILE DOWNLOAD WITH THE PROGRAM TO TRANSFER ALL LOCK/SECURITY CONTROLS

TO YOUR CONSOLE. IF YOU CHANGE YOUR MIND.

OUTSIDE CONTROL ON-SITE CONFIRMS THE MAIN AIR-LOCK FROM OUTSIDE INTO POD 1 IS INTACT. SEALS ARE GOOD. SHOULDN'T BE ANY RISK OF LEAKAGE. AS LONG AS YOU DON'T OPEN THAT DOOR.

I'LL KEEP IN TOUCH AS LONG AS WE HAVE POWER. WISH I HAD SOME KIND OF BETTER NEWS. GOD BLESS YOU GUYS. YOU'LL NEED IT. ALL FOR NOW. ::
JOHN

Jimmy found the depressing message about 2:00 p.m. Against his better judgment, he made a copy for the team to read, then committed it to data storage.

"Clayton," he called over the intercom.

"Yeah?" His purple dot blinked in Pod 11.

"They're switching lock controls over to us tonight."

"What time?"

"Nine."

"Be sure you're there."

"John is transmitting the programming changes now. I can preload them."

"Be there anyway. We can't afford for anything to go haywire."

"Right."

"I'll be there, too. Remind me at dinner. I'm busy with bunny rabbit poop at the moment."

"Can we afford a swim this afternoon?"

"No reason why not. If the monitors look OK."

"I'll let the ladies know."

The team gathered about 5:00 by the pool. Jimmy brought the message from Haskins. They passed it around, each face absorbing with unique emotion the latest news.

"How much bad news does he think we need?" Pam asked.

Block read it last.

"Keep the hard copy, Jimmy. Historical record. For old times' sake."

Mai Ker gave him a quizzical look.

"I keep hearing this, I don't understand. Times get old?"

"No. Just us. It's just an expression," he said.

After a half hour of swimming, Jimmy and Mai Ker went and sat on a bench in the aviary in #6. They counted 16 birds, though some may have been flying in other pods. Jimmy's mind wandered. Mai Ker watched the birds intently.

"You know, only some of them can mate," she said.

"Who?" Jimmy paused, and thought. "Clayton and Bridget?"

"The birds, dummy."

"Oh. Yeah," he said, looking up. Jimmy's mind had obviously been not on birds, but birds and bees.

"What were you thinking just now?" she asked as if she didn't already know.

"Everything."

"That's nice and specific." She waited. "Anything besides everything?"

"Well, you know," he said. "When we were working on the animal husbandry. You talked about the importance of . . . how'd you put it? Crisscrossing the gene pool? Like that?"

"Yes."

She continued looking at the birds. She wasn't going to help him.

"I've been thinking about that," Jimmy admitted. "And us. And, of course, you're right."

"Of course."

"I mean, you know how I feel. If we could get married this minute I would. But that doesn't solve it."

"What?"

"Crisscrossing," he repeated.

"Do you want to explain what you're thinking or make me guess?"

"Well, it's really awkward, you know. There's you and me. There's Clayton and Bridget. Then there's Pam. I'm sure she feels like the odd man out."

"Odd woman out."

"Whatever. But that still doesn't solve the problem."

"Crisscrossing?"

"Yes."

"We need more than two lines in the gene pool, you mean," she said.

"Unless we want a very shallow pool."

"I see."

"You do?" he asked, relieved.

"Well, it means even if we marry—and I think Clayton and Bridget are thinking the same—even then, it's not enough. I mean, assuming any of us can even have children."

"Exactly my point."

"So. Crisscrossing," she repeated.

"Seems very immoral."

"Yes." She pondered. She looked at Jimmy. "Isn't letting the human race die out immoral?"

Jimmy looked at her. It was another new question.

"Too many questions," he muttered. "Maybe I should talk to Clayton first."

"He's not your type," Mai Ker laughed satirically.

"Funny, Mai Ker. You know what I mean. About Pam."

"I knew."

"It's really his thing you know. He's the leader. And he can talk to Bridget. I can't do that."

"You want me to?"

"No, Block's the leader. Let him deal with it. First."

"OK with me," she said.

They continued to watch the birds.

"Jimmy?"

"Yeah?"

"It's OK."

"What?"

"I think we have to do this. It's OK with me. For you to have children with the others. I don't think we have really a choice. Need to stir the gene pool."

"Thanks, Mai. But it's still awkward. Just thinking about it. Makes me feel—I don't know. Sad. You're my girl. My love. Anything else, it'd just be mechanic work, you know?"

"I don't know any mechanics like that," she laughed.

"You know what I mean. If I gotta do this, I've just gotta woo one of the ladies into the bedroom some night. The old-fashioned way."

"For 'old times'?"

"Cut it out, Mai Ker. This is difficult enough."

"Only if you make it that way."

"Well, then, go ahead and talk to Pam and Bridget, if it's so easy."

"I could."

"Well, go on."

"Maybe they'd rather talk to a man."

"I doubt it. We're the enemy, remember?"

"Sometimes I forget." Her eyes smiled merrily at him, though he wasn't watching. She kissed him on the cheek. They were silent for a moment then Mai Ker nodded her head. "But I'm first."

"Of course you are. You'll always be first." He thought a moment. "You know, Clayton's like a ship's captain now. No reason he can't marry us. If that's what we want."

"Is it what you want?"

"I already told you."

"Me, too."

"Tomorrow morning."

"My gosh, Jimmy, what's the rush!"

"Several rushes. Time's wasting. Tomorrow."

MAI KER went back to the pool. Fortunately, Block had gone to the house and changed clothes so the two women were alone.

"We need to talk, girls."

The conversation was embarrassingly short. Mai Ker explained. She told them Jimmy agreed. She just had to talk to Block.

Bridget pondered things for about a minute. She looked at Pam, who was looking away. Finally, she spoke.

"I agree. We have to consider the future. If we have one. I think Mai Ker's right, Pam."

"Not even remotely interested in taking part in something like that," Pam said, almost chewing her lips. "Sounds like some kind of lab experiment."

"Well, would you at least think about it?" Bridget pleaded.

"What's there to think about? I'm not a Petri dish."

"We don't have to decide this second," Mai Ker said. "Like Bridget said, let's just think about it."

"Anybody want a snack?" Pam asked as she got up and went to the house.

Mai Ker went to the Comm. Center and saw Block's purple dot blipping in the far end of a storage shed in #13. She caught up to him there. He was rooting around in half-opened cardboard boxes and crates and had the lids off several huge blue plastic barrels.

"What are you looking for?"

He turned to her, vaguely shaking his head.

"Oh, nothing special. Swimming was fun. But my mind's elsewhere. Thought it'd be a good time to look through some of the junk the project planners thought we'd need. Did you know we have three boxes of tweezers and six boxes of fingernail clippers? Must've thought we were going to eat them for snacks. Oh, and that doesn't count four boxes of toenail clippers. Can't believe they thought we'd ever open up half this stuff."

"Things break," she said.

"Yeah. But four boxes of toenail clippers?"

"Or maybe somebody had a sense. That we might be here longer."

Block wondered.

"I doubt it. But then, Haskins knew. Even if he didn't share it widely, he might have ordered in some extra supplies. Who knows." He shook his head glumly. "If we live, at least we'll have nice toenails."

"Clayton, I have to talk to you about something." He caught the muted tone of her voice. "Something personal."

"Yeah?"

"It's about Pam. And Jimmy. And me."

"Sounds interesting."

"Don't joke, please. This is very clumsy for me. Jimmy and I have talked, see. About—well, about how we're going to sustain ourselves."

"Sustain?"

"You know what I mean. About how we're going to reproduce."

"Hey, you and Jimmy are free to do whatever you want. Just keep it private. I'm the team leader. I'm not gonna play priest or judge."

"Well, that's another part of it. You have to understand, it doesn't just affect Jimmy and me."

"Why's that?"

"Come on, Clayton, you're the one with the degree in Life Sciences. Haven't you thought about this at all?"

"About you and Jimmy?"

"No, dummy, about all of us. Pam, you, Bridget." There was an poignant pause. "Me," she said halfheartedly.

"Wait a minute," he said. He was putting a large lid back on a barrel. "You're suggesting that we all—"

He stopped and looked at her. Then he turned a little and looked off into the distance, focused on nothing in particular. He actually had *not* thought about this. He wanted to marry Bridget. He knew Mai Ker and Jimmy had grown close. But it never crossed his mind that any other relationships were even possible, let alone necessary. As it dawned on him, he was suddenly very uncomfortable. He took a few steps away from Mai Ker toward the door of the shed as if to escape.

"You mean—" He looked back at her. "I see what you mean. You're saying we all—what do we call it? Interbreed?"

"I think we have to," she said. Her tone was thoroughly pragmatic, devoid of sexuality or suggestiveness.

Block suddenly felt like the rusted tin man in Oz, except his feet felt like lead. He looked at her lovely face and those beautiful brown eyes in a completely new way, realizing that in a very roundabout way she was asking him to please sleep with her and get her pregnant someday.

When he was finally able to move he turned away from her again and plopped down onto a wooden crate, narrowly missing a large brass staple sticking out of the wood. He sat staring at four cartons of candy bars. He talked to the candy bars.

"You think we all have to have—" He started to say "sex" but then said "—babies." It was a statement rather than a question. "You and me?"

"I think so. For genetic reasons."

Block realized he would really like to have a child with Bridget but beyond that his mind had entirely dodged any thought of another generation. Suddenly he felt ashamed. *How completely self-centered can I be?*

he wondered. Mai Ker was right. These were not small stakes. The survival of the human race was up for grabs. It was an ugly realization, one he had successfully avoided thinking about in any depth.

"For genetic reasons." He hesitated. "You're right of course."

"Yes. For example, if you and Bridget have a baby, and Jimmy and me have a baby, well, someday—if the sexes are right—those two could have a baby. But then what? Either their children would have to reproduce with each other—not a good idea—or with their own parents. Worse idea. It would all end up one family genetically. And it wouldn't last. There'd be serious problems."

"Kinda like, after Adam and Eve, who did Cain marry?"

"I'm sorry. I don't know that story."

"Never mind."

"I think we all have to interbreed as far as possible. And as quickly as possible. Pam is 36, going on 37. If we wait very long, she runs huge risks. For herself, for the baby. We need her genes in the mix, to produce different strains."

"Variety is the spice of life."

"Now you're making fun of this."

"No. I meant genes. Variety. It's the key to a healthy gene pool," he smiled at her.

At least he wasn't looking at the candy bars anymore. She continued.

"So you and Jimmy both have to try to produce a child with her at least once. That'll take over two years, if we're lucky. And maybe more than once."

"And you? And Bridget?" he asked.

"The same," she said matter-of-factly. "With you and Jimmy both." She was playing hard at being the scientist but this was working on her emotions, too. But she managed, barely, to keep them at bay.

Block could see those emotions bubbling under the surface though. She was beautiful, yes. But at the moment that seemed neither here nor there. He knew how attached she was to Jimmy. He couldn't picture himself disturbing that love. It was more than he could think about at one sitting.

"I think I have to talk to Bridget about this."

"I already have. She gets it. Pam wasn't too crazy. You've got to talk to them both," she said in a very polite and sweet voice, but a voice full of insistence.

She went over and sat beside him on the scratchy edge of the crate and put an arm around him as far as she could reach.

"This won't be that difficult," she assured him.

"Oh yes, it will."

She kissed him on the cheek. He half-smiled, blushed bright red, got up and left.

WHEN BLOCK got to the house Bridget and Pam were making supper. There was a stony silence in the kitchen. *Not surprising,* he thought.

This was not the time.

Instead, he decided to take Caroline for a walk. The air quality had been holding steady. It was now or never. Sink, or swim.

He went up and untaped her oxygen tent from the floor. She just sat, looking at him. She expected seed. He put his finger by her. She pecked at it. He nudged her onto the finger and walked downstairs.

"Clayton?" Bridget said as he came through the kitchen with Caroline perched on his finger.

"Sooner or later, I gotta chance it. She's been cooped up a long time."

Caroline rode his finger all the way to the aviary. Jimmy was still sitting on the same bench, pondering their mess.

As soon as she saw the other birds, Caroline flew

off Block's finger and circled the main cage. Then she flew in. She perched. She looked around. No other nuthatches. Hers had been a very lonely life.

Jimmy had been grappling with the deep questions they now faced. *Why in the world was it me who ended up here?* He thought of all the others who had applied for a job in Solarium-3. And all those who hadn't. *How come I'm sittin' here, not them?* As usual, there seemed to be no real answer.

It doesn't matter diddly, he told himself, *because here I am.*

He was so engrossed he hadn't heard Block walk in but he did notice Caroline fly into the aviary cage. He turned and saw Block, who walked to the cage and ran fresh water into two little troughs. Caroline stayed in the open cage, enjoying the company of the other few birds.

"Hey, Clayton."

"Hi, Jimmy. Almost time for supper. You hungry?"

"Not really. But we gotta eat. I guess." He hesitated. "You and Mai Ker talk?"

"Yeah. Sort of."

"You talk with the others yet?"

"Working on it." He frowned. "I'm not very hungry, either."

"Yeah. But the ladies are expecting us."

Neither was sure whether to nod, or shake his head. In other circumstances, both would have felt some sense of jealousy, or rivalry. As it was, neither knew what he felt.

"Let's go get supper," Block said.

AFTER SUPPER Block pulled Bridget aside in the living room where they would not be heard. But as soon as they sat on the couch Mai Ker walked in and sat opposite, picking up a book.

"Can we go for a walk?" Block said to Bridget.

"Sure."

"I want to check some lima beans in number ten."

She looked at him, knowing this was just a lame excuse to get her out of earshot of the others.

"Mai Ker was talking to me earlier," he said as they walked toward #10.

"I know. We talked by the pool this afternoon."

"So you know what this is about?"

"It's about babies." They came up to one of the large lima bean plots.

"These the ones?" she joked.

"Forget the lima beans." He was frazzled. "Mai Ker says we all need to have children," he said, as if Mai Ker had suggested they all have their livers removed.

"All. Can you be more specific?"

"If I have to."

She gave him an odd look.

"I've thought it over, too," Bridget said. "She's right, you know."

"It's going to be very awkward. Very. For all of us."

"Yes it is."

"I was kind of astounded. She just bought it up—out of the blue."

"You haven't thought about it?"

"I've only been thinking about you and me. And maybe a child."

"Really." She smiled. "All since you gave me that lovely paper ring?"

"No. Long before that." He waited but she didn't jump in. "So you OK with that? Us having one?"

"Of course, Clayton. It's not like I'm totally over the hill."

"But that's the thing," he said, "Mai Ker was pretty insistent that Pam needs to get pregnant as soon as possible. That means either me or Jimmy . . ."

"You'd rather it was Jimmy."

"Yes, I would. I don't feel right about marrying you

then hopping in the sack with Pam. It's not right."

"Normally. I mean, normally I'd agree. But our situation isn't exactly normal."

"Exactly the problem."

"Have you talked to Jimmy?"

"No. Mai Ker did."

"Maybe he would father a child with Pam."

"I know Jimmy. He'll probably feel just like I do."

"There's always artificial insemination." She paused. "But I can pretty much guess Pam would never agree. And none of us is really qualified to try it."

"Well, I'll talk to Jimmy some more," Block said. "And we need to do this marriage thing. Whatever else happens, we need to make babies. You and I."

She reached down and picked a lima bean and handed it to him.

"Our child will start out looking kind of like this."

He laughed.

"Fine with me." He looked at the bean. "She has your eyes."

Bridget jabbed his arm.

"Who's going to marry us?" she asked. "You're the team leader. Can you do it?"

"Well, I think Jimmy and Mai Ker are ready, too. I thought I'd ask John if he could get someone to do it by teleconference."

"Then we don't have much time."

"No. We don't."

They went straight to the Comm. Center and sent Haskins an urgent message.

"Must have gone home," Block said. "He's not answering."

"We can check in the morning," Bridget said. "I'm tired." She looked at him for a moment with a twinge of guilt on her face. "Clayton, we'll work the rest out. Mai Ker, Pam. We'll figure this out. Nobody gets pushed. Things have a way of working out. The main thing is we respect each other, and everybody's conscience. If we fail, we fail. Hardly our fault."

Block got up from the console and hugged her. His emotional balloon was finally rising. He broke into a beaming smile. For half a moment, there was a tingling in his fingers and a slight tremor in his chest.

"I do love you," he told her.

"And that's good." She kissed him.

"A father." It came out like a mystical statement. His mind flashed back briefly to his first wife, Michelle, who had died giving birth to his first child, who was stillborn.

"You know, I lost my first wife in childbirth. Lost the baby, too."

"We'll do better this time," she assured him, and kissed him again.

"What a strange place to bear children."

JUST BEFORE 9:00 p.m. they called everyone to the Comm. Center. Jimmy keyed up the new security program Haskins had sent them. Drives whirred and screens momentarily flickered.

"We losing power?" Pam asked in a brief panic.

"No, it's all right," Jimmy said. "The lock transfer required a complete restart of our main computer. Before it could accept the new codes."

A monitor flashed a series of codes and graphics. An icon of a little door appeared at the upper left of the main screen. One beep. A blue lever on the door icon switched from vertical to horizontal. A second beep. MAIN LOCKS SECURE, the screen told them in large green letters.

"And that's that," Jimmy said. "We're now in full control."

Block shook his head.

"Wouldn't that be nice." He paused. He looked at each of them. "We could just leave now, you know."

There was just a moment's pause. But all four heads shook *No*. Block tackled the other subject.

"Since we're all here, Bridget and I have been talking. We're going to be married. If we can get Haskins to arrange it. And we wondered if Mai Ker and Jimmy want to join us."

To everyone's surprise, Pam beamed.

"So I get to be maid of honor twice, and best man twice—all at the same time?"

"At least maid of honor," Bridget laughed.

"Mai Ker and I thought you could do it, Clayton. Like captain of the ship."

"Except I'm getting married, too. Don't know how that works."

"If John can find someone, that's OK." Mai Ker said. "We want to do it tomorrow."

"As soon as we can," Block said. "I sent John a message. We should know pretty quick. Let's get some sleep."

20

Sunday, May 11th

Clayton Block was staggered by how his life had changed so rapidly. "A strange place to bear children," he had said to Bridget three days ago, a prophecy so bizarre even he could not yet imagine it.

What had started out as a complex, highly controlled scientific excursion into a well-planned future had been twisted into a radically unpredictable venture into the unknown. He had arrived here almost a year ago as a scientific researcher and a confident team leader. Now he felt like a befuddled comic trying to come up with one-liners to explain life.

The expansive Solarium-3 manual had not envisioned reproduction—at least on the human level. The plan had changed. It was as if they had just crested the top of a Ferris wheel and a whole new view of the ground—a view that included bearing and raising children under pods of Stellar plastic—was rushing up at them in a whirl.

John Haskins emailed them late Saturday to say he had found someone to do the weddings. The team gathered around the Comm. console at 10:30 this morning.

"Strange looking church," Jimmy commented, looking around at the familiar surroundings with entirely new eyes.

"Ready?" Bridget asked with clear excitement in her eyes. Nods all around. She flipped the teleconference switch and Haskins appeared on a single monitor left of the main ones, which were now constantly showing air sensor readings.

"Good morning, everybody. The lock switch-over went as planned, I see," Haskins said.

"Smooth as glass," said Jimmy. He was in the cleanest slacks and nicest shirt he could find, which wasn't saying much. The rest of the team had likewise dressed as best they could for the occasion. Wedding garb was not in their inventory.

"I tried to find a priest or pastor," Haskins said. "But they're all overwhelmed. Last rites, burials, grief counseling," Haskins said.

"We understand, John," Block said. "We just wanted to make this kind of official. If we can."

"Judge James Mariano is here," he said, pulling the judge into the picture and moving aside. "He's a municipal judge up in Blair. Was able to get enough gas to drive down this morning."

"Good morning, everyone. Happy to meet you," Judge Mariano said.

"Thanks for helping," Block told him. "This means a lot to us. I'm sure you've got better things to do."

"No problem. We've kind of given up trying cases. Not much point. Everything's too chaotic. Glad I could do this. It's actually an honor."

"Are you married, too?" Mai Ker asked innocently.

There was a pause. The judge's face changed.

"I was. She died last Monday. My two kids are still hanging on."

The dreadful reality of life OUTSIDE once again settled over the Solarians like a poisonous cloud.

"I'm sorry, I didn't mean—" Mai Ker said, almost choking.

"No. No." He managed a slight but genuine smile. "It's all right. No, it would have been more rude if you hadn't asked. Thank you for asking."

"Well," Haskins said. "We should move along. I've got a couple of things to update you on when we're done.”

The ceremony was brief, just the basics. Betrothals. “Will you have this man, this woman . . . until death do you part?” It rang with fresh meaning. In succession Bridget, Block, Mai Ker and Jimmy said, “I will.” Some prayers followed that the judge had borrowed from his pastor at First Lutheran. Then the vows.

“Repeat after me.”

Block and Bridget went first. Then Jimmy and Mai Ker.

“Sorry I can’t give you some kind of blessing,” the judge said.

“You’ve already done that,” Jimmy said. “We are honored, too, your Honor.” Jimmy wiped back tears from his cheeks.

“I guess you can all kiss,” the judge added. He smiled. “John, thank you for calling me. This was really something. Maybe there is still order somewhere in the world.”

Haskins clasped him into a hug on the monitor and sent him off with a handshake.

“I don’t want to mess up the moment, folks,” he then told the team. “But can you sit down for a minute?”

They all sat.

“Go ahead,” Block said, still holding Bridget’s hand.

“Just need to let you know, we’re getting close. Like the judge said, it’s totally chaotic. Riots, killing. Suffocation deaths. By the millions. You can’t imagine it. I’m archiving a lot of the news reports and video. It needs to be preserved. I’ll send it all in to you before long. But frankly, I’d tell you not to watch or read this stuff anytime soon. In fact, don’t look at it. Just better to let it go. Store it. You’ve got your own troubles enough. Focus on that.” He took a breath. “That’s your only responsibility now.”

"John," Bridget said, her insides doing somersaults, "you know if there was a way—any way . . ."

"I know. I know. No, like we said, we're not going to jeopardize any chance you have of making it. Just be prepared. It's not over yet."

"How do you mean?" Pam asked with deep furrows over her eyes.

"Just be prepared," was his only comment. "I'll be in touch."

"John," Block said at the last, "thanks again for finding Judge Mariano. Thanks."

Haskins gave them a nod, and half-a-smile, and switched off his camera.

DESPITE WHAT they planned, the newlyweds did not run straight to the house to consummate the marriages. Haskins' sobering report had thrown ice water on the whole day. Instead, they made a late brunch and headed off to routine chores.

Many of the plants were beginning to thrive again. As the air sensors showed daily improvement in their atmosphere, the animals also were acting more lively. But after repeated discussions, on Friday they implemented the slaughter plan, butchering the cattle and hogs that looked least likely to thrive. Several carcasses were still hanging in walk-in coolers in Pod 13 so Jimmy and Mai Ker headed there after lunch to keep cutting and packaging.

The killing was the hardest part. The usual slaughter house routine of a sledgehammer to the skull didn't sit well with any of them. So they brought each animal into a "clamping" stall, as Pam called it, and killed it with a large injection of nicotine. The nicotine was normally used to tranquilize small animals for tests. But, they found, in a large enough dose, it would do in the biggest ones, also. The downside was the nicotine would leave a bitter taste in some of the meat. But death was quick enough that it didn't affect the whole carcass.

Friday night they grilled up large quantities of beef and pork ribs and stored these in the house refrigerators and small freezers. From then on, everything they packaged went to the big freezers in Pods 8, 13 and 14. It was difficult work, but would keep them supplied with meat for months to come.

By Saturday morning the air sensors already showed the strategy was working. The elimination of 30 beef cattle and a dozen large hogs had helped. The sensors showed significantly lower oxygen consumption in the animal pods, a consumption rate that would give their atmosphere a chance to heal further.

SUNDAY AFTERNOON raced by. They broke from chores for supper. They all half-stared at each other across the table, and there wasn't much talk. What small talk there was acted as a diversion from what was on everyone's mind, including Pam's.

"You up for some more cutting?" Block asked Bridget as he finished dessert.

"Maybe for a little while," she said, giving him an inquiring look. *Is he actually trying to avoid this?* she wondered.

As the others cleaned up dishes, the couple went to the butcher tables set up in Pod 8.

"Sure tired of smelling raw beef," Bridget said as she pulled on rubber gloves.

"You know, this is still going to be tough."

"The meat?"

"No," Block said with an exasperated look, "you know what I'm talking about."

"Actually, I don't."

"About me and Pam. And Mai Ker."

Bridget was starting to get irritated with the whole topic.

"Only tough if we make it that way," Bridget said. She looked at him with piercing eyes. "And you sure seem to be making it that way. Clayton, I don't object about them. If that's what you're worrying about."

"Well, so you don't. But I do," he admitted sheepishly.

"You really are an old-fashioned guy, aren't you?"

He pulled at the back of his neck. It was aching from standing over the cutting tables all afternoon.

"I think you're going to have to talk to Pam. I can't."

"Clayton, if you can't talk to her, how can you do the rest?"

"Fear and trembling," was all he said.

Bridget smiled with her face away from him so he wouldn't think she was making fun of him. This was a unique man she had married. He was hesitating at what many men would have leapt at.

"I'll talk to her," she said, still grinning to herself. "I love you, Clayton Block."

"You're just saying that to get me in bed."

"I'm starting to wonder if *that's* ever gonna happen." She turned to him. He pulled her into a loose hug.

"Shall we? I'm tired," he said.

"I'm not."

This was it, he realized. No bushes to run and hide under in Washington Park. No blanket to pull over his head like he used to do when his parents fought. Just the huge pods of Solarium-3, which were growing smaller by the second. The whole world, in fact, was shrinking. As they walked arm in arm toward the house, the world they had known was changing into an alien planet, inhabited OUTSIDE by strange beings who didn't seem to know who they were, or how they came to be here, or where they fit in, or why they were still killing each other.

PAM, JIMMY and Mai Ker were planted in porch chairs when Bridget and Block walked up to the house. They figured Mai Ker and Jimmy would rather be somewhere else but Pam seemed to have them captured.

". . . how that makes any sense?" Pam was saying. "And there's something else I don't understand. About OUTSIDE."

"Go on," Mai Ker said.

"What Haskins said, about the ionosphere 'raining' nitrogen ions into the lower atmosphere. I wasn't very good at geology, or chemistry for that matter. Even when I studied for nursing. Thick-headed, I guess."

"Don't feel bad," Jimmy said, "because *they* still haven't figured it out. I got a report from Daniels Wednesday. The air's still deteriorating. It's like a freight train nobody can stop. What Haskins gave us was a very cut-down version."

"I just want to understand," Pam said. "I feel so helpless. If I can just understand it, it feels like I'm helping. You know?"

Jimmy shifted into teacher mode, giving her more detail.

"Well, the basics. The atmosphere is just a thin shell of gases enclosing the earth, right? It's got several layers—depending on how you look at them. Each layer serves a certain purpose. Helps keep us alive. If you picture the earth as an orange the whole atmosphere would be only as thick as the skin. The lowest layer—what we breathe—is a mixture of gases, mostly nitrogen—and about twenty-one percent oxygen. Because they're the heavier elements. There's a few other gases, argon, carbon dioxide and some others—and lots of water vapor."

"This sounds like tenth-grade science," Pam said.

"Close," Jimmy said. His arms made some large

circular motions in the air. "The atmosphere's not fixed, it's like an organism. Always moving relative to the earth, and the oceans, changing, interacting with the earth's rotation. There's heating, cooling, weather patterns. That's what causes winds, storms, that stuff."

"That part I get," Pam said. "But what's happening now?"

"Well the atmosphere is classified into different layers, depending on how you look at them—whether you're talking about temperature, or composition, or electrical properties. If you look at the layers from an electrical point of view, there's basically two layers. There's a pretty much electrically neutral layer closest to the ground. Goes up about 40 miles. Above that, for miles and miles, is the ionosphere. But it's made up of sub-layers of different gases and gas ions. Oxygen and nitrogen ions lower down, helium and hydrogen ions higher up."

"How high?" Pam asked.

"The helium dominates to about 600 miles up. The hydrogen dominates to about 1,500 miles up."

"An ion is just an electrically charged particle," Mai Ker said.

Despite their intentions, Bridget and Block were now sitting on the porch swing, listening. Which, for the moment, was all right with Block.

"Right. Put simply," Jimmy said. "Anyway, if I understand Haskins, when we glided through this cloud in space—this cosmic whatever-it-was—something triggered a breakdown in the upper regions of the atmosphere. Daniels thinks the hydrogen and helium ions have increased in volume. His theory is, nitrogen ions further down are neutralizing—losing their charge—by picking up free electrons. That's why nitrogen pressure has increased so much. The increased nitrogen pressure is cascading into what we breathe. At the same time, oxygen molecules are breaking down."

"And that's what ruined our air?" Pam said. "In here?"

Jimmy nodded.

"Yes. Our air was contaminated, remember. Before Seal-In. Those tests they had us do made it worse. But since we're protected from the increasing damage OUTSIDE, we should be able to stay stable."

"And," Block added, having read the same report from Daniels, "ozone is increasing out there—rapidly. Ozone's denser. And unbreathable."

"I don't remember what ozone is either," confessed Pam.

"An allotropic form of oxygen," Block said.

"An al-lo . . . what?"

"A variant form of oxygen. Tri-atomic," Block said.

"Which means?" Bridget asked.

"O_3 instead of O_2," Mai Ker explained.

"I thought ozone was a good thing," Pam said doubtfully.

"It is good, in certain places," Jimmy said. "Like Clayton says, it's denser than oxygen. Where it's usually concentrated, high up, it absorbs lots of ultraviolet radiation. So it acts like a giant sun-screen. But you can't breathe it. Too much down here, at ground level, it's toxic. It's poisoning the air OUTSIDE even more."

"Forget it. I've heard enough," Pam groaned. "I never realized plain old air was so sensitive," she said wistfully.

"Actually, it's miraculous stuff," Jimmy said. "It's almost alive. Like a chameleon. Temperature changes, gas densities, changing pressures. That's why the weather reports are never perfect. You just can't predict it."

"So why has the sky been getting more bluish and purple?" Bridget asked.

"Good question," Block said. "I don't remember

that in Nathan's report." He looked at Jimmy.

"My guess is the ozone," Jimmy said. "I didn't notice it at first. Mai Ker pointed it out. I think it was the night Sarajane died."

"Why ozone?" Bridget asked.

"Not sure that's it. Just a guess. The heavier concentration of nitrogen and ozone would diffuse light differently. There may be more dust and moisture in the air, too. Don't know. Whatever it is, the atmosphere is diffusing more of the longer red waves of the spectrum, so the sky's shifting from mainly bluish to more of a purple. It shows up most at sunrise and sunset. The low angle of the rays diffuses the light even more."

"I'm not following," Pam said.

"Well, sunlight is white. But the layers of the atmosphere diffuse it. The shorter light waves, in the blue part of the spectrum, get scattered the most. So normally the sky looks blue. Now more of the longer waves are diffused—near ground level—so it's looks more purplish. In space, with no atmosphere, the sun's light looks pure white, and the sky looks black."

"You're amazing, Jimmy," Pam told him.

Jimmy looked a little embarrassed.

"Just basic earth science," he said.

"Well, now I feel even more stupid," she said

"Hey, Pam," Block said, "there's a difference between stupid and just not knowing."

"You think?"

"Yeah. Ignorance asks questions. 'Stupid' would just as soon not know."

Pam felt better. She smiled.

"It's late," she said. "I shouldn't be keeping you guys up." She swallowed a little giggle. "Go on." She shooed them away like pesky chickens. "We'll worry about me later."

Another embarrassed silence.

But this gracious permission was exactly what they

needed. Pam sometimes seemed simple, but she was actually a very complicated woman.

WHEN BRIDGET and Block reached the bridal chamber they heard the familiar *whi, whi, whi.* Caroline was back, sitting above the bathroom light fixture.

"How'd you get back here?" he said.

"She obviously flew," Bridget said.

"I left her in the big cage in the aviary. Must have found a way back into the house. Probably hungry."

"Never seen her sit there before," Bridget said. "You'd think the heat would bother her."

"Nah, she used to be up there all the time, before I put her in the tent." He made a *snitch-snitch* sound with his tongue and teeth and Caroline flew to him, perching on an outstretched finger.

"Tamest bird I ever saw," Bridget said with genuine wonder. "How'd you get her to do that?"

"Don't know. She just does it. Like I'm her dad."

"Didn't know you could lay eggs, Clayton."

"No. The question is, can you?"

Caroline fluttered down onto his headboard. He pulled Bridget onto the bed. His shyness was evaporating.

"Don't watch this," he ordered Caroline.

She was walking headfirst down the headboard, more interested in the bag of seed under the bed.

"It amazes me how she does that," Bridget said.

"It's genetic. All nuthatches do it."

"It's still incredible."

"You ain't seen nothin' yet, lady," Block said.

THE HONEYMOONS were short lived. Sometime just after midnight, Block bolted straight upright in their bed, startled out of his wits, his heart pounding. Bridget was instantly alongside him, also startled out of sleep— by what, they weren't sure.

Barely awake, they sensed something was horribly wrong. Then it came again. A tremendous flash of yellowish-purple light flooded the windows and the door, saturating the air of their room like a brilliant strobe light triggered in complete blackness. Another hellish flash followed. Then another, and another.

Pam, shaking violently in her nightgown, was suddenly in their doorway, clutching the door jamb. A stifled scream came from Jimmy's and Mai Ker's room.

"Clayton?" Pam demanded, as if this was his fault.

Still trying to orient himself, he pulled himself from the bed, pulled on some shorts, and ran downstairs, passing Jimmy and Mai Ker in their doorway. The front door, which faced east, revealed the ricochet of bright flashes and left ghost-like negatives in his eyes. The blinding flashes were coming from behind the house, toward the north and west.

Block ran onto the porch and around to the back of the house, the other Solarians close on his heels. The expansive view through the pod dome toward the west and northwest was unobstructed by the lower tops of Pods 1 and 2. There was a lull in the flashes. Then without warning, the pod roof shook violently with a groaning, wrenching sound. The support beams quivered and the great plastic shell seemed to cower. It felt as if some cosmic giant had struck the pod with a monstrous sledgehammer, once, twice, three and four times, as if to an echo.

The next nightmarish flash came quickly. Reacting in complete disbelief, the team shielded their eyes from the devastating brilliance. Block's jaw snapped shut like a bear trap. Even the trailing radiance that followed the flash was like staring at the sun. When they uncovered their eyes, they saw the inconceivable. Far in the distance, above the outline of the front range of the Rockies, a half-dozen ashen-gray mushrooms sprouted. Thousands of feet across at their crowns, they rose hideously into the sky, far above the 14,000-foot summit of Pike's Peak.

"Cheyenne Mountain," Block said stunned, as if to himself.

"NORAD?" Jimmy asked.

Block nodded silently.

Two more stuttering flashes followed, slightly to the south. More giant mushrooms shot toward the heavens, then slowly bled together.

No one asked what they were seeing. They knew the monstrous spectacle from movies in school. What had been projected on a classroom wall was now projected on the sky in abhorrent reality.

"This is insane." It was all Bridget could squeak out.

"I can't believe it!" Jimmy was saying over and over. "Why now? What the hell is going on out there?"

The pods shook violently again from the concussion of several rapid fire explosions whose light they had seen several minutes ago. Even the floor of the porch, safe within the protective strength of the pod, shook with the ground underneath them.

Five or six more blistering mushrooms lit up almost due west of them.

"Pueblo Army Depot," Block said.

Three dimmer but still distinct, strobe-like flashes belched far to the north.

"Denver."

"Shut up, Clayton!" Bridget protested. She threw herself onto a porch chair and pulled the cushion over her face.

Jimmy was dumbfounded.

"I thought all those weapons had been disarmed! Destroyed!"

"You're kidding, right?" Block said.

"What about START-3?"

"Never started. Russian Parliament refused to ratify

it."

"Damn it, damn it all!" Jimmy shouted as if this would have some effect.

"Quit swearing, Jimmy! It's stupid," Mai Ker snapped. Tears broke from her eyes.

The bursting mushrooms subsided quickly. Several far-off flashes twinkled like bursting novae in faraway galaxies.

"I'm going to Comm.," Block announced, not knowing what else to do.

Bridget took the cushion from her eyes. She and the other's followed.

Block punched keys madly.

TO HASKINS: PRIORITY — PRIORITY
:: JOHN, WHAT'S GOING ON? WHY THE ATTACK? ::
BLOCK & TEAM

The response was slow in coming. Forty minutes later, words rolled down the screen:

TO BLOCK AND TEAMMATES:
:: SORRY FOR SLOW RESPONSE. NO ONE AVAILABLE RIGHT NOW.::
CONTROL—OMAHA

Block keyed up the CHAT mode and punched out a message to whoever had answered.

:: WHO'S NOT AVAILABLE? CB::
:: HASKINS IS NOT HERE. CJ::
:: WHO IS CJ? CB::
:: I'M OPERATOR/TECH SUPPORT NUMBER 43, CARL JENKINS. CJ::
:: CARL, WHAT HAPPENED? CB::
:: DON'T KNOW. NO ONE HERE BUT ME

TONIGHT. CJ::
:: YOU DON'T KNOW WHAT'S HAPPENING IN COLORADO SPRINGS?? CB::
:: PROBABLY WHAT'S HAPPENING AROUND SAC HEADQUARTERS HERE IN OMAHA. RIGHT? CJ::
:: MUSHROOMS? CB::
:: BIG ONES. CJ::
:: CAN YOU FIND HASKINS. GOT TO TALK TO HIM. CB::
:: DON'T THINK SO. CJ::
:: WHERE IS HE? CB::
:: NO LONGER WITH US. CJ::
:: HE QUIT?? CB::
:: NO. HE DIDN'T QUIT. CJ::

Block fingers stumbled against the keys. He sat stunned, taking this in, his heart recoiling.

"Oh, dear God," Bridget said with dismay.

:: WHEN? CB::
:: JUST GOT NEWS TONIGHT. HAPPENED LATE TODAY. CJ::

All five Solarians stared at the screen. They felt a new sense of abandonment, and knotting stomachs. Block forced himself to continue.

:: CONFIRM—DEAD? CB::
:: YES. CJ::
:: WHAT ABOUT NATHAN DANIELS? CB::
:: DON'T KNOW. LOOK, THEY JUST PUT ME IN HERE AT NIGHT. TOLD ME TO KEEP COMMUNICATION OPEN AS LONG AS WE CAN. THEY'VE GOT ME IN AN UNDERGROUND SHELTER. FILTERING IN AIR FROM THE STORM DRAINS. IT'S A

LITTLE CLEANER. THEY DON'T TELL ME MUCH. JUST KEEP THE LINE OPEN. CJ::
:: WHAT'S GOING ON OUTSIDE? CB::
:: UPSTAIRS TOLD ME A LITTLE. MUSHROOMS STARTED SPROUTING ABU--, ABOUT 20 MINUTES AGO. ALL OVER THE PLACE. CJ::
:: WHAT PROVOKED IT? CB::
:: PROVOKE? YOU KIDDING??? THE WHOLE WORLD IS PROVOKED. CJ::
:: SORRY. CB::
:: WHO CARES. PROBABLY SOME BOMB JOCKEY OVER IN RUSSIA OR UKRAINE GOT BORED. MAYBE THEY DECIDED WHAT THE HECK, NOTHING TO DO, LET'S SEE IF THESE STUPID THINGS REALLY WORK. CJ::
:: CAN YOU ESTIMATE LOSS OF LIFE? CB::
:: IMPOSSIBLE. DON'T KNOW. NO IDEA HOW MANY WERE LEFT BEFORE THIS. COMMUNICATION DOWN. NATIONALLY & INTERNATIONALLY. CAPUT. CAN'T EVEN GUESS HOW MANY LEFT IN OMAHA. CJ::
:: WE DON'T UNDERSTAND. CB::
:: JOIN THE CLUB. I WAS IN SATELLITE RECONNAISSANCE IN THE MILITARY. STILL LOTS OF ACTIVE SILOS OVER THERE. THOUSANDS. THEY COULD NUKE THE WHOLE PLANET. SO? ONES WHO GET BLASTED MAY BE THE LUCKY ONES. CJ::

"Let it rest Clayton," Bridget said.
He kept typing.

:: THAT BAD? CB::
:: BAD? KIDDING, RIGHT? WE HAD SOME BOTTLED AIR. UP IN THE LABS. ALMOST GONE. AFRAID TO LEAVE WHEN MY SHIFT

ENDS. BUT THEY WON'T LET ME STAY.
GOING OUTSIDE IS LIKE CRAWLING INTO A
BIG COFFIN. CJ::

"Good Lord," Jimmy said dazed, "why?"

Mai Ker held him, looking at his wrenched face, not understanding why he asked this.

"Come on. Clayton—this just can't happen," Jimmy insisted.

Everyone was acting as if Block was in control of something. They were desperate for something—someone—to cling to, to reassure them life was not over.

"Why didn't the military prevent this?" Jimmy almost shouted. "There's people out there who're supposed to watch out for this!"

"Are there?" Block almost whispered it.

His question hit Jimmy and the others like another sonic sledgehammer. They had desperately clung to the belief that somewhere, somehow, someone was still watching over them. They knew now this was an illusion. They really were alone. Humankind OUTSIDE was being torn away from them. They were totally on their own.

Block's own guts were tearing inside but he tried to finish the CHAT with Carl Jenkins.

:: SORRY TO SOUND CRABBY, CARL. WE'RE
JUST IN THE DARK IN HERE. CB::
:: JOIN THE BIGGER CLUB. CJ::
:: ANYTHING ELSE YOU CAN TELL US? CB::
:: NO. SITTING HERE PRAYING. THAT I
DON'T GET BLOWN OFF THE FACE OF THE
EARTH. DON'T KNOW WHY I CARE. BUT I'M
SCARED TO DEATH. CJ::
:: I'LL SAY A PRAYER. CB::
:: THANKS. PROBABLY WON'T HELP. NEVER

UNDERSTOOD WHY HE LETS THIS STUFF HAPPEN. UNDERSTAND LESS NOW. CJ::
:: TAKE CARE. CB::
:: SURE. DON'T KNOW HOW I'D DO THAT. CJ::
:: TALK TO YOU LATER. CB::

Block gently tapped the END key. The CHAT log disappeared.

He sat very still, rocking slightly in his desk chair. Everyone was silent. What could be said?

The macabre flashes OUTSIDE had petered out to an occasional blink, blips on a radar screen pinpointing—as if for some distant observer—the last few pockets of humanity. The abyss of evil in the human heart had opened, and was on full display.

Bridget took hold of Jimmy's arm, which was wet with sweat.

"He's right. I don't get it. Why did God let this happen?" she asked.

"No way, Bridget," Pam shot back. "That's an excuse. *People* pushed those buttons."

"That's harder yet," Jimmy said. "What sick minds would do this?" He became rigid and wanted to scream. He pulled his arm free and walked out of the building.

It was obvious no one could go back to sleep. The joy of this morning had crashed into the wreckage of this night. The emotional devastation was complete. Every hope seemed lost. In their hearts, each felt it. It was pointless to go on—though no one dared say it aloud. The idea of children suddenly seemed perverse. They were a new sprig off humanity's trunk, a small shoot that could ensure the survival of mankind. But that shoot was festering at the moment under a sense of loss so pervasive it overwhelmed every other thought or feeling. Fear spread like a silent plague in their souls. What kind of children would they create?

Block couldn't take it any longer, and broke the silence.

"Anybody want a drink?"

No one answered.

"Let's go somewhere, Clayton," Bridget said. "I just need quiet."

He nodded, took her hand, and followed. Pam went to the kitchen and sat, trying to think about a menu for tomorrow. But food seemed suddenly obscene. What right did they have to eat?

Jimmy wandered the pods trying to convince himself that this was his usual early morning walk. Mai Ker caught up to him near the horse corral. The horses were still skittish, reacting to the hammering of the pods and the repellant flashes of light. One colt munched some hay. Jimmy stroked its broad neck.

"You OK?" Mai Ker asked.

"I'm lost. Really lost."

"We all feel it Jimmy. But we have to go on. You know it."

"I've never felt suicidal, Mai. But tonight, in there, looking at Carl's words—I felt it. It's like, I don't deserve to live."

"Who does?" she asked with an insight she didn't intend.

He turned to her, and pulled her close.

"I guess it was making love to you earlier. It was so beautiful. Our wedding night. Somehow it made it even more rotten. All the suffering out there. And us safe in here."

"We're only safe if we want to be. We could give up." She looked into his eyes. "We could go."

"I know. We could still leave. But I know we can't. In some way, I don't want any kids. In another, I know it's the only choice. The only right thing."

"We always have to choose. Even when it seems there's no real choice."

"See, that's it. In a sense, I chose to be here. In another, I didn't. None of us did. Not like this. But here we are."

"Life was a mystery before we were born. It'll be a mystery after we're gone."

"Wanna walk to the ocean?"

"Yes."

ABOUT 4:30 that morning, Block and Bridget returned to the house. Pam had fallen asleep on a kitchen stool, her head down on the butcher block countertop. Block picked her up, her leaden arms and legs hanging off him like draperies. Bridget steered her feet through the doorways as they carried her upstairs and safely into bed. She barely stirred.

The two of them collapsed onto their own bed. They wrapped themselves together like needlepoint and fell asleep.

Jimmy and Mai Ker had fallen asleep on the beach in #12 an hour before.

Nightmares haunted all but Pam as they slept beyond daylight, vague, disturbing sequences of evil attacking their restless souls. Unidentifiable figures warred, pummeling the good. Lightning-like swords clashed in silent combat. Malignant, desperate foes fought through their dreams for supremacy, steadily losing ground. It all made no sense, even less had they been awake.

21

Tuesday, May 27th

There had been no more nights of terror. In one futile outburst, the remnants of mankind had burned what they could of their nuclear arsenal. The Solarians would never be sure if the U.S. had even bothered to retaliate. With John Haskins dead, there would be no more news files funneling in.

Omaha, in fact, had been silent now for two days. Repeated efforts to communicate with the OUTSIDE failed. They tried email, CHAT, and video-conferencing. None brought any response.

They wondered about Carl Jenkins. Block pictured him wandering out of his basement shelter at project headquarters. And not returning. Had he gone as he feared? Slow, irrevocable suffocation? Did it come when he was awake, or in his sleep? Try as he may, Block could not keep such thoughts at bay. They pestered him like a cloud of locusts, devouring his mental energy.

Similar troubled thoughts preoccupied the other teammates, too. The days seemed longer.

"What do you think's happened?" Bridget asked Block at the control console this morning. "Think they lost power?"

"Dunno."

She put the more unthinkable question.

"Are they *all* dead?"

Block shook his head with a shrug of his shoulders. His gaze remained glued to the empty computer monitor. He remembered how irritated he had been at

Haskins' messages over these last months. Today he'd settle for anything, irritating, banal or otherwise, just to know someone was still out there. An eerie sensation ran through him. He finally responded to her question.

"I don't know." His chest heaved an empty sigh, like wind escaping from an open window in his soul. "Maybe it's like with parents. You know? You're going on and on with your own life, then one day it hits you. They're not there anymore."

This pierced deeply into Bridget. Her father had died just a few years ago of a stroke at a fairly young age, hundreds of miles from where she was living. Her mother was still living. At least, she had been when Bridget arrived at Solarium-3.

Block typed in another pointless message, one he learned as Morse Code in the military:

:: C.Q. C.Q. C.Q. BLOCK ::

"Seek you, seek you, seek you . . ."

When he couldn't raise Omaha yesterday, Block tried repeatedly to reach someone in OUTSIDE Control under the Visitors Center. No response there either. The Control Room in the basement was well-disguised and well-secured. If anyone was there, they would respond. If they could. Block was sure the Control Room still had electricity because the security lights around the Visitor Center still burned nightly.

There were two employee cars and two company guard trucks still in the parking lot but no cars had come or gone since Saturday afternoon, as far as they had noticed. Their last link to OUTSIDE had apparently failed. It was too grim to think about. No one spoke of it.

It seemed like a perpetual funeral wake in the house, in the fields, in the sheds. Life went on hour by hour but with no clear purpose. Block spent most of his time here in the Comm. Center, hoping against hope for some kind of contact. Though just wed, Bridget had to work at getting his attention. When he was not at the console, he would go out and stand for long periods staring through the wall of Pod 2, watching the cars in the parking lot, hoping someone might come out and at least drive away. Any sign of life.

Much of their time was consumed with building the new solar panels. They knew the power could go down any minute. Their backup generators scattered around the complex and the large storage batteries in the equipment shed would carry them only a day or two. They wanted to be ready. Block oversaw the work but frequently excused himself to go to Comm. Jimmy and Mai Ker did most of the work, though Pam lent a hand when she could.

The OUTSIDE security lights around the Visitors Center had a battery backup, also. When those ran dry, there would be total darkness out there, except for whatever moon or starlight might filter through the sickly air over the pods.

"Can't you give it a rest for a while, Clayton?" Bridget asked. "If anything comes in, it'll stay on screen till we respond."

"I'd just like to be here if something happens."

"I know. When my dad died I wanted to be right there. But I was six states away. The stroke was completely unexpected. I felt so bad. Mom called and said don't worry, the doctors said he'd snap right back. Eighteen hours later he was gone."

She stopped. It seemed like death was the only subject they could find to talk about. She thought Block might pick up the conversation with details about his own parents' deaths. He didn't.

"Want to take a break with me?"

"I guess." He was still elsewhere. "In a while."

"I'm going to go do some weeding," she said,

giving up. *A man this big ought to have a lot of feelings in there,* she told herself. *You'd never know it.*

Block listened to her walk away. He felt like he should turn and follow, but didn't. He stared at the screen with vacant eyes. He was struggling with the emptiness, trying to work through it, but not sure how. He scratched the whiskers he hadn't bothered to shave for two days. That was very unlike Clayton Block. His mind tried to latch onto something concrete, something that possessed reality. Nothing came. He may as well have been at the bottom of their ocean. *Or OUTSIDE,* he thought.

Since Sunday night, he had been overcome by a sense that it was all so pointless. His own sense of helplessness had returned with a vengeance. When all else failed him he conjured up his old Sunday school image of God Almighty, sitting in some distant, abstract heaven on a big white-painted throne, watching all this.

"I simply don't understand," Block told this image. "I'll never understand you at all. How could you let this happen?" He expected some kind of response. A lightning bolt, a thunderclap. An earthquake. A still, small voice. Anything would be better than this silence.

Unexpectedly, his childlike God stared back. He didn't smile. He didn't frown. He didn't say a word. Just sat attentively, looking at Block. Then, just as unexpectedly, he leaned forward a little from his big white throne and picked Clayton Block up in his hand. Block rocked gently as if on the swing set back at his grade school. An intense sense of relief seared through him. The strange sensation was not physical, it was more real. Whether it was love, or something else, he couldn't tell. Then the image—great hand and all—was gone, and all was absolute stillness, and silence. Even the cooling fans on the many computers seemed silent. They were running, but Block couldn't hear them.

He rocked back and forth in the swivel chair, his hands clasped loosely on his stomach. A warm shiver ran up his back. He flashed back to his Sunday school lessons again. His favorite parable came to mind. The lost sheep. *Is that it,* he wondered, *riding on the shoulder of God?*

22

Wednesday, June 4th

The team finished up a delicious Sloppy Joe lunch made with some of the tomato sauce Pam had been canning all morning and hamburger from what was now a huge supply of frozen beef. They left a pile of dirty dishes in the sink and headed for their afternoon chores around the complex.

Jimmy and Pam walked over to #10 to water and cultivate a newly planted bean crop in the area where they had dumped all the soda pop. Before planting, the team had brought wheelbarrows of fresh dirt from other areas in the pod to provide a more tillable soil. The young beans were just beginning to sprout and needed tender, loving care.

Bridget went to #11 to care for a ewe that had borne a lamb Monday evening. There was also a new litter of kittens whose mom loved being near the other animals. "Barn kitties," Pam called them. Bridget checked the mother cat, making sure nursing was going smoothly and none of the little creatures, as often happens, was being ignored.

Across the complex in #13, Block was in the equipment shed welding one of the new steam turbines while Mai Ker screwed a cover into place on a new solar panel.

The constant, low drone of the ventilating fans circulating the air and the warm afternoon sun pouring into the pods from behind a light cloud cover was starting to make the Solarians long for a nice afternoon nap. It was as routine a day as they were likely to see.

Jimmy and Pam, on their knees weeding the new bean plot, were the first to notice the unusual noise. A sudden banging startled them, a hammer-like noise from one of the other pods.

"What in the world is Clayton banging on over there?" Jimmy asked her.

"I don't think it's coming from there. It's over that way," Pam said, pointing in the direction of Pods 6 and 4. She stood and walked to the podwalk that led to #6. She stopped, hesitating.

"It sounds like banging from OUTSIDE, Jimmy. Near the entrance."

Their view was obstructed by the buildings in the pods between them and Pod 1, but she could see vague movement in that direction.

"Who could—?"

Both their hearts started pounding.

"Our security guys?" Pam asked.

"Let's see," Jimmy said, running past her and pulling her along by the arm.

They ran through the aviary into #4, then around the house. As they rounded the back, they saw a line of rough looking vehicles streaming into the Visitors Center parking lot. Forty or fifty people had already climbed out of the vehicles and a dozen of them were peering into the pods closest to that end of the Solarium.

When Jimmy and Pam came around the house all eyes of the OUTSIDErs went straight to them like arrows zeroing in on their prey. A flood of people gushed around Pod 1 and pressed toward the pod wall of #4, facing the two Solarians.

Block and Mai Ker had also come running and appeared from the other corner of the house. Bridget was not far behind. Slowly, as if pulled by magnets, the five Solarians drew closer to each other, an unconscious defensive maneuver.

This mass of OUTSIDErs was as rough and dirty looking as the cars and campers they rolled up in. Three larger trucks were just slowing to a stop. Two were military vehicles, either surplus or stolen. The third was a beat-up delivery van. Across its side in chipping paint was "JUST DESSERTS SNACKS & BAKERY".

The team stood motionless, uncertain what to do. The OUTSIDEers all began pounding on the solid plastic, almost in unison.

"Jimmy," Block said, "get on the link to the Control Room under the Visitors Center, try to raise somebody."

"Clayton, we haven't had any response from them for weeks."

"Try anyway!"

Jimmy ran to the Comm. Center and tried to make contact. Nothing.

It looked like a riot was developing OUTSIDE. Everyone—the oldest to the youngest—was pounding, pounding on the plastic pod. More faces arrived by the minute. The crowd swelled to over a hundred in two minutes. A few cars were still turning into the parking lot. Then, like the Red Sea parting, the bodies folded back as two men in fatigues walked toward Pod 4, each carrying a large scoped rifle.

One of the men waved a command at the Solarians to walk toward the pod wall. Jimmy rejoined the others, but all stood still. The man motioned angrily at them again.

"Stay put," Block told them.

In the brief seconds that followed, the two men pointed their rifles straight at the team. A nearly inaudible "crack, crack" was heard as two dark spots appeared in the pod wall directly in front of the Solarians. Each of the team was sure they felt a bullet, but this was only illusion. The impenetrable, one-inch

Stellar plastic stopped the high-powered bullets easily, deforming them into lead blobs as they melted less than a sixteenth of an inch into the plastic.

Jimmy stood frozen. Mai Ker had ducked behind him. Block, Pam and Bridget were picking themselves up off the ground. The two men disappeared back into the crowd, the waves closed behind them, and all streamed back toward the far side of the Visitors Center.

"Everybody all right?" Bridget asked.

"That's some tough plastic," Jimmy said in amazement.

"They shot at us!" Mai Ker said in disbelief. "Why would they shoot at us?"

"You all right?" Bridget asked again when she saw how Mai Ker was shaking.

"Everyone into the Comm. Center," Block commanded.

Mai Ker was still gulping air as Jimmy led her in through the side door.

"Where'd they all come from?" Pam asked, squinting out a window.

"Wherever," Block replied with a deadpan. He was trying to digest the fact that some were still alive OUTSIDE. "Who knows?"

"Clayton," Bridget said, "that message from Haskins. Remember? He said something about a bunch of refugees who came through Omaha."

"That was almost a month ago!" Mai Ker said.

"Well, gas is probably hard to find—for a bunch like that," Jimmy said. "Maybe they've got some pirated oxygen tanks in those trucks."

"This must be the bunch," Block said.

The pounding against the pod walls started again, just outside the Comm. Center. Then, from the direction of Pod 1, they heard what sounded like a heavy object banging against something. Block peered out the door of the Comm. Center. In the walk between the Visitors Center and the entry pod about twenty of the crowd had gathered. A man with a large crow bar was hammering away with all his might at the outer air-lock door. The door was half-inch-thick steel with a Stellar window in the top. It was secured by multiple safe-like deadbolts on all sides. Despite his best efforts, the assailant was making no progress on breaking it open.

"What're we going to do?" Bridget asked.

"What can we do?" Pam asked. She turned to Block. "Come on, Clayton, you're in charge. You're not going to let them in are you?"

"Maybe we should . . ." Mai Ker started to say.

"No way!" Jimmy thundered. "No way! We don't open that door for no one. Nobody comes in—nobody goes out."

"Jimmy," Mai Ker screeched, "look at them! They're dying. There's little kids out there. We can't just stand here and—and watch—and not help."

"I know, honey, but—"

"What if it was *you* out there?" she cried.

"Well, it's *not* me out there!" he said angrily. "Mai, we can't help them! We've got no choice. You know it." He shuddered like an oak in a wind storm. "I know what you're feeling. But *no*. We can't take the risk. If we crack that seal, we're all done!"

Block stepped between them and put his arms around Mai Ker. His face was beet red, tension written in every line.

"He's right, Mai Ker," Block told her, trying to calm her, and himself.

"Mai, we just got the air somewhere close to normal. It's poison out there," Jimmy said. He looked at the floor, shaking his head, then looked back at her with sorrow in his eyes. "We can't risk it!" He took her from Block's arms as if they were passing an infant between them. He held her tight. "It's terrible. I know. But we can't." He was choking down emotion.

"I know," she finally said, sobbing. She pulled herself free. "But I don't like it."

"Like you said the other day. We have to make choices."

"I never thought of this one."

She pulled away and walked to a window, looking out toward the pod wall. It was ghastly. OUTSIDE was a sea of angry faces, sad faces, blank faces, bitter faces, small weeping faces. She broke down completely.

"We *want* to help," she whimpered through the glass with hiccup-like sobs. Her own reflection, like a ghost, cried back at her.

"Pam," Block said, "take her over to the house, would you?"

Pam nodded voicelessly. As she led Mai Ker out a back door toward Pod 4, there were two sets of sobs.

"Maybe we can try to talk to them," Block said. "Try to explain."

"We could write notes," Bridget suggested. "Through the pod."

"Good idea," Jimmy said.

Bridget dragged a large easel pad out of a storage closet at the end of the room and grabbed a marker.

"Wait," Block told her. "Stay in here for a few minutes. Jimmy and I'll go over to number one and see if we can get them to stop beating the door."

They walked cautiously across the short podwalk into #1. They knew the plastic was safe but the rifles still had them rattled. They motioned to the man with the crow bar but he ignored them, still swinging at the door but not with as much force. He was wearing down. The two men with rifles stood not far behind him.

Block tried yelling but the thick doors blocked most of the sound. He tried waving again. One of the women

OUTSIDE grabbed the man's shoulder and got him to stop. He looked up. His eyes met Block's, then Jimmy's. Block waved an arm, motioning them back toward Pod 2, where another part of their crowd was still hovering on the sidewalk. The man with the bar scowled at Block. Block held his arms up and apart in a gesture of helplessness, then motioned for them to follow. The man gave Block the finger, then spoke to his part of the crowd. They all moved toward Pod 2.

"OK, Bridget," Block said coming into the Comm. "Bring the pad."

The three Solarians went out and walked across the yard to the pod wall. They approached the plastic wall near the two black spots left by the bullets. The rifles were out of sight.

Block made a "time-out" gesture with his hands. Most of the faces scowled at him but a man in fatigues nodded *OK*. He gestured for the others to sit on the ground, which they slowly did in clumps.

"Hold this for me, Jimmy," Bridget said. "What do I say?" she asked Block.

"I was hoping you'd tell me," he said grimacing at her. "This was your idea."

"You're the boss."

"Yeah, thanks," he said. "OK. Tell them there's no point beating on the door and the pods. This place is indestructible. They'll never get through."

Bridget scribbled.

YOU CAN'T GET THROUGH THE PODS. OR THE DOOR. NO POINT BANGING ON IT.

The man still holding the crow bar let loose a crashing blow against the pod. All his might produced only a sickly thud and not the slightest dent. His hands recoiled in pain. One of the men in fatigues grabbed his arm and took the bar from him. It was clear this guy was in charge.

"Tell them we know about the air. But there's

nothing we can do."

KNOW YOUR AIR IS BAD, Bridget scribbled in large letters. *CAN'T HELP.*

From the crowd a teenaged boy walked up to the leader and held out a ratty-looking spiral notebook in his hand, a pencil in the other hand. The man in the fatigues pulled him forward toward the pod wall. The man's lips moved. The boy watched him, then scrawled something. He held the notebook against the pod.

SEEKING REFUGE.

The boy's expression was pitiful. It looked like he hadn't eaten well for weeks. In the boy's face Block saw a wimpy little kid who used to run around Washington Park in Denver.

"Good God . . ." Block murmured, choking back his feelings. He was shaken to the core. "Bridget," he said in a dry whisper, "tell them we understand—but we can't help. We can't open the door. Tell them *something.* Tell them the lock's busted." His heart ached with every syllable.

"That's a lie, Clayton."

"Then tell them the damned truth!" he shouted, clenching his fists at his waist. His face turned redder. "Tell them we're gonna sit in here on our butts and let their lungs fry!" he hollered. "Tell the kid *that!*"

Now Bridget was crying, but trying mightily to hide it. Block turned and started to storm away, his eyes burning.

"Clayton!" she shot after him.

He stopped abruptly, and turned.

"Act your age," she said.

It was the perfect rebuke. He tried to compose himself.

"I'm sorry," he said, lumbering back like an injured porcupine, its quills turned inward. "This is just—" His voice broke. He was about to pour out a bucket of profanity. He looked at Bridget. "It's just a nightmare."

"And we're awake," Jimmy said.

Bridget's wet eyes met Block's with the same profound sadness. She nodded her understanding. He summoned up his last ounce of courage.

"Tell them we've stabilized our air, but if we open up we'll poison the whole complex. There's no point. There's no refuge."

AIR IN HERE WAS BAD TOO. JUST GOT IT STEADY, she wrote. *OPEN UP, RISK RUINING IT AGAIN.* She underlined the last word. *THAT WON'T HELP YOU.*

The man in the fatigues, his face scruffy with curled black and white whiskers, shook his head miserably from side to side. He raised his arms and circled them slowly over the heads of his people.

Block held up his hands up in despair. The man looked at him. He nodded very slowly. He said something to the boy, who scribbled, and held up the one word.

UNDERSTAND.

"Jesus," Jimmy said in a hush. It wasn't a curse, but a prayer.

Block's eyes went to his feet. He would've crawled into his boots if he could have.

"Tell them we're sorry."

Bridget turned to a fresh sheet.

SORRY.

The skinny, tired-looking boy with the notebook turned a page and in small, perfect letters wrote:

ME TOO.

Bridget had to turn her face away.

"Clayton. I've got an idea," Jimmy said. He ran back into the Comm. Center and queried up the security files. He scanned several coded documents and jotted brief notes.

"Here," he told Block, coming back into the yard. "These numbers will get 'em past the security locks into the Control Room under the Visitors Center. This second sequence—here—will get them online with us from out there."

"But they'll have access to the control computers down there. What if they figure out how to unlock the main doors?"

"Can't. When we switched the lock controls INSIDE we blocked out the computers in the basement, too. They won't be able to bypass that."

"You're sure?"

"Positive."

"OK," Block said, still skeptical. "If you're absolutely sure."

Jimmy gave him an exasperated look, wondering why Block didn't fully trust him by now. Block read his face.

"Sorry. Let's do it."

Bridget wrote brief instructions on the pad, with the series of numbers. The boy copied them down. Their leader read over his copy, compared it to Bridget's numbers, and nodded *OK*.

"Better warn them there may be bodies in the Control Room," Block said.

Bridget scribbled *BODIES.*

The boy frowned, but wrote it down. He handed his notebook to the leader. The man made a gesture toward Block that said, *SO?*

The man turned and said something to the crowd, then waded through them toward the far end of the Visitors Center. He and two others went in. Inside they found the nondescript door leading to the basement.

"This is worse than being in a monkey house," Bridget said. She looked over the faces of the refugees. All looked forlorn. Their clothes were a mess, their hair unkempt and scraggly. Many of the faces bore the telltale reddish pocked hue of deepening radiation burns.

"They must have got caught near one of the blasts,"

she said.

"Yeah," Jimmy replied, almost wishing he was out there with them.

The three went inside to the Comm. console, waiting to see if a message would appear. The codes worked. A CHAT log came up on the right hand monitor.

:: WE ARE DESPERATE. YOU MUST HELP US. YOU MUST LET US IN. ::

Block sat and typed.

:: WHAT IS YOUR NAME? ::
:: PAUL BISHOP. ::
:: WHERE ARE YOU ALL FROM? ::
:: ILLINOIS MOSTLY. CHICAGO AREA. ::
:: HOW MANY? ::
:: 227. ::

Block shook his head. He tried to change the subject.

:: CAN YOU TELL US WHAT HAPPENED? THE BOMBS? WHAT STARTED IT? ::
:: DON'T KNOW. UNPROVOKED PROBABLY. SOMEONE SAID MAYBE MILITARY PEOPLE IN THE UKRAINE. PART OF THE OLD SOVIET ARSENAL. MOSCOW WAS ATTACKED, TOO. ::
:: FALLOUT? ::
:: TERRIBLE. WORSE EVERY DAY. FALLOUT CLOUDS SPREADING. EVERYWHERE. SOME OF US WERE BURNED. ::
:: COULD TELL. ::

As Block wrote this, Bridget, standing behind him,

gripped his shoulder.

"What do we do?" she pleaded.

"Nothing, Bridget. There's *nothing*. Drop it." He resumed typing.

:: PAUL, WISH WE COULD HELP. WE FOUGHT THE SAME AIR PROBLEM IN HERE. FOR WEEKS. DIDN'T KNOW UNTIL RECENTLY WHAT WAS ACTUALLY HAPPENING. WE'VE STABILIZED IT. THE COMPLEX IS AIR TIGHT. IF WE OPEN THE PODS, WE'RE DEAD, TOO. ::
:: DON'T YOU HAVE AN AIR-LOCK? ::

Block hesitated, then answered.

:: YES. ::
:: LET US COME THROUGH A FEW AT A TIME. IF WE'RE CAREFUL WE CAN DO IT. ::

"No, Clayton," Jimmy insisted. "Out of the question. Even if there's a small pass-through leak. It could throw everything out of whack again."

"You're certain, Jimmy?" Bridget asked.

"Not one doubt."

:: SORRY PAUL. CAN'T BE DONE. ::

There was no response. After a minute and a half came this.

:: THEN WE'LL LAY OUT HERE AND DIE IN FRONT OF YOU. ::

The awful image formed in Bridget's mind, and was unbearable.

"They can't do that, Clayton. You can't allow it."

"Can't allow it! Whad'a'ya expect me to do?"

"We'd be living forever with piles of corpses! Right under our noses."

"And how do you suggest I stop them?" he asked caustically.

"I don't know," she said, defeated. "Just talk sense to him."

"I'm not sure that's possible." He got up and pointed at the chair. "You want this?"

"Sit down," she said. "Don't be ridiculous."

"Bridget, he's right. How do you tell dying people what to do?" Jimmy asked.

"Maybe we should rethink this," she said. "What if we agreed to let just some of them in? Think about it. It might enhance our own chances of survival."

Jimmy was losing control.

"I'm only gonna say this one more time. Is everybody listening?" he asked as if addressing second-graders. "We cannot open the door! No door. No open. Please raise your hands if you understand me."

"All right, Jimmy. We get it," Block said.

"I'm sorry, Bridget," Jimmy said. "I can't stand the idea of them lying out there dying either. Anyway, who would you let in?" he pressed. "Which ones?"

She tried to speak but was stopped cold. She had not considered this.

"See?" Jimmy said bitingly. "It's unthinkable. What? Five? Ten? Women? The little ones? Do we take the children who are dying, or some adults who might reproduce quicker?"

Bridget stood silent, her eyes wet and glazed. Through a door she could see the people huddled together, anxious, waiting for answers. Her heart broke into agony. Two hundred and twenty-seven anonymous souls in their own purgatory. *Why'd they have to come here?* her mind demanded.

Jimmy put an arm around her shoulder.

"Just accept it. There is no good way out of this."

She was stifling tears again.

"Go ahead and cry. Probably what we all ought to do," Jimmy said.

The muscles in Block's taut fingers were trying to bend the steel arms of his chair. He was holding tears back, too. He tried again for a message that might end this standoff.

:: PAUL. PLEASE UNDERSTAND. IF THERE WAS ANYTHING WE COULD DO, THAT WAS SAFE, WE'D DO IT. BELIEVE ME. CAN'T EVEN GUARANTEE OUR OWN SURVIVAL. IF WE OPEN THE PODS, ALL BETS ARE OFF. WE DON'T LIKE IT EITHER. I'M TELLING YOU, THERE IS NO CHOICE. ::

After a moment the reply came.

:: WHAT IS YOUR NAME? ::
:: CLAYTON BLOCK. TEAM LEADER. ::
:: HOW'D YOU LIKE TO LEAD MY TEAM, CLAYTON BLOCK? ::
:: I KNOW WHAT YOU'RE THINKING - - - ::

The computer squealed several loud beeps like a stepped-on cat as Bishop's reply overran Block's typing.

:: - - - BULL! NO YOU DON'T. ::

Block tried to keep calm. It was a losing battle.

:: PAUL, LOOK - - - ::
:: YOU DON'T HAVE THE FIRST CLUE. ALL YOU'RE THINKING IS YOU'RE GOING TO LIVE. WE DON'T MATTER. ::

"Ahggg!" Block croaked, unable even to form profanity. *Blang!* yelled the foot panel. "What's the point?" *Blang!* "This is useless!"

"Clayton, stop it!" Bridget cried, even more agitated. "Please. Just try to get them to leave. They can't make us sit here and watch them die."

"Yes, they can."

"Clayton!"

"You do it!" he demanded. He got up and stood like a statue.

This time Bridget took the keyboard. Her lips trembled. She looked at the screen, fingers poised for several seconds.

:: PAUL. I'M BRIDGET LISTNER. PLEASE LISTEN. I KNOW YOU THINK WE'RE AWFUL. CALLOUS. THAT'S NOT IT. WE JUST CAN'T RISK OPENING THE PODS. WE DIDN'T CHOOSE THIS. BUT YES, WE WANT TO SURVIVE. NOT JUST FOR OURSELVES. FOR YOU, TOO. IF WE OPEN THE AIRLOCK WE COULD ALL BE GONE IN DAYS. NOT JUST THE AIR. THE RADIATION. ::

This made Bishop think. It had not occurred to him how easily the radiation could infect the pods. In fact, it hadn't occurred to Jimmy or Block. Bridget, despite her desperation and tears, was thinking more clearly than all of them. Bishop's reply finally came back.

:: DON'T WANT TO SAY THIS. YOU ARE RIGHT. MOST OF US ARE VERY SICK. HORSE RACE WHETHER AIR OR RADIATION KILLS US FIRST. ::
:: WE CAN'T CHANGE PLACES PAUL. THAT'S THE UGLY FACT. ::
:: YOU STILL MAY HAVE TO WATCH US GO.

MANY ARE WEAK. DON'T KNOW IF I CAN GET THEM TO MOVE ON. YOU WERE THEIR LAST HOPE. VERY LAST. ::

Three short beeps followed, and the screen went blank. The three Solarians were silent.

As they watched out the windows of the Comm. Center the man in the fatigues—Paul Bishop, they assumed—emerged with the two others from around the corner of the Visitors Center and walked toward the crowd. He stood close to the pod, his back to the Solarium. He waved his arms with various gestures, including one pointing toward the highway. Some heads nodded "Yes," some shook "No." This went on for nearly half an hour.

The man who had wielded the crow bar came up and stood by Bishop, speaking to the crowd. As he spoke, Bishop was clearly not happy. Some of those seated began pulling themselves to their feet, with great difficulty. They fanned out around the perimeter of Pod 2 along the sidewalks. Others slowly moved toward other pods, doing the same. Soon a line of refugees encircled the whole complex. All sat, forlorn, like abandoned cattle. Paul Bishop walked away shaking his head and disappeared into a pickup camper near the Visitors Center.

"Great," Bridget said, dejected. "Exactly what we *didn't* want."

"Nothing we can do," Jimmy said. "Let's go to the house."

Block nodded, though his face was still red and he looked like he might vomit any second. They crossed self-consciously through the podwalk into #4 and into the house, eyes watching their every movement.

Mai Ker and Pam were in the living room looking miserable. They all talked. No one had any suggestion how to deal with this latest crisis. One crisis too many.

They now felt like bacteria under a microscope.

Periodically, like fish to the edge of their aquarium, they looked out a door or window, watching the grim sentries. The refugees were still unmoved at their assigned positions around the pods. A few acting as servants were walking from person to person with pails, pouring what was either water or very weak soup into people's cups.

As hard as it was, the team decided to eat supper. They had to carry on, even with everyone staring. And they would have to try to sleep, knowing as they did that men, women, children could be dying on the sidewalks just the other side of the pod walls.

"Don't know who has it worse," Pam said during the meal.

"They do," said Mai Ker. "We have time. They don't."

Block wasn't able to eat much. When they had finished supper he felt much sicker than during the afternoon. What he had thought were nerves and anxiety turned out to be more. He and Bridget went to sit on the love seat but in two minutes he was running up to his bathroom. She followed and arrived at the bedroom door to the sounds of violent vomiting.

"I don't feel good," he said, emerging from the bathroom.

"Lay down for a while"

"Yeah."

She felt his forehead which was hot. He felt like his head would split. Bridget helped him undress and tried to make him comfortable.

"I'll get something from the infirmary."

"Thanks."

Despite a throbbing headache and twisting stomach, he was asleep before she returned. She set the analgesics on the dresser and sat opposite on Willy's bed, and watched. She left the bathroom light on.

Caroline was above the light fixture again, nibbling a fresh supply of sunflower seed Block had set there just before supper.

Bridget went down to help clean up. When she returned an hour later she found him bathed in sweat. She roused him.

"How you feel?"

"Like three-day-old dog dump."

"You're sweating."

"Yeah. Feel really hot."

She touched his skin. It was hotter. She bathed his face with a cool wash cloth, as well as his chest. She kissed him and got undressed and crawled in next to him.

Just my luck, she thought, *a nursemaid already.*

Exhausted from their day, she soon dozed off, though it was like sleeping next to a fireplace.

By 2:00 a.m., Block was burning up. He had roused himself three times, barely making it to the toilet with increasingly severe bouts of diarrhea. These were followed by a violent vomiting, though nothing much was left to come up.

At 2:25, Bridget found him on the john again, the waste can stationed in front of him.

"You gonna make it?"

"I'll be OK."

"You eat something bad?"

"Don't know. When we were butchering the other day I chewed some raw bacon. Used to do it as a kid. I should know better by now."

"Could be the tomatoes Pam was canning this morning. Maybe some bacteria. Bet it was in the Sloppy Joes."

"Whatever it was, it doesn't like me."

She helped him back to bed.

"I'm going to get Pam. Maybe she can help." She plodded to Pam's room and woke her.

"I need your help. Clayton's really sick."

Pam shook herself awake and followed Bridget. She checked Block's temperature. 105.8 degrees.

"Keep trying to cool him down," she instructed Bridget. "I'll get some antibiotics from the infirmary."

"I brought some analgesics."

"Maybe just some acetaminophen for the fever. Probably has an infection."

She returned in a few minutes with a syrupy anti-diarrhetic, an antacid, and a syringe of high-potency antibiotic. They propped Block up enough to help him swallow the syrup and the chalky antacid. Pam gave him the shot. He was in so much pain he didn't even feel it.

"Need some water," he managed to say through the goo.

Pam brought him a glass. He tried to swallow it. Before it was half gone, he lunged sideways, spewing it back up. His stomach was not accepting visitors at the moment.

"We need to get him to the infirmary," Pam said. "Get Jimmy."

With Jimmy and Mai Ker helping—and it took all four of them—they manhandled Block over to the infirmary. Pam put an IV into each of his arms.

"He's dehydrating. We've got to pump as much saline into him as we can. Nothing by mouth right now. He probably can't keep it down."

"Even water?" Bridget asked.

"No."

Jimmy and Mai Ker went back to bed, neither having really gotten fully awake. Pam and Bridget sat by Block on either side of the infirmary bed, bed pans at the ready. He would shiver and they would try to steady his hulky frame.

"Just rest, Clayton," Pam told him, trying to comfort him.

"Anything we can do?" Bridget asked.

"We can rub him down a little with alcohol."

"Will that help?" she asked, beginning to sound desperate.

"No. But he'll feel cooler."

"I think he'd rather have a stiff drink."

"No booze," she warned Bridget. "It would make it worse. He'd never get it down anyway."

Pam turned down the infirmary lights so Block could rest. Bridget periodically wiped him down with a wash cloth soaked in cold water and rubbing alcohol. She hummed soft melodies to him and kissed his forehead every few minutes, an attempt to hold on to the thin shred of her own sanity. Her emotions had reached the breaking point this afternoon. Now she was sinking toward numbness. Pam propped a pillow behind Bridget in her chair. Pam sat and said a quiet prayer, but not loud enough to disturb Bridget, who was drifting off.

23

Friday, June 6th

Since Wednesday night, Block had not improved. The gut-wrenching diarrhea gave way to repeated stomach cramps. Every three to four minutes he doubled up in pain.

Pam tried other treatments, and a second antibiotic. Nothing seemed to stem the progressively worsening pain. The IVs were keeping fluid in him but the cramps were increasingly severe.

"It's like labor pains," Pam told Bridget. "But they won't quit!"

Pam was sure it was a bacterial infection but not sure what. She had taken a stool sample Thursday morning which Mai Ker used to start cultures in the lab. If they could identify the particular bacteria, they had a better chance of fighting it. But there was blood in the stool, too. This meant intestinal bleeding, which was weakening him even faster. What they would not discover for several days, once the cultures grew out, was that Block had a severe, aggressive salmonella infection.

Everything he attempted to eat, whether solid or fluid, was instantly rejected. Despite an IV in both arms to rehydrate his system he continued to sweat heavily, loosing much of what he gained. His fever hovered between 105 degrees and 107 degrees.

To add to turmoil, at about 3:30 this afternoon a huge racket erupted. The refugees, either out of frustration or collective rage, began pounding on the tough plastic pods with sticks, rock, boards, pipes, hands, anything. Tough as they were, the pods transmitted the deadened sound like muffled machine gun and cannon fire.

Jimmy and Mai Ker went to the yard in Pod 2, hoping to spot Paul Bishop. If they could get him back to the Control Room under the Visitors Center, maybe they could persuade him to stop this incessant but pointless protest.

Bishop was nowhere in sight.

Bridget and Pam were running shifts with Block, taking only necessary breaks to eat or rest briefly. Neither had slept completely since Wednesday night. By 5:00 p.m., Block's temperature spiked to 107.5 degrees. Pam had given him another injection of antibiotics just after noon, hoping this would break the siege. Bridget continued to bathe his head and whole body with cool cloths, trying to help ease the fever. Pam had considered an ice bath, but as weak as he was she was afraid the temperature shock could kill him.

He opened his eyes every few minutes but his throat was so parched he could hardly speak. His voice was like sandpaper scraping a cactus. Now he managed a few words.

"What's the noise?"

"Bishop's people. Banging on the pods," Pam told him.

"Sorry I'm so much trouble," he squawked. His voice trembled like a frightened prairie coyote seeking shelter from an impending storm.

Bridget kissed him.

"You're no trouble," she said. "You're just not used to having someone take care of you, are you?"

He shook his head feebly from side to side.

"No," he managed. "I don't know what I am . . ." His breathing was shallow and tired.

"Just rest. Pam thinks it's an infection. We're trying to figure out what. Then we can help more."

He nodded.

THE PODS continued to rumble under hundreds of angry hands. Mai Ker and Jimmy set out in opposite directions, walking the pod perimeters, searching for Paul Bishop. The infernal racket was driving them crazy and something had to be done to stop it. If Bishop was still among the living, he was out of sight. Jimmy spotted the crowbar man sitting with a small group on the south side of Pod 14. They were eating something. He got the man's attention and tried to motion him back toward the Visitors Center. The man shook his head "No" and went on eating. Jimmy moved his hands and fingers as if typing. A girl sitting by the man pointed. Jimmy had not brought anything to write on, so he tried to spell out B-I-S-H-O-P-? in large letters in the air. The man shook his head, *No,* again. Jimmy didn't know if this meant, *No, he's gone,* or, *No, I'm not going to get him for you.*

Jimmy walked on, finally meeting up with Mai Ker in the podwalk between #10 and #11.

"Any luck?" he asked.

"No."

"Me either."

The appearance of the two Solarians walking the pods had drawn some interest from OUTSIDE, which itself had somewhat quieted the protesters.

"Let's go home, I'm hungry," said Jimmy.

As they walked toward the house in Pod 4, eyes followed them. When it became clear they were not headed to Pod 1, the pounding got louder again.

IN THE infirmary, Block lay very still. His fever seemed, to Bridget's touch, to have fallen slightly. He opened his eyes briefly, a few inches beneath Bridget's loving face. His body quaked suddenly with a pain that was different from the abdominal cramps. His shoulders rolled together as if they would pull away from his spine, and he gasped for a breath. His shoulders relaxed. He got half a breath in but even this obviously hurt.

Parched tears squeezed from his eyes. They stared helplessly up at Bridget. She clutched his hand. Fear rose in her own eyes.

"Clayton?"

The remains of the half-breath escaped gradually from his lungs. His jaw relaxed. He was completely still.

She began to speak his name again. She couldn't get it out. She stiffened and stopped breathing, the shock unthinkable, the reality impossible.

He was gone.

Every fiber of her being seemed at war. Several emotions raced for the surface, then ran and hid. She clutched at his arm. She would have gone with him—in that instant—if she could.

Finally, the pent-up emotions erupted. She gasped for breaths between angry sobs. She lay across Block's still chest, clutching at him with anguished cries.

Her agony was so loud Mai Ker and Jimmy heard it as they passed through Pod 3. They ran to the infirmary. Mai Ker stopped abruptly in the doorway. Without asking a word, the tortured expression on Bridget's face told what they did not want to hear. Jimmy stepped passed Mai Ker and checked Block to be sure. Mai Ker remained immobile in the doorway, her legs starting to shake.

"Pam," he said quietly, keying his intercom radio. "Get over here."

"My God," Mai Ker said in complete disbelief. Her heart came into her throat. "Oh my God . . ." Her voice shrank into a whisper. She sank to her knees. Slowly her hips sank onto her heels and she rocked back and forth. She felt dizzy and sick to her stomach.

The ominous pounding continued from OUTSIDE. Pam arrived.

"What's wrong?" She got the words out, then, seeing Block, an icy chill ran through her. The hulking man who had been writhing and twisting just an hour earlier lay there perfectly still, every muscle relaxed. She rushed to the bed, checking for a pulse at his neck. Nothing.

"How could this happen?" Jimmy said numbly.

"I don't—" Pam could not finish her sentence. Her mind flew into a whirl of what more she might have done, what she possibly missed, whether she was even competent to nurse anyone at all. The room around her seemed to darken and a terrible sick feeling plowed her stomach.

This was the last thing she expected. Not Clayton. He was too strong for something like this to take him. She gently lifted Bridget's head off his chest.

"Bridget." They looked at each other, shaking their heads. What could be said? It was better to keep quiet.

Jimmy helped Mai Ker up. She held him so tight he thought his spine would crack. Jimmy looked at Pam. He looked at Block's lifeless face. No more of his unsettling frowns. No more of his comely smiles. This face was strange, foreign.

For a full minute, no one said a word. But all four locked onto the same thought. *What happens now?*

Pam finally broke the wall of silence.

"Let's leave him for a bit. Go over to the house. There'll be time later."

Jimmy nodded. They walked to the house as the refugees continued to pound, and sat in the living room, trying to absorb what had happened. Willy. Sarajane. Now Block. The shock settled in. Their thoughts ran laps. *How do we go on? What's the point?* And inevitably, *Who's next?* And with it all, incessant pounding, pounding, like a fibrillating heart, no direction, no rhythm, no purpose.

Jimmy was sitting next to Mai Ker on the couch. He pulled her close and kissed the side of her head. Emotionally he pulled her inside himself. Could he protect her?

The light OUTSIDE was fading as sundown approached. Purplish light streamed through the house. They sat together as it got dark, no lights on.

"We'll bury him tomorrow," Jimmy said. "I'll move him to one of the coolers for tonight."

"Just as well," Bridget said, sitting alone in a chair. "But I need some time with him. I'll clean him up."

Pam said she'd help clean him and dress him. The other three watched Bridget, the sympathy in their eyes helping hold her upright. They tried to talk about how they would go on. Without him.

In the middle of a sentence, Bridget got up.

"I'm going to go over now."

Pam followed her to the infirmary. They took out the IV lines, bathed Block's body and wrapped it in two large, clean sheets.

WITHOUT THE last four Solarians really noticing, the pounding had gradually subsided. The protesters were settling down. Fatigue, the rotting air or the radiation poisoning made it impossible for them to go on tonight.

After a sandwich and some stale potato chips, Jimmy went to the infirmary, where Pam and Bridget were just finishing. They loaded Block onto the wheeled gurney.

"I need to walk for a while," Bridget said.

Jimmy guided the gurney slowly through the pods to #13, where he parked it in the largest walk-in cooler, one that would keep the body cool but not freeze it. He closed the heavy door carefully, so that it made no noise.

He went over to find lumber in the workshop in the

same pod. He started cutting up plywood and pine boards for the next coffin and worked for three hours putting it together. His mind hit idle, thinking of nothing but the tools at hand, nails, exact measurements. Making it just right.

Has to be right. And nice, he was telling himself. He even took a power sander to it, and finished it with a light coat of varnish. "Buff it in the morning, when it's dry," he said to no one in particular. He began to put the tools away. A glint of light flickered behind his left shoulder just for a moment. He looked, but saw nothing. He was exhausted and assumed his eyes were playing tricks.

BRIDGET WALKED to what had been her favorite place with Block, the ocean in Pod 12. A few huddled faces peered in from OUTSIDE but she never noticed them. The dim night lights of the pod had come on, bathing the water with a very dim shimmer as the artificial waves lapped the sand.

She found the spot where she and Clayton had often sat, near the rocks at one end of the swimming beach. It seemed like the right place to be. She sat very still, once rubbing at her stomach gently. It had been in knots, for one reason or another, all day. She had thought the worst was behind them. Now she no longer wanted to speculate. One day at a time. That's how it would have to be. Anything else was too frightening to think about.

PAM WAITED back at the house in case Bridget returned. When she had not come back by 9:30, Pam and Mai Ker went looking for her. They knew where to look. They found her lying on her side in the sand, an abandoned beach towel rolled under her head, sound asleep. The tears and sand had left tracings on her cheek like those left by the waves on the beach.

"Bridget. Come home," Mai Ker said.

Bridget stirred. The voice seemed far off.

"Too tired," she said groggily.

"You'll sleep better in bed," Pam said.

This seemed to register.

"My old bed," Bridget said.

They helped her up and the three walked very slowly back home. It seemed to take forever. But then, so did everything else.

WHEN JIMMY came back from #13, he found Pam alone on the porch swing. It was obvious she had been crying.

"What's wrong?"

She didn't answer. He tried again.

"Tell me."

"It's my fault, Jimmy. It must have been something I cooked."

"You don't know that. And we all cooked for ourselves, too. Especially lately."

"It must've been food poisoning."

"We don't know that."

Jimmy sat and tried to hold her gently but she rebuffed him. She slid away to the end of the swing. He reached over and touched her shoulder lightly. Finally she took his hand and held it there on her shoulder.

"If it was me, I'll never forgive myself."

Jimmy thought about this.

"But Clayton would," he said.

Pam looked straight ahead for several moments, into the darkness OUTSIDE the pod. "Isn't that something?" she said. She nodded. "You're probably right."

After ten minutes of silence, Pam got up without another word and went up to bed. Jimmy went in and snacked on some more stale chips and some orange juice, then went up.

Bridget was sound asleep in her old room that she

had shared with Mai Ker. He stopped and looked into Block's room. Willy's bed was stripped, Block's was still a disheveled mess from two nights before. The empty room looked harsh. He walked over and straightened the bedclothes on Block's bed. Then he noticed, in the dark bathroom, a *click, click* up near the light. He switched it on. Caroline sat atop the light fixture, pecking around for seed that wasn't there.

"Kind of forgot you, didn't we?" Jimmy said. He extended a finger toward the light. She didn't move.

He searched around the bedroom, finally spotting an edge of the seed bag under one end of Block's bed. Finding a small silver plate on the top of Atchison's dresser, he put some seed in it and set it near the foot of the bed. He backed away to the door. Caroline flew to the plate and feasted. She flew back to the sink for several drops of water from the tap that lay pooled near the drain. Then she flew back up onto Block's bed and perched on the bedspread. A few suitable pecks made a small indentation, then she snuggled down onto the fabric nest.

Jimmy watched, and considered it all.

"Here you are. And him gone," he told Block's little friend. "And life goes on."

He found Mai Ker fast asleep in their room. He sat on the bed quietly, took off his shoes, then curled up beside her.

24

Saturday, June 7th

"You hungry?" Pam asked Jimmy as he came downstairs. It was just after 6:00 o'clock, but she had been up nearly an hour.

"No."

"Eat something."

"Maybe later. I gotta finish Clayton's coffin."

"He'll wait."

Jimmy sat and ate the eggs and bacon Pam had made. Bridget came down a few minutes later. She had slept some, but you couldn't tell. She sat.

"Coffee?" Pam asked her.

She nodded, and stirred brown sugar into the coffee. She looked at the two of them, her eyes bloodshot.

"What do we do now?" Bridget asked as if she expected some miraculous answer. She was ready to give up after asking herself this same question throughout a night of soul searching with little breaks of sleep.

"We do what we've been doing," Mai Ker said, coming through the door from the living room. She had been up before any of them but had been quietly reading. "We try to go on. We sleep, we eat, we work. And we take care of ourselves."

"Try to survive," Pam said.

It was simple, but hollow, advice. They watched Bridget closely but could not distinguish the pain from the skepticism sculpted into her face.

"And if we don't?" Bridget asked. They were words she didn't want to speak. But they were pressing in on everyone.

"Then it makes no difference," Jimmy said, chewing his last few bites and setting his fork down carefully. "We'll be gone. They'll die out there." His voice became almost inaudible. "We'll all be gone," he told his plate.

They looked at one another. Searching, fearful, anxious. But groping for the last impossible shred of hope. A faint chorus of hushed breathing was the only sound in the room.

Ironically, it was Bridget who spoke.

"We have to try," she said finally. "You're right. We have to go on—as long as we can. If we don't make it, it can't be because we didn't try." Out of nowhere, out of the vacuum inside her, this unexpected sense of determination sprang forth. "Life is no different today than it was yesterday. True? Yesterday we were determined to go on. Today has to be the same."

Mai Ker walked over and hugged her shoulders from behind. Bridget gave a little smile. Forced. But a smile nonetheless.

"Well, we've got lots to figure out. That's for sure," said Jimmy. He watched Bridget. "You OK if we go ahead and bury him today?"

She winced and bit at her lower lip.

"I guess. Don't really want him in that stupid cooler anymore." Her face softened. "I love you guys. Thanks for getting me through this."

The three women continued their breakfast as Jimmy headed for Pod 13 to polish Block's coffin. As he was buffing down the finish a thought skipped through his mind, uninvited. *Might just as well build four more.* But he kicked it away. The last thing they needed was to feel sorry for themselves. *If you want to feel sorry, feel sorry for them out there,* he reminded himself. He was one of four lucky ones.

When they finished eating, Pam and Mai Ker went to Willy and Sarajane's plot in #10 and began digging the grave. Bridget brought clean clothes from the house and she and Jimmy dressed the body, and managed to get it, somewhat awkwardly, into the coffin. Enough time had passed that rigor mortis was gone and the limbs were at least movable, if still incredibly heavy.

About 8:30, Jimmy and Bridget wheeled the coffin, atop the gurney, into #10 for the burial. Small clumps of OUTSIDEers, having slept under blankets on the grass OUTSIDE, watched with curiosity.

The Solarians gathered inside the white fence Jimmy had made for the grave yard. The third hole in the ground gave the little plot a foreboding sense of permanence.

There was no formal service. Jimmy brought his Bible along and read some verses from the Psalms, and a short bit from the end of Revelation that he had once heard at a funeral.

Mai Ker listened with curiosity to words that seemed to make little sense.

"'. . . and He will dwell among them, and they shall be His people, and God himself will be among them. And He will wipe away every tear from their eyes. There will no longer be death, there will no longer be mourning, or crying, or pain, for the first things have passed away . . .'"

Bridget, trying to listen but her heart rebelling, shook her head very slightly. As badly as she wanted to believe these words, she could not see past the loss of her new husband. Life seemed just one loss after another. *How can anything ever go right again?* she wondered. With a small embroidered handkerchief, a gift from her father, she wiped her face.

Not knowing what to say, they each prayed silently for several minutes as best they could. Then Bridget stepped closer and laid a hand on the coffin.

"I guess I'm not sure I'm really a Christian, Clayton. Not sure what I am. So I don't know what you want me to say. We all became close." She looked at the others. "But Clayton and I found a very special love. I'd hoped we'd have a child. God knows our little world here needs one. But God—" She sobbed. "—this God we talk about so easily—who I frankly don't much understand—I guess he's got some other plan. I wish he would tell us."

She went quiet. Everyone waited.

"Clayton was my husband, but he was our guiding force, too. Even when we all disagreed with him. He knew how to hold us together." She brushed tears from beneath her eyes. "Our marriage was very short. But those few days with him were . . ." She searched for a word. ". . . reassuring."

She rubbed her hand along the top of the coffin.

"He said something the night before he got sick. Bet he never told you. Said as desperate as everything was, he was glad it was me, and all of you, he was stuck with." Her voice broke. "Sorry, Clayton. I love you. If you see your God, tell him to have a little mercy on the rest of us. We need it."

Mai Ker put her arm around Bridget's waist and comforted her. Then with two on each side of the grave they struggled with the ropes and lowered the heavy box into the grave. Mai Ker lost her grip as it neared the bottom and the coffin bumped hard onto the soil and rocked to a rest. Bridget threw on the first few shovels of dirt, then stopped. Her breaths came in little, short catches.

"You finish it," she said. She walked quietly away.

"Pam, go with her?" Mai Ker pleaded.

Sweating like bears in a sun-baked desert, Jimmy and Mai Ker finished shoveling in the grave. They repeatedly wiped sweat from their face and arms. The pods were hot today, the sun intense. The cooling system probably needed adjustment, but Jimmy had been too preoccupied to notice, until now.

A larger crowd had collected OUTSIDE Pod 10 watching the burial. Some looked surprised. Some, sadly, looked pleased. Jimmy recognized the face of Paul Bishop near the back of the group.

Mai Ker packed large rocks over the grave to secure it from the few small animals that still roamed loose. These were always filching crops in #10 so the fresh dirt would be too inviting.

The two stood by the grave a few more moments, a last bit of respect for their leader. They ignored the people OUTSIDE.

MAI KER went to the Research Center to check the bacterial cultures taken from Block. Not that it mattered now, but they wanted to know. Mainly they wanted to know if it was something they were all exposed to, or something more random. But the cultures still had not completely grown out. She would have to check again in a day or two.

Jimmy worked around in Pod 10 some more, watering, cultivating several corn rows, trying to ignore the eyes that pried through the plastic walls.

Bridget helped Pam clean around the house and then went up for a much-needed nap. Her brain had filled with cobwebs since the burial. Pam devoted herself to the very neglected kitchen, deciding that more than anything today they needed a really good meal.

At lunch they reassigned duties again. They had never fully adjusted after Willy and Sarajane died, just limped along day-to-day and improvised. Now, with Block gone, they had to make some essential changes. There was no arguing, not the slightest disagreement. They all agreed to the adjustments, even though it meant a lot more work for each of them.

When the meal was cleaned up, they went into the

living room for a brief siesta. Everyone but Bridget fell asleep quickly in the cozy chairs. Yesterday had been very long, last night very short.

About 2:15, Mai Ker woke Jimmy, who was snoring so loudly it had awakened her and Pam. Mai Ker punched him lightly in the side. Bridget laughed, which was a welcome relief.

"We need to check the cooling, Jimmy," Mai Ker said, "or we're going to roast. It's too hot in here."

They went out on the porch, down the steps and started across the yard toward Pod 2. Mai Ker lurched to a stop, looking around.

"Where are they?" she said.

Jimmy, not watching, almost bumped into her. He didn't see what she meant.

"What?"

"Look." She pointed OUTSIDE in several directions. "They're gone."

Jimmy glanced around the perimeters of the nearest pods. Not a person was in sight. He called into the house.

"Pam! Bridget!"

They appeared on the porch, frightened by the excitement in his voice. Jimmy looked toward the Visitors Center and the parking area. Not a person, not a vehicle in sight.

"Weird," Jimmy said.

"What?" Pam asked anxiously.

"I wonder. Come on," he said.

They hurried to the Comm. Center. Jimmy went to the terminal Block had used to talk with Paul Bishop. A fresh message had filled the screen. He scrolled through the message as the women read over his shoulders.

:: GOODBYE. THANKS FOR YOUR HOSPITALITY. IT WAS LOUSY. TOOK SOME

SUPPLIES FROM YOUR VISITORS CENTER. AND TWO CARS. THESE GUARDS DOWN HERE WON'T NEED THEM.
WE WATCHED THIS MORNING. QUITE A SIGHT. LIKE A MOVIE. THERE YOU WERE BIG AS LIFE, BUT WE COULDN'T TOUCH YOU. ::

Jimmy paged down to the next screen.

:: YOU'RE RIGHT. NO POINT. WE'RE ALL DYING. YOU. US. WHAT'S THE DIFFERENCE?
PREACHER WITH US SAYS WE'LL SEE YOU AGAIN SOMEDAY. HOPE NOT. YOU WOULDN'T LIKE WHAT I'D SAY.
WE BURIED ONE OF OURS LAST NIGHT. PUT THE GRAVE ACROSS FROM THE VISITORS CENTER SO YOU WON'T HAVE TO LOOK AT IT.
GOOD LUCK. PAUL BISHOP. ::

Bridget and Mai Ker held back tears, mixed with relief. Pam dropped into a chair.

"It's for the best." She hung her head. "I guess." She pictured the ragged crowd driving on down the highway. No place to go. No home anymore. "Will the air out there stay like this forever?" she asked vaguely, for anyone who might have an answer.

"No way to know," Jimmy said. "Could last forever. Or it could come back. Or it could mutate into something worse. Different gases, different kind of atmosphere. We're dealing with the unknown." He looked at Bishop's leftover words frozen on the screen. "Since we can't go OUTSIDE, I guess we'll never know."

They went back to the house and changed into work clothes. Their new work assignments were waiting.

25

Monday, June 9th

Mai Ker awoke late. Their alarm had not gone off. She got up and stumbled toward the bathroom. She flipped the light switch, but no light. She looked at the bed stand. The LED on the clock was out. She went to the bedside and jiggled Jimmy's shoulder.

"Jimmy?" she said. He stirred but didn't awake. "Jimmy. Get up. The power's out."

One eye opened to investigate.

"Turn it back on." He rolled toward the wall.

"Jimmy, the power's *out*. It's all out."

He managed to come around. Seeing her drowsy face over his, he pulled her toward him.

"Good, we can sleep all day."

"You sleep. I'll go check."

She went and woke Bridget and the two women went around the house, finding everything off. Bridget started to open the refrigerator to get some milk.

"Wait, keep it shut until we know how long this will be," Mai Ker told her.

They walked to the Research pod. No power. They jogged to the Comm. Center. Everything dead. Computers. Everything.

"Oh no," Bridget said. Her eyes became intense.

"What?"

"Everything's out, the computer's down—that means the outer doors could be unlocked."

They both rushed through the podwalk that linked Pod 2 to #1. Bridget was about to try the inner door that led into #1. Mai Ker jerked her arm back.

"Bridget, no! The bolts might have flipped open."

Bridget realized she was right. Both the inner and outer doors looked like they were shut tight. But if the lock bolts had unset, air movement from opening the inner door might crack the seal on the outer door. It was too risky to even check.

"We are on really thin ice," Bridget said.

"Let's get Jimmy. We've got to get the generators on line."

They started for the house but saw Jimmy and Pam crossing the podwalk from #4 to #2. They all met in the Comm. Center.

"Something's really wrong," Jimmy said, realizing finally that the whole complex was down.

"You don't know half," Bridget said. "The door locks in Pod one are offline. They look secure. But they may not be."

"I don't understand. If the OUTSIDE power went down, everything should have kicked over to backup generator automatically," Jimmy said. "If that failed, it should have switched to the master battery backup."

"Well, whatever," Bridget said, "we've got to fix this quick. What if more refugees show up—"

"—or the others come back?" Pam finished. "And the door's not secure?"

Jimmy and Bridget ran to Pod 13, where the huge bank of storage batteries was built into one whole wall of the equipment shed. Jimmy checked the indicators. Everything was totally dead.

"I know those check lights were on when I was in here yesterday," he said. "I don't get it."

He opened several panels and used a tester to check for voltage. Nothing. He traced the wires between the battery packs and where they connected into the main system. No juice anywhere. He quickly scanned down the electrical schematic drawing inside one of the panel doors. He retraced the connecting wires.

"There's a wrong connection," he told Bridget.

"Where?"

"Here. See this large green wire. That's hooked into the feeder to the pods. But it should be the ground wire. This black one here to the ground—that should feed into the system."

"And?"

"Well, for some reason the auto-start on the backup generators didn't kick in. Could be a bad switch. Could have been a programming error. Anyway, when that failed, the computer would have a couple of hours on its own battery. When the computer tripped the system over to these batteries and closed the circuit, it grounded out. Sucked the batteries dry."

"That quick?"

"If you ground them completely, they die quick."

"But why were your indicators showing good yesterday?"

"Well, all that showed was there was juice in the batteries. It was after the computer tried to switch the batteries into the main system that the short happened."

"What else can go wrong in this place? How could the wiring be wrong?"

"Whoever did the final wiring must've had too many beers that afternoon."

"The idiots never tested it?"

"Guess not."

"So, what now?" Bridget asked, still worried about the locks on the outer door.

"We have to go around and manually start the backup generators. I'll have to jumper these batteries into the system so we can recharge them. And I'll have to figure out the programming error. Why the generators didn't kick in when they should have."

"Not like you have anything else to do."

"This is our only priority right now. The crops will have to make it on their own. Till we fix this."

There would be no breakfast today. Jimmy fixed the wiring in the battery panels, then he and Bridget fired up the main backup generator outside the back of the equipment shed. He checked to make sure voltage was feeding into the storage batteries. Slowly, the indicator lights showed them coming back to life and starting to recharge.

Next he reset the circuit breakers on the main power system that had kicked out during the night. He called Mai Ker and stationed her by Pod 1 to listen for any action in the locks while he and Bridget went to the Comm. Center. Lights were on. An indicator light on the backup battery for the main systems computers showed these recharging, also.

The two sat at separate consoles and manually restarted the main and redundant system computers. Monitors came to life and programs began to boot up.

As soon as his console was online, Jimmy went immediately to the security program that controlled the door locks in Pod 1. To his horror, icons on the screen showed that all the deadbolts on both the inner and outer doors had unlocked when the system went down.

"Bridget. Look."

She rolled her chair by his, looked and gasped.

"What about the seals?"

Jimmy flipped to a different screen.

"Shows they're intact. No leaks."

"Get 'em locked!"

He flipped to the previous screen and keyed the locking commands. Nothing happened. The icons still showed both doors unlocked.

"Oh man," he whined.

"Why isn't it working?!"

"I don't know!"

"Do something. Kill all the fans! A pressure change in here could break those seals!"

Jimmy slid to a second computer and shut down the

whole air circulation system in the pods.

"How do we lock the doors?" Bridget prodded.

"I don't know. Let me think." He pounded a fist on the console. "Maybe there was a power spike or something when the computer tried to switch to backup."

"Could have corrupted a program file," Bridget said.

"Yeah. Let me think." He worked his fingers open and shut nervously. "Maybe I can pull up the change-over program. The archived one Haskins sent us when we took over lock control. It wouldn't have been running. It might be OK."

"Do it!" Bridget urged pointlessly, since Jimmy was already searching for the file.

He found the program and loaded it. He read several lines of instructions. Then he shook his head.

"Not that easy," he said.

"Why?"

" 'Cause when we took the locks over, our computer INSIDE had to talk with the one OUTSIDE, over there in the basement. If the OUTSIDE power went down, the Control Room is dead, too. That computer is dead. When this program tries to talk to it, it'll hit a road-block."

"Let me sit," Bridget said. "Let's see if all those programming classes paid off." She clicked to another screen and translated the locking program from English back into programming language. She searched for digital access codes. Several number strings popped into the search window. "Here goes nothing . . ."

"What are you doing?" Jimmy asked, worried.

"I'm deleting the routing and access codes to the Control Room computer in the basement. And now—" she said, quickly typing some new programming instructions into several lines, "—we're going to make our computer talk back to itself." She made some additional changes to remove the run-verification sequence. "We just took out the garbage," she said. "The program should be able to run internal-only."

"Don't lose anything crucial."

"Too late, Jimmy. I don't have a manual on this. I'm winging it. You like to pray. This would be a good time."

For nearly 10 minutes, she searched and rescanned the program, looking for any dead-ends or mistakes.

"OK," she finally said, drawing a long breath. "Save. Done." She translated the program back into English and graphics. "What now?"

"Just click the two door icons. Outer first, then inner. See, where they show UNLOCKED. The little red levers should move."

Bridget clicked the outer door icon. Two loud bird-like chirps sounded, the lever flipped from vertical to horizontal. A message popped onto the screen, LOCKING IN PROGRESS. DOOR SECURE. She drew another long breath and clicked the inner door icon. Two more loud chirps. The red lever flipped. LOCKING IN PROGRESS. DOOR SECURE.

Jimmy let out a hoot.

"You're brilliant!" he shouted, pulling her up. They danced in a small circle and he hugged her. "You get the award today. I'll even do the dishes!"

Bridget laughed. Mai Ker came through the podwalk from #1.

"I heard some moving. Did they lock?"

"Yeah!" Jimmy said. He pulled Mai Ker into the dance. "Solarium-3 is back to life!" he shouted.

Winded, they went to tell Pam who was at the house checking to make sure food in the freezers hadn't thawed. It was nearly 11:00 o'clock and all were starved. Sandwiches were thrown together and they ate with new vigor.

"That was way too close," said Pam. "What if it happens again? And we don't find it in time?"

"It won't happen again," Jimmy said confidently. "I've got the battery wiring straightened out. And after lunch Bridget and I will check all the switch-over programs. My guess is when we took over control from OUTSIDE, we may have created some programming conflicts with our INSIDE systems. We just need to find that and fix it. Our computer might still have been looking for some link to an OUTSIDE power supply. We have to reprogram that."

"Can we?" Mai Ker asked.

"I can't. Bridget the Master can. Apparently she can do anything," he smiled.

"We need to get those new solar panels wired in," Mai Ker said.

"Yes," Bridget agreed. "We'll work on them as soon as we fix the computer problems."

"I wish Block was here," Jimmy said. "He had the master plan for the solar panels in his head."

"We'll figure it out," Bridget said. "He kept a little notebook up in our old room. I'll check it. Might have left some ideas there."

It hit them again how impossibly difficult life had become. The team of seven was now four. It wasn't just the gene pool. It was the energy pool, the mind pool, the emotional pool. The need to depend on each other had grown geometrically as their numbers had shrunk. The question was, could they go on this way?

AT THE Research Center lab, Mai Ker pulled out the Petri dishes with bacterial specimens from Block. She examined them as Jimmy watched. The color of two specimens had changed slightly. She carefully scraped a small sample from one dish and placed it on a slide under the microscope. She studied it intently for several minutes, making some hieroglyphic like sketches in a notebook.

"Well?"

"I think I know," she said. "Give me a minute."

She read the sample for a few more minutes, adding detail to the sketches, then went to a book shelf and pulled down a thick biology reference. She flipped through many pages until she found the picture she was looking for.

"Look," she showed him. "Now, see if you can see it," she said, directing him to the microscope.

Sure enough, there it was. Hundreds of the bacteria pictured in the book swarmed in the culture sample. He looked again at the color photograph in the book.

"Salmonella," he said, reading the caption.

"Yes," she said, nodding. "Very common. Very deadly. We missed it."

"Would it have helped if we'd known?"

"Maybe." She looked at the floor. "Maybe not. Depends on if Pam gave the right antibiotics or not. When you do not know it is just a . . . crap—? What is the saying?"

"Crapshoot."

"Yes. But there's no way Pam could know. Shooting in the dark."

"What caused it?" he asked.

"I do not know. Lot of things could. Could have been touching raw meat when we were slaughtering. Or handling meat in the kitchen. But it could have been something he ate."

"Pam worried it was something she cooked."

"It could have been those awful raw eggs he was always drinking for breakfast."

"So we'll never be sure."

"No. But you should mention the raw egg thing to Pam. It might make her feel better."

Jimmy nodded.

"Thank you, 'wife.'" It still sounded very foreign to him. "Back to work."

"This is work."

"You know what I mean. There's animals to be fed, plants to water. That work."

She laughed as they went to change clothes.

"I'm be in number nine and number eleven working with the animals," she told Jimmy.

"I'll join you as soon as Bridget and I check those control programs we talked about."

"Ooh," she teased, "sounds like 'work'!"

BRIDGET AND Jimmy found several more programming errors in the computer files that controlled the electrical system of the complex. They fixed these, then added several new computer-controlled access points in the system for the new turbine-powered generators they had built. With the new generators, the Solarians would be able to offset some of the loss of electrical power from OUTSIDE.

Still, they knew their make-shift adjustments would not fully replace the power supply they had relied on from OUTSIDE. This was the one major failure of the whole project design. The planners had built Solarium-3 as a closed, self-sufficient eco-system, with one exception. Operation of all the electrical equipment, including the sophisticated computer systems, relied heavily on power from the OUTSIDE. Now, because of the catastrophe that had hit the planet, the Solarians would have to become truly independent of the OUTSIDE world. They would become entirely self-sufficient, or they also would die. This presented formidable mental and emotional challenges. Could they make those adjustments quickly enough?

As all four of them tended the cattle and horses in Pod 9 this afternoon, the conversation quickly focused on confronting this reality. Mai Ker, who stayed quiet during much of the discussion as she brushed one of the horses, finally spoke up with an idea that might help them survive.

The plan was simple and would help conserve electricity. Why not, she suggested, consolidate all their daily activities as far as possible into Pods 9, 10, 11 and 12? Here they had plenty of land to cultivate, the ocean for seafood, and room for all of the animals. Routine supplies they would need from Pods 13 and 14 could be stored in the agriculture barn in #10. Basic medical supplies could be brought from the infirmary in Pod 7, but #7 could still be used in an emergency. They could close off the other pods with one exception. The air would still be fully circulated throughout the whole complex. Since little or no oxygen would be consumed in the closed pods, the air circulating through those pods might help sustain the delicate oxygen pressure balance in their atmosphere, circulating back into the four pods they were using.

"Except for the master computers in the Comm. Center, we could shut down most of the electrical equipment in the other pods. That would reduce the load, right?" Mai Ker said. "So maybe the original solar panels coupled with the new generators could keep up."

"It might work," Bridget said. "Conservation, sort of."

"I don't know," Pam said. "I feel pretty cooped up as it is."

"But it doesn't mean we could never go into the other pods," said Mai Ker. "Just when we really have to."

Pam's face suddenly brightened a little.

"Wouldn't have to clean the house anymore," she smiled.

"Where do we live?" Jimmy asked.

"Jimmy, where did people live before we had houses?" Mai Ker asked.

"Caves?"

"Tents, dummy. I always loved camping. In fact my

last camping trip was interrupted to come here."

"Do we have tents?"

"We can make some. We've got a lot of plastic tarps. And some rolls of canvas." For Mai Ker, whose ancestors had lived a fairly simple life for centuries, this did not seem like much of a challenge. "We could set up a living compound in number ten."

"We'd still have to be in Pod two once in a while," Bridget said, "to check the circulation systems, air sensors, that stuff."

"You could set up a couple of laptops in number ten, with a wireless link to the main computers," Jimmy said. "Most of the stuff could be checked that way."

"Yeah," Bridget said. Her expression became dispirited. "And let's face it. I don't think we need to try to communicate with OUTSIDE anymore." Her observation was unsettling and held an unwelcome ring of finality. But they all knew she was right.

"Tents. Kind of like living outdoors," Pam said.

"Yes," Mai Ker said.

Living "outdoors" INSIDE seemed a new idea, even though they had been working "outdoors" for a year.

"We can use the Research Center in number three when we have to," Mai Ker continued. "We'll still have to keep up certain crop tests, make sure things aren't going wrong with them genetically. And blood work on the animals maybe."

"Or us, maybe," Jimmy added.

They talked over details of Mai Ker's plan for several hours as they moved into the fields in #10 to work crops. Saving on light usage would pay off in the long run. Light bulbs for the various fixtures were a limited item. While they still had a large supply, cutting use would preserve that supply much longer than originally planned.

Because the sky had gradually become darker, "purpling" as they called it, sun rays had grown fainter, impeded by the denser air. One trade-off—and a positive one—was that the sunlight was less intense so it was easier to cool the pods in the warmest months. This would conserve electricity. A negative effect was that they would need to build more, or larger, solar panels to run the turbines for the new electrical generators.

With no team leader, it was difficult to come to a final decision about every detail of the plan. But consensus was reached. As soon as the new solar panels and electrical components were built and in place, they would begin the process of moving outdoors, shutting down all nonessential equipment, and closing off pods.

As the afternoon wore into early evening, a severe thunderstorm brewed OUTSIDE, driven from the west. The trees along the river began to bend violently under its force and large thick rain drops were blown up and down the pods, driven by the violent wind.

INSIDE, the Solarians were warm and dry. A gentle wind from the circulating system and overhead fans swirled gently around them. They were safe, and secure, in their protective shells.

26

The thunderstorm became more violent and continued overnight. The purpling air gave the lightning an even more eerie look. Rain mixed with large hail pounded the pod roofs into the morning hours but from INSIDE it sounded like nothing more than a gentle sprinkle.

Jimmy and Pam worked today on completing the new solar panels. Block, before his death, had finished welding the new turbines, and the linkage needed for the bike-driven generator Mai Ker had suggested, although the bike was not set up yet. Instead of ruining one of the seven bikes the planners had given them, they decided to use one of the exercise bikes from the Recreation Pod since it already had a stationary frame.

Bridget and Mai Ker spent most of the day in #10 working crops. Most of the plants had fully recovered from the corrupted air. But they still needed care, weeding, and watering. Several plots of sweet corn were ready to harvest. As these could not be ignored very long, they began hand-picking bushel after bushel and stored them in the artificially cooled "root cellar" that was actually above ground in the back of the barn.

By early afternoon the violence of the storm OUTSIDE had let up but the rain continued. Rays of sun tried to break through the thick clouds but much darker clouds to the west showed more rain was on the way.

They worked into late afternoon with no break. As they got ready to head to the house for supper, Bridget triggered the large overhead sprinklers in #10 to give the crop plots a much needed rain of their own. Jimmy and Pam joined them and they went home and made supper.

AFTER SUPPER and dishes, Jimmy headed upstairs to shave and clean up, anticipating another night with his new wife. Mai Ker beat him to the shower, changed into her PJs, and was now curled up on the bed singing quietly to herself. Then, for some reason, she remembered she had left her favorite work gloves hanging on a fence rail in #9 yesterday. She slipped her shoes back on. Jimmy was just coming out of the bathroom.

"I left my good gloves over at the corral yesterday. I'll be right back."

"Pretty obsessed with a pair of gloves," Jimmy laughed, drying his hair.

"They're the only ones that really fit me."

The lights in other pods were all off, saving energy, so she carried a flashlight. The sky was black, punctuated by occasional purple-hued lightning. As she picked up her gloves at the horse corral and started back to the house, two or three drops of water splashed down on her head, startling her to a stop.

She took a step back. *That's funny,* she thought. *Did Bridget leave the sprinklers on in here, too?* She realized this couldn't be it because there were only a few drops, and a very small wet spot on the soil near her feet.

She looked up with the flashlight. The sprinklers were off. She looked again at the damp spot by her feet. She peered toward the pod roof again. A flash of lightning momentarily illuminated something wet near the crest of the pod. She shined her flashlight on the spot as several more drops of water sped from the pod roof toward her face. She ducked sideways. The drops splattered silently onto the ground. She hurried into the stable and found a more powerful floodlight and raced back to the spot. The tricks of the distance to the roof, the lightning, and the floodlight beam made it hard to focus. She could just make out the area of moisture near the top of the pod but she couldn't tell where it was coming from. On a dry night OUTSIDE, she would have assumed the drops were just condensation dripping from the pod roof. The fact that it was still pouring OUTSIDE made her suspicious.

She ran back to the house and found Jimmy in his pajama shorts on the bed, reading computer printouts. A heavy smell of aftershave lotion filled the bedroom. She tried to catch her breath and spoke.

"Jimmy—quick—come on!"

She was already pulling him forcefully toward the stairway.

"Hey, this is different," Jimmy said with a big grin. "You're never this excited," he laughed, thinking of something entirely different from what was on Mai Ker's mind.

She dragged him without another word all the way to Pod 9.

"Here," she ordered him, "look." She picked up the flashlight again and pointed it to the ground. They were both panting now. "Look!" she said again sharply.

Jimmy saw the damp spot. He had no idea what to make of it. His mind was still on his beautiful bride.

"Stand still," she said. She looked up, and repositioned him. "Now look. Right there." She pointed.

"What's the idea?" Jimmy said playfully. "I gotta run laps around the corral first?" he laughed loudly.

Several drops of water hit his head. He looked up into the darkness. "What the—?"

"Here," Mai Ker said, handing him the flashlight. "Look."

The silly, playful grin was gone from his face in an

instant. An uneasy scowl replaced it.

"Condensation?"

"I don't think so," she said. "That would be spread all around."

He looked more intently. She was right. The entire pod roof was dry except for one small area. As he moved the flashlight around, Mai Ker picked up the large floodlight and searched. Several flashes of lightning competed for their eyes. Jimmy squinted. The flashlight's beam flickered. He smacked it lightly and the bulb brightened.

"Cheap junk," he said under his breath.

"What is it?"

"Dunno," he said still squinting. "I can't see where it's coming from."

"It's raining awfully hard. It made me wonder."

"Be right back." He ran to Pod 3, grabbed a pair of binoculars, and ran back.

"Hold your light real steady," he said, "right up . . . there."

The large floodlight illuminated several glistening droplets of water clinging to the roof of the pod, sixty-five feet up. Jimmy looked carefully through the high-powered lenses. His hands began to shake as anxiety welled up in him. He crouched by the corral fence, resting his elbows on the top rail to steady the binoculars. Several more drops fell.

"There," he said almost swallowing the word.

"What?"

"I think we have a hairline fracture."

"A leak?"

"I think so. Very small. Maybe just a crack."

"Crap!" she said, a word out of character for Mai Ker, and used very differently than the last time.

"We have a big, big problem." He shook his head slowly, still looking up. "If water can get in—"

"—air can, too," she finished.

"Sweetie, go get Pam and Bridget."

She set down the floodlight, took the flashlight from Jimmy and ran for the house. Jimmy went to the control shed in #9 and flipped on every light in the pod. The three women were back in two minutes, all winded.

"Where is it, Jimmy?" Bridget demanded, angry that another crisis was brewing.

"Up there," he pointed. "I think we got a leak."

He handed Bridget the binoculars and shined the powerful floodlight on the spot where the droplets were hanging. Pam coughed, a tremor of terror catching her throat.

"Impossible. Impossible!" Bridget hollered. She could see the droplets pooling inside the roof, dropping one and two at a time.

"I guess I don't think anything's impossible anymore," said Jimmy.

Bridget scowled at the pod roof through the glasses. She flopped back against a corral rail.

"Now what?" she asked despondently. "This is too much."

"I thought they couldn't leak," Pam said.

"Anything humans can make can break," Jimmy said.

"What could have caused it, Jimmy?" Bridget asked.

"Maybe the violence of the storm last night. But my guess, it's been there a long time. We just didn't know it."

"You mean the nuclear blasts," Mai Ker said.

"Most likely."

Panic was settling in all around. Pam was nearly in tears and Bridget was tightly gripping the corral rail.

"So we've had bad air seeping in all that time?" Mai Ker asked.

"Maybe. Don't know. If water's coming through, air

could. Looks like maybe there's a hairline crack under that seam cover. Where the panels join," Jimmy said, pointing. "That would be the weakest point."

"So air could get in," Mai Ker repeated.

"Yeah. Air could leak in. But our atmospheric pressure in here is basically steady. It'd be a standoff. Except, like with low pressure OUTSIDE before a storm, actually, our air could leak out."

"Nothing on the air sensors though?" Bridget asked.

"No. No alerts. If anything major was happening, we'd have gotten an alert," Jimmy answered.

They were quiet for a few moments.

"Is it safe to leave it?" Mai Ker wondered.

Jimmy considered this, but shook his head.

"I don't think we can risk it. It may be a hairline crack now. In a week or a month it could widen. The compression weight of the arch is probably all that's keeping it tight. So we've got drops, instead of a steady shower."

Without anyone noticing, Pam was suddenly on the ground, sitting limp-legged. Her eyes were vacant. Mai Ker knelt and shook her gently.

"You need to lay down?"

Pam looked at her as if through a window.

"I can't believe it. Everything is going wrong. Isn't anything ever going to go right?" Pam whimpered.

Bridget helped her up to a bench by the stable.

"Rest for a bit, Pam. While we figure this out."

Pam nodded weakly and leaned her head back against the wall.

"What do we do, Jimmy?" Mai Ker asked. "I know tents. I don't know buildings."

"Can we fix it?" Bridget wondered.

"Maybe patch it," he said.

"Patch it? *How?*" she asked. "Way up there?"

"Oh, there's a way," he said with absolutely no enthusiasm.

"You don't mean—?" Bridget stopped. "Go up there?"

"How else you think we're gonna fix it?"

"Jimmy, how are you going to get up there?" Mai Ker asked.

"You mean, how are *we* gonna get up there," he said. "I can't do it by myself." He stared into Mai Ker's beautiful brown eyes. "You afraid of heights, sweetie?"

"I don't know," she said, worried.

"Well, I am," Bridget said. "You couldn't pay me enough to go up there." This last comment was now a defunct expression but Bridget wasn't thinking about such technicalities at the moment.

"Maybe we could try in the morning," Mai Ker pleaded.

"You kidding? We can't wait till morning, Mai. You want to risk some of that poisonous air getting in?"

"No."

"Me either!"

"So how do we fix it?" Bridget pressed.

"We have small sheets of Stellar over in one of the sheds in number thirteen. Not sure why—since they insisted we'd never need it."

"'Never' has arrived," Pam said from her bench.

"The seam covers—if that's where the leak is—are on the OUTSIDE. The inner surface is smooth. So we try to glue a patch on the INSIDE. Everything we need is over in the main supply. Some 4-foot by 4-foot sheets of half-inch Stellar. And some special epoxy glue that's supposedly made just for this stuff."

"Aren't we—?" Bridget corrected herself. "Aren't you going to have to dry the roof somehow. Before you can glue it?"

"Yeah. We need some kind of dryer."

"A hair dryer work?" Pam asked. She had found the strength to get back on her feet.

"Something hotter."

"In the maintenance shed in number eight," Mai Ker said. "Those little propane torches."

"Yeah," Jimmy nodded. "Maybe a couple of them."

"I'll get them," Pam said, walking that direction.

"So, how are we—? How are *you* going to get up there?" Bridget asked. "We don't have any extension ladders that tall."

"Climbing ropes. A harness. And carabiners."

"What?" Mai Ker asked.

"Snap rings, Mai. For mountain climbing. Oblong rings you snap into the eye of a piton—"

"A pee-what?"

"It's a wedge. A spike you drive into the rock."

"You can't go driving spikes into the pod," Bridget said incredulously, envisioning more leaks.

"Don't have to," he said, pointing. "The support beams were designed for this, for climbing. Just in case. That's why there's all those holes along the bottom edge of the beams."

"I thought they were just for looks," Bridget admitted.

"The architects knew we might have to get up there sometime. Equipment change-overs, repair fans— whatever."

"And you're not afraid of heights?" Bridget asked him.

"Actually, I am."

"Jimmy," Mai Ker insisted, "then you can't go up there!"

"Yeah. I can. And I will. And you or Pam is going with me."

"I'm what?" Pam asked, just returning with the two small propane torches.

"Somebody has to climb up there with me," Jimmy said, pointing at the roof.

Pam looked up, then looked at the other three, and

didn't say a word. She just went back and sat on her bench, weighting herself down with the torches. She wasn't going anywhere.

"You're elected, sweetie," Jimmy said, and kissed Mai Ker. "Pam, we'll need you and Bridget on the ground. We're gonna need those two big lights, too. The 500,000-watt ones."

He looked up. Occasional lightning continued to flash across the sky, illuminating the steady rain peppering the OUTSIDE of the pod.

"I hope this works," Bridget said, obviously not convinced.

They scurried about the pods assembling the necessary materials and equipment. Jimmy found the needed climbing ropes and supplies in a box that had never been opened in Pod 8: twenty 100-foot coils of climbing rope, six full-body harnesses, eight boxes of 6-inch pulleys, and twelve boxes of carabiners. He piled ten ropes, the carabiners and two harnesses on a large cart and wheeled them to the spot. He and Mai Ker jogged back to the house and changed into shorts, T-shirts, and good tennis shoes.

Pam and Bridget meanwhile brought four 4-foot-square sheets of Stellar from Pod 13 along with a pile of liquid epoxy glue guns. They weren't sure how long the crack might be and wanted to have enough material. They also brought the two 500,000-watt floodlights that were mounted on small, light-weight trailers.

"How'd you know about the climbing gear?" Bridget asked Jimmy when he and Mai Ker returned.

"Saw it on the master inventory, that day we were looking for air sources."

"Someday we really ought to go through that whole mess in number thirteen and find out what's really here," Bridget said. "I'm beginning to think we don't know half of the stuff those project planners stored up in here for us."

Jimmy directed the placement of all the materials. He strapped on a climbing harness and then fitted Mai Ker into the other. She watched his eyes.

"This thing safe?" she asked.

"Mai, would I put you in it if it wasn't?"

She gave him a look that said she wasn't that certain.

"Is that a trick question?" she frowned.

Jimmy shook his head. He tightened the straps around her chest. Then he and Bridget cut several lengths of rope to make slings for the sheets of Stellar so he and Mai Ker could pull up the pieces they needed once they were up there.

"When we get to the leak," he told Pam and Bridget, "I'll lower a rope and you're gonna hook a sheet onto it with these snaps."

He looked at Mai Ker.

"You want to climb with me? Or you want me to fly you up once I'm up there?"

For a split-second she pictured herself dangling from a rope as Jimmy pulled her sixty feet into the air.

"I'll climb."

"OK," he said. "I'll have you on a safety tether all the way. If you slip, I'll catch you."

"What if you slip?"

"Think I've never climbed before, huh?" He grinned. "I go a little way, then secure myself to a beam. You move up, then snap this carabiner on your safety line—here," her showed her, "into the beam before I move again. One of us always stays secure. When I move, you're hooked. If I fall, your rope'll catch me."

"She's been hooked on you for a long time," Pam smiled. A little thread of hope returned to her face, forced as it was.

"Like leap frog," Jimmy said.

"Leap what?"

"Never mind."

"OK," Mai Ker said with lingering uncertainty.

"These short ropes with the loops are climbing stirrups. Anywhere you need to climb with your feet, or just need to rest, you hang one from the beam with a carabiner. Once you're above them, unhook them and pull them up for the next part." He tied a bundle of carabiners to the belt of her harness.

"OK," she said again, only slightly reassured.

"Time's a wastin'."

Jimmy put the two propane torches and flint starters into a backpack along with four of the epoxy guns and strapped the pack to his back. He put another pack on Mai Ker with six more epoxy guns. He looked over the beam system, planning their ascent, and hooked a long tether between himself and Mai Ker.

The pod skeleton INSIDE was built of I-beams made of a special aluminum alloy. Along the bottom flange of each beam was a continuous line of 1-inch holes drilled about 16 inches apart.

Jimmy free climbed about 12 feet, the length of their tether, up a support leg. He snapped one of the spring-locking carabiners through a hole and hooked his safety line.

"Come on," he urged Mai Ker. "Don't think about it. Just start up."

Fortunately, she was very agile and in great physical condition. As she started up, it looked as if she might be climbing a palm tree on a beach. When she got just below Jimmy, she quickly snapped her safety line to the beam.

"You done this before?" he asked, somewhat amazed.

"No. But I have a good instructor."

They leap-frogged their way up slowly, very cautiously and with great effort. They slowed more the higher they got. Mai Ker surprised Jimmy with her stamina. She struggled, but she continued to climb. His arms and legs were getting strained half way across a main lateral beam, but Mai Ker said nothing and showed no signs of letting up.

"OK?" Jimmy called up to her as she leap-frogged over him.

"Good," she said. "Keep going."

It took them nearly 50 minutes to reach the transverse beam just under the leak. An angled cross-member ran off it to another upright. The cross-member angled upward very near the top and would enable Jimmy to get within arm's reach of the roof. When he reached it, he told Mai Ker to tie off on the transverse beam just below him.

Pam and Bridget watched from below, the powerful work lights illuminating the pod roof from two angles. The lights were so bright it made it hard for Jimmy and Mai Ker to see the ground. But this was just as well. Each time Jimmy hazarded a glimpse downward, his stomach tried to change places with his brain.

Mai Ker surprised herself, realizing she had almost no fear at this height, although she had never climbed anything like this before. Dangling from the two stirrups she had secured in place, she remembered the high-wire circus performers she had seen as a child in California. Now she knew how they felt.

Jimmy kept feeling sick. He secured his safety rope, got his stirrups in place, and struggled to get the backpack off.

"You OK?" he asked Mai Ker, his chest thrusting in and out.

"Yeah. Are you?"

"Yeah," he lied.

The rainstorm continued unabated. Heavy sheets of water streamed down the pod OUTSIDE. On the ground Pam and Bridget couldn't tell the leaking rain from the drops of sweat pouring off Jimmy and Mai

Ker.

They were right under the drip. Jimmy shined a small hand-held laser light on the leak. As he had suspected, the drips were coming from a seam between the plastic panels. It appeared the seam cover OUTSIDE had separated from the main Stellar panels along one edge. It was hard to tell the extent of the damage. The drips came from a 12-inch section of seam, but because of the slope of the pod the actual crack might have been much smaller. An inch or two. The compression pressure from the arching weight of the pod was partially sealing the leak. Looking it over with the laser, Jimmy was confident that a single 4-foot by 4-foot sheet would repair the problem.

He handed the laser down to Mai Ker to examine the fracture from her angle. She agreed the crack was very small.

"One piece should cover it," he said. He lowered a long rope to the ground and shouted for Pam and Bridget to hook on a piece of Stellar. He tried not to look down.

"I was on this giant Ferris-wheel once," he told Mai Ker as he got a propane torch ready. "At a fair in Georgia. Eighty feet high. At night, kind of like this. The third time we came over the top I puked—really bad!"

"Why are you telling me this?"

He realized the mistake.

"Never mind," he said, looking up at the crack again. As he tested the flint starter though, he couldn't help finishing the story. "A couple of little old ladies were in the seat right below us. I felt really bad."

"Oh, thank you, Jimmy." For the first time, Mai Ker, several feet below him, felt queasy.

"You ready?" he asked.

"Yeah."

He handed down the other torch and a starter.

"I think I can dry it OK with mine. But you may have to help heat the glue with yours. Strap it to your harness."

She did this. He swung across several feet and snapped a free safety rope to the cross beam where Mai Ker would be able to reach the roof. He threw her a short line.

"Bring your stirrups. You've gotta get right up there," he pointed.

"Let's get it done and get down from here," she said.

"Ready," Bridget yelled from the ground.

Jimmy pulled the long rope and the piece of Stellar started up.

"Mai, help pull!"

She grabbed the rope and they pulled together. Although only 4-feet by 4-feet, the half-inch panel was dense and weighed almost 80 pounds. Jimmy's arms were tired and straining. Mai Ker's strength made the difference.

Jimmy rested the bottom edge of the Stellar patch on the beam in front of him.

"OK. Climb on up here," he said, indicating another safety rope he had secured across from him.

Mai Ker unhooked both stirrups and tossed them to him. She unhooked her safety and climbed as far as she could. Just as she leaned toward the new safety line, her leg cramped.

She missed.

Jimmy, steadying the sheet of Stellar, was momentarily looking up. All he heard was the shriek. Before he could look, Mai Ker snapped to a stop at the end of their tether. At the same instant, he lost hold of the repair patch. The edge of the heavy Stellar narrowly missed her face as she spun helplessly in a small, wobbling circle. He winced, then his mind recoiled with a second shot.

"Bridget—run! Pam!" Jimmy shouted.

The Stellar sheet flew blindly toward the ground, the rope longer than the distance. Pam and Bridget panicked as they saw it coming at them through the brilliant lights. They peeled off in opposite directions like two maniacs escaping the asylum. The Stellar sheet, with the slack rope trailing like an enraged rattlesnake, hit the ground with terrifying force but— true to its name—didn't shatter. The impact cut its rope sling. With a ghastly screeching noise, it flexed like the string of a bow and shot through the air sideways, loosed from the cut sling.

If Bridget had seen it coming she would have frozen with fright. But moving like a bat out of hell, she didn't take time to look back. The sheet fired past her like a 4-foot by 4-foot bullet, missing her back by just 18 inches. It landed and dug a gouge in the dirt almost twenty feet in front of her. The propane torch that Jimmy also dropped hit the ground almost simultaneously. It didn't explode, but the neck ruptured and the gas turned it into a jet flying across the grass until it slammed into the side of the metal stable.

Bridget stopped dead, staring. Pam turned, frozen in mid-step, and yelled "Bridget!" She broke her feet loose and ran toward Bridget who was still staring at the plastic sheet embedded catawampus in the dirt in front of her. The brilliant shadows from all this, cast by 500,000-watt lights, would have created a grotesque mime show had anyone been OUTSIDE the pod to watch.

In his panicked attempt to rescue Mai Ker, Jimmy forgot he was in his foot stirrups. One pulled loose, one didn't. He twisted and swung sideways. His chin crashed against the beam, sending shock waves through his skull which arrived like the sound of a freight train in his brain. It nearly knocked him out. His safety strap caught him. It was holding him and holding Mai Ker at the bottom of the tether. She was still trying to breathe, or cry, or both.

"Jimmy?" she gulped, too terrified to scream a second time. She could see he was stunned, squirming mindlessly like a worm on a hook. Every muscle in her body tensed. Without even thinking, she swung her head upward and with both hands gripped the tether line and began pulling herself up to him. His right foot was still caught in the stirrup. Drops from the roof leak dripped down on her. She thought it was blood. It was hard to breathe. A lonely, wretched feeling came over her.

"Hold still," she cried, "let me get above you."

The burst of strength in her arms would have enabled her to bend the beam if she had wanted. She got above him and snapped her original safety line to the beam. Jimmy was coming around but still half-dazed. Mai Ker planted both feet on the horizontal beam.

"Feels like I was hit with a fast ball," he mumbled. He pulled on the tether and realized it was slack. "Mai!" he shouted with new panic.

"OK," she said. "I'm up here."

Jimmy, still disoriented, looked up. Lit by the bright lights she looked like an angel, though he had never seen one.

Holding his safety rope he worked his foot free. Using the tether Mai Ker pulled him up until he had hold of the beam. With great effort he got a foot onto the beam and she helped pull him to his feet. He leaned toward her but the safety rope held him back.

"Mai—baby—you OK?"

"Are you?"

"Don't do that anymore," he said.

"You either," she said.

"OK, OK. We're not goin' anywhere."

"You mean we are staying up here forever?" she

asked, trying to laugh.

He belched out a spasmodic laugh.

"Look at you. How'd you get up here?" He was completely dazzled. Unconsciously he unhooked his safety and slid toward her. "I knew there was a reason I married you!" he said, trying to kiss her.

Then he realized what he'd just done. He looked at the limp safety line in his hand. His eyes went toward the lights 60 feet below. He almost threw up. Mai Ker snapped his safety line to the beam.

"Not now," she said, "I have a headache."

He swallowed the contents of his stomach back down.

"Come on," he said. "Heck with it. I'm taking you back down."

"No you're not."

"I'm taking you down!"

"No, Jimmy! We have to finish this." She frowned. "No choice."

He collected himself.

"OK. Let's try this again. Bridget!" he hollered.

"Yeah?"

"Tie on a new sheet."

"You wanna try to kill us again?"

"Sorry. Had a little spill," he shouted.

"Cryin' out loud. Be more careful! Pam and I aren't going to run this place by ourselves!"

Jimmy worked back along the beam and got in position. He tied another 100-foot rope to the beam at his feet and let it down to Bridget.

"Got it," Bridget shouted. A minute later she called "Pull!"

He squatted to the beam and pulled. Mai Ker tried to lean forward to help.

"I'll get it," he said. "Sit tight." He yelled back down to Bridget. "Don't stand under it this time!"

"Don't worry," Pam said under her breath.

The new sheet came into sight through the brilliant lights below them, like a giant, translucent fish being reeled in. Jimmy rested it on the beam and braced it between his knees.

"This should be good." He pulled his pack around again and got two epoxy guns out. "OK, since I lost my torch, here's how we're gonna do this. Light your torch and reach up and dry the water best you can. While you do that, I'm gonna get glue on the back of this patch. Then you've got to quick shut the torch off and help me lift it into position."

"I'm ready."

"Watch it, the torch will be real hot. See that ring by the valve? Hook a carabiner in there, then you can snap it to the beam when you're done."

"OK." She lit the torch and started moving it slowly back and forth below the pod roof. It was a stretch for her short arms, but she made it.

"Dry?" he asked.

"Yes. If we work quick." She shut off the torch and hung it from the beam.

"OK, epoxy's on. Take your side. Ready?"

"I guess."

"I'm gonna untie the sling. Then we gotta level it and raise it at the same time. Don't want one end touching before the other."

They executed the maneuver very cautiously. Juggling the 80-pound sheet in the air was trickier than he expected. It flexed slightly, and his arms and legs felt like gelatin.

"Got it?" he asked Mai Ker.

"Keep going!" she said with a hoarse whisper.

The thing seemed to gain weight as they raised it toward the roof. Mai Ker's arms began to burn, finally overcome by the strain. Veins bulged out on Jimmy's arms. His shoulders were cramping up. He held his end level as Mai Ker stretched up with every inch she had toward the roof.

"Now!"

They got under it and pushed up. Mai Ker's side was an inch shy.

"More, Mai Ker! Just a little more!"

She strained onto her tiptoes and pushed. The panel made even contact.

"Keep pushing, but move it back and forth a little," Jimmy said. "It'll help spread the glue."

They did this, then rubbed their hands across the patch, pressing it into place, all the time keeping their balance on the beam. The glue began to set quickly.

"Now the torch," he ordered.

She re-lit it and started heating the exposed side of the panel. The epoxy thinned slightly. Blobs transformed into big, flat, glue amoebas. Jimmy pulled a rag from his backpack, wrapped it around his hand and rubbed it over the hot plastic, pushing out small air bubbles where he could reach.

"Hand me the torch."

She tossed the still burning torch. Jimmy made a major-league catch and finished heating his end of the patch.

"I want to epoxy the edges, too. Can you reach?" he asked her.

Mai Ker was feeling the fatigue.

"I'll try."

Jimmy shut off the torch, hooked it to the beam, then stood midway under the patch to hold it. Mai Ker took an epoxy gun from her pack and opened the cap. Stretching again, she ran a thick bead of glue along the edges she could reach, trying to keep her free hand against the patch on her end.

"Good," he said. He took the epoxy gun and finished sealing the edges toward his end. Sweat was streaming from most of his body. "Man, it's a lot hotter up here in the dome. I'm cookin'!" Holding the patch with one arm, he put the glue gun in his pack.

"We have to hold it up here all night?" Mai Ker complained.

"Just a little more. Till I'm sure it's set."

She strained on her tip-toes again. They held this position, frozen, for over a minute.

"I can't hold anymore," she said. She sat on the beam, exhausted.

"It's good. It's good." His arms were rubbery. He leaned back and watched. Three more minutes went by.

"Everything OK up there?" Bridget yelled.

"Good," Jimmy shouted. "Just checking the seal."

He was only now beginning to breathe normally again, his chest heaving more slowly. Mai Ker had slumped over like a wilted flower on the beam. But her safety line was secure. Jimmy watched the patch another five or six minutes. No drips.

"We did it."

Mai Ker hurt so much she wanted to cry. With Jimmy's help she sat up. He pulled her to her feet.

"I love you! You're fantastic!" Jimmy said with glee.

"OK." She started giggling like a teenager at her first prom as happiness, fear and joy bubbled out. "If you say so. Can we please get down now?"

Jimmy started laughing, too.

"Hey, wanna do this again tomorrow night?"

Tears broke from her eyes.

"No, I don't think so."

Jimmy collected stray gear and carabiners around him and shoved them in his pack.

"You rested? This is gonna hurt more going down that it did coming up," he warned her. "We're worn out."

They rubbed the muscles of their arms and upper legs for a few seconds, and started down. It was like a choreographed dance. As tired as they were, they moved fairly gracefully, leap-frogging their way down the beams. The descent took only 20 minutes. As they reached the ground, Bridget and Pam grabbed them into a group bear hug, like two lost children just emerging from a very dark wood into the desperate arms of their parents.

Jimmy's legs shook with fatigue. When Pam and Bridget finally let go, he dropped to his knees. Mai Ker plopped onto the ground, smelly and wet. Both felt like old, wrung out dish rags. Pam and Bridget helped them walk to the house. As badly as the two climbers needed a shower, they were too tired. They fell into the twin beds Jimmy had pulled together the night of their wedding, and curled up, and shut out the world. Had the universe ended that second, they would not have cared.

Although Bridget was exhausted, too, she was not done.

"You rest," she told Pam. "I'm going around to inspect the rest of the pods."

"Can't we do that tomorrow?" Pam protested, not feeling well herself. The adrenalin pumping through her system over the last couple of hours had left her nauseated, with a growing headache.

Bridget shook her head.

"I want to do it while it's still raining. That's our best chance of spotting any more leaks."

Pam nodded.

"I'll help. You don't need to do it alone."

They went to the maintenance shed in #8 for freshly charged, handheld flood lights, flipping on lights in each pod as they went. For the next three and a half hours, they walked every pod, running the flood lights along every seam in the pod roofs, watching the ground and concrete for telltale spots of moisture. Finding spots in #10 was impossible since they had run the sprinklers for several hours earlier this evening and the whole ground was still damp. But to their great relief they spotted no more leaks. They double-checked every seam in #10 with the lights, carefully watching for a single new drop. Nothing.

When they got to the house they stopped in the kitchen for ice cream, which would soon be a thing of the past because of energy conservation. Their necks ached from looking up at pod roofs. They treated each other to a neck and shoulder massage, then headed to their own rooms.

Bridget laid on her bed a long time, exhausted, but unable to fall asleep. She peeked in on Pam, who was snoring softly. She went a few steps down the hall to the room she had briefly shared with Clayton, his and Willy's old room. She threw a single blanket and pillow onto Clayton's stripped bed. She laid down. Though gone, she still sensed his presence. She sobbed. To her surprise, Caroline lit on top of the footboard. The little creature sat very still. A silent sentinel. Bridget finally closed her eyes, said a brief, nebulous prayer of thanks to someone, and slept.

27

Tuesday, June 24th

Two weeks had passed since the night Jimmy and Mai Ker had walked the tightrope-like beams high up in Pod 9. Much work had been done since.

The Solarians sat eating lunch in their new outdoor dining room, shielded from the sun by large tarps supported by 2-by-4s, plywood framing and some metal scaffolding. Jimmy had finished wiring in the new electrical generators yesterday and they spent this morning uncovering the new solar panels that would feed steam to the turbines that would drive those generators.

Bridget sat looking pensive. She chewed slowly around the outer edges of her sandwich, her eyes drifting thoughtfully from face to face. Out of the blue, she sprang an unexpected question on them.

"Who'll be our new team leader?"

The quiet chatter stopped. Chips and parts of sandwiches dangled in the air between mouths and the table. The others looked at Bridget blankly. The question hadn't occurred to any of them.

"What does it matter?" Jimmy asked, analyzing the bite marks on his sandwich.

"It matters because I think we should still have a leader," Bridget said.

"Can't we all just kind of lead?" Pam asked.

"What happens if we disagree?" Bridget said.

"What do you mean?"

"Every family has disagreements. Sooner or later something will come up. And we won't agree. There's four of us, remember."

"Yes, you are right," Mai Ker said. "There could be many tie votes."

"We need to agree on a leader. Who can settle disputes," Bridget went on. "A judge, you might say."

While it seemed petty at the moment, and awkward this soon after Block's death, they realized there was a certain wisdom in Bridget's suggestion. But they were reluctant to try to fill Clayton Block's shoes. He had led them through several near-disasters.

"Why don't you do it?" Mai Ker asked Bridget. "You were closest to him. You know best what he thought—and how he thought. You knew his feelings."

"I don't know if I could say that," Bridget said. Her face showed a certain indistinct sadness. "We all knew how he thought. In some ways. But I don't know if I really understood Clayton's feelings—any better than you." She was quiet for a moment. "There was so much in him that never showed through."

"Still, you were his wife," said Mai Ker.

"Just do whatever you think Clayton would have done in a situation," Pam said.

"Meaning I can't think for myself?" Bridget said sourly.

"'Course you can," Jimmy said, trying to mend Pam's blunder.

Bridget considered this. Then shook her head.

"I don't want to. I nominate Jimmy."

His eyebrows squinted together.

"Nah," he said, taking another bite of sandwich. "You can do it."

"No, Jimmy. You're the natural. Look how you took charge when we found the leak. You have the talent for it."

"I don't think I do," he said.

"All in favor?" Bridget asked, her hand already in the air.

Pam raised her hand. Mai Ker hesitated.

"I'm biased. I'm married to him."

"Does that mean 'biased for' or 'biased against'?" Pam laughed.

"For," she smiled.

"Three in favor, Jimmy," Bridget said. "You're elected."

So, despite his own resistance, it was agreed. Jimmy said he would accept only on the condition that they always try to make every important decision unanimous. They all agreed this was wise.

"See," Pam said, "you are a natural."

Bridget looked around, with relief on her face.

"There's something else. Not a decision. But important." She had the look of some corporate executive whose company's stock just shot up.

"What?" Mai Ker asked.

"I'm going to have a baby."

Pam stared at Bridget. Mai Ker turned and stared at Jimmy.

"Hey," he said. "I'm innocent!"

Mai Ker turned to Bridget.

"You are sure?"

"Yes. Something else the planners left us in Supply. Pregnancy test kits."

"Well. I guess they planned better than we thought," Pam said.

"So," Mai Ker began to think back. She hesitated a little. "So, really, you and Clayton had been together before you got married. I mean—you know."

"Actually, we weren't," Bridget said, to everyone's amazement.

Pam in particular looked skeptical.

"You were only married—how long, before he got sick?" Pam asked.

"We were married May 11th. He got sick on June 4th."

"That's nearly impossible odds," Pam said. "Three and a half weeks?"

"Maybe someone's looking after us after all," Bridget said, wanting in her heart to believe this.

The other two women sandwiched her in a hug. Jimmy sat still, thinking to himself what a failure their new leader was. He and Mai Ker had been married the same day but so far she didn't have this kind of joyful news. It didn't help when Pam, with no idea what he was thinking, blurted out,

"You got some catching up to do, Jimmy!"

He tried to smile. And he remembered uncomfortably a conversation they had a week earlier.

THE CONVERSATION had occurred the day they began building their tent village. They decided to build it in Pod 10 since they would have to be here caring for crops much of the time anyway, and it was close to the chickens and small animals in #11. There was enough wood, ladders, and metal scaffolding to the erect basic structures. They collected all the tarps and sheets of canvas they could find for roofs and walls.

As they began work that day, Pam seemed lost in thought.

"It'll be like an extended camp out," she mused.

"Very extended," Jimmy said.

"Like nomads in the desert," said Bridget.

"Very few nomads," Mai Ker said. She cleared her throat quietly. "We are going to have to talk more. About reproducing."

Jimmy stopped hammering, his back to the women. He turned toward Mai Ker with a look that said, *You don't need to keep bringing this up.*

"We're not trying hard enough?" he said, with an exasperated smile. "Don't know about you. I'm about wore out."

"Not just me, Jimmy. Pam, too. And Bridget."

Jimmy stared at all three women for a moment with a mix of frustration and agitation in his eyes. He turned away, back to nailing a brace at the bottom of what would be a kitchen wall. He offered a little prayer. He felt surrounded, and hemmed in. But Mai Ker looked very serious. Pam smiled at him. Bridget grinned a little, though her smile was different and no one else saw it.

"I know, I know," he said, reaching for more nails, his back still to the women. "Gimme a chance, huh?" His face glowed brightly with embarrassment. They could see it even on the sides of his face. "I gotta get a new saw blade," he said, a sudden excuse to leave.

"So that's the problem?" Pam joked.

The women all laughed.

"I'm not busy tonight, Jimmy," Pam called after him with a cooing in her voice. She laughed lightly when he didn't respond.

Jimmy intended to head into Pod 8 to the maintenance shed. He was so distracted he walked into #9 instead. A lone stallion stood in a corner of the corral, his tail fanning away flies.

"Man, know just how you feel, fella," he said to the horse.

NOW, AT the lunch table, Jimmy thought over that conversation of last week. He was trying to smile at Bridget's announcement but all three women were buzzing like queen bees.

"How long do we have to wait?" Mai Ker asked Bridget.

"How far along are you?" Pam overlapped.

"Just three or four weeks I think."

"How long before we know if it's a boy or girl?" Mai Ker asked.

"By 16-17 weeks we can tell with an ultrasound," Pam said. "The body parts will tell us."

"Body parts?" Jimmy asked, not paying very close attention.

Bridget, never one to mince words, gave him a "stupid" look.

"His male parts, Jimmy," she said bluntly.

"Oh." His face turned a deep, dark purple. He tried to think of a reason to excuse himself again. He couldn't think of a thing.

"Hey, Pam," Mai Ker whispered loudly, "you think that ultrasound thing could help me find Jimmy's?"

Too late. The women laughed hysterically. Jimmy shook his head in disgust, turned a darker shade of purple, and left to vent his anger on some helpless little weeds in a new corn plot at the other side of the pod.

As if similarly embarrassed, the air OUTSIDE the great pods had continued to turn a darker shade of purple. The catastrophic changes described by John Haskins were working their horrible destruction, turning life-giving air into toxic, poisonous gas. Day by day the air darkened slightly, almost unnoticeably.

But as Jimmy stood and stretched between rows of infant corn and looked up, he remembered how the sky right after the heavy rains two weeks ago had seemed a little less purplish. Maybe, he thought, the rain still had some kind of cleansing effect.

Guess we'll never know, he told himself.

Eventually the three women came to help with the weeding, all looking a little ashamed, but still enjoying themselves.

"Sky's looking darker again," Jimmy commented, hoping for a change of subject, at least for the rest of the day.

"Yes. And this is not good," said Mai Ker. "Everything depends on enough sunlight in here."

"The plants still seem OK," Bridget observed.

"Yes, we have enough heat," Mai Ker said. "But if the sky is darkening, we're losing some of the radiant energy. That could slow photosynthesis—if it slows too much and we don't generate enough oxygen."

Pam, as usual, looked particularly worried.

"Can we compensate?"

"Write the sun and tell him to burn brighter," Jimmy said with mild sarcasm. "Or—I know—we could send an email to the sky and tell it to stop turning purple."

"Don't have to be smart, Jimmy," Mai Ker chided.

"No, Mai Ker, it's OK," Pam said. "That's exactly what he does need to be. We all do."

Jimmy continued looking up at the sky.

"The heavens," he said. "Gone to hell."

"Don't swear," Mai Ker said.

"I don't think he did," Bridget said.

As the day wore on the sky darkened even more as a bank of nearly black clouds moved up from the southwest, bringing distant lightning and promising more rain.

"Good," Jimmy said as they noticed it. "We can check for leaks again. We're not taking any more chances."

THE RAIN came in heavy, rolling waves for several hours. After two hours checking the pod roofs after supper, the four Solarians settled into chairs in their new, makeshift living room. The women had talked privately after Jimmy had bolted from lunch today. Mai Ker enjoyed teasing him, but she could also see something was really bothering him.

"Jimmy," she said when they were all together, "let's talk."

"Talk, talk, talk . . ."

"I'm serious. We have to talk about this. About having children."

Though he felt the urge to escape again he quelled it.

"So talk. Wife."

"Well, we've been trying. Maybe it's not going to happen. Maybe something's wrong. With me."

"Or me."

"Yes. Possibly. But we don't know. But see, we will—when you try with Pam."

"Jimmy," Pam said with a very loving tone, "we've talked. We all know the reality. We've all got to . . ." She searched for words. ". . . support this. To try. It's our only hope."

"So you don't mind?"

"I'm not sure 'mind' is the right word. I feel funny. Yes."

"I'm not sure 'funny' is the right word. From where I sit," he said.

"So what will make it work?" Bridget asked.

"You're going to think I'm a stick-in-the-mud," he said. He sat up straighter and looked at them intently.

"No we won't," Mai Ker said.

"Mai Ker's my wife. I want to have a child with her. First."

"But we can't sit around and wait. We don't have the luxury," Bridget reminded him.

"It's because you two are married. And we're not," Pam said, speaking what she was certain he was feeling.

"That's part of it. A big part," he admitted.

"Can't undo that," Pam said. "And we don't want to."

"But maybe we can, kinda, fix it," he said.

"How?" Bridget asked.

"You'll think I'm really old-fashioned."

"No," they all murmured.

"Well. Why can't I marry all of you?"

The women's expressions vacillated between stunned, surprised, pleased, and uncertain. They glanced at each other. They had not considered this.

"You mean—?" Bridget looked uncomfortable for

the first time in the conversation. "But, I'm already married."

"Yes. You were. But remember, 'Until death do us part'?" Jimmy repeated.

Her eyebrows went down. Her mouth twisted sideways and quivered slightly.

"Yes. I remember." It was a crushing reminder. She didn't like to think of it.

"Well," Jimmy stumbled on, "I don't believe in polygamy. This 'group marriage' stuff. I mean, normally. But—well, I don't know what 'normal' means now." He frowned. "I'm like you. I don't know what else to do. I mean, even in the Bible, in my Sunday school lessons, you know, some of those guys had more than one wife. And that's when there was still plenty of men around."

The women nodded, watching him grasp for answers, but they said nothing.

"Well, I always thought that was wrong," he went on. "But when I think what we're left with, I mean, I don't think there's any choice. But I don't feel right, unless we actually get married."

"Afraid I might run off with another man?" Pam laughed.

Jimmy gave her a look that would have melted a glacier.

"Serious, Pam. I'm being serious."

She stopped snickering.

"I know, Jimmy." Then without thinking, she helped break down the barrier. "I guess I'm uncomfortable, too." She watched his reaction. "You're a very lovable guy. I think you're an actual gentleman."

"So, you mean you want to marry Pam? And me?" Bridget asked.

All the uncomfortable joking was over.

"I guess so," he said.

"Not much of a proposal, Jimmy," Bridget replied.

"I mean, I guess there's no reason not to."

"Worse," Pam commented.

"You are not making this easy," Jimmy said, thinking of leaving the room again.

"Neither are you," Bridget said.

"Are you all right with this, Jimmy?" Mai Ker asked.

"Yes. I guess so."

"Then I say we plan a wedding," his first wife said.

"Who will marry us?" Pam asked.

"Have to do it like in the old times," Mai Ker said. "Do it yourself."

"I remember a wedding at our church when I was little," Jimmy said. "The pastor said something, that in a wedding the man and woman are the actual ministers. The pastor just sort of gave a blessing."

"So who's going to bless us?" Pam asked.

"Maybe whoever it is who's kept us alive," Bridget said with just a shade of sarcasm.

AS JIMMY walked by himself late tonight trying to sort through all this, his mind kept going back to those Sunday school lessons. He walked again to #9. He leaned on a fence rail. He looked up at the patch on the pod roof. For several minutes he watched the horses wander aimlessly from side to side in the corral.

I'm no Abraham, he kept telling himself. The stallion whinnied softly as if to agree. *Or King David,* Jimmy thought. *And sure as heck no Solomon!* Yet in some way he could not grasp, he felt he *was* like them, suspended between a wish and a promise, dangling for an impossibly long time from finger tips that just barely seemed to hold him.

"I don't understand. I can't see it," he said aloud to the air. Then he brought quiet to his mind and settled it. "But I can't see anything else, either." He would marry them. They would raise up as many children as they could. And even if those children could never reproduce, it would extend the human race at least one more generation here in the pods. If that was it, that would have to be enough.

28

Wednesday, July 2nd

They were finished with the process of moving "outdoors." The basic tents were complete enough to live in and Jimmy had run power cables to each tent so necessary lights and appliances could be run. By using a few small lights in their new home, they could shut down all the overhead lights in Pod 10 at night, saving more energy.

Bridget had installed three laptop computers linked by a wireless connection back to the main console in the Comm. Center and to a second console in the Research Center. From the laptops they could manage most of the environmental controls, keeping Pods 2 and 3 closed off except for emergencies.

Their new village took shape nicely. It was somewhat haphazard, pieces of structures and tents being added as they thought of a particular use. They initially created three tents for sleeping. Now that the marriage plan was moving forward, Jimmy decided to build a fourth, for himself, for times when he just might want to have peace and quiet. The women all agreed this was smart.

Last night, once the pod lights were completely shut down and the village lights were off, they saw, clearer than they had for many months, the faint light of several stars shining through the pod roof. Even though the purpling effect had muddied the air OUTSIDE, the brighter stars continued to penetrate the haze. This brought a sense of reassurance to the Solarians in the coming months, as they gazed up at the stars reaching out to them from distant galaxies. Amid the catastrophe that had engulfed the earth, these stars, light-years away, seemed solid, fixed, reliable.

Bridget pointed to one star that seemed to shine extra brightly.

"That's weird. Must be millions of miles away," she said, pointing. "But looks like it's just inches above the pod." As quickly as she pointed to it, though, it seemed to flicker out. "Sky's playing tricks," she said to the others. She assumed a cloud took it.

THE WEDDING, only a few days in the planning, was upon them, set for 3:00 p.m. today. Jimmy wanted a real celebration, so this morning he made up a special party drink, dumping together the remains of several nearly empty liquor bottles he found shoved to the back of a kitchen cabinet in the old house. To this mix he added sugar and water.

"Rocket fuel," he called it. "Learned to make it in college."

"So it wasn't a total waste?" Mai Ker laughed.

"The rocket fuel?" he frowned.

"College," she said.

Jimmy offered her the first glass just after lunch, a taste test.

"Pretty weak," she said.

"Well, I don't plan to get hammered. Just happy."

This was part of the truth. Mai Ker knew the other part. There was a lot more liquor in the main supply in Pod 13 but Pam had made them promise it would all be kept for emergency, for antiseptic. It was off limits, so Jimmy had to suffice with the dregs he had found in already opened bottles.

Each found special clothes for the occasion. Pam opted for a skirt, one she had brought when she first came to the Solarium. All three women, in bridal party fashion, spent a good deal of time preening and primping, wanting to look their best for the festive day, the only festive day they had seen in a while.

Jimmy shaved and showered in his new plastic tarp "camp" shower right after chores. He had created his own little toilet and dressing area near the stable over in #9 so he would have some privacy, except for a few nosy horses.

It was an outdoor wedding. They set up an arbor woven with flowers near the front of their new village late yesterday. At 3:00 p.m. they gathered. As Jimmy walked into #10 wearing shorts, a collared shirt and a somewhat disheveled handmade cravat, his wife and two brides appeared from their new "house" tent, walking arm in arm. Jimmy was already nervous but the scene of the three of them linked together made a sudden and indelible impression of what it was going to be like having three wives instead of one. His anxiety tripled.

They came together by the arbor and stood facing each other. Mai Ker had been tapped to lead the ceremony since she was the only one who didn't have a new part. They remembered a little from the ceremony before Judge Mariano, and of course from movies. None, however, had ever seen a man marry two women at once, let alone with his first wife leading the ceremony. So they just made it up as best they could to suit the circumstances.

"Pam, Bridget. Jimmy has asked you to marry him," Mai Ker said as if this were news, or some noble proclamation. "We've all agreed. As Jimmy's first wife, I give my consent. So I now ask you to pledge yourselves to him."

Jimmy smiled, but the cravat was choking him a little. Or maybe it wasn't the cravat.

"Who's first?" he asked.

"You first, Pam," Mai Ker instructed her. "This is your first marriage. Take Jimmy's hand and repeat after me."

Pam repeated the words slowly, thoughtfully.

"I, your new wife, Pam, give you my love, and will try to love you, even when you are being unlovable. I will honor you with my body and give you children if I am able, for the good of humanity. I will not desert you when you are old. I will teach our children to love all their brothers and sisters." Pam choked up as she came to the end. On her own she added, "All this I will do with God's help."

Bridget took her turn, holding Jimmy's right hand, following Mai Ker with the same words. She even added Pam's last part, though she wasn't sure who this God was she was asking for help.

"Now you, Jimmy," Mai Ker said.

Jimmy had written out his promises. The women hadn't seen them. He hoped they would understand. He offered a hand to both Pam and Bridget. Mai Ker held his little piece of paper where he could read it.

"Mai Ker, my first wife, I love you best, and always will." He gave her a long and sincere look. "But I also take you Pam, and you Bridget, to be my wedded wives. I will love you also with all I have. I will respect each of you. I will honor you with my body and give you children if I am able. I will not desert you." He nodded soberly. "Any of you." He looked around, laughing. "Anyway. Where would I go?"

Mai Ker suppressed a grin. Jimmy regained his seriousness, taking a deep breath.

"I will never leave you. Until I die. And I ask the Good Lord for his help. Because I am surely going to need it."

All three wives grinned at this one. They stood in silence. The weight of the moment settled in. To his surprise, Jimmy felt an irresistible sense of love pouring over him.

"Very nice, Jimmy," Bridget said.

Jimmy kissed Mai Ker, then Pam, then Bridget. They joined in another great hug, as they had three weeks ago under very different circumstances.

"Now," Jimmy said, something dawning on him, "who's gonna give the big toast? It's usually the Best Man."

The women looked at each other.

"Guess you're elected again," Pam said. "You're the best man around."

Jimmy laughed. Glasses of "rocket fuel" were poured all around and raised in a circle.

"OK," he said. He thought for a moment. "Here's to the best years of my life, spent in the arms of another man's wife. My mother."

The women all hooted. They clinked the wine glasses together and toasted their new and even stranger life together.

The festivities went on for several hours. First they sat down to a picnic supper. The only bother was a few mosquitoes, who were also hungry. Some things never change. They had tried for months to eradicate them from the pods, without success.

The supper was roast turkey that Bridget had prepared, starting early this morning. This was followed by singing the few songs most of them knew in common. Here Mai Ker was at a disadvantage, as her traditional family songs were quite different. They then moved into the "Meeting Tent," as they now called it, for dancing. None of them, as it turned out, were much good at it. Pam seemed very worried about this.

"Who'll teach the kids?" she asked after a third glass of rocket fuel.

"They'll teach themselves," Bridget said. "Haven't they always?"

More laughter.

When it was well past dark they turned the overhead pod lights completely off. A few dim lights glowed in the tents, augmented by a dozen candles set around the Meeting Tent. Made from the tallow of the many slaughtered animals, their supply of candles would likely outlast their supply of light bulbs. It was wasteful, they knew, to burn so many tonight. But there was something about the soft, natural light that brought a sense of healing to their wounded hearts.

In the middle of a waltz, Mai Ker switched the music to a fast rock and roll band and wiggled around the dance floor by herself. This lasted only a few minutes before quieter music was back. The women took turns dancing with their husband. Mai Ker cut in on Pam and, standing on Jimmy's feet, rested her head on his chest as they made slow circles around the tent. She soon dozed off, and Jimmy carried her over and propped her gently sideways on a chair like a large rag doll.

Pam took Jimmy's arm and began to dance again. She was quiet and somber, and keeping a little space between them. There was a look of apology in her face.

"I like you Jimmy. I do. It's just—" She sighed quietly. "—it's hard for me to be real close to anyone," she confided. "And I know how difficult this is for you."

"Well, my mom used to say love can always make a way." He chuckled, lost in a distant memory.

"What're you laughing at?" Pam asked.

"Then there was what my dad always said back."

"What did he always say?"

"Just do our best, love will do the rest." He held her closer and gently kissed the side of her face. It was the best either could do at the moment.

On the chair, Mai Ker's eyes drifted open and shut. Jimmy saw this, helped her up and walked her toward her tent. To no one's surprise, Jimmy slept with Mai Ker tonight. Though the marriages were now official, it would be days before Jimmy mustered the courage to sleep with either of his new brides.

They all knew it would take time. Their predicament was beyond anything they could have imagined. Monogamy, in all their minds, was still not just the norm, but the right thing, even though none had ever been married before arriving at Solarium-3. Bridget, as a teenager, had a daughter out of wedlock but had given her up for adoption. Her marriage to Block had been a great joy. The tragedy that ended it would leave deep pain for years to come. Her marriage to Jimmy was one of necessity. Still, in the recent weeks she had developed a real love and respect for him, which, once her baby was born, would make their times of love-making more genuine, if not less awkward.

But there would be no love-making tonight, just a very somber sense of peace and a growing sense of joined solitude that settled over the four remaining Solarians.

Jimmy looked out at the sky as he helped Mai Ker to her tent.

"What are you thinking?" she asked drowsily.

"Where do you think they all go?"

"The stars?"

"No," he said. "Them. All those people OUTSIDE. Who died."

Mai Ker pondered this in her half-awake state.

"I guess they know, and we do not."

"That's no answer."

"Then, I do not know," she said.

"Do you think they're still conscious, somehow?"

She thought about this for several unsteady steps.

"Most wise people thought so," she said.

"But what do you think? Do you believe there's something else?" He asked because they had never really talked about all this.

"I think so."

"I wonder if they know what's happening down

here."

Mai Ker didn't respond. Her mind went off in several directions at once. Fatigue, months of anxiety, and rocket fuel had turned her brain to wool.

"Life's so strange," she mumbled with a tongue that felt like it was held on with glue.

They reached her tent and cuddled together on the bed. After several minutes, Jimmy thought she was asleep. Her breathing was slow, rhythmic. Then she stirred with a little sudden jerk.

"Are we going to make it?" she asked, about to drop into deep sleep.

"Hard to know," he whispered. And he wondered.

Overhead, beyond the tent, a full moon shone more dimly through the darkened sky, riding sidesaddle on a timorous cloud. Jimmy laid there a long time, Mai Ker in his arms, but unable to sleep. He knew all hope for the OUTSIDEers was gone. Any scrap of hope they held for communication from OUTSIDE would meet with disappointment. The insurmountable combination of a poisonous atmosphere coupled with spreading radiation had been, he was sure, universally fatal to mankind, the animal world, and probably most plant species out there. The trees along the banks of the Arkansas had withered rapidly over several months, despite the rains. The prairie grasses, bushes and scrub oaks around the pods were drier and browner than normal, and looked to be dying.

The world they had known was gone. What lay in the future—as unknown as always—was beyond their sight, beyond, in fact, what any of them could conceive.

29

Tuesday, December 9th

Mai Ker was rubbing down two of the horses. She and Jimmy had just finished a ride around the pods to exercise the animals. As she unsaddled and groomed them, Jimmy went to adjust the cooling controls. Sensors showed the OUTSIDE temperature at 56 degrees. INSIDE Pods 9 and 10 it hovered at 89 degrees.

When Jimmy returned, glasses of lemonade in hand, Mai Ker greeted him with an unusually large smile.

"So what's the big grin?"

"You, Mr. Jimmy, are a father."

It took a moment for this to sink in. He grabbed her and lifted her a full foot off the ground, then stopped and set her down as if she were a 200-year-old China doll.

"Then why in the world are you riding a horse?" he demanded.

"I'm perfectly fine," she assured him. "Maybe I'll stop in another month or two."

"How far?"

"About five weeks I think. You and I were together on November first. I think that might have been it."

"This is fantastic! Have you told Pam and Bridget?"

"Of course not, silly. I wanted to tell you."

"We gotta tell them! Bridget's little boy is going to have a buddy!"

They had learned from an ultrasound at the end of September that Bridget was carrying a boy. Jimmy already could see his own son playing games with

Block and Bridget's boy.

"Or a girlfriend," Mai Ker said.

He stopped his little dance.

"Huh?" He looked puzzled. "Oh, yeah. Oh yeah, maybe so." Still full of joy at the news, the thought was somehow unsettling to him. "I always thought of having a boy first. 'Course, a girl would be great, too."

"Better," she said.

His nod admitted this was true, in the overall picture. He broke into a smile again and picked her up and carried her through the podwalk back into #10, as if carrying her across the threshold one more time. She broke the good news to Pam and Bridget, who were equally elated. After months of desperation and no hope, the thought of a second child in the Solarium raised everyone's spirits enormously.

Pam and Jimmy had also been trying to conceive, so far without success. They had their first official "date" a week after their wedding last July. Neither had particularly looked forward to it. It felt almost like work, a part of the job so to speak. They both felt dreadfully awkward. It was like an unplanned meeting between two high school sweethearts who hadn't seen each other for twenty-five years.

Jimmy only kept the date because Mai Ker made him. At that point Mai Ker was seriously worried she would never conceive, and Pam was the only other hope. The lovemaking between Pam and Jimmy was pleasurable but stifled by an undercurrent of obligation. It was not like his times with Mai Ker. Jimmy had to fight against feeling like a mechanic with Pam. Just work. Job done. Time to go.

After that first night, neither Jimmy nor Pam said a word about it until several days later. Jimmy broached the subject as he and Pam were cleaning and restocking shelves of canned goods in the new kitchen tent.

"You feel funny about this?" he asked.

"A little," she admitted. "But I'm committed to it, Jimmy. I'm committed to you."

"Yeah."

"This is how life will be now. For us."

"I worry about Mai Ker," he confided.

"You don't need to. I've talked with her. Her eyes are wide open. She knows what's at stake."

"Yeah. Everything."

"Exactly. She told me, 'You and Jimmy being married, sleeping together—it's strange. More than strange. But it has to be.'"

Still, it was awkward. Jimmy couldn't convince himself to be intimate with Pam in her tent when Mai Ker's was just a few feet away. He insisted that he and Pam walk to the ocean. Here they had some privacy. He would bring some blankets so they could make love on the beach. Despite what he'd seen in movies, it was actually rather bizarre, water lapping near their feet.

If I didn't feel like a fish out of water before, I do now, he said to himself.

IN THE months since, he and Pam had been together many times, to no avail. She wasn't pregnant and didn't seem hopeful. She and Jimmy talked, and they would not give up. But Pam was starting to feel like an auto mechanic, too.

Besides this problem for Jimmy, intimacy with Bridget was out of the question until her baby was born. He would have to get over these same hurdles again when that time came. He tried not to think about it.

Unbelievably, life in the pods was working into a regular routine again, even if a very different routine from that which had been planned out for them. Daily chores and routines helped them keep their minds focused, and off the OUTSIDE world. Nightmares of piles of corpses, worse than anything the Black Death had wrought, and more mind-boggling than the Holocaust, had ruined their sleep more than once. Gradually though, the horrors inevitably began to fade as they became engrossed in their own survival.

Bridget's pregnancy and now Mai Ker's were like eddies of fresh air seeping in around them. Hope was budding, even in the midst of so much tragedy.

The new inspection routine continued, from the ground and higher up. Jimmy and Mai Ker made regular trips up the skeletal beams of the pods about once a month, including the pods that were now closed off most of the time. Having found one leak, they knew they couldn't afford to miss another. Jimmy, as the new team leader, was not willing to take any chance on this. Even a slow leak, over time, could cause irreversible damage to their atmosphere. Their heat sensors on the OUTSIDE of the pods were their only scientific link to that immense ghost town. They had no way of knowing, with all the changes caused by the atmospheric catastrophe, if the outer air pressure was still constant. If the OUTSIDE pressure increased it would intensify any leak into the pods. The inspections would continue. They had to be sure.

"I guess no more beam climbing for you for a while," Bridget said as she worked alongside Mai Ker in Pod 11 later in the afternoon.

"I think I can still climb. But I know Jimmy won't want me to. Ever since I told him this morning, it's like I'm made of glass or something."

"You're not. But your baby kind of is," Bridget said. Here she was, feeling and talking like a mom. It brought back sad memories. She had given up her first baby, a girl, for adoption. Since then she didn't think she could ever be a mother again. Now she felt differently. Now so much was at stake. She rubbed her stomach. Her middle seemed to be growing by the hour. She was anxious for her child to arrive. Yet she still had fears.

"I wonder," she said, "if it's right. You know? How we can even think of bringing babies into this place. But in another way, it seems the rightest thing in the world."

"It will sure change things, won't it?" Mai Ker said.

"I can't even imagine."

"Do you think Pam will be upset? Jealous I mean?"

"I don't think so. She's so gracious. I mean, think about it. Ever since we came to the Solarium, if anyone has kept her senses—and her joy for life—it's been Pam."

"Maybe one exception."

"Oh, yeah. The day she tried to escape. Well, we were all at the end of our rope that day."

MORE TENTS had sprouted up in Pod 10, more "permanent" housing for their daily activities. The women even convinced Jimmy they needed a craft and sewing tent where they could "escape all the testosterone around this place." He didn't get the joke for 10 minutes. When he finally did, and stopped laughing, he agreed to build the craft tent.

They continued to move furniture from the old house, also. The familiar pieces gave a sense of permanency to their flimsy new digs and maintained a connection with their past.

Since all the pods had been built with electrical, water, and sanitation facilities, the place was very flexible in what spaces they could use. The one exception was the far end of Pod 12 where their self-contained sewage plant continuously treated and recycled water into the ocean. Sewage first went through a standard skimming and chemical treatment system. The waste water was pumped through extensive deep earth filters in the catchment basin under the complex. From there, the water was circulated back into their miniature ocean. "New" water from the ocean was regularly pumped through large pipes that linked the ocean to purifying and desalinization equipment in Pod 13. After salt removal and several more filter stages, fresh water emptied back into huge, elevated storage tanks in #13 and #14.

The water system, in fact, had worked better than any system in the complex. It required little attention or maintenance, except that over time the salinity of the ocean would gradually drop. Every two months the team took the salt residue produced by the desalting works in #13 and used it to keep the water balanced in the ocean. Other than that, water flowed throughout the pipes, drains and treatment systems of Solarium-3 without a glitch.

With water as well as sewage lines in Pod 10, they were able to move the washing machines out there as well. A new laundry tent was going up near the lavatory tent bringing everything they needed close at hand. It also changed the routine of the last several months of washing all their clothes, towels and bedding by hand.

Like his private bath and shower in #9, Jimmy rigged up complete "indoor" plumbing for the women in their lavatory tent. The women still cared about how they looked and how they smelled. With the kind of physical work they did every day, the showers were a must.

The air quality in the Solarium had remained stable, aided, no doubt, by the fact that they were mostly using only four pods. Using the laptops setup in a new Comm. tent in #10, Jimmy or Bridget checked the air daily, if not twice a day. They had reconfigured the air alert sensors so an air problem in any pod would trigger an audible alarm in #10. So far, the alarms had been silent. The oxygen and nitrogen pressures stayed within normal limits.

The master heating, cooling and ventilating system, now running entirely off internal solar panels and the new generators, continued to circulate air through the whole complex, even the unused pods. As hoped, this helped their atmosphere to self-regulate.

What had surprised them was that by November oxygen levels actually increased just slightly above normal. With three fewer humans and several dozen fewer animals, the oxygen consumption assumed by the planners had dropped enormously. The levels had remained steady.

The little group sat and rested from their afternoon in the shade of the house tent. Jimmy beamed with obvious relief as he and Bridget reported how well the oxygen levels were doing.

"You know, maybe we could afford to scale back on food crops for a while," Mai Ker said. "Slow the oxygen production rate."

This bothered no one since it meant less labor and less worry. They had food in storage to carry them many months. The simple realization that they could, if they wanted, overproduce oxygen was a huge relief.

"But you know this will change again," Mai Ker said, popping the bubble she had just floated. "When the children are born. Extra lungs breathing, extra mouths to feed."

But this, finally, was a good problem, one they actually looked forward to handling.

30

Thursday, March 5th

It was staying cooler INSIDE now, so much so that they found themselves wearing sweatshirts and running the heating system more often. The air and sky OUTSIDE continued to darken as if the whole Solarium was trapped in the cellar of an ancient, haunted house nearing sundown. Less of the sun's radiation was making it to ground level. Even with the greenhouse effect INSIDE, the temperature often dropped at night below what was comfortable—or at least what they had become used to—especially living outdoors in the tents.

The need to provide heat over the winter months was creating an energy drain. The entire heating system in the complex was electric, designed by planners who assumed it would rarely—if ever—be used and who, moreover, counted on an endless supply of electricity. Their planning vision was filtered through lenses for the nearsighted. They never saw this coming.

So when the heaters started kicking on at night in late January, the Solarians had to find a way to compensate. They didn't want to run the gas-powered generators. Fuel was too precious. This meant the heat had to be powered entirely by the solar panels and turbine-driven generators.

After a long debate, they had decided to draw on one of the large storage batteries if needed to provide adequate heat during the night. But that meant assuring the battery got recharged the following day. This was the first time Jimmy had to cast a tie-breaking vote.

Mai Ker and Bridget opposed the idea. What if they suddenly needed all the backup power, and the storage batteries were down?

Jimmy helped resolve the dispute by promising to finally finish the bicycle-driven generator that Mai Ker had suggested long ago. They had made the linkage for the second exercise bike but had still not hooked the generators up to the two bikes. Like some projects, it was just one that always got pushed to the rear. Now it was pushed right to the front. While at it, they built a second, since there were two exercise bikes sitting in the Rec. Pod. These had been nothing but dust collectors for months since the four Solarians found more exercise than they needed each day.

With some creative wiring and a relay, Jimmy and Bridget set the two-bike system up so that two peddlers could charge the same battery at once. They found that by taking turns on the bikes the four of them could recharge one of the large storage batteries in about seven hours. The downside was this would keep them from other responsibilities. The upside was that winter would once again become a season. The bicycling season.

They saved power where they could by burning candles in the evenings and using only the necessary lights in the pods. And since the tents blocked little light, they were generally up with the sun, as sunrise began to rewarm the complex each morning.

THE TEAM was taking a mid-morning break, munching snacks. Bridget was so huge every bit of field work was a strain. She continued to work, though, trying to hurry the birth along. She was on schedule but like every expectant mom could not wait to get past the pain that was about to come crushing in.

Jimmy chose this moment to bring up a subject that had dogged them since their arrival at Solarium-3. As their new leader he had suggested—several times—that they should think about some kind of religious life. This had been a big part of his life growing up, although he largely abandoned the practice of his faith in college. Still, something nagged at him. Having lived through the greatest crisis in mankind's history, he felt they were neglecting the more serious side of life, not trying to understand what had happened. But the subject was touchy each time he brought it up.

Bridget, with her token Christian background, said she didn't object if he wanted to read aloud from his Bible in the Meeting Tent on occasion. She said it wouldn't bother her, although something in her tone said it might. Mai Ker still had trouble conceptualizing the whole notion of a single God that Jimmy's Bible spoke of. Pam, by contrast, said she would enjoy talking about all this, even though she couldn't see where it would get them.

"I'm like Pam," Bridget said as they sat resting. She chewed half a pear. "What good is it? Why talk about things we can't change? We've done pretty well. We've made it through—what—three funerals without any outside help?"

"Guess that depends on how you look at it," Jimmy answered.

"I have my own beliefs," Pam said with a little hesitation. "But I was always taught it's not right to push our beliefs off on others." She waited for some kind of approval but no one said anything to this. "I know what I believe. That's what's important."

"Seems religion just always made people hate each other," Bridget added. "Why encourage that?"

"That is true," Mai Ker said. "When my people lived in the old lands, there were many different gods— no one could get along."

Clearly Jimmy was outnumbered.

"I know," he admitted.

He let the conversation drop. This was not the time. Maybe the time would never come. But Pam unwittingly picked up the torch.

"Don't you feel, sometimes," Pam asked, "as if the whole world is just kind of—I don't know—winding down? Like going to sleep?"

"How do you mean?" Bridget asked.

"I'm not sure. Almost like it was planned this way? The end of the human race?"

"And we are it?" Mai Ker asked, unable to draw any insight from her own words.

"I don't know," Pam said, obviously feeling in over her head. "Maybe we've outlived our usefulness?"

The others looked at her as if to say, *Continue.* Pam looked out at them from the recesses of her mind like a drowning woman crying for rescue.

"I've thought about this a lot," she confided to them. Her voice was subdued. "But I don't really have the words. If it's the end—it makes no sense. No purpose. Or, have we come to a sort of bridge? The four of us. And we have to decide."

"Decide what?" Jimmy asked.

"If we want to cross it."

"I do not see any bridge," Mai Ker said. "Just the end. Last chapter, last sentence. Period."

"But here we are," Pam said. "No explanation. What? Just four leftovers?" Her voice dropped to a starched whisper. "It's very frightening to think of."

"Why so frightening, Pam?" Bridget asked sympathetically.

"Because . . . I can't understand it."

They sipped cups of water and worked on scraps of fruit left on each plate.

"I think sometimes we worry too much," Mai Ker finally said.

Bridget smiled with palpable relief.

"Mai," Bridget said, "you always have a way of

putting the needle on just the right spot on the record."

"What does this mean?"

"Maybe you'd have to be a little older," Bridget chuckled. "Guess I'm showing my age."

"You're only four years older than me," Mai Ker pointed out.

"Yes," Bridget said, "and sometimes that seems like an eternity."

PAM AND Jimmy were feeding chickens and rabbits in Pod 11 about 2:00 p.m.

"So. Do you think I worry too much?" Pam asked him as she poured water into a tank in the rabbit hutch.

Jimmy didn't get to answer. For on this day, at this particular unpredictable moment, Mai Ker began shouting from #10.

"Come quick, guys!"

"Oh God—it's starting," Bridget blurted out as she went down to her knees, rolled and sat. Jimmy and Pam arrived. Together they lifted Bridget and helped her toward the Infirmary.

Pam the nurse played doctor, Mai Ker the genetics specialist played nurse, and Jimmy played the father, holding Bridget's hand, encouraging her, supporting her head. And without letting on, he said frequent little prayers for her as the labor progressed.

Since this was not her first child the labor went more quickly than they expected. The baby crowned just after 9:00 p.m., and was delivered ten minutes later.

Clayton Block had a successor, a baby boy, as the ultrasound had predicted. They had been discussing a name for weeks. This was a major crossroads and the decision took on epic-like proportions.

Now the baby was here and they were still undecided.

After cleaning up Bridget and the baby, they

gathered around her on the Infirmary bed. Bridget was too exhausted at the moment to hold her son. Pam was cuddling the new arrival. Here he was, bright and sleepy, and they had no name.

"I have an idea. One we haven't thought of," Pam said. She had quickly snapped out of the morose mood of earlier this afternoon.

"What?" Bridget groaned. She was more anxious than anyone to name her beautiful son.

"Herald."

"Harold!" Jimmy blurted out, almost laughing. "My grandfather's name?"

"Not o-l-d," Pam said, "a-l-d. You know. Like 'herald of good tidings.'"

"It is good," Mai Ker said. "A name with meaning."

"I'm just glad he's here," Bridget smiled, looking at her reddish-purple, rubbery looking infant. "Herald?" she said looking at him, as if asking the baby's permission.

"Herald Block?" Jimmy said.

"I don't know," Bridget said. "Maybe Herald Listner."

"Herald List-en-er," Jimmy said, trying it out.

"Herald Listner-Block," Bridget said with finality. "He is Clayton's only living child."

That settled it.

Jimmy pulled Mai Ker to him. He rubbed her bulging belly. An ultrasound two weeks ago had revealed their baby was a girl.

"And who is this gonna be?" Jimmy asked. "Little Mai Mouuu-ahhh?" he said, playfully stretching it into the sound of a cow.

"Don't make fun of my name," Mai Ker told him. "Doesn't sound as funny as Alllll-Gooooooddddy," she teased.

"Have you picked a first name?" Bridget asked.

"I have," she said.

"You have?" Jimmy said, surprised.

"Yes. Sing."

"Sing what?" Jimmy asked.

"No dummy. 'Sing.' That is her name."

Jimmy realized how perfect this was, for a child of Mai Ker.

"OK. Done." He hugged her again.

"Good," Pam said. "It's been a long day. I'll stay with Bridget and the baby for a while. Why don't you two get some sleep."

There was melancholy sense in her voice. Pam still had been unable to conceive. She was beginning to worry that her age, or her system, was going to make it impossible. They knew it was important that she have a child if possible, another piece of the genetic puzzle. A third family line would make a huge difference—perhaps a critical difference—to their survival.

But with little Herald cradled in her arms, her anxiety passed quickly. She lowered herself into the rocker they had ready at hand and played grandma, a role with which she would be content, if need be.

"It is so amazing," Mai Ker said as she and Jimmy walked slowly through the fields to her tent.

"What?" Jimmy asked.

"We were so worried. Think back. I thought we would all be dead by now."

"Well, I've never admitted it. But, honestly? I did, too."

"And now there's a baby. And another soon. It is amazing." She stopped and looked up at him. "What is your English word? 'Wonder-full?'"

Jimmy smiled at her unintended innocence.

"Proves what my dad always said."

"What did he say?"

"Us humans—we were never really in charge of anything."

31

Saturday, August 8th

Just over two years had passed since the team entered Solarium-3. First they were seven, now they were five. Four implants from OUTSIDE, one native.

The one native, five-month-old Herald Listner-Block, was growing like a garden weed and mimicking all the sounds around him. Within a few months he would be crawling, pulling things over on himself, then walking, then talking. None of this would be a surprise. These were some of the few predictable events in what had become their thoroughly unpredictable world, a world of life quarantined within a world of death.

What would be a surprise—and a happy one—was how long baby Herald would live, and what he would live to see.

While little Herald slept contentedly under a purple-hued moon at 3:12 a.m. early on this warm August morning, his first "cousin," Sing Moua-Algood, was born to Mai Ker and Jimmy. She arrived as a five-and-a-half pound baby girl with beautiful dark skin, sweet brown eyes avoiding the light, with nearly a full head of fine, dark brown hair, and all her fingers and toes. She made her entrance into Solarium-3 a full week early, for which Mai Ker was thrilled. Another week of pregnancy would have been agony to Mai Ker's tiny frame.

Although Sing's arrival was early, she seemed perfectly healthy. Jimmy played dad more perfectly this time, watching the fascinating drama again as Pam and Bridget helped Mai Ker give birth. Throughout fourteen long and painful hours of labor and delivery, Jimmy watched in wonder and said his little prayers. As with Herald's birth, Jimmy was overcome by a sense of awe at how beautiful this old world was, after all, even trapped INSIDE their artificial pods. *Like the ark in the days of Noah,* he thought, a microcosm of what their world had been. Yet forced as it was, it was home.

Mai Ker had suffered a lot in the past two weeks, heavy and uncomfortable and barely able to move some days. With Sing delivered, she finally rested. Jimmy cradled his daughter in his arms, humming some tune that he must have known but didn't recognize. He loved her name already, and it fit so perfectly. The tiny cries and squeaks that came out of her were like those of a baby songbird trying, for the first time, to reach the world's deafened ears.

IN THE months since Clayton Block left her, his treasured friend Caroline continued to roam the Solarium, even though her flights were now restricted to the four open pods. She would alight occasionally for a snack in a field or perch on a branch, as if on an inspection tour. Once in a while she would perch near one of the Solarians as they worked, or played. Swim parties were now in the ocean and Caroline would regularly show up for those. Cracker crumbs from picnic lunches made delectable fare for the little nuthatch.

Bridget kept a small dish of bird seed by the base of the lamp on the bed stand in her tent. Caroline now treated this room as her own. Bridget would talk with Caroline if she came by for a late night snack. She spoke of how much Caroline must miss Clayton. In all the months since Block had disappeared, Caroline had landed on her finger only twice. Each time she pecked at Bridget's hand and forearm as if there should have been more seed there. Disappointed, she flew on.

Yesterday afternoon, unseen by the Solarians, Caroline faltered over the ocean in Pod 12. She landed briefly on a rock by the beach and sat as if collecting her wits. Intent on making it back to her nest in Pod 11, she flew off, but faltered again and fell gracefully into the cool water. Her frail, soggy carcass floated on the artificial waves through the night. She washed ashore early this morning but no one noticed. No one ever found her. She bounced gently there by the shore for several days, waves caressing her, until an undertow finally pulled her out to sea and buried her among long arms of seaweed lapping against the base of several large rocks. She decomposed slowly into the sea and its cycle of regeneration that helped support the six Solarians now trapped here.

THE BIRTH of Sing, like that of Herald, was bittersweet for "Aunt Pam" who had still not conceived. At the best times of the month, Jimmy would spend every night with her but so far their efforts were fruitless. Jimmy prayed for a miracle.

He had shared his thoughts, and his prayer, with Bridget two weeks ago as they cleaned cricket remains from the corners of a storage shed.

"So, you believe in miracles?" she asked, looking at him with genuine curiosity.

"Do you?" he asked.

"If there was any evidence," Bridget said.

"We're still here. Evidence enough?"

The reaction on Bridget's face conceded the point. In the midst of so much death, grief, and catastrophe, she had to admit it to herself. Life itself is the grand miracle, and the most inexplicable.

AT THE moment of Sing's arrival in the middle of the night none had been to bed and all were exhausted. Mai

Ker laid like wreckage on the Infirmary bed, physically and emotionally drained but resting, trying to replenish her system and corral her stampeding feelings. Pam helped Bridget sponge her down. The pods had been unusually warm yesterday and Mai Ker sweated profusely throughout her labor.

Pam had wrapped the baby in a huge diaper-like towel to keep her warm. Jimmy took her for a round-about walk through Pod 10 so she could see her new home, even though her eyes could barely open and could not begin to focus. The birth of Herald had been grand, but the birth of his own daughter was far grander. He circled back to the Infirmary and gave Sing to Mai Ker, who had regained enough strength to hold her. Mai Ker's eyes seemed bigger than ever as she beheld the incredible sight of the fruit of her own body.

Since babies had never been part of the Solarium-3 plan, there was a complete lack of the needed equipment. Just before Herald's birth, and expecting the birth of Sing, Jimmy built a large, oval bassinet big enough for both babies. It was a traditional wicker-like affair, woven of small green branches and strong pieces of straw. They had no baby mattress so they had to fabricate this, too. Mai Ker was the artist here. She had created a soft oval-shaped pallet of fine wheat straw and cotton fragments sewn into a doubled-up blanket. This they tucked beneath a folded twin bed sheet. Herald was sound asleep there at the moment, with no idea he would have an even smaller neighbor by daybreak.

After a half hour, Mai Ker fell fast asleep holding Sing in her arms. Bridget carried Sing home to their village and placed her in the bassinet, being careful not to disturb her son. Herald moved ever-so-slightly, made one of those unintended half-smiles that babies make as they sleep, and rolled his head sideways.

Not long after, Jimmy carried Mai Ker back to her

tent so she could rest in her own bed and heal from the trauma of childbirth. Pam followed along to help get her settled.

"You go on, Pam," he said. "I need to just sit and be with her awhile. I don't know how women get through this."

Pam smiled.

"But," Jimmy added with genuine earnestness, "I really hope you get to find out."

"Me, too," she nodded.

She kissed Jimmy, then walked over and joined Bridget in the nursery. One dim candle burned nearby. Light and shadows danced against the canvas walls.

Within a half-hour, Jimmy could not resist his next look at his beautiful daughter. He found Pam and Bridget still standing by the bassinet, arms around each other's waist, supporting one another so they didn't fall over from their own exhaustion.

Jimmy joined them, wrapping his arm behind Pam. Nearly delirious with fatigue, their gaze was transfixed by the children in the wicker crib.

A contented silence prevailed for several minutes. Herald rolled toward Sing and they nestled together, blankets just touching.

"Congratulations, Dad," Bridget said, beaming.

"You, too," he nodded.

The three pulled each other closer, interlaced arms holding them like a rescue net. Herald plugged a thumb into his mouth. Sing fussed quietly but intently, no doubt complaining about how cold her new home was.

Pam was overcome with inexpressible relief and joy as she watched them.

"The most precious thing in the world," she said.

"Beyond price," Bridget said with wind-chimes in her voice. "So beautiful. Like two little birds in a nest."

Look for **Haeven,**
Book Two of the Solarium-3 Trilogy
wherever books are sold

Hanging by a thread . . .

Everything went wrong.

INSIDE *Solarium-3* (Book One) a research team was to sustain life in a completely closed, man-made environment.

Then came devastation. Earth's atmosphere turned toxic. Ruin has taken the world.

Trapped in their air-tight sanctuary, the Solarians cling to life. Now two children have been born. Is there hope? Can they survive?

But something goes wrong, a possible leak of poisonous air from OUTSIDE. Time is running out.

If it's no longer safe INSIDE, what will they risk?

Haeven
Book Two of the Solarium-3 Trilogy

Venture OUTSIDE

www.solarium-3.com

About The Author

JOHN R. SPENCER grew up in Kansas and Colorado, and holds a degree in English Literature from the University of Northern Colorado, where he was, for two years, editor-in-chief of the campus literary magazine *NOVA*.

In addition to writing, he has enjoyed a diverse career as a police detective, emergency medical technician, coroner's investigator, social worker, and community corrections supervisor. He has also worked as a dramatic director for several community and children's theaters in Colorado, Wisconsin and Illinois.

The father of three grown children, he lives with his wife, Candice, in eastern Iowa.